Jesus of Nazareth, the Messiah or Christ

*Thirty-two Textual Sermons on Proving
Jesus of Nazareth as Messiah or Christ,
with an Essay,
'A Theological Significance of Forty Days'*

Jesus of Nazareth, the Messiah or Christ

Thirty-two Textual Sermons on Proving Jesus of Nazareth as Messiah or Christ, with an Essay, 'A Theological Significance of Forty Days'

DANIEL D. RUPWATE

2018

Jesus of Nazareth, the Messiah or Christ: *Thirty-two Textual Sermons on Proving Jesus of Nazareth as Messiah or Christ, with an Essay, 'A Theological Significance of Forty Days'* - published by the Rev. Dr. Ashish Amos of the Indian Society for Promoting Christian Knowledge (ISPCK), Post Box 1585, 1654, Madarsa Road, Kashmere Gate, Delhi-110006.

© Author, 2018

ISBN: 978-81-8465-680-0

Cover picture credit: Internet Sources

Laser typeset at **ISPCK,** Post Box 1585, 1654, Madarsa Road, Kashmere Gate, Delhi-110006.

Tel: 23866323, Fax: 91-11-23865490

e-mail: ashish@ispck.org.in • ella@ispck.org.in

website: www.ispck.org.in

Dedication

This book is dedicated to my grandfather, my mother's father, late Mr. Dhondiba Sadu Salve (ca.1885-1950). He had no opportunity to be schooled. Yet he was wise and enterprising. He formed a team from his village Kotul, taluka Akole, District Ahmednagar. The team went from vilages and talukas to demonstrate their polular art (*tamasha*). My grandfather was also a religious man; he used to worship his gods every morning. As he toured Ahmednagar district, he saw big churches building and their missionary works in terms of schools, boarding schools for boys and girls, medical schools, and hositals. He was impressed by the evidences of Christian faith. He formed his opinion that Christianity was a great religion.

My father late Mr. David A. Rupwate (ca. 1904-1965) went to work in Khirkee, Pune. He was converted to Christianity. His conversion to Christianity was not appreciated by his family, because of fear of being excommunication of the family from the community or caste. My grandfather, late Mr. Dhondiba salve, advised my mother late Mrs. Siatbai D. Rupwate (ca. 1914-1971) that Christianity was a great religion; and she should embrace Christian faith also. After the death of my grandfather, my mother embraced Christianity, with other children in the family.

My grandfather late Mr. Dhondiba S. Salve realized Christianity as a great religion, because he saw a great missionary works of the churches. The real greatness of Christianity lies in the fact that the LORD God became the Messiah or Christ in the person of Jesus of Nazareth to give salvation to the entire world. Jesus of Nazareth was born a prophesied Messiah; He was welcome by the crowds in Jerusalem and its temple as the Messiah; He was resurrected from the dead on the third day, according to the scripture. My grandfather did not know these scriptural facts. Yet he had a vision or insight to know the greatness of Christianity; therefore, I dedicate this book to my grandfather, late Mr. Dhondiba Sadu Salve in appreciation of his admirable opinion of Christianity, which was rare.

Rt. Rev. Dr. Daniel D. Rupwate,
Hamilton, Ontario, Canada.

Contents

Part - I

Jesus as the Messiah at His Birthday: Celebration of the Birth of Jesus Christ, The Saviour of the World (*Muktidata*): Sixteen Textual Sermons on Christmas

PART - II

Jesus as the Messiah at the First Palm Sunday:
The Trimphal Entry of Jesus Christ into Jerusalem:
Seven Textual Sermons on the Palm Sunday

PART - III

Jesus as the Messiah at His Resurrection:
The Ressurection of Jesus Christ
and its Implications for Believers:
Nine Textual Sermons on the Easter Sunday

Acknowledgments

T he picture on the front cover is a traditional picture which can be justified on the basis of the scripture (Mt. 21:6-11; Mk 11:1-10), indicating that Jesus of Nazareth was given a royal welcome by crowds in Jerusalem and in the temple. The people were shouting loudly "Hosanna to the son of David! Blessed is he who comes in the name of the Lord! Hosanna in the highest!" (Mt. 21:9)

The quotations in the book are adopted from the Revised Standard Version, unless otherwise stated.

Mr. Ravindra H. Rupwate, my nephew, collected information about my grandfather late Mr. Dhondiba S. Salve. The writer is grateful for his service.

Preface

Christmas is a joyful festival for the hope   of the resurrecton of the believers in the Lord and Saviour Jesus Christ. This is a biggest festival celebrated universally. Chistmas day is the day when Jesus Christ was born. Christians celebrate this day as the birth-day of Jesus Christ. This day makes children, adults, and neighbours very happy when they give gifts to one another and wish Merry Christmas to one another.

Jesus Christ was an anticipated Messiah. The Old Testament prophets prophesied that He would be born of a virgin and of the Most High. The place of His birth and time of His birth were also prophesied. He would preach in the parables. He would be rejected and crucified by the people; and He would be resurrected on the third day and would ascend to heaven.

The WORD of God (*Logos* in Greek) became incarnate in a male baby named Jesus of Nazareth. His date of birth and the date of His crucifixion were not correctly and accurately registered. There are internal evidences in the Bible and external evidences in political life of the people. These evidences can help us to roughly determine these dates.

Jesus Christ, a king of the Jews, was born before the spring of 4 B. C. or in the final year of King Herod the Great (37-4 B. C.). King Herod the Great heard the news of the birth of a king of the Jews from the Magis or three wise men from Persia. He was upset by the news. (Mt.2:2-4) When Magis returned to Persia by another route, without seeing him, he ordered to kill infants in and around Bethlehem. Joseph, Mary, and Jesus went to stay in Egypt, as an angel of the LORD God asked them. They returned after the death of King Herod the Great. (Mt. 2:14)

John the Baptist was the forerunner of the Messiah. He was born six months before Jesus of Nazareth was born. It means he was born in 5 B. C. He was baptizing the people in the river Jordan. Jesus of Nazareth went to John the Baptist to be baptised. Jesus was baptized in A. D. 28/29. After being baptized and receiving the Holy Spirit, Jesus began His teaching, preaching, and healing ministry. His ministry lasted about three and half years. Jesus was put on trial by the Jews. (Mt. 27:1-2) He was examined by Pontius Pilate (in office A. D. 26-36) and was delivered to be crucified. (Mt. 27:26) This suggests that Jesus was crucified in A. D. 30.

Jesus Christ did not allow His disciples to declare that He was the Messiah or Christ. He was waiting for an appropriate day to publicly declare His Messiahship. He made an arrangement to lend Him a colt on the Sunday. His disciples and crowds welcomed Him in the city of Jerusalem and in the temple with enthusiasm. The crowds shouted that He was the Messiah, who came into the name of God. His triumphal entery into Jerusalem became the reason to celebrate Palm Sunday in the churches. On the following day, He went to the temple in Jesrusalem and purified the temple by removing the tables of money changers. The scribes and Pharisees were angered by His actions and words. They plotted to kill Him.

Jesus of Nazareth was sentenced to die on a cross by the Jewish council and the Roman authority, mentioned before. The scribes and Pharisees were successful to kill Jesus Christ on the cross. They thought it was an end to His life and His mission.

With the power of the LORD God, Jesus of Nazareth was raised from the dead, according to the plan and promise of the LORD God. Resurrection of Jesus Christ proved His victory over sin and death.

His resurrection gave hope for Christians to be resurrected at the second coming of Jesus Christ and to be with Him forever. Resurrection of Jesus Christ and the hope of the resurrection of the believers to be resurrected are celebrated on the Easter Sunday.

Jesus Christ was raised from the dead on the third day, the Easter Sunday. His disciples and followers were eye-witnesses of His appearances for forty days. He was ascended to heaven. Before His ascension, He gave a great commission to His apostles to preach the gospel of the kingdom of God and to baptize the people in name of God, in His name, and in the name of the Holy Spirit (Mt. 28:19) .

The LORD God exalted Jesus Christ as the Lord of lords and King of kings. God bestowed on Him the highest title which is above every title. (Phil. 2:9-11)

Christmas, the day of the virgin birth of Jesus Christ ,the Messiah, Palm Suday, the way of the triumphal entry of the Messiah in Jerusalem, and Easter Sunday, the day of the resurrection of Jesus Christ are most important days in the life of Churches. These days are joyous days in the life of believers, therefore, they should be celebrated with joy and zeal.

PART - I

Jesus as the Messiah at His Birthday:
Celebration of the Birth of Jesus Christ,
The Saviour of the World (*Muktidata*):
Sixteen Textual Sermons on Christmas

Chapter - 1

Titles of the Sermon

'The Ruler from the Least,'

'The Ruler from Antiquity,'

'Everlasting Ruler of Israel,'

'Ancient and everlasting Ruler,'

'Jesus Christ, the Ancient and Everlasting Ruler,'

'The Birth-City of the Messiah, Jesus Christ.'

Scripture

Micah 5:1-5

Genesis 2:8; 3:1-24; 14:18-20; 48:7-8

Ruth 1:19; 2:1-23; 4:21-22

II Samuel 5:6

I Kings 2:11-12; 10:2

Psalms 110:1,4; 119:105

Isaiah 1:1; 7:1; 9:6-7; 11:1-2

Micah 1:1

Matthew 1:1-17; 27:11

Luke 3:23-38; 23:3

John 1:1-3, 14; 17:34; 18:35-37

I Corinthians 1:26-30

Hebrews 7:2-3

Revelation 1:8

Text: Micah 5:2

A Few Versions of the Text, Micah 5:2

But you, Bethlehem Ephrathah, Though you are little among the thousands of Judah, Yet out of you shall come forth to Me the One to be Ruler in Israel, Whose goings forth are from of old, From everlasting. *The New King James Version*

But thou, Bethlehem Ephrathah, which art little to be among the thousands of Judah, out of thee shall one come forth unto me that is to be ruler in Israel; whose going forth are from of old, from everlasting. *The Wesleyan Bible Commentary*

But you, O Bethlehem Ephrathah, who are little to be among the clans of Judah, from you shall forth for me one who is to be ruler in Israel, whose origin is from of old, from ancient days. *Revised Standard Version*

But you, Bethlehem Ephrathah, though you are small among the clans of Judah, out of you will come for me one who will be ruler over Israel; whose origins are from of old, from ancient times. *New International Version*

But you, Bethlehem in Ephrathah, small as you are among Judah's clans, out of you shall come forth a governor for Israel, one whose roots are back in the past, in days gone by. *The New English Bible*

O Bethlehem Ephrathah, you are but a small Judean village, yet you will be the birthplace of my King who is alive from everlasting ages past. *The Living Bible Illustrated.*

You, Bethlehem Ephrathah, are too small to be included among Judah's cities. Yet, from you Israel's future ruler will come for me. His origins go back to the distant past, to days long ago. *God's Word*

Introduction

Christians understand the word of God in two different senses. The first meaning is that all Christians believe the Bible, the holy scripture, as the word of God. The word of God means spiritual teachings or the biblical doctrines, religious laws, and practices of the Bible. In this precise sense, the Bible is like a lamp to the feet of believers (Ps.119:105), that the believers may walk in the righteous path, which is prescribed by the LORD God Himself.

The second meaning of the word of God is the incarnation of God in Jesus Christ or the embodiment of the Biblical teachings in the person of Jesus Christ. St. John wrote about it, as follows:

> In the beginning was the Word [*Logos*] and the Word was with God, and the Word was God. He was in the beginning with God; all things were made through him, and without him was not anything made that was made. (Jn 1:1-2) And the Word became flesh and dwelt among us, full of grace and truth; we have beheld his glory, glory as of the only Son from the Father. (Jn 1:14)

In these words, St. John spoke of the pre-existence of Jesus Christ before the creation of the world or rather the universe, and also of the role of Jesus Christ in creating the world. When the Word of God became a man, named Jesus, he manifested God's glory and truth to the people. St. John, other apostles, and believers bore the witness about Jesus Christ, that He is the Word (*Logos*) of God.

In Jesus Christ, God's plan of redeeming mankind from sin was fulfilled. God had been revealing His plan of redemption to His servants, since the fall of Adam and Eve in the garden of Eden (Gen. 2:8; 3:1-24). God's plan of salvation became very specific in His promise that He would send the Messiah to be the ruler over His chosen people, Israel. Jesus Christ is the Messiah, through whom God's plan of redemption is achieved.

Introduction of the Text

There are many prophecies about the Messiah in the Old Testament. In the eighth century B. C., prophets Isaiah and Micah prophesied about the birth of the Messiah. Prophet Isaiah wrote that the Messiah would be born in the lineage of David (Is. 9:6-7). Prophet Micah prophesied as which place or town the Messiah would be born, in these words:

> But you, O Bethlehem Ephrathah, who are little to be among the clans of Judah, from you shall come forth for me one who is to be ruler in Israel, whose origin is from of old, from ancient days. (Mc. 5:2)

This is the text of our mediation now.

The Context of the Text

Prophet Isaiah referred to the kings of Judah or Southern Kingdom, namely, Uzziah (Azariah) (783-742 B. C.), Jotham (750-742 B. C.), Ahaz (735-515 B. C.), and Hezekiah (715-687 B. C.), in the beginning of his book (Is. 1:1). Prophet Micah did not mention Uzziah; but he referred to Jotham, Ahaz, and Hezekiah, the kings of Judah, in the beginning of his book (Mic. 1:1). This indicates that Isaiah was older than Micah. Isaiah mentioned Pekah (737-732 B. C.), the son of Ramaliah, a king of Israel or the northern kingdom (Is. 7:1) This means that these two prophets were contemporary, who saw the invasions of the kingdom of Israel by Tiglath-pileser II of Assyria in 738 B. C. and in 732 B. C., and the fall of the northern kingdom, or Israel. They also witnessed the invasion of Judah by Sennacherib of Assyria (705-681 B. C.) in 701 B. C., when King Hezekiah was ruling Judah. They saw political powers, destroying the kingdoms of the people of Israel. Nevertheless, they had hope that God would save His chosen people or remnant. They believed that the State might perish; but a sacred remnant, chosen by God, would survive. Therefore, the prophet Micah prophesied, saying:

> But you, O Bethlehem Ephrathah, who are little to be among the clans of Judah, from you shall come forth for me one who is to be ruler in Israel, whose origin is from of old, from ancient days. (Mc. 5:2)

In these words, Micah proclaimed the plan of God to restore the kingdom of the people of Israel.

An Analysis of the Text

This text has three ideas. (A) The first idea is that the town of Bethlehem was little or insignificant among the other towns, which were occupied by the people of the clan of Judah.

(B) The second idea is that a ruler or governor of Israel would be raised from Bethlehem.

(C) The third idea is that the origin of the ruler is from the ancient days.

Exposition of the Ideas

(A) The first idea of the text is that the town of Bethlehem was little or insignificant among the other towns, which were occupied by the people of the clan of Judah. We should know the reasons why was the town of Bethlehem considered insignificant among other towns or cities of Judah, with reference to history, given in the Old Testament.

(1) The town of Bethlehem is on the south of Jerusalem, five miles away from it. It remained under the shadow of Jerusalem, which was a very important city of Judah. Jerusalem or Zion was the capital of King David (1002-962 B. C.), who was an ideal and very important king of the united kingdom of Israel. King David ruled Israel and Judah thirty three (33) years from Jerusalem (II Sam. 5:6; I Kg. 2:11). His successor and son, King Solomon (962-922 B. C.) kept Jerusalem as his capital city (I Kg. 10:2; 2:12). Thus, Jerusalem became a royal city; moreover, it was a strategic city from a military point of view.

(2) Jerusalem was the city where King Solomon (962-922 B. C) built the first temple of the LORD God. Therefore, Jerusalem became the central place of worship for the Jews. Thus, Jerusalem gained religious significance for the Jews. But Bethlehem did not get either royal or strategic significance as Jerusalem had got. It remained an insignificant village, with reference to Jerusalem.Even though Bethlehem was of less significant than Jerusalem, some important events took place at Bethlehem. (1) Jacob's wife, Rachel, was buried at Bethlehem (Gen. 48:7-8). (2) Ruth was the great-grandmother of King David (Ruth 4:21-22); she returned to Bethlehem and met Boaz (Ruth 1:19; 2:1-23), when she was gleaning in a field of Boaz. However, these things of Jewish heritage

could not make Bethlehem a very important city. It remained an insignificant town of Judah.

God chose Bethlehem, a little town of Judah, to be the town where His Son, Jesus Christ, was to be born. Prophet Micah (800 B. C.) prophesied that the Messiah would be born in Bethlehem. Jesus Christ was born in a manger in the town of Bethlehem. Magis, the wise men of the East, came seeking Jesus Christ, the Saviour of the world in Bethlehem.

There are some archaeological evidences to confirm that Jesus Christ was born in Bethlehem.

(1) At the time of Emperor Constantine the Great (305-337), Christianity became a state religion. Helena was the mother of the Emperor Constantine the Great. She built the Church of Nativity in 324-330 over the traditional site, believed then as now to be the place of Christ's birth in Bethlehem.

(2) The Emperor Justinian (527-565) rebuilt the Church of Nativity in the sixth century. This building still stands in Bethlehem.

(3) In 1934, Mr. William Harvey carried excavations, eighteen inches under the floor of the present Church. He discovered portions of the mosaic floor of the original church built by both Helena, the mother of the Emperor Constantine the Great, and the Emperor Justinian.

Under the choir area, at the east end of the church is a flight of steps leading down to the grotto of the Nativity, twenty feet below the floor level. This cave-like chapel room measures 12' x 42'. At the eastern end of the chapel is an inscription in Latin saying, "Here Jesus Christ was born of the Virgin Mary." Near by the inscription is a manger where Jesus was born. [1]

As Jesus Christ, the Saviour of the world, was born in Bethlehem, the village has gained a religious importance for the world. God made an insignificant village to be a significant city. The scripture tells us that God always chooses weak and unwise to serve His purpose. This divine practice is applied when God chooses His Christian believers. St. Paul spoke about this fact when he wrote to the Corinthians the following words:

> For consider your call, brethren; not many of you were wise according to worldly standards, not many were powerful, not many were of noble birth; but God chose what is foolish in the world to shame the wise, God chose what is weak in the world to shame the strong, God chose what is low and despised in the world, even things that are not, to bring to nothing things that are, so that no human being might boast in the presence of God. He is the source of your life in Christ Jesus, whom God made our wisdom, our righteousness and sanctification and redemption; therefore, as it is written, 'Let him who boasts, boast of the Lord.' (I Cor. 1:26-30)

May God be gloried for His achievements through insignificant persons and places! Bethlehem was an insignificant place; and its residents were insignificant people among other clans of Judah. But the Lord God made Bethlehem a very significant city.

(B) The second idea of the text is that a ruler or governor of Israel would be raised from Bethlehem. God revealed His plan to His chosen people, who were facing political and spiritual problems, that He would raise the ruler or the Messiah from the village of Bethlehem, which was of little importance among the tribes of Judah. Prophet Isaiah (800 B. C.) prophesied this, in these words:

> There shall come forth a shoot from the stump of Jesse, and a branch shall grow out of his roots. And the Spirit of the LORD shall rest upon him, the spirit of wisdom and understanding, the spirit of counsel and might, the spirit of knowledge and the fear of the LORD. (Is. 11: 1-2)

The phrase 'stump of Jesse' implies that the tree of Judah was chopped by the foreign powers; and the remnant was surviving barely. God revealed His plan to prophet Isaiah that He would revive the kingdom of Judah by raising the Messiah or Ruler from the remnant. Therefore, Isaiah prophesied in the verses, quoted above, that the Messiah would come from the lineage of King David (1002-962 B. C.).

Prophet Isaiah described the Messiah as a man filled with knowledge, understanding, and the fear of God, in these verses. Isaiah shortened this description of the Messiah this time, because he had described the Messiah in more details, when he wrote previously, as follows:

> For to us a child is born, to us a son is given; and the government will be upon his shoulder, and his name will be called 'Wonderful Counsellor, Mighty God, Everlasting Father, Prince of Peace,' Of the increase of his government and of peace there will be no end, upon the throne of David and over his kingdom, to establish it, and to uphold it with justice and with righteousness from this time forth and for evermore. The zeal of the LORD of hosts will do this. (Is. 9:6-7)

Prophet Isaiah herein spoke that the Messiah would be born in the lineage of King David (1002-962 B. C.). St. Matthew traced the genealogy of Jesus Christ back to Abraham (Mt. 1:1-17). According to this genealogy, Jesus was born in the house of King David. Similarly, St. Luke traced the genealogy of Jesus Christ further back to Adam (Lk. 3:23-38), for the same purpose.

Jesus Christ was born in the royal lineage of King David; and He was born to be the King for David's throne for eternity. When Jesus Christ was arrested by the Jewish religious authority and was presented to Pontius Pilate (A. D. 26-36) to be tried and sentenced, Pilate, in the trial, asked Jesus Christ, "Are you the king of the Jews?" (Mt. 27:11; Lk. 23:3) Jesus Christ answered him, "You have said so." (Mt. 27:11) St. John recorded the answer of Jesus Christ to Pontius Pilate, in these words, "Do you say this of your own accord, or did other say it to you about me?" (Jn 17:34) Pontius Pilate replied to Jesus Christ, saying, "Am I a Jew? Your own nation and the chief priest have handed you over to me; what have you done?" Jesus answered, "My kingdom is not of this world; if my kingship were of this world, my servants would fight, that I might not be handed over to the Jews; but my kingship is not from the world." Pontius Pilate said to Jesus, "So you are a king?" Jesus answered, "You say that I am a king. For this I was born, and for this I have come into the world, to bear witness to the truth. Everyone who is of the truth hears my voice." (Jn 18:35-37) Thus, Jesus Christ told Pontius Pilate that He was the King of the heavenly kingdom. He was born to be the King of that everlasting kingdom.

(C) The third idea of the text is that the origin of the ruler is from the ancient days. In other words, the Ruler or Governor or the Messiah, who was to be the King of the everlasting kingdom, was Himself of the ancient days or antiquity.

Jesus Christ claimed to be the King of the heavenly kingdom in His discourse with Pontius Pilate; He is the King or the Lord of the spiritual world. His lordship and priesthood are joined together. This was the way King David perceived the Messiah. He mentioned these two positions of the Messiah in a psalm, as follow: "The LORD says to my lord: 'Sit at my right hand, till I make your enemies your footstool.'" (Ps. 110:1) Herein King David spoke of the Messiah as his LORD.

Then King David added, "The LORD has sworn and will not change his mind, 'You are a priest forever after the order of Melchizedek.'" (Ps. 110:4) The name of Melchizedek is first mentioned in Genesis 14:18. When Abram defeated Ched-or-laomer and other kings, Melchizedek, the king of Salem, went to meet Abram. Melchizedek was not only a king of Salem, but he also was a priest of God Most High. He blessed Abram and said, "Blessed be Abram by God Most High, maker of heaven and earth; and blessed be God Most High, who has delivered your enemies into your hand." (Gen. 14:19-20)

King David recognized the importance of Melchizedek as an ancient king and a priest of God Most High for ever. He compared the Messiah, the everlasting Lord of Israel, with the order of Melchizedek. Similarly, the writer of the Letter to the Hebrews spoke of Jesus Christ as a high priest, who was designated by God, after the order of Melchizedek, as follows:

> He is first, by translation of his name, king of righteousness, and then he is also king of Salem, that is, king of peace. He is without father or mother or genealogy, and has neither beginning of days nor end of life, but resembling the Son of God he continues a priest for ever. (Heb. 7:2-3)

Melchizedek resembled the Son of God. His roles as a king of peace and as a priest of God Most High foretold the roles of the Messiah,

Jesus Christ. Jesus Christ was God; and was instrumental to create the universe (Jn 1:1-3); He is the beginning (*Alpha*) and the end (*Omega*) (Rev. 1:8).

Conclusion

Bethlehem was an insignificant town of Judah in comparison with Jerusalem, the capital city, and the holy city. But in this unimportant town, Jesus Christ, the Saviour of the world, was born, according to plan of God; thus, God enhanced the religious importance of Bethlehem. The Messiah was born in the lineage of King David. He was born to be the Ruler or the Lord of the kingdom of God. He was to be a priest of God for ever. His lordship and priesthood remind us of Melchizedek, who was a king of Salem (i.e., peace) and a priest of God Most High. Jesus Christ was God; He was with God; and He created the universe. He is the beginning and end. He was from antiquity; and He was born to be the Lord or Ruler forever over the kingdom of God.

Let us recognize the eternity of kingship and governorship of the Lord Jesus Christ over the world. As the Old Testament prophesied the coming of the Messiah, who is the eternal Ruler of the kingdom of God, Jews should recognize Jesus Christ as the Messiah. The universal Church has a mission to proclaim the Messiahship of Jesus Christ to all and especially to the Jews. Moreover, Christians should recognize the Rulership of Jesus Christ on their personal life. By this recognition, Christmas will be joyful to them and to us.

Recommended Hymns from the Methodist Hymnal

117   'Hark! The herald-angels sing'

118   'O come, all ye faithful,'

124   'See, amid the winter's snow,'

125   'O Little town of Bethlehem,'

139   'The race that long in darkness pined'

Recommended Responsive Reading from A Worship Manual for A Scriptural or Methodist Order of Service

65 (pp.170-171).

Endnotes

[1] The Thompson Chain-Reference Bible (Indianapolis, Indiana: B. B. Kirkbride Bible Co. Inc. and Grand Rapids, Michigan: Zondervan Bible Publishers, 1983), p. 1634.

Chapter - 2

Titles of the Sermon

'Jesus Means Saviour'

'Awareness of Salvation-Purpose,'

'Consciousness of Purpose of Life,'

'Preordained Purpose of Life.'

Scripture

Matthew 1:18-25

II Samuel 7:12-14, 16

II Kings 24:8-16

II Chronicles 28: 5-7, 10, 14; 36:22-23

Ezra 1:1-4

Psalms 10:2; 12:5; 14:6; 35:10; 37:10; 72:4, 12-14; 110:1;
146:8

Isaiah 10:1-2; 14:1-2; 29:19; 35:5; 43:4-7; 45:1-6; 49:1-6,
25; 54:24; 58:6-7; 59:6, 7; 61:1-3

Jeremiah 1:5-10; 24:4-6; 33:20-22

Ezekiel 37:24-28

Matthew 8:20; 9:27-30; 12:8, 40; 13:41; 14:33; 16:27; 19:28; 20:18;
22:44; 24:30; 25:31; 26:31

Luke 1:30-33; 7:22

John 1:12-13; 8:12; 9:1-41; 11:25; 14:6

Romans 5:18-19

I Corinthians 15:22, 45-49

Galatians 3:26-28

I John 1:12-13

Text: Matthew 1:21

A Few Versions of the Text, Matthew 1:21

And she will bring forth a Son, and you shall call his name Jesus, for he will save His people from their sins. *The New King James Version*

And she will bring forth a son, and thou shalt call his name Jesus; for he will save his people from their sins. *Explanatory Notes Upon the New Testament*

she will bear a son, and you shall call his name Jesus, for he will save his people from their sins. *Revised Standard Version*

She will give birth to a son, and you are to give him the name Jesus, because he will save his people from their sins. *New International Version*

She will bear a son; and you shall give him the name Jesus (Saviour), for he will save his people from their sins. *The New English Bible*

And she will have a Son, and you shall name him Jesus (meaning 'Savior'), for he will save his people from their sins. *The Living Bible Illustrated*

She will give birth to a son, and you will name him Jesus [He Saves], because he will save his people from their sins. *God's Word*

Introduction

Many sincere people search for meaning and purpose of their life. The traditional and well established religions are expected to provide the meaning and purpose to those, who search for these spiritual things. When the traditional religions cannot provide these things, the people go to various cults, demonic worship, spiritual experiments, and even drugs.

Some religious philosophies teach that man has to save himself by realization and by good deeds. Hindu philosophy of non-dualism (*Advaita*) teaches that there is an identity between an individual self or soul (*Jiva* or *Atman*) and the supreme Self or Soul (*Paramatman* or *Brahman*); and man has to realize this spiritual identity by meditation; and he should not seek liberation coming from outside. Man is the Supreme God (*Paramatman* or *Brahman*) himself.

Similarly, Hinayana Buddhism teaches that man should enlighten himself by meditation; and there is no god to save man.

Christianity does not subscribe to these aforesaid religious philosophies or theologies. It believes that man is made by God in His image (Gen. 1:26, 27). Man is different from God, as an image is different from the original thing; they are different in essence. Man is sinful by nature; and he cannot save himself by good deeds. Man is saved by the grace of God in Jesus Christ. St. Augustine (354-430), in his book '*Confessions*' wrote: "Thou hast made us for Thyself; and the heart of man is restless until it finds its rest in Thee." [1] This theological statement implies that man can find purpose and meaning for his life, when he sees his salvation in God in Jesus Christ.

Many religious people have to find the purpose and meaning for their life. But in some cases, God assigns the mission to man, and that mission provides the purpose and meaning for him. There are some examples in the Bible, illustrating the point.

(1) Jeremiah (Jer. 1:2-3, period of his prophecy 627-587 B.C.) responded to the call of the LORD God; and he was asked to be a prophet of God, delivering divine messages to the people of Israel. He reviewed his career as a prophet. He was convinced that his commission as a prophet was preordained. He heard God saying to him:

> Before I formed you in the womb I knew you, and before you were born
> I consecrated you; I appointed you a prophet to the nations. (Jer.1:5)

Jeremiah was not ready to respond to God's call immediately. He was aware of his weakness or inadequacy. When God asked him to be His prophet, he said to God: "Ah, LORD God! Behold, I do not know how to speak, for I am only a youth." (Jer. 1:6) Then God said to him:

> Do not say, 'I am only a youth'; for to all whom I send you you shall go, and whatever I command you you shall speak. Be not afraid of them, for I am with you to deliver you. (Jer. 1:7)

Then God touched Jeremiah's mouth and said:

> Behold, I have put my words in your mouth. See I have set you this day over nations and over kingdoms, to pluck up and to break down, to destroy and to overthrow, to build and to plant. (Jer. 1:10)

Jeremiah was convinced of his divine call; and he remained faithful to his call.

(2) In a similar way, Isaiah (Is. 1:1; 7:1, his period of prophecy 783-687 B.C.) became a prophet of God. Concerning his divine call, Isaiah wrote:

> Listen to me, O coastlands, and hearken, you peoples from afar. The LORD called me from the womb, from the body of my mother he named my name. He made my mouth like a sharp sword, in the shadow of his hand he hid me; he made me a polished arrow, in his quiver he hid me away. And he said to me, 'You are my servant, Israel, in whom I will be glorified.... I will give you as a light to the nations,that my salvation may reach to the end of the earth. (Is. 49:1-6)

Prophet Isaiah then spelled out his commission in these words:

> The Spirit of the LORD God is upon me, because the LORD has anointed me to bring good tidings to the afflicted; he has sent me to bind up the brokenhearted, to proclaim liberty to the captives, and the opening of the prison to those who are bound; to proclaim the year of the LORD's favour, and the day of vengeance of our God; to comfort all who mourn; to grant to those who mourn in Zion- to give them a garland instead of ashes, the oil of gladness instead of mourning, the mantle of praise instead of a faint spirit; that they may be called oaks of righteousness, the planting of the LORD, that he may be glorified. (Is. 61:1-3)

(3) St. Paul received the call of Jesus Christ to work for Him. He was changed from being a persecutor of the Church to becoming an outstanding apostle of Jesus Christ. His first name was Saul. He was zealous to defend Judaism and to oppose Christianity, as a

cult, threatening Judaism. He obtained an official permission from the Sanhedrim at Jerusalem to persecute Christians. On his way to Damascus, Jesus Christ appeared to him. That appearance of Jesus Christ to Saul caused him to change completely. (Acts 9:1-20) He became a most dedicated servant of Jesus Christ. He reviewed his career in the light of his divine commission; and said these words:

> For you have heard of my former life in Judaism, how I persecuted the church of God violently and tried to destroy it; and I advanced in Judaism beyond many of my own age among my people, so extremely zealous was I for the traditions of my fathers. But when he who had set me apart before I was born, and had called me through his grace, was pleased to reveal his Son to me, in order that I might preach him among the Gentiles. (Gal. 1:13-16)

From the life and career of these servants of God, we can conclude that they reviewed their entire life with reference to their divine mission. They realized that they were predestined to serve God. They understood that the ultimate purpose and meaning of their life were spelled out for them in terms of their commission. The divine commission provided them the purpose and meaning for their life.

Introduction of the Text

As the divine commission was preordained for prophet Isaiah, prophet Jeremiah, and for St. Paul, the same was true in the life of Jesus Christ. His divine commission was spelled out for Him in His very name, "Jesus." Mary was betrothed to Joseph, who was a righteous man. When he found Mary pregnant, he wished to divorce her privately. An angel of God appeared to Joseph; and he told Joseph that Mary was pregnant with a baby boy by the Holy Spirit; and he should not be afraid to take her as his wife. Then the angel said to Joseph:

> **She [Mary] will bear a son, and you shall call his name Jesus, for he will save his people from their sins.** (Mt. 1:20-21)

This is the text of our meditation now.

The Context of the Text

The birth of Jesus Christ was the divine intervention in the history of mankind. Jesus Christ was predestined to be the Saviour of the world. Therefore, the birth of Jesus Christ was a unique or supernatural fact. God was born as a man, called Jesus. The name 'Jesus' was given to the firstborn son of virgin Mary by Joseph, a human parent, because an angel of God asked him to do. This name has a special significance.

How the supernatural birth of Jesus Christ took place is told by the gospel writers in a few versions. Before Jesus was conceived in the womb of the virgin Mary, an angel of God appeared before the virgin Mary and said to her:

> Do not be afraid, Mary, for you have found favour with God. And behold, you will conceive in your womb and bear a son, and you shall call his name Jesus. (Lk. 1:30-31)

Mary was betrothed to Joseph. When Joseph found Mary carrying a baby in her womb, he resolved to divorce her quietly. Then an angel of the Lord appeared to Joseph in a dream and said to him:

> Joseph, son of David, do not fear to take Mary your wife, for that which is conceived in her is of the Holy Spirit; she will bear a son, and you shall call his name Jesus, for he will save his people from their sins. (Mt. 1:20-21)

The appearance of the angel to Joseph was very important, because Joseph became doubtful of Mary's virginity or chastity. If he had brought the matter to the public attention, Mary could have been charged with adultery; and she would have been sentenced to death (Lev.20:10) by stoning (Jn 8:5). Joseph did not wish to do so. But he thought of divorcing her privately. Therefore, the angel had to come to Joseph and to explain him that Mary was conceived by the Holy Spirit, and she was not pregnant of any man. Joseph was told to name the baby boy "Jesus," because the child was going to save His people from their sins. In other words, Jesus Christ was born of the virgin Mary and of the Holy Spirit, for the divine commission of saving the world.

An Analysis of the Text

The text, "She [Mary] will bear a son, and you shall call his name Jesus, for he will save his people from their sins," (Mt. 1:21) has two ideas.

(A) The first idea is that the virgin Mary would bear a son.

(B) The second idea is that Joseph would name the child "Jesus," because he would save his people from their sins.

Exposition of the Ideas of the Text:

(A) The first idea of the text is that the virgin Mary would bear a son, a male child. Jesus Christ is called the Son of God or the Son of Man, several times in the scripture (Mt. 8:20; 12:8, 40; 13:41; 14:33; 16:27; 19:28; 20:18, 28; 24:30; 25:31; 26:31; 27:54).

From theological points of view, the Saviour had to be a male child. (1) Adam, the first male, disobeyed God; and he sinned against the Creator. Subsequently, he brought death on himself and his descendants. God, in His grace, had to redeem the mankind from sin and death, through the sinless Man. St. Paul described Jesus Christ as the new or last Adam (I Cor. 15:22, 45-49). He argued how God would redeem mankind, in the following words:

> Then as one man's trespass led to condemnation for all men, so one man's act of righteousness leads to acquittal and life for all men. For as by one man's disobedience many were made sinners, so by one man's obedience many will be made righteous. (Rom. 5:18-19)

Though the last Adam or Jesus Christ was a male, He is not the Saviour of males only, but also He is the Saviour of both males and females (Gal. 3:26-28). Further, there is no distinction among the children of God, on the basis of sex. St. John made this point, in these words:

> But to all who received him [Jesus Christ] he gave power to become children of God, who were born, not of blood nor of the will of the flesh nor of the will of man, but of God. (Jn 1:12-13)

(2) Secondly, God was pleased with King David (1002-962 B. C.) and He promised King David that his kingdom shall be established

forever through his offspring, who would be the Messiah (II Sam. 7:12-14,16). King David, being filled with the spirit of God, addressed the Messiah, the Son of God, as his Lord (Ps. 110:1; Mt. 22:44; 26:44). God repeated the words of the covenant, which He made with King David, through prophet Ezekiel (Ezek. 37:24-28) and prophet Jeremiah (Jer. 33:20-22), after passing away of King David. St. Luke saw the fulfilment of the prophecy in the birth of Jesus Christ, which was heralded by an angel (Lk. 1:30-33). Prophet Isaiah prophesied that the Messiah would be a son (Is. 9:6) and His name will be called "Wonderful Counsellor, Mighty God, Everlasting Father, Prince of Peace." (Is. 9:7). In short, the Messiah would be a son, a male child; and He would be the Saviour of all.

(B) The second idea of the text is that Joseph would name the child "Jesus," because He would save His people from their sins. In other words, the meaning of the word "Jesus" is the Saviour of the people from their sins. This meaning was given by the angel to Joseph. Both name and meaning of Jesus were originated from the heaven or from the LORD God. In spelling out the meaning of the name 'Jesus,' the angel announced preordained commission of Jesus Christ.

Jesus Christ knew the divine purpose and commission of His life from His adolescence. Before He started His career as a preacher, He went to a synagogue at Nazareth and read a passage from the book of prophet Isaiah, as follows:

> The Spirit of the LORD is upon me, because he has anointed me to preach good news to the poor. He has sent me to proclaim release to the captives and recovering of the sight to the blind, to set at liberty those who are oppressed, to proclaim the acceptable year of the LORD. (Lk.4:18-19 cf. Is. 61:1-2)

Having read the scripture, Jesus Christ gave the book to the attendant and said to the people, "This day is this scripture fulfilled in your ears." (Lk. 4:21) This event tells us that Jesus Christ reaffirmed the purpose of His life and the divine commission of His life, with reference to the word of God.

Let us analyse the divine commission of the life of Jesus Christ, which was prophesied by Isaiah, eight centuries before Jesus Christ was born.

(1) First, Jesus Christ was anointed to preach good news to the poor. The poor were waiting to hear the good news from the Messiah, because the Messiah was their hope of the rescue and of salvation. In general, the poor in every society are always maltreated and exploited. They are deprived of justice and economic fairness by the wicked persons. The wicked persecute the poor (Ps. 10:2) and they fight against the poor (Ps. 37:10). But God saves the fatherless and the needy from the hand of the mighty; therefore, the poor have hope of the rescue (Job. 5:15; Jer. 20:13). The LORD God is just and righteous. He commanded the people of Israel not to be partial to the poor in suit (Ex. 23:3; Lev. 19:15). He also commanded them to give liberally to the poor (Deut. 15:7-11). He also asked them to leave gleaning for the poor (Lev. 23:22), and to leave grapes for the poor (Lev. 19:10). He asked to give gifts to the poor, when they celebrate happy events (Est. 9:22). Thus, God made provisions for the poor in the land.

As the poor are not able to negotiate for their daily wages, they are at the mercy of their employers. They cannot fight back, if their unjust employers deny their claims of wages. God commanded His people not to oppress the poor, but give their wages on the same day (Deut. 24:14-15). God takes up cause of the poor (Ps. 12:5); and He redeems them from the strong (Ps. 35:10). He is their refuge (Ps. 14:6). In addition to giving His protection to the poor, He commands the kings to defend the cause of the poor and to deliver the needy (Ps. 72:4, 12-14).

God condemned those who exploit the poor, through prophet Isaiah, in these words:

> Woe to those who decree iniquitous decrees, and the writers who keep writing oppression, to turn aside the needy from justice and to rob the poor of my people of their rights, that the widows may be their spoil, and that they may make the fatherless their prey! (Is. 10:1-2)

God explained to His people as to what is true religious life in terms of doing right and just things, in the following words:

> Is not this the fast that I choose: to loose the bonds of wickedness, to undo the thongs of the yoke, to let the oppressed go free, and to break every yoke? Is it not to share your bread with the hungry, and bring the homeless poor into your house; when you see the naked, to cover him, and not to hide yourself from your own flesh? (Is. 58:6-7)

God protects the poor from exploitation and oppression in His way. He commands His people to be just and fair to the poor; and He asks the kings to do justice to the poor. Furthermore, God was going to send the Messiah to assure His care and protection to the poor. Prophet Isaiah prophesied about this, in the following words:

> The meek shall obtain fresh joy in the LORD, and the poor among men shall exult in the Holy One of Israel. (Is. 29:19)

God kept His promise of sending the Messiah, Jesus Christ, to the poor. As part of His Messiahship, Jesus Christ preached the good news to the poor. When John the Baptist (ca.5 B. C.-A. D. 28) was in prison, he sent his disciples to ask Jesus whether He was the Christ, the anticipated Messiah. Jesus Christ asked the disciples of John to tell him the following things:

> The blind receive their sight and the lame walk, lepers are cleansed and the deaf hear, and the dead are raised up, and the poor have good news preached to them. And blessed is he who takes no offence at me. (Mt. 11:5-6; cf. Lk. 7:22)

Jesus Christ preached the good news to the poor; and He fed the hungry occasionally. He gave them the assurance that He came into the world for the poor and the neglected to save them from sin and sufferings.

(2) Secondly, Jesus Christ was anointed to proclaim a release to the captives. The captives were those, who were defeated on the battlefield, and who were subjugated by those who won the war (I Sam. 30:2). In the captivity, people lost their rights and privileges; they were treated as slaves (II Chr. 28:10); they were ruled over mercilessly; they were reduced to subhuman beings. Nebuchadnezzar, the king of Babylon (605-562 B. C.), besieged

Jerusalem and carried ten thousand people as captives to Babylon (II Kg. 24:8-16) in 598 B. C.. The people of Israel defeated the people of Judah and took King Ahaz (735-715 B. C.) and his people as captives to Damascus (II Chr. 28:5-7). Prophet Obed of Samaria denounced the action of the people of Israel; and caused them to release and to send the captives back to Judah (II Chr. 28:14). When the people of Israel and of Judah were in captivity, prophet Jeremiah prophesied that God would take them back to their lands, when they would repent (Jer. 24:4-6). He said that God would be their Redeemer (Jer. 50:33-34). Prophet Isaiah also prophesied that God would bring back His people to their land (Is. 14:1-2; 43:4-7); and God would rescue them (Is. 49:25). God released His people from the hand of Babylonian and Assyrian powers; and He brought them back to their promised land, through King Cyrus of Persia (539-530 B. C.) (II Chr. 36:22-23; Ezra 1:1-4; Is. 44:28, 45:1-6). The work of releasing the captives was to be carried out through the Messiah, Jesus Christ. Jesus Christ proclaimed the good news to the captives; and He gave them the hope of better days ahead of them.

(3) Thirdly, Jesus Christ was anointed to recover the sight of the blind. This mission of Jesus Christ was prophesied by psalms writers and prophets. A psalm writer wrote: "the LORD opens the eyes of the blind. " (Ps. 146:8) Prophet Isaiah prophesied about the healing ministry of God, in the following word:

> Then the eyes of the blind shall be opened, and the ears of the deaf unstopped; then shall the lame man leap like a hart, and the tongue of the dumb sing for joy. (Is. 35:5 cf. Is. 42:7)

Jesus Christ fulfilled the promise of God, when He restored sight of the blind persons. Jesus Christ opened the eyes of two blind men (Mt. 9:27-30); and He did the same with many blind (Mt. 20:30-34; Lk. 18:35; Mk. 8:22-25). Jesus Christ gave sight to the man who was born blind (Jn 9:1-41). He performed this miracle on a Sabbath day; therefore, many scribes and Pharisees were offended. This event has spiritual implication. The man, who received sight, met Jesus Christ and worshipped him. Then Jesus Christ said:

> For judgment I came into the world, that those who do not see may see,
> and that those who see may become blind. (Jn 10:40)

The mission of Jesus Christ was not limited to recovering physical sight of the blind; it went beyond that. It included giving the spiritual insight to the people, who were sitting in darkness of sin, of ignorance and prejudices. His mission was to give the spiritual insight to the people. This was the mission of God. Prophet Isaiah (800 B. C.) prophesied about the mission in these words:

> And I will lead the blind in a way that they know not, in paths that they have
> not known I will guide them. I will turn the darkness before them into light.
> (Is. 42:16)

Jesus Christ said to the people, who were groping in darkness in the temple at Jerusalem:

> I am the light of the world; he who follows me will not walk in darkness,
> but will have the light of life. (Jn 8:12)

In other words, Jesus Christ is the light for the spiritual life of the people. He also said that He is the way, the truth, and life. He is the only way to God. (Jn 14:6; Jn 11:25) God is light, and there is no darkness in Him; and believers are exhorted to walk in the light of God, and have fellowship with one another (I Jn 1:12-13).

(4) Fourthly, Jesus Christ was anointed to set at liberty those who were oppressed. The people of Israel were oppressed by many kings. They were oppressed by Jabin, the king of Canaan, who reigned in Hazor (Jud. 4:2); they were oppressed by the people of Midian (Jud. 6:5), by the Philistines and Amorites (Jud. 10:7-9), and by the king of Syria (II Kg. 13, 4, 22). When the people of Israel cried to the LORD for liberty from their oppressors, God sent judges, like Barak, Gideon, and Jephthah to deliver them from their oppressors. God has been the stronghold of the oppressed (Ps. 9:9), because of His love and covenant with the Israel (Ps. 106:7-10). God has been their Redeemer (Jer. 50:33)

Apart from political oppression, God wanted to save man from the spiritual bondage of sin. God created man in His image, a free being (Gen.1:26-27). When man lost his spiritual freedom, because of his sins, God sent His Son, Jesus Christ, to set man free from the spiritual bondage (Rom. 8:1-3; 6:17-18) and oppression. It has been the work of God to redeem man from the spiritual bondage and oppression. Concerning this divine mission, God spoke through prophet Isaiah, as follows:

> Is not this the fast that I choose: to loose the bonds of wickedness, to undo the thongs of the yoke, to let the oppressed go free, and to break every yoke? (Is. 58:6)

The yoke represents bondage and oppression or social and spiritual slavery. Jesus Christ came into the world to put an end to the bondage or slavery to sin and set people free to walk in godly way. Bondage of sin brings death; but bondage to righteousness gives life to the spirit. St. Paul made this point in his letter to the Romans, in the following words:

> But now that you have been set free from sin and have become slaves of God, the return you get is sanctification and its end, eternal life. For the wages of sin is death, but the free gift of God is eternal life in Christ Jesus our Lord. (Rom. 6:22-23)

Jesus Christ spoke about two types of yokes, resulting into oppression and rest respectively. He invited people to take His yoke upon them and to find rest in Him. He said to the people:

> Come to me, all who labour and are heavy laden, and I will give you rest. Take my yoke upon you, and learn from me; for I am gentle and lowly in heart, and you will find rest for your souls. For my yoke is easy, and my burden is light. (Mt. 11:28-30)

Jesus used the term "rest" in terms of freedom from oppression. His yoke is His discipleship, which requires man to walk in righteousness. The reward of His yoke is rest or freedom from oppression.

Conclusion

God sent His Son, Jesus Christ, into the world. He gave the name to His Son and told the meaning of Jesus to Joseph. In this way, God predestined the mission for Jesus Christ. His life mission was to preach the good news to the poor, to proclaim liberty to the captives, to give sight to the blind, and to set the oppressed free. The mission is given to those who profess to be Christians. The Christmas greetings come to Christians with challenges of their age.

Recommended Hymns from the Methodist Hymnal

82   'Hark! The glad sound! the Saviour comes,'

117   'Hark! the herald-angels sing'

120   'Christians, awake, salute the happy morn,'

143   'Good Christian men, rejoice'

373   'Lord, I was blind!' I could not see'

Recommended Responsive Reading from the Methodist Hymnal

5 (p. 386),

Recommended Responsive Reading from A Worship Manual for Scriptural or Methodist Order of Service

79 (pp. 193-194).

Endnotes

[1] Frank S. Mead (ed.) The Encyclopedia of Religious Quotations, (Old Tappan, New Jersey: Fleming H. Revell Company, 1965), p. 165.

Chapter - 3

Titles of the Sermon

'Emmanuel's Virgin Birth,'

'Virgin Birth of Jesus Christ,'

'Virginity as the Necessary for the Divine Incarnation,'

'God with Man,'

'Divine Incarnation.'

Scripture

Matthew 1:18-25

Genesis 8:1-9:17

Exodus 3:1-12; 14:5-31; 13:18-20

Leviticus 26:3-12

I Samuel 3:3-14

II Samuel 7:12-14,16

Job 25:4

Psalms 23:1; 34:10; 51:5; 53:3; 110:1; 130:3

Proverbs 20:9

Ecclesiastes 7:20

Isaiah 6:1-8; 7:7, 9,14; 9:6-7; 43:2-5

Jeremiah 1:4-8; 33:20-22

Ezekiel 2:1-3:3; 37:24-28

Matthew 8:20; 12:8, 40; 13:41; 14:35; 16:27; 19:28;
20:18, 28; 24:36; 25:31; 26:31; 27:54

Luke 1:30-35

John 1:12-14

Romans 3:23; 5:18-19

I Corinthians 15:22, 45-49

Galatians 3:26-28

Text: Matthew 1:23

A Few Versions of the Text, Matthew 1:23

"Behold the virgin shall be with child, and bear a Son, and they shall call His name Immanuel," which is translated, "God with us." *The New King James Version*

Behold the virgin shall be with child, and bring forth a son, and they shall call his name Emmanuel, which is, being interpreted, God with us. *Explanatory Notes Upon the New Testament*

"Behold, a virgin shall conceive and bear a son, and his name shall be called Emmanuel" (which means, God with us). *Revised Standard Version*

"The virgin will be with child and will give birth to a son, and they will call Emmanuel" — (which means, "God with us.") *New International Version*

'The virgin will conceive and bear a son, and he shall be called Emmanuel,' a name which means 'God is with us'. *The New English Bible*

'Listen! The virgin shall conceive a child! She shall give birth to a Son, and he shall be called "Emmanuel " (meaning, "God is with us").' *The Living Bible Illustrated*

"The virgin will become pregnant and give birth to a son, and they will name him Immanuel,"which means "God with us." *God's Word*

Introduction

Rationalism, thinking led by human reason, is good, as long it leads people to think rationally and logically. But it turns out to be disadvantageous, when it fails to know its limits and becomes arrogant. A liberal way of thinking has come out of human rationalism. Following a fashion or fad of liberal thinking, many Christian preachers doubt traditional biblical doctrines, such as resurrection of Jesus Christ and subsequently belief in resurrection of believers, God's power to perform miracles, and the virgin birth of Jesus Christ, etc. Their blatant denials of the virgin birth of Jesus Christ have influenced many Christians to doubt the necessity and factuality of the virgin birth of Jesus Christ. Therefore, it is necessary to reemphasise the biblical doctrine of the virgin birth of Jesus Christ.

Introduction of the Text

Our rational thinking is limited by natural laws, which govern nature; therefore, it cannot conceive that beings, including human beings, are born without sexual acts. Our human rationality does not recognize the supernatural power, which can bypass natural laws in order to serve its purpose. Biblical faith recognizes supernatural interventions in the natural realm; we call them miracles or the divine acts. We experience miracles, yet not knowing how the miracles take place.

It is a distinctive faith of Christianity that Jesus Christ, who saves mankind form sin, was born of the virgin Mary. Mary was a virgin before Jesus was conceived in her womb. Her husband Joseph did not know her, in a biblical sense, after Jesus Christ was born. Mary became pregnant with Jesus, not by Joseph, but by the Spirit of God. Jesus Christ was the Son of God, as He was born of the Spirit of God; He was born in a supernatural way.

That Messiah, the Christ, would be born in the supernatural way, was prophesied by prophet Isaiah (800 B. C.). St. Matthew, in his narration of the birth of Jesus Christ, quoted the prophesy of Isaiah, as the fulfilment of the prophesy. He quoted:

"Behold, a virgin shall conceive and bear a son, and his name shall be called Emmanuel" (which means, God with us.) (Matthew 1:23)

This is the text of our meditation now.

The Context of the Text

St. Matthew explained the virgin birth of Jesus Christ with reference to the prophesy from the Book of Isaiah 7:14:

> Therefore the LORD himself will give you a sign. Behold, a young woman [or virgin] shall conceive and bear a son, and shall call his name Immanuel [that is God is with us].

Prophet Isaiah (his period of prophecy 783-687) told this prophecy to King Ahaz, who began to reign Judah at his twenty. He was born in 755 B. C. He ruled Judah for twenty years, from 735 to 715 B. C. The capital of Judah was Jerusalem. During the reign of King Ahaz, King Pekah was reigning over Israel from 737 to 732 B. C. The capital of the kingdom of Israel was Samaria. These two Jewish kingdoms were hostile with one another. The kingdom of Israel planned to destroy the kingdom of Judah. Pekah, the king of Israel, asked Rezon, the king of Syria, to attack the kingdom of Judah and to annex it to his kingdom. Damascus was the capital of Syria. When King Ahaz and the people of Judah heard about this plot, they were terrified. Pekah, the king of Israel, and Rezon, the king of Syria, combined their armies and besieged Jerusalem, the capital of Judah in 734 B. C. The people of Judah were afraid of being destroyed. They cried to the LORD God for help. God sent prophet Isaiah, with the assurance that the plan of King Pekah and King Rezon to destroy the kingdom of Judah would fail; but the people of Judah should trust God. Prophet Isaiah said to King Ahaz:

> It [the plot] shall not stand, and it shall not come to pass.... If you will not believe, surely you shall not be established. (Is. 7: 7, 9)

After these words, Isaiah told King Ahaz God's plan to save the people of Judah, in these words:

> "Behold, a young woman shall conceive and bear a son, and shall his name Immanuel." (Is. 7:14)

This prophesy was fulfilled when Jesus Christ, the Saviour of mankind, was born of the virgin Mary. This is how St. Matthew explained the virgin birth of Jesus Christ to the believers. This is a historical background of the text of our meditation.

An Analysis of the Text

This text has three ideas. (A) The first idea is the prophesy that a virgin shall conceive.

(B) The second idea is that the virgin shall give birth to a son, a male child.

(C) The third idea is that the son, born of the virgin, shall be called "Emmanuel" (which means, God with us.)

Exposition of the Ideas of the Text

(A) The first idea of the text is the prophecy that a virgin shall conceive. Prophet Isaiah told King Ahaz that God would give him a sign of the immediate and future relief from the siege. That sign could be a greatest sign; it could be deep as Sheol or high as heaven (Is. 7:10). In other words, it would be most incredible sign or miracle.

The LORD God had been giving signs of relief or liberation to the people, who cried for His divine help. There are many examples to prove the point.

(1) The LORD God gave sign of assurance to Noah that He would never destroy the world by flood; God put rainbow in the sky as the sign of His covenant with Noah. (Gen. 8:1-9:17)

(2) When the Hebrews were at the seashore of Red Sea and Pharaoh's army was behind them, they cried for help and relief, God heard their cry. God asked Moses to hold the staff upon the Red Sea. When Moses did so, the Red Sea was divided; and the people escaped from danger and they were saved. (Ex. 14:5-31)

The Bible has recorded many miracles, which are the evidences how God uses the nature in mysterious ways. Man has not yet understood how God works miracles. It is beyond our ability to comprehend rationally. We somehow have to believe in the works of God. If we believe in God, we will experience how God works in us, without our understanding of His mysterious ways.

The virgin birth of Jesus Christ is a deepest miracle; it is a supernatural fact. St. Luke recorded this supernatural event, as follows: Gabriel, an angel of God, appeared to a virgin called Mary and said to her, "Hail, O favoured one, the Lord is with you!" (Lk.1:28) Mary was puzzled over the greetings. Then the angel added:

> Do not be afraid, Mary, for you have found favour with God. And behold, you will conceive in your womb and bear a son, and you shall call his name Jesus. He will be great, and will be called the son of the Most High; and the Lord God will give to him the throne of his father David, and be will reign over the house of Jacob for ever; and of his kingdom there will be no end. (Lk. 1:30-33)

The virgin Mary, like any other woman, questioned a possibility of being pregnant without having her sexual relationship with a man. She asked the angel: "How shall this be, since I have no husband?" (Lk. 1:34) The angel told the virgin Mary how that would take place, in these words:

> The Holy Spirit will come upon you, and the power of the Most High will overshadow you; therefore the child to be born will be called holy, the Son of God. (Lk. 1:35)

Thus, Jesus Christ was born of the Holy Spirit or God and of the virgin Mary.

God favoured Mary to be the mother of the Messiah, because Mary kept her virginity or purity of her body and character. She must have been religious maiden; and she had the fear of God in her heart. Therefore, God considered her to be worthy to conceive His Son in her womb. Mary was divinely chosen to be the instrument to fulfil the purpose of God. God had been choosing persons, who were walking in His way, as His servants for fulfilling His purpose. God chose Moses (Ex. 3:1-12), Joshua (Jos. 1:1-9), Samuel (I Sam. 3:3-14), Isaiah (Is. 6:1-8), Jeremiah (Jer. 1:4-8), Ezekiel (Ezek. 2:1-3:3), etc. because they were righteous in His sight.

Someone might ask a question: Why Jesus Christ, the Saviour of the world, had to be born in this supernatural way? What is a theological reason of the supernatural birth of Jesus Christ? If Jesus Christ had been born in the natural way, as we all are born, He would have been subjected to sin and death; subsequently, He would not have been resurrected. Moreover, He would not have been able to make atonement for our sins; subsequently, He could not have become our Saviour.

The Bible often talks about man's sinful condition. Bildad, a friend of Job argued, in these words: "How then can man be righteous before God? How can he who is born of woman be clean?" (Job 25:4) David described the sinful condition of his birth, in these words: "Behold, I was brought forth in iniquity, and in sin my mother conceived me." (Ps. 51:5 cf. 53:3; 130:3) King Solomon (962-922 B. C.) asserted sinful condition of human life, in these words: "Who can say, 'I have made my heart clean; I am pure from my sin?" (Pr. 20:9) The preacher of the Bible wrote: "Surely there is not a righteous man on earth who can do good and never sins." (Eccl. 7:20) St. Paul similarly wrote to the Romans: "Since all have sinned and fall short of the glory of God." (Rom.3:23) In short, man is born in sin and remains sinful until he dies.

As the mankind remains sinful, there is no possibility that a sinless man be born of mankind to redeem it from sin. It is beyond man to save himself. Only God, the supernatural and caring Spirit can do something to save man from sin. God, out of love and grace, wished to redeem man from sin; therefore, God planned a sinless Man to be born for redemption of mankind. This is why Jesus Christ, the only Saviour of the mankind, had to be born of the Holy Spirit and of the virgin.

(B) The second idea of the text is that the virgin shall give birth to a son, a male child. Jesus Christ is called the Son of God or the Son of Man several times in the scripture (Mt. 8:20; 12:8, 40; 13:41; 14:33; 16:27; 19:28; 20:18, 28; 24:30; 25:31; 26:31; 27:54).

From theological points of view, the Saviour had to be a male child. Adam, the first male, disobeyed God and sinned against the Creator; subsequently he brought death on himself and his descendants. God, in His grace, had to redeem the mankind from sin and death through the sinless Man. St. Paul described Jesus Christ as the new or last Adam (I Cor. 15:22, 45-49). He argued how God would redeem mankind, in the following words:

> Then as one man's trespass led to condemnation for all men, so one man's act of righteousness leads to acquittal and life for all men. For as by one man's disobedience many were made sinners, so by one man's obedience many will be made righteous. (Rom. 5:18-19)

Though the last Adam or Jesus Christ was a male, He is not the Saviour of males only; but He is the Saviour of both males and females (Gal. 3:26-28). Further, there is no distinction among the children of God, on the basis of sex. St. John made this point, in these words:

> But to all who received him [Jesus Christ] he gave power to become children of God, who were born, not of blood nor of the will of the flesh nor of the will of man, but of God. (Jn 1:12-13)

Secondly, God was pleased with King David (1002-962 B. C.); and He promised King David that his kingdom shall be established forever through his offspring, who would be the Messiah (II Sam. 7:12-14,16). King David, being filled with the Spirit of God, addressed the Messiah, the Son of God, as his Lord (Ps. 110:1; Mt. 22:44; 26:44). God repeated the words of the covenant, which He made with King David, through prophet Ezekiel (Ezek. 37:24-28) and prophet Jeremiah (Jer. 33:20-22), after passing away of King David. St. Luke saw the fulfilment of the prophecy in the birth of Jesus Christ, which was heralded by an angel (Lk. 1:30-33). Prophet Isaiah prophesied that the Messiah would be a son (Is. 9:6) and his name will be called "Wonderful Counsellor, Mighty God, Everlasting Father, Prince of Peace." (Is. 9:7). In short, the Messiah would be a son, a male child; and He would be the Saviour of all.

(C) The third idea of the text is that the son, born of the virgin, shall be called "Emmanuel" (which means, God with us.) It means that

Messiah, in the form of Jesus Christ, will be with the people. Jesus Christ is none other than God Himself. When God was incarnated in Jesus Christ, He would be with the people. The name of the Messiah would be called "Emmanuel," because the actual presence of the Messiah would be the presence of God with the people.

God being present with the people in the form of Jesus Christ was a special manifestation of God. This was the promise, which God gave to King Ahaz (735-715 B. C.) and the people of Jerusalem, when they cried for God's help. This promise was fulfilled, when God became incarnate in Christ Jesus. Apart from the special manifestation or revelation of God in Jesus Christ, God demonstrated His presence with the people on various critical occasions. Let us recall a few events.

(1) When the people of Israel went out of Egypt, the LORD God guided them through the wilderness, leading them to the promised land. The people of Hebrews were travelling day and night. God went before them as a pillar of cloud in day and as a pillar of fire by night (Ex. 13:18-22). When Pharaoh's army drew near and the people were at the seashore of the Red Sea, people cried to the LORD God for His protection and relief, God asked Moses to stretch out his hand over the sea and divide it. At the same time, the angle of God and the pillar of cloud went behind the people of Israel; and they stood between the army of Pharaoh and the host of Israel. The army of Pharaoh (Ramses II, 1301-1234 B. C.) did not catch the people of Israel, because God protected them (Ex. 14:19-20).

Afterwards God gave the people of Israel His commandments and statutes. He made His presence with them conditional, when He said:

If you walk in my statutes and observe my commandments and do them, then.... I will have regard for you and make you fruitful and multiply you, and will confirm my covenant with you.... And I will make my abode among you, and my soul shall not abhor you. And I will walk among you, and will be your God, and you shall be my people. (Lev. 26:3-12)

(2) On another occasion, the LORD God repeated His promise to protect the people of Israel, through prophet Isaiah (800 B. C.), in these words:

> Fear not, for I have redeemed you; I have called you by name, you are mine. When you pass through the waters I will be with you; and through the rivers, they shall not overwhelm you; when you walk through fire you shall not be burned, and the flame shall not consume you. For I am the LORD your God, the Holy One of the Israel, your saviour....Because you are precious in my eyes, and honoured, and I love you, I give men in return for you, people in exchange for your life. Fear not, for I am with you. (Is. 43:2-5)

(3) God promised the people of Israel that He will be always with them through the Messiah, who would be born as a Son of a virgin, in these words:

> Behold, a virgin shall conceive and bear a son, and his name shall be called Emmanuel (which means, God with us.) (Is. 7:14)

This promise was fulfilled when Jesus Christ was born, as the first son of the virgin Mary and of the Son of the Most High. St. John wrote about the incarnation of God in Jesus Christ, saying:

> And the word became flesh and dwelt among us, full of grace and truth; we have beheld his glory, glory as of the only Son from the Father. (Jn 1:14)

Conclusion

God chose Mary to be the mother of the Messiah, Jesus Christ, the Saviour of the world, because of her virginity or holiness of life. We can apply this fact to our life. If our hearts are pure, free from wicked thoughts, God will use us to be His instruments in order to fulfil His purposes. Let the Holy Spirit overshadow us. We will be bearing divine ideas and plans to save the sin-sick world.

God became flesh or incarnate in Jesus Christ; and He abided among the people. We can experience this spiritual reality that Jesus Christ abides in us and we abide in Him, as branches and vine abide together (Jn 15:4-5) This experience can be our everyday experience. The name of the Messiah is Emmanuel, which means God is with us. The same Messiah, who is eternal God, can be with us at all times.

Recession started in the U. S. A. in December 2007 and its severe effects on the economy of the world has been felt in 2008. Nobody knows when there would be economic recovery. Canadian economy has been effected by the recession in the U. S. A. Many people in the U. S. A. and Canada have become unemployed. Many have become bankrupt and lost their homes. In this critical time, we should have an assurance that God is with us; He is our Immanuel. We should have belief in the providence of God in Jesus Christ. We should believe that God is our shepherd and we will not want. (Ps. 23:1). Again King David wrote: "The young lions suffer want and hunger; but those who seek the LORD lack no good thing." (Ps. 34:10) May God be with us; He be our Immanuel in the difficult times.

Recommended Hymns from the Methodist Hymnal

117   'Hark! the herald-angels sing'

118   'O come, all ye faithful,'

124   'See, amid the winter's snow,'

128   'A virgin most pure, as the '

140   'God from on high hath heard;'

Recommended Responsive Reading from A Worship Manual for Scriptural or Methodist Order of Service

87 (pp. 208-209).

Chapter - 4

Titles of the Sermon
'King Herod's Reaction to the Good News,'

'Troublesome News to King Herod,'

'Reaction of Magis and of King Herod,'

Reaction of Salvation-Seekers and of King Herod,'

'Positive and Negative Reactions to the News
of the Birth of Messiah'.

Scripture
Matthew 2: 1-18

I Kings 21: 1-16

Micah 5:2

John 3:16-21

Text: Matthew 2:3

A Few Versions of the Text, Matthew 2:3
And when Herod the king heard this, he was troubled, and all Jerusalem with him. *The New King James Version*

When Herod the king had heard these things, he was troubled, and all Jerusalem with him. *Explanatory Notes Upon the New Testament*

When Herod the king heard this, he was troubled, and all Jerusalem with him. *Revised Standard Version*

When King Herod heard this, he was disturbed, and all Jerusalem with him. *New International Version*

King Herod was greatly perturbed when he heard this; and so was the whole of Jerusalem. *The New English Bible*

King Herod was deeply disturbed by their question, and all Jerusalem was filled with rumours. *The Living Bible Illustrated*

When King Herod and all Jerusalem heard about this, they became disturbed. *God's Word*

Introduction

It is generally true that every news produces both negative and positive reactions; the following are the examples to make the point.

(1) In 1990 January it was officially declared that the economy, based on the principles of communism in the United States of Soviet Russia, was in a great trouble and the U. S. S. R. was disintegrating. This news was a good news to the United States of America and other democratic nations in the west. But it was a bad news to eastern block countries in Europe, China, and Cuba. It was a good news to the Russians, who were seeking political, economic, and religious freedom. But it was a bad news to the leaders of the communist party in Russia, as they had to lose their hold on the political power. It was a good news to the nations, seeking independence from the Russian dictatorship. But it was a bad news to the U. S. S. R., because it was losing power and its recognition as a world power.

(2) The United Nations decided to send peace making and peace keeping force in Somalia in 1990. This mission was called "Operation Restore Hope." Somalia has become a field of civil wars over last ten years. War lords are fighting to gain control of Somalia. Civilians were being killed, and subjected to starvation and sufferings. Women and children suffered more than men. The nations in the world were watching the deplorable, dehumanizing effects of the civil war in Somalia, for such a long time. Finally,

the United Nations sent its troops to restore order in Somalia, and to feed the Samalians. Canada also sent its troops under the mandate of the United Nations. Arrival of the forces of the United Nations was a good news to the majority of Samalians, who wish to end the civil wars and to restore democracy in Somalia. But it was a bad news to those who were greedy for political power namely, war lords.

(3) Canadians voted on a national referendum in October 1992. Majority voted against the proposed changes in the Canadian constitution. Majority votes against the referendum had produced both negative and positive reactions among Canadians. The decision of Canadians had effects on lowering value of Canadian dollars and on increasing loan and mortgage interest. The banks were happy to increase interest rates; it was a good news to the banks and lending institutes. But it was a bad news to the borrowers or customers. One man's opportunity becomes another's misfortune.

Introduction of the Text

It is proven that every news produces both negative and positive reactions among the people, because their interests, which are mutually exclusive, are affected by the news. This fact is also applicable to the spiritual world. The news of the birth of Jesus Christ had produced a negative reaction on King Herod and some people. It is stated in these words:

> **When Herod the king heard this, he was troubled, and all Jerusalem with him**. (Matthew 2:3)

This is the text of our meditation now.

The Context of the Text

When Jesus Christ, the Messiah, was born in Bethlehem of Judea, Herod the Great was the king of Judea (37-4 B. C.). The wise men, who were the astrologists, saw the star in the East, indicating the birth of the Messiah. They started their journey, guided by the star. They entered Judea. They went to the capital city of Judea, i.e.,

Jerusalem. They were asking the people at large, 'where is he who has been born king of the Jews? For we have seen his star in the East, and have come to worship him.' (Mt. 2:2) They went to see King Herod the Great (37- 4 B. C.) and inquired about the baby king. The news of the birth of the king of the Jews, or the Messiah, produced a negative reaction in the heart of the king, Herod the Great. He was disturbed by the news, and his disturbance affected all Jerusalem. This historical fact is told to us in these words:

> When Herod the king heard this, he was troubled and all Jerusalem with him. (Mt. 2:3)

This is the historical background of the text.

An Analysis of the Text

This text has two ideas. (A) The first idea is that King Herod heard the news of the birth of the king of Jews from Magi, the wise men from the East.

(B) The second idea is that King Herod was troubled and all Jerusalem with him.

Exposition of the Ideas of the Text

(A) The first idea of the text is that King Herod the Great (37-4 B. C.) heard the news of the birth of the king of Jews from Magis, the wise men from the East. Herodotus (484-425 B.C.), a great historian of the Greek world, said that Magis were originally of Median tribe. The Medas was a part of the Persian Empire. The Medas failed to attain their political freedom from Persia. They became teachers and priests in Persia. They were men of holiness and wisdom.

When the Magis saw the star, they interpreted the appearance of the star as indicatiion that a king of the Jews was born; they were happy and excited to see the baby king. They travelled from Persia to Jerusalem about 1000 miles or 3850 k.m. to see the baby king of the Jews. They went to the palace of King Herod the Great to inquire where the king of the Jews was born. King Herod met them and believed them. Then he called the chief priest and scribes in order to ascertain the place of the birth of the king of the Jews, or Messiah, as prophesied by the prophets. They quoted King Herod the Great the prophecy of Micah, the prophet, as follows:

> But you, O Bethlehem Ephrathah, who are little to be among the clans of Judah, from you shall come forth for me whose origin is from old, from ancient time. (Micah 5:2)

King Herod called in the wise men of the East and told them to go to Bethlehem to find the child and to report him so that he might go to see the child and worship him.

King Herod the Great was a son of Antipater, who was a dominant political figure and an Edomite prince in the troubled Palestine.[1] He was a man of keen intellect. He helped the Romans in the wars and civil wars of Palestine. The Roman Senate trusted Herod; and appointed him the governor of Coele-Syria in 47 B. C. He advanced from one position to another until the Roman Senate made him the king of an extensive territory in 40 B. C. He ruled Judea until 4 B. C.; he ruled over Judea thirty-six years, as a king.

Herod was called "Herod the Great." He deserved the title for the great things he did during his reign. He was the only ruler of Palestine, whoever succeeded in keeping peace and bringing order into chaos. He built streets and gardens in Jerusalem and in Judea. He began to rebuild the temple with great splendour in 19 B. C., as a part of his policy of winning the favour of his unwilling subjects, the Jews. The actual temple building was completed in eighteen months; but the building work went on for many years. It was fully completed until 60. This temple was destroyed by the Roman in 70, ten years after its completion.

In times of economic crises, King Herod the Great reduced the taxes to make things easier for the people. In 25 B. C. there was a big famine. King Herod the Great melted down his own gold plate to buy corn for the starving people. However, King Herod the Great had one terrible flaw in his character. He had been suspicious of anyone to be rival to his power. He was regularly eliminating his rivals. He had three sons- Antipater, Alexander, and Aristobulus. When Antipater became eager, with his mother's help, to succeed his father, King Herod the Great, instructed his servants to drown Antipater. His wife Mariamne accused Herod of contriving her son's death. Herod murdered his wife and his mother-in-law, Alexandra. Later on, he stated in his will that his two sons-Alexander and Aristobulus- were to inherit his kingdom. But when rumours reached King Herod the Great that his sons were conspiring against him, he put them to death likewise. Augustus, the Roman Emperor (31 B. C-A. D. 14), had bitterly said that it was safer to be Herod's pig than Herod's son.

The older King Herod the Great became, the more suspicious he grew. In his old age, he became 'a murderous old man'. When King Herod the Great was in this state of mind, the Magis went to meet him and delivered the news that a king of the Jews was born in Judea.

(B) The second idea of the text is that King Herod the Great was troubled, and all Jerusalem with him. Herod the Great was holding unto his throne and the kingly power so adamantly that he was never in a mood to hear a news that someone was attempting to take away his throne from him. He eliminated his sons, his wife, and mother-in-law when they conspired against him to take away his throne. This was said before.

He was greatly disturbed, when the Magis told him that a king of the Jews was born in Judea. He was threatened by the news. He was doubly disturbed by the news, because he was half Jew and half Idumaean (or Edomite) from his father's side. He suspected that the Jews would prefer a king, who was a pure Jew. They would remove him from his throne. Secondly, King Herod the Great was disturbed, because the child was destined to be the king of the Jews. He wanted to eliminate or kill the potential king of the Jews. He secretly summoned the Magis. He ascertained from them what time the star appeared to them so that he would be able to calculate the age of the child in question. King Herod the Great told the Magis to diligently search the child. When they had found the child they should return to him with the report so that he too would go to see the baby king and worship him. King Herod the Great was deceitful in his talk with the Magis; he was troubled in his heart.

When the Jews of Jerusalem heard the news that a baby king was born in Judea, they were troubled and panicked. They knew how King Herod the Great eliminated his own sons, who tried to succeed him as kings. If King Herod the Great did not spare his own sons, he would not spare any other child, who would become a rival to his throne. They were frightened that King Herod the Great could do anything to get rid of that baby king. He was a murderous old man. They were anticipating King Herod's cruel reaction to the news at any time. All people of Jerusalem were afraid of what King Herod the Great would do in order to maintain himself in power.

The Magis followed the star to Bethlehem; and they found the baby king of the Jews. They were exceedingly happy to see the child Jesus with his parents. They fell down and worshipped the child. They offered the baby Jesus gold, frankincense, and myrrh (Mt. 2:11): gold for a king, frankincense for a priest, and myrrh for one who was to die. By offering those gifts to the baby Jesus, the Magis foretold that Jesus Christ would be the true King, the perfect High Priest, and the Supreme Saviour of mankind.

After paying their homage to the baby king, the Magis departed to their own country by another way, as they were instructed by God in a dream (Mt. 2:12). After this, an angel of God appeared to Joseph in a dream. He asked Joseph to flee to Egypt, with the baby and Mary (Mt. 2:13).

Bethlehem is five miles away from Jerusalem, the capital of Judea. King Herod the Great was waiting to hear from the Magis for a long time. Then he realized that he was tricked by those wise men. He became furious. He sent soldiers to kill all male children in Bethlehem and the region, who were two years old or under, as King Herod the Great had ascertained the time of the birth of the baby king from the Magis (Mt. 2:16). This date implies that Jesus the Christ was born before 4 B. C. King Herod the Great thus killed the innocent male children in order to keep his throne secured.

Herod the Great proved himself to be a wicked king by murdering innocent children. He did not care what was right and just. His wicked acts remind us how King Ahaz (735-715 B. C.) took possession of Naboth's vineyard by conspiracy and murder. Elijah, the prophet of God, confronted King Ahaz and denounced his wicked action (I Kg. 21:1-16).

The birth of Jesus Christ (before the spring of 4 B. C.), the spiritual king of the Jews, or the Messiah, created both positive and negative responses from the people. The Magis, the wise men of the East, were very anxious to meet the baby Jesus. They travelled a thousand miles from Persia to Jerusalem to see the baby king of the Jews. When they met the baby Jesus and his parents, they bowed down and worshipped the baby and offered precious gifts as the symbols for which the baby would stand for. The Magis were filled with the divine knowledge. They were very happy to see the spiritual King or the Saviour of the world. They honoured the baby Jesus as a spiritual King. They were Godfearing men; and they obeyed the word of God, as it was revealed to them in a dream. They were pious men. Because of their piety, they worshipped the baby Jesus as the spiritual King of the Jews.

When King Herod the Great heard from the Magis that a baby king was born for the Jews, he was troubled by the news. He thought of baby Jesus as a threat to his throne and kingly power. He was planning to eliminate the baby Jesus. His response was negative. He was not pious, but wicked in his heart. Therefore, his response to the news of the birth of the Messiah was negative. The people in Jerusalem were disturbed by the news, because they knew King Herod the Great that he would do any cruel act to maintain his kingship and throne. The people of Jerusalem responded to the news of the baby king of the Jews negatively.

These were the two types of responses to the news of the birth of Jesus Christ. As the people responded to the news of the birth of baby king, Jesus Christ, they would keep responding to the teaching and works of Jesus Christ. St John wrote about this spiritual fact, in these words:

> For God so loved the world that he gave his only Son, that whoever believes in him should not perish but have eternal life. For God sent the Son into the world, not to condemn the world, but that the world might be saved through him. He who believes in him is not condemned; he who does not believe is condemned already, because he has not believed in the name of the only Son of God. And this is the judgment, that the light has come into the world, and men loved darkness rather than light, because their deeds were evil. For every one who does evil hates the light, and does not come to the light, lest his deeds should be exposed. But he who does what is true comes to the light, that it may be clearly seen that his deeds have been wrought in God. (Jn 3:16-21)

Conclusion

The Magis, the wise and pious men, responded to the news of the birth of the baby king very positively. They were anxious to see the king; and they were delighted to see and worship the Lord Jesus Christ. Their piety was responsible for their positive response to the Saviour of the world. On the contrary, King Herod the Great, impious king, responded the same news negatively. His impiety was responsible for his negative response to the spiritual Lord of the world. If we have righteousness of God in our hearts, we will rejoice at the good news of the birth of the Saviour of the world. On the other hand, if we are filled with wickedness, we would hate the news of the birth of the Saviour of the world. We pray that God grant us real joy, and happiness, because Jesus Christ was born for us to save us personally from sin and the spiritual destruction.

Recommended Hymns from the Methodist Hymnal

124   'See, amid the winter's snow,'

131   'The first Nowell the angel did say'

132   'As with gladness men of old'

133   'From the eastern mountains'

143   'Good Christian men, rejoice'

242   'Come, Thou long-expected Jesus,'

257   'O come, O come, Immanuel,'

Recommended Responsive Reading from the Methodist Hymnal

5 (p. 386).

Recommended Responsive Reading form A Worship Manual for Scriptural or Methodist Order of Service

79 (pp.193-194).

Endnotes

[1] The Wesleyan Bible Commentary, (Peabody, Massachusetts: Hendrickson Publishers, Reprinted 1986), Vol. IV, p. 15.

Chapter - 5

Titles of the Sermon

'Man's Travel to See the Saviour,'

'Divine Guidance to Meet the Saviour,'

'Reverential Visit to the Saviour,'

'Worshipping the Baby King.'

Scripture

Matthew 2:1-12

Genesis 37:5-11; 43:29-30; 45:4-8, 12

I Samuel 9:6, 19

John 1:35-45; 4:25-26, 42

Acts 9:1-8, 25

Text: Matthew 2:10-11

A Few Versions of the Text, Matthew 2:10-11

And when they saw the star, they rejoiced with exceedingly great joy. And when they had come into the house, they saw the young Child with Mary His mother, and they fell down and worshipped Him. *The New King James Version*

And seeing the star, they rejoiced with exceeding great joy. And being come into the house, they saw the young child with Mary his mother; and falling down, they did him homage. *Explanatory Notes Upon the New Testament*

When they saw the star, they rejoiced exceedingly with great joy; and going into the house they saw the child with Mary his mother, and they fell down and worshipped him. *Revised Standard Version*

When they saw the star, they were overjoyed. On coming to the house, they saw the child with his mother Mary, and they bowed down and worshipped him. *New International Version*

At the sight of the star they were overjoyed. Entering the house, they saw the child with Mary his mother, and bowed to the ground in homage to him; *The New English Bible*

And look! The star appeared to them again, standing over Bethlehem. Their joy knew no bounds! Entering the house where the baby and Mary his mother were, they threw themselves down before him, worshipping. *The Living Bible Illustrated*

They were overwhelmed with joy to see the star. When they entered the house, they saw the child with his mother Mary. So they bowed down and worshipped him. *God's Word*

Introduction

In our era, people would like to travel and visit many places in the world. Canadians would like to see the Disney World in Florida; and see the national monuments in Washington, D. C. Similarly, Americans would like to see Rocky Mountains in British Columbia, and C. N. Tower in Toronto. As the people are interested in travelling, tourism has become a big industry. Tourism is a top industry in Florida, Nevada, and Hawaii. The tourist industry in the U. S. A. employs four million Americans; and grosses more than $ 61 billion a year. [1]

(2) St. Paul (ca. 2 B. C. -67) was an apostle of Jesus Christ. He travelled extensively. His previous name was Saul. He was born in Tarsus. He went to Jerusalem for his advanced studies (Acts. 7:58- 8:1). He went from Jerusalem to Damascus to persecute Christians (Acts 9: 1-8). He had a vision of Jesus Christ on his way to Damascus; he was converted there (Acts 9:25). After his conversion, he made three journeys to preach the gospel and to

establish churches. His last or fourth journey was from Jerusalem to Rome. When he returned from his journeys, he wrote a good deal. His letters or epistles were widely read among churches. It is surprising to note that in all his writings he did not describe the scenery of the countries he passed through; he did not mention the wonders of the architecture of his time; and he did not describe customs of the people he met. It seems strange to many people why did St. Paul fail to describe or mention these important things in his letters. There was a reason for his omissions. As he travelled about, he was blind to all else but one thing. On the way to Damascus, when he met the Lord Jesus Christ, he was blinded by the vision of Jesus Christ and His great glory. From that moment onward, he could see nothing but Jesus Christ; and tell of nothing but the gospel of Christ. [2]

Introduction of the Text

Before the time of Jesus Christ, people were travelling for various purposes such as trades, learning, and seeing famous sites. As the travel in the old world was not safe and convenient, very few would venture to travel. Their trips were not for pleasure; but they were motivated by specific purposes, which are mentioned early. When Jesus Christ, an anticipated King of the Jews, was born (4 B. C.), the Magis of Persia saw the star of His birth. They wanted to see the King of the Jews, who was a special King. They decided to travel from Persia to Palestine, a distance about a thousand miles, to see the King and to worship Him. Their journey was guided by the star. They went to Jerusalem to inquire about the place, where the anticipated King of the Jews would be born. They met King Herod (37- 4 B. C.). He asked the scribes and high priest as to where the Messiah would be born. He passed on the information to the Magis; and they went to Bethlehem. The star appeared again in Bethlehem. They went to the house, and saw the baby King, Jesus Christ, and his parents; and they worshipped the child, the Messiah or the Saviour of the world. This joyous event is described by a writer of the gospel, in these words:

When they saw the star, they rejoiced exceedingly with great joy; and going into the house they saw the child with Mary his mother, and they fell down and worshipped him. (Mt. 2:10-11)

This is the text of our mediation now.

The Context of the Text

The Magis of Persia are also called 'wise men' by the translators. Herodotus (484- 425 B. C.) was an ancient historian. He wrote about the Magis that they were originally a Median tribe (1:101, 132). The Medes were part of the Persian Empire. The Median tribe tried to overthrow the Persians; but it failed in its attempt. The Medians had no ambition for power or prestige; they became a tribe of priests, of teachers and instructors of the Persian kings. They became men of holiness and wisdom.[3]

In the olden days, all people believed in astrology, a branch of knowledge, which believes that man's destiny is settled by the star, under which a man is born. The stars follow their route. If suddenly a brilliant star appeared on the horizon, it was believed that God was breaking into His own order to announce some special events.

The Magis of Persia saw an unusual astronomical phenomenon, a brilliant star. They understood that the heavenly brilliance told them of the entry of a King into the world. They wanted to see the King of the Jews. The distance between Persia and Palestine is about 1000 miles or 3850 k.m.. It was a very long distance for them. They used camels, the ships of a desert, for their journey.

Their journey was guided by the star, which appeared at the birth of Jesus Christ. They went to Bethlehem; and they met the baby Jesus and his parents. They worshipped the child. This important event is described by St. Matthew in these words:

When they saw the star, they rejoiced exceedingly with great joy; and going into the house they saw the child with Mary his mother, and they fell down and worshipped him. (Mt. 2:10-11)

This is the text within its historical setting.

An Analysis of the Text

This text talked three things about the Magis, the wise men. (A) The first thing about the wise men was that when they saw the star, they rejoiced exceedingly with great joy.

(B) The second thing about the wise men was that they entered the house and saw the child with Mary his mother.

(C) The third thing about the wise men was that they fell down and worshipped the child.

Exposition of the Ideas of the Text

(A) The first thing about the wise men was that when they saw the star, they rejoiced exceedingly with great joy. In other words, when the Magis saw the star again in Bethlehem, they rejoiced greatly, because that star pointed out the place, where the anticipated King of the Jews or the Messiah was born. St. Matthew told us that the Magis or three wise men of the East, who saw a star in their country Persia, indicating that a King of the Jews was born at that particular time. They interpreted the appearance of the star as a divine intervention in human history. They put aside all their daily concerns and prepared themselves for a long journey in order to see the King of the Jews.

Their journey from Persia to Palestine was a very long journey, about 1000 miles or 3850 k.m. journey. Their journey was tiresome and uncomfortable; they had to ride on camels. As it was through a desert, there were no marked high ways or resting places on their way. Their journey was risky; they could be robbed and beaten. Those wise men knew the dangers and risks of such a long journey. Yet they decided to undertake the journey at any cost.

The star, which they saw in Persia, in their country, became their guide. They followed the star throughout their journey, until they reached Jerusalem; and met King Herod the Great (37- 4 B. C.). A hymn-writer composed a hymn about that guiding star, as follows:

O Star of wonder, star of night,

star with royal beauty bright,

westward leading, still proceeding,

Guide us to Thy perfect light.

Those wise men followed the direction of the star; and they went to Jerusalem and to the palace of King Herod the Great, inquiring: "Where is he who has been born king of the Jews? For we have seen his star in the East, and have come to worship him." (Mt. 2:2)

When they met King Herod the Great, they asked the same question to him. King Herod the Great was troubled by the news. He called the high priest and scribes to ascertain the prophecy about the place where the Christ or Messiah was to be born. They quoted him Micah 5:2, prophesying that the Christ was to be born in Bethlehem of Judea. King Herod the Great passed on this information to the wise men; and he asked them to go to Bethlehem and to bring back the word about the baby King so that he might go and worship the baby King.

As the Magis started their journey from Jerusalem to Bethlehem, the star appeared to them again. They were following the star. The star rested over the place, where the child, the baby King of the Jews was with His mother Mary. Thus, the star guided their journey from their country Persia to the house in Bethlehem where Jesus Christ was as an infant. God guided the Magis to see His Son, the Saviour of the world, by the star, an external sign. He can guide man without external signs. God guides His servants, when they submit themselves into the hands of God, because God controls and directs their destiny. There are a few examples in the Bible to illustrate the point.

(1) Joseph had two dreams, which were interpreted that he would be a great person; and his brothers and parents would bow down before him (Gen. 37:5-11). His brothers were angry at him, because of those dreams. They sold him to Midianite traders. Joseph was taken to Egypt; and sold as a slave to an official of Pharaoh. He was falsely accused of rape; and was put in a prison of the king. He had no hope to be a free man to rise to any position in life. He

interpreted two dreams to Pharaoh; and he was given the highest position to Joseph; he was next to Pharaoh. He himself experienced the divine guidance in his life. He witnessed this to his brothers, when he met them third time. He said to them:

> I am your brother, Joseph, whom you sold into Egypt. And do not be distressed, angry with yourselves, because you sold me here; for God sent me before you to preserve life. For the famine has been in the land these two years; and there are yet five years in which there will be neither plowing nor harvest. And God sent me before you to preserve for you a remnant on earth, and to keep alive for you many survivors. So it was not you who sent me here, but God; and he has made me a father to Pharaoh, and the lord of all his house and ruler over all the land of Egypt. (Gen. 45:4 - 8)

(2) Saul was the first king of Israel (1040-1004 B. C.). Before he was anointed as a king, he was looking after his father's herds. He lost his donkeys on a day. He and his servant went in search of them. When they went to Zuph, Saul's servant asked Saul to see prophet Samuel, saying: "Let us go there; perhaps he can tell us about the journey on which we have set out." (I Sam. 9:6) They met prophet Samuel, who invited Saul to attend the sacrifice and told him not worry about the asses, because they were found (I Sam. 9:19). On the following day, Saul was anointed to be the king of Israel (1044-1004 B. C.). Samuel further foretold Saul the future events, which would take place (I Sam. 10:2-7). These events tells us that God directs human destiny.

Whenever our destiny is fulfilled by the divine guidance, we become exceedingly happy. When the journey of the wise men came to an end, in terms of seeing the King of the Jews, they were exceedingly happy.

The excessive joy makes one to burst into tears, because the words fall short of expression. In the second visit of Joseph and his brothers, Joseph saw his brother Benjamin, and he said to them: "Is this your youngest brother, of whom you spoke to me? God be gracious to you, my son!" (Gen. 43:29) Then Joseph made haste, for his heart yearned for his brother, he sought a place to weep. And he entered his chamber and wept there. (Gen. 43:30) In their third visit, Joseph could not control himself before all those, who stood by him; and he asked others to leave the room; and then he made himself known to his brothers and wept aloud. (Gen. 45:12-15)

(B) The second thing about the wise men was that they entered the house; and they saw the child with Mary his mother. The star, which guided the wise men to the house where Jesus Christ was born, definitely pointed out the birthplace of the King of the Jews or the Saviour of the world. It was left to the Magis to convince themselves of the good news. They entered the house in order to convince themselves of the good news.

This idea teaches us that God points out to the Saviour; but He leaves up to man to see and then to accept the Saviour for himself. Man has a role or responsibility to do so. Each individual is accountable for his / her salvation. There are some examples to confirm the idea.

(1) Andrew was a disciple of John the Baptist (ca.5 B. C-A. D. 28). When John the Baptist looked at Jesus, he said to his disciples, including Andrew: "Behold, the Lamb of God!" (Jn 1:35) Andrew then followed Jesus. Andrew met his brother Simon; and told him that he and another disciple of John the Baptist had found the Messiah. Thus, Simon was brought to Jesus by Andrew. Simon believed Jesus to be the Messiah. The next day, Jesus met Philip; and asked Philip to follow Him. Philip found Nathaniel; and told him that they have found Messiah, Jesus of Nazareth. Philip told him to "come and see." After a brief conversation with Jesus Christ, Nathaniel said: "Rabbi, you are the Son of God! You are the king of Israel!" (Jn 1:49) This is how the disciples were brought to Jesus Christ; and everyone was convinced that Jesus was the Messiah.

(2) Jesus Christ met a Samaritan woman at Jacob's well. In the process of their conversation, Jesus told her that He was the Messiah, who would show the Samaritans all things.(Jn 4:25-26) The woman went back to her town called Sychar; and she asked the people to verify whether the Jew, whom she met at the well, was the Messiah. She led her people to Jesus Christ. Her people asked Jesus Christ

to stay with them; Jesus and his disciples stayed there two days. Many people believed in the teaching of Jesus. They said to the woman who led them to Jesus Christ:

> It is no longer because of your words that we believe, for we have heard for ourselves, and we know that this is indeed the Saviour of the world. (Jn 4:42)

(C) The third thing about the wise men was that they fell down and worshipped the child. The Magis were not the spectators of the house, where the baby king was born; they were not only curious to know the birthplace of the King of the Jews; they entered the house to see the child and to worship Him. Those wise men were not inquisitive of inquiring into the lineage of Jesus Christ; they were not concerned about the exact time of the birth of the baby King; they were not mindful of the circumstances under which the child was born. They did not talk about the hardships they had to face on their way from Persia to Bethlehem; they did not talk about themselves in terms of their vocation, wealth, or their learning to anyone. Their main and only purpose of the long journey was to see the baby King and to worship Him.

Those wise men teach us about the right attitude to enter the house of God and to worship God. They entered the house, where the long anticipated King of the Jews was. They entered the house reverently; and they worshipped the baby King, the Saviour of the world. They worshipped the child with three gifts - gold for a king, frankincense for a priest, and myrrh for one who was to die. Their gifts foretold the destiny of the baby King that he would be the King or the King of kings, the perfect High Priest, and the supreme Saviour of the world. The wise men worshipped the baby King with meaningful gifts. It can be speculated that they chose those meaningful gifts, because God guided them to choose those gifts; and He guided them to worship the child reverently.

Conclusion

The Magis, the three wise men, were from the East. They travelled to west to see the baby King of the Jews. They were pagan, non-Jews.

They were divinely guided to see the Saviour of the world. These two features of the wise men point to the fact that Christianity was going to be a world religion, embracing people from the east and from the west, as well as people from the north and the south, embracing the Jews and the Gentiles. Jesus Christ is the Saviour of the world. God in Jesus Christ entered the world to save all people, irrespective of countries, colours, and creeds.

The Magis entered the house, where they saw the baby Jesus with his mother Mary. They worshipped the baby King, the Saviour of the world. Let all church buildings be filled with the divine presence of the Saviour so that all worshippers worship the Lord Jesus Christ with reverence and with meaningful gifts to Him.

It is needless to say that the Magis must have returned to their country with exceeding joy. Let the worshippers return to their homes with true joy of salvation today.

Recommended Hymns from the Methodist Hymnal

125   'O Little town of Bethlehem,'

132   'As with gladness men of old'

133   'From the eastern mountains'

Recommended Responsive Reading from A Worship Manual for a Scriptural or Methodist Order of Service
65 (pp. 170-171).

Endnotes

[1] Paul Lee Tan, Encyclopedia of 7700 Illustrations: Signs of the Times, (Rockville, Maryland: Assurance Publishers, Ninth Printing, 1985), # 6738.

[2] Ibid., # 3447.

[3] William Barclay, The Gospel of Matthew (Edinburgh: The Saint Andrew Press, Sixth Impression, 1965), Vol. 1, pp. 16f.

Chapter - 6

Titles of the Sermon

'Divine Direction,'

'Divine Direction to Change the Way of Travel,'

'Divine Direction and Cleaver Counsel,'

'Conforming with the Divine Direction.'

Scripture

Matthew 2:1-12

Genesis 28: 10-19; 37:5-11, 28; 39:20; 40:1-22; 41:2-7, 41

Daniel 2:1-47; 3:15-18; 6:6-13, 19-23

Matthew 1:18-24; 2:13-15, 21-23

Acts 5:17-29

Text: Matthew 2:12

A Few Versions of the Text, Matthew 2:12

Then, being divinely warned in a dream that they should not return to Herod, they departed for their own country another way. *The New King James Version*

And having been warned of God in a dream, not to return to Herod, they retired into their own country another way. *Explanatory Notes Upon the New Testament*

And being warned in a dream not to return to Herod, they departed their own country by another way. *Revised Standard Version*

And having been warned in a dream not to go back to Herod, they returned to their country by another route. *New International Version*

And being warned in a dream not to go back to Herod, they returned home another way. *The New English Bible*

But when they returned to their own land, they didn't go through Jerusalem to report to Herod, for God had warned them in a dream to go home another way. *The Living Bible Illustrated*

God warned them in a dream not to go back to Herod. So they left for their country another road. *God's Word*

Introduction

A question as to what do we dream about is more important that why do we dream. We dream not of the past or present but of the future. A dream world is different from reality. A person, who lives in a dream world, lives in the world of illusion or in the world of magic. Many dreams are creations of our subconscious mind. Some dreams are realized in the near future.

We dream about our future or what would happen to us in the future. Dreams are considered as a means of divine communication with us, or divine revelation for us. God directs us or foretells us about our future. There are some dreams, which are written in the Bible.

(1) Joseph had two dreams as to what he would become in the future, while he was young. He dreamed that his sheave of grain stood upright and sheaves of his brother bowed down to it. He again dreamed that the sun, moon, and eleven stars bowed down to him. When he told his dreams to his brothers, they were offended; and they became jealous of him. (Gen. 37:5-11) His parents were angry at Joseph, when they heard his dreams. He was sold into slavery by his brothers (Gen. 37:28). He was taken to Egypt, and was sold to Potiphar, an officer of Pharaoh. He was falsely accused

of adultery; and he was put behind the bar, among king's prisoners. (Gen. 39:20)

(2) Joseph was in a prison of Pharaoh with the cup-bearer and the backer of Pharaoh, who had dreams at the same night. They were dejected and puzzled about by those dreams. Joseph went to see them next day; and he saw them to be sad. He asked them why they were sad. They told him that they had dreams; and there was no one to interpret those dreams to them. Joseph asked them to tell him their dreams. The cup-bearer dreamed that he saw a vine with three branches. The vine blossomed and its grapes ripened. The cup-bearer squeezed the grapes into Pharaoh's cup and gave the cup to him. Joseph interpreted that dream to the cup- bearer, saying that after three days the cup-bearer would be restored to his position by Pharaoh.

Then the chief baker told his dream to Joseph. He dreamed that there were three baskets of bread on his head. In the top basket, were all kinds of baked goods for Pharaoh; but the birds ate them out of the basket. Joseph interpreted that dream to him, saying after three days, the baker's head would be lifted off; and birds would eat away his flesh.

These dreams were realized on the birth day of Pharaoh, after three days. (Gen. 40:1-22)

(3) Pharaoh had two dreams about the future prosperity and famine of his land (Gen. 41:2-7). Pharaoh told his dreams to the magicians and wise men of Egypt; but no one was able to interpret those dreams to him. His cup- bearer recalled how Joseph interpreted his dream and of another prisoner; and those dreams came to be fulfilled. Pharaoh called Joseph; and Joseph interpreted those dreams to Pharaoh. Pharaoh appointed Joseph to the highest position in the land. (Gen. 41:41) Joseph's dreams came to be true, which he had when he was young.

(4) Nebuchadnezzar (605-562 B. C.), the king of Babylon, had a dream in which he saw a large statue. The statue's head was made of

pure gold, its chest and arms of silver, its belly and thighs of bronze, its feet partly of iron and partly of clay. The rock struck the statue, and destroyed it completely. The rock became a huge mountain, and filled the whole earth. Daniel told this dream to the king and interpreted it, telling how his empire could disappear gradually. (Dan. 2:31-45)

Through those dreams, God foretold the future events to the dreamers. God thus spoke to them through those dreams. Dreams are considered to be a means of divine revelation.

Introduction of the Text

There are many dreams, recorded in the Bible. The intention of those dreams is to tell us how God reveals His will and purpose to persons and nations; and thereby He guides many people. On this Christmas day, we will reflect on such a kind of event, stated in the following words:

> And being warned in a dream not to return to Herod, they departed their own country by another way. (Matthew 2:12)

This is the text of our meditation now.

The Context of the Text

When Jesus Christ, the Messiah, was born in Bethlehem of Judea, three Magis, or wise men of Persia, saw a star of His birth in the East. They were astronomers; they interpreted the rising of the star as indication of the birth of a great king of the Jews. They were anxious to meet the baby king of the Jews, and worship him. They reached Jerusalem, the capital of the kingdom of Judea; they went to see King Herod the Great (37- 4 B. C.), inquiring about the birthplace of the king of the Jews.

When King Herod the Great heard the news of the birth of the king of the Jews, he was disturbed, because he would not tolerate anyone to take away his throne from him. He eliminated his three sons, who attempted to replace him. He was known for his cruelty; therefore, Romans used to say, "it is better to be born as pigs than to be born as sons of Herod." As King Herod was perturbed by the news, all people of Jerusalem were disturbed, because they feared King Herod very much.

King Herod the Great called the chief priest and the scribes; and he asked them where the Christ would be born. They quoted him the prophesy of Micah 5:2, foretelling that he would be born in Bethlehem of Judah. Then King Herod called the Magis; and he secretly told them to go to Bethlehem, and diligently search the child, and bring him a word that he too might go and worship the baby king. Those three wise men found the baby king, Jesus with his parents. They worshipped the child and offered some gifts to him.

The Magis were thinking of returning to King Herod, and to give him the news about the whereabout of the baby king. They were warned by God in a dream not to go back to King Herod the Great, but to take another route to their country. This is the background of the text of our mediation.

An Analysis of the Text

The text has two ideas. (A) The first idea is that the Magis were warned by God in a dream not to return to King Herod.

(B) The second idea is that they were advised to depart to their own country by another way.

Exposition of the Ideas of the Text

(A) The first idea of the text is that the Magis were warned by God in a dream not to return to King Herod. Those wise and pious three men saw the star in the East or in Persia. They interpreted the rising of the star as a sign of the great king, being born among the Jews. They followed the star and went to Jerusalem, the capital of Judea. They went to see King Herod; and they inquired of him where the baby king of the Jews would be born. King Herod the Great helped them through the scribes.

King Herod had a secret meeting with the Magis. He asked them when they first saw the star of the baby king of the Jews. He asked this question to them so that he could be able to know the age of the child approximately. He had a plan to eliminate the baby king, because he thought of the baby as a serious threat to his throne and power. His intention was evil and God knew it. The wise men were not able to read the mind of King Herod the Great.

King Herod the Great asked the Magis to seek the child diligently, and to immediately report him about the child, child's parents, and place where they were abiding; so that he too might go and honour the baby king. King Herod was hypocritical and pretentious, as far worshipping the baby king was concerned. King Herod was a deceitful man. He had a vested interest in asking the Magis to do the diligent search for the child. The Magis were foreigners, visiting Judea; they might not have much knowledge about King Herod and his cruel way of dealing with his opponents.

The Magis might have promised King Herod the Great to return to him, and to report him about the baby king. Being religious and honest, they were thinking of going back to King Herod. Then God spoke to them in a dream; and He warned them not to return to King Herod, and to take different way to their country. Those wise and pious men had to decide either to obey King Herod the Great or to God. They finally decided to obey the command of God; and they took another way to their country.

When wise and pious persons are perplexed by difficult problems, God directs them as to what they should do or choose. God directs them through dreams or visions; we will limit our meditation to dreams only. There are a few examples in the Bible to confirm the idea.

(1) Isaac and Rebekah sent their son Jacob to take a wife from the house of Bethuel, who was a brother of Rebekah, and who was living in Padan-aram. On his way to Paddan-aram, Jacob stayed at a certain place over night. He took a stone, and used it as his pillow. When he slept, he had a dream that there was a ladder, set up on the earth, and reached to heaven. Angels of God were ascending and descending on it. God promised Jacob that He would

be with him and would give the land to him and to his descendants. The next day, Jacob set the stone, which he had used as a pillow, as a pillar and named the place "Bethel." (Gen. 28:10-19)

(2) In the second year of the reign of King Nebuchadnezzar (605-562 B. C.) he had a dream; and he was troubled to know the meaning of his dream. He commanded the magicians, the enchanters, the sorcerers, and the Chaldeans to tell his dream and its interpretation; otherwise he would kill them and destroy their houses. The king was so much furious that he commanded that all the wise men of Babylon be destroyed. Among those wise men were Daniel, and his companions - Hananiah, Mishael, and Azaria. Daniel asked his companions to seek God's mercy concerning that mystery. God revealed the mystery to Daniel in a vision, at the night. Daniel saw the great image, which King Nebuchadnezzar saw in his dream; and he interpreted the dream as to what would happen to the empire in the future. King Nebuchadnezzar was convinced that the God of Daniel is the God of gods and a revealer of mysteries. (Dan. 2:1-47)

(3) Joseph, a parent of Jesus Christ, was a godfearing and just man. He was betrothed to Mary. He found that his wife Mary was pregnant with a child. He decided to divorce her quietly. When he thought of this, an angel of God appeared to him in a dream and advised him not to fear to take Mary his wife; and she was conceived of the Holy Spirit. Joseph did as he was commanded to do. (Mt. 1:18-25).

(4) When the Magis departed from Bethlehem, an angel of God appeared to Joseph in a dream; and he asked him to take the child and his mother, and go to Egypt because King Herod the Great was about to search for the child and to destroy him. (Mt. 2:13-15) Joseph obeyed the command of God and went to Egypt and stayed there until an angel of God appeared to him in a dream to return to the land of Israel; and he went to Galilee, as he was warned by an angel of God. (Mt. 2:21-23)

(B) The second idea of the text is that the Magis were advised by God in a dream to depart to their own country by another way. The Magis had a dilemma either to yield to the royal demand of King Herod the Great, to return to him and report where they saw the baby king of the Jews, or to follow the divine directive to take another way and to deliberately avoid seeing King Herod. They chose to follow God's directive; they decided to obey God rather than to obey man. They knew that God directed their journey from Persia to Bethlehem of Judea, over about a thousand miles journey, as they followed the star. They reached safely to Bethlehem and saw Jesus Christ, the Messiah, or long expected king of the Jews. They worshipped the baby king of the Jews. They experienced God's presence and protection throughout their long journey. By the grace of God, their tedious journey was a success, because they met the baby king of the Jews, who was to be the Saviour of the world. It was a great privilege for them to see the Messiah. They were exceedingly happy to see and worship the Saviour of the world. For all these reasons, they obeyed God rather than man.

The Magis, or three wise men, took another route to return to their country. They went a few miles to the northwest, then turned down to the Jericho Road, crossed Jordan, and went up the east side of the river. Thus, they avoided going to Jerusalem and passing through central Palestine. This was a probability of another way going to Persia.

The Magis obeyed God rather than man. This is a practice of saintly people. There are a few examples to confirm this point.

(1) King Nebuchadnezzar (605-562 B. C.) made an image of gold; and he ordered the people to worship the image; and whoever would disobey the royal command was to be thrown into a burning fiery furnace. Shadrach, Meshach, and Abednego did not worship the image, because it was against their religion to worship any other god. King Nebuchadnezzar was angry at them because they disobeyed his command. He said to them:

> Now if you are ready when you hear the sound of the horn, pipe...to fall down and worship the image which I have made, well and good; but if you

do not worship, you shall immediately be cast into a burning fiery furnace; and who is the god that will deliver you out of my hands? (Dan. 3:15)

Those devoted servants were ready to face death rather than to please the king against their religious conviction. They boldly replied to the king in these words:

> O Nebuchadnezzar, we have no need to answer you in this matter. If it be so, our God whom we serve is able to deliver us from the burning fiery furnace; and he will deliver us out of your hand, O king. But if not, be it known to you, O king, that we will not serve your gods or worship the golden image which you have set up. (Dan. 3:17-18)

(2) King Darius I (522-486 B. C.) was persuaded to sign a decree that whosoever makes petitions to any god or man for thirty days, except King Darius I, shall be cast into the den of lions. Daniel heard that the king signed the document. He continued his religious practice to pray to God and praise Him three times a day. The officials, who were envious of Daniel, reported the king that Daniel disobeyed the command of the king; and he should be thrown into the den of lions. (Dan. 6:6-13) Daniel obeyed God's law more than a law of the king. God spared Daniel's life. (Dan. 6:19-23)

(3) The apostles of Jesus Christ followed this way in their life. When the apostles of Jesus Christ were preaching in the name of Jesus, the high priest and his associates were offended by their preaching. They put them in a public jail. God's angel opened the gates of the prison and they were freed. After the release from the prison, the apostles resumed preaching in the name of Jesus. The high priest prohibited them to preach in the city. (Acts 5:17-24) St. Peter and other apostles said to the high priest and others: "We must obey God rather than men." (Acts 5:29)

An Application and Conclusion

What can we learn from the three Magis or the wise men of the East? Those wise men were religious or just. They were guided by the star to the place, where Jesus Christ, the Messiah, or the Saviour of the world, was born. They were happy to meet the anticipated king of the Jews; they worshipped him. As they were warned in a dream not to return to king Herod but to take a different way for their country. They obeyed God rather than King Herod, a powerful and cruel man. These wise men have set an example before us that we obey God rather than man.

In our primary schools and high schools, many teen age students are under a peer pressure. A group of students puts a pressure on other students to conform to the lifestyle of the group. The group prescribes a code of behaviour such as to smoke cigarettes or marijuana, to drink beer and alcohol. Other students who refuse to conform to the lifestyle of the group are labelled as "not cool" or as "weird." The group has no code of morality; it lacks discipline, and it spreads promiscuity. The group produces unproductive and useless teenagers. The teenagers, who have heard about Jesus Christ, as the Saviour of the world, should not yield to the peer pressure; but they should follow the voice of God or the voice of their pure conscience.

Adults form their clubs in order to enforce their lifestyle upon other adults. There are nude clubs, which have no code of decency. There are some clubs, whose code of behaviour is to exchange life-partners. They have no moral values such as sanctity of marriage and mutual faithfulness. They perpetuate promiscuity. Adults should be mature enough not to conform to this immoral lifestyle; let them hear the voice of God or the voice of their conscience.

Let us be wise and godly people by imitating the three wise men, who took another way and avoided the evil path of life, and who listened to the voice of God.

Recommended Hymns form the Methodist Hymnal

116   'Sing we the King who is coming to reign,'

118   'O Come, all ye faithful,'

131   'The first Nowell the angel did say'

132   'As with gladness men of old'

133   'From the eastern mountains'

143   'God Christian men, rejoice'

Recommended Responsive Reading from the Methodist Hymnal

15 (p. 389),

Recommended Responsive Reading from A Worship Manual for Scriptural or Methodist Order of Service

8 (pp.88-89).

Chapter - 7

Titles of the Sermon

'No Room for Jesus Christ'

'Rejection of Jesus Christ.'

Scripture

Luke 2:1-20

Job 13:20

Proverbs 24:23-24

Malachi 2:9

Matthew 2:1-8; 8:10-20, 28-34

Mark 5:1-20; 15:10, 15

Luke 5:16-17; 8:30-37; 9:57-58

John 1:1-2, 9-11, 14

Philippians 2:5-11

Hebrews 1:1-3

Text: Luke 2:7

A Few Versions of the Text, Luke 2:7

As she brought forth her firstborn Son, and wrapped Him in swaddling clothes, and laid Him in a manger, because there was no room for them in the inn. *The New King James Version*

And she brought forth her son, the firstborn, and swathed him, and laid him in the manger; because there was no room for them in the inn. *Explanatory Notes Upon the New Testament*

And she gave birth to her first-born son and wrapped him in swaddling cloths, and laid him in a manger because there was no place for them in the inn. *Revised Standard Version*

And she gave birth to her firstborn, a son. She wrapped him in cloths and placed him in a manger, because there was no room for them in the inn. *New International Version*

And she gave birth to a son, her first-born. She wrapped him in his swaddling clothes, and laid him in a manger, because there was no room for them to lodge in the house. *The New English_Bible*

And she gave birth to her first child, a son. She wrapped him in a blanket and laid him in a manger, because there was no room for them in the village inn. *The Living Bible Illustrated*

She gave birth to her firstborn son. She wrapped him in strips of cloth and laid him in a manger because there wasn't room for them in the inn. *God's Word*

Introduction

Majority of Canadians have come to Canada from other countries, for various reasons. They have some common experiences in finding jobs and apartments. Many of the immigrants were well qualified for good jobs in the country of their origin. They had hopes to find similar jobs in Canada, which is considered to be a land of opportunities for everyone. When the immigrants, who have different skin colour, culture, and accents, go in the search of jobs, they are told there is "no vacancy" or "no room" for them in factories, firms, and even in religious institutes. If positions were advertised, and immigrants aspire for the positions, they are told in their first meeting with hiring persons that they are over qualified; therefore, there is "no room" for them. If professional qualifications of the immigrants were adequate, they are asked whether they have Canadian work experience. If they have no Canadian work experience, they are told there is "no room" for them. The phrase of having Canadian work experience is subtly discriminatory, and it is a cruel joke. How recent immigrants can have Canadian work experience unless they are given opportunities to work in Canada? When job-opportunities are deliberately and inconsiderately denied to persons whose responsibility is to feed their families, the families face many hardships. Those hardships are created for others, who are struggling to survive in the new land, by hardness of the hearts of those, who are in position to employ others.

When immigrants or new Canadians are given jobs, and they serve employers faithfully and devotedly for many years. When the top or executive positions are available, the new Canadians are denied those positions, because there is "no room" for them in the firms as executive officers. If those positions are reluctantly given to the new Canadians, the executives of those positions become eye sore to many. Therefore, their personal life and administration are made difficult, only because they are racially and culturally different persons.

All immigrant families have to find a shelter, a house or an apartment to live in. When apartments or suits are vacant, and new immigrants personally go to see superintendents of the building, they are told lies that vacancies were filled an hour before; therefore, there is "no room" in that huge building. Houses on sale in particular areas are not sold to the new immigrants, because there is "no room" for them in those areas, because they are culturally and racially different.

The Bible, the word of God, denounces partiality, based on race and culture, as a sin (Job 13:10; Pr. 24:23-24; Mal. 2:9). The churches profess to be guided by the word of God. They are to uphold spiritual equality of all believers, irrespective of cultures and colours, and to provide equal opportunities in serving God. These principles are upheld by church administrators in principle; but those administrators are not ready to encourage new Canadian believers to be in the services of the Lord. New Canadian Christians are denied those opportunities, because there is "no room" for them in the offices. Canadian Churches are ready to accommodate new Canadian Christians in the pews but not in the pulpits and in high positions.

It is a wide spread belief among the people of eastern-hemisphere that countries in the western hemisphere, such as Britain, France, Germany, Italy, Switzerland, Canada, and the U. S. A., are Christian countries, where Christian symbols and principles are honoured. This belief may not be true in many respects. It has been a policy of the U. S. A. Post Office to issue Christmas stamps every year to encourage first class mail for Christmas greetings. In 1962 the postal authorities of the U. S. A. rejected a special Christmas stamp, on the ground that its design looked like a cross. The design in question showed a candle burning in a window framed by a wreath. The window panes were thought to resemble a cross. The final design, chosen for 1962 stamp, shows a simple holy wreath and two tapers. The reason for rejecting the first design was as stated: "Rejection of the design emphasized the fact that no religious symbol or apparent religious symbol will be permitted on the Christmas stamps..." [1] It is a modern policy of the post office; it is due to the influence of non-Christian religions or secularism.

The policy of not having cross on the postal stamp is new; it was not the policy a century before. On October 12, 1892, a stamp was issued in two century commemoration that Columbus planted the cross in the New World. The cross on the stamp was not central. On July 30, 1966, a stamp was issued in commemoration of the birth of the Polish nation and introduction of Christianity to the Polish people. On that stamp was a cross with the inscription' Poland's Millennium 966-1966.' [2] In general, crosses have appeared in the background of other U. S. A. stamps, on church steeples and the like; but they were not as part of the central design. These designs of the stamps, not giving central place to cross of Jesus Christ, can be understood that Jesus Christ has no central room in the life of so-called Christian countries.

Introduction of the Text

Jesus Christ and His teaching have no central or prominent place in the life of the countries in the western hemisphere. This is the Christian belief that Jesus Christ is the Saviour of the world; He is the Lord of lords, and God of gods. Nevertheless, when Jesus Christ was born, He was not born in a palace; He was not born in the home of rich and powerful man. He was born of a poor and ordinary parents. This indicates humility of the Saviour of the world. He was not born in the house of His human parents. But He was born in a manger, the shelter for animals. The birth place of Jesus Christ indicates humility in terms of lack of proper shelter at His birth. Mary was the mother of Jesus Christ. She had to give birth to her firstborn son in a manger. The reason why Jesus was born in the manger is given in the following words:

> **And she gave birth to her first-born son and wrapped him in swaddling cloths, and laid him in a manger because there was no place for them in the inn.** (Luke 2:7)

This is the text of our meditation now.

The Context of the Text

Caesar Augustus (31 B. C. -A. D. 14), a Roman Emperor issued an order that all people in Palestine be enrolled. According to this order all persons had to go to their ancestral town to be enrolled. Joseph and Mary were the parents of Jesus Christ. They were residing in the city of Nazareth of Galilee. They had to go to Bethlehem of Judea, because Joseph was of the house and lineage of King David (1002-962 B. C.). Mary was betrothed to Joseph; and she was pregnant with her firstborn child. When Joseph and Mary reached Bethlehem, it was the time for Mary to deliver a child. The people, who were of the house and lineage of King David, came to Bethlehem to be enrolled, from all over Palestine. Those visitors went to the inn to stay in it. It was overcrowded. Joseph and Mary did not get a room in the inn, because of the crowd. There was no room for them in the inn. A home owner or the owner of the inn offered a manger to Mary to deliver a child.

Mary gave birth to her firstborn son, Jesus, in the manger. She wrapped her baby son in swaddling clothes; and she laid him in a manger. This is why Jesus Christ was born in the manger.

An Analysis of the Text

The text has one idea which gives a reason why Jesus Christ was born in the manger and the reason was that there was no room in the inn for Mary to deliver her first born son.

Exposition of the Text

The Bible teaches that Jesus Christ is the only begotten Son of God. He is the manifestation of God in the unique and most authentic form of revelation. The writer of the Letter to the Hebrews began his letter, speaking about Jesus Christ in the following words:

> In many and various ways God spoke of old to our fathers by the prophets; but in these last days he has spoken to us by a Son, whom he appointed the heir of all things, through whom also he created the world. He reflects the glory of God and bears the very stamp of his nature, upholding the universe by his word of power. (Heb. 1:1-3)

Herein we find that Jesus Christ was the final means of God's revelation to the people of the world, because Jesus Christ reflects the very nature of God. The writer of the letter to the Hebrews said that God created the world through His Son, Jesus Christ, and all things are created for Jesus Christ (Heb. 2:10). In other words, Jesus Christ pre-existed before He was born as a child of the virgin Mary.

St. John shared the same point of view about Jesus Christ. He wrote about this unique status of Jesus Christ in the introduction of the gospel, as follows:

> In the beginning was the Word, and the Word was with God, and the Word was God. He was in the beginning with God; all things were made through him, and without him was not anything made that was made. (Jn 1:1-2)

Then St. John said:

> And the Word became flesh and dwelt among us, full of grace and truth; we have beheld his glory, glory as of the only Son from the Father. (Jn 1:14)

Jesus Christ, who is God the Son, who had no beginning, and who was instrumental to create the world, became incarnate or was born as the firstborn son of the virgin Mary. St. Paul reflected upon the pre-existence of Jesus Christ and His humility in the following words:

> Jesus Christ, who, though he was in the form of God, did not count equality with God a thing to be grasped but emptied himself, taking the form of a servant, being born in the likeness of men. And being found in human form he humbled himself and became obedient unto death, even death on a cross. Therefore God has highly exalted him and bestowed on him the name which is above every name, that at the name of Jesus every knee should bow, in heaven and on earth and under the earth, and every tongue confess that Jesus Christ is Lord, to the glory of God the Father. (Phil. 2:5-11)

St. Paul spoke in this passage about the pre-existence of Jesus Christ and His extreme humility. Because of His extreme humility and death, God bestowed on Him the name viz. the Lord of all.

It was said before that when Jesus Christ, the Son of God, was born on the earth, He was not born in a palace; He was not born in the home of rich and powerful man. But He was born of a poor and ordinary parents. This indicates humility of the Saviour of the world. Further, He was not born in the house of His human parents. But He was born in a manger, the shelter for animals. The birth place of Jesus Christ indicates humility in terms of lack of proper shelter at His birth. Mary was the mother of Jesus Christ. She had to give birth to her firstborn son in a manger, because there was no room in the inn for Mary and her firstborn son.

We have to imagine or think of the possible reasons why there was no room for Jesus Christ in the inn, when He was born. The first reason might be that the inn keeper was following a general rule, 'first come, first served'; it is a fair rule in general. The inn keeper gave rooms to those who came first; it did not matter him who were the guests, asking for accommodation. The inn had limited rooms. Anyone, who came after all the rooms were taken, was told that the inn was full and there was no room for him / her. If Mary and Joseph had gone earlier to the inn, the inn keeper might have accommodated them. Mary and Joseph were late to reach the inn. They could not go faster, because Mary was pregnant and her days of delivery were fast approaching. In that condition, Mary and Joseph had to be very careful in their journey. By the time they reached the inn, the inn was overcrowded or full. Therefore, Mary and Joseph could not get a room in the inn.

Mary and Joseph were poor ordinary persons; they were not popular persons or celebrities to receive a preferential treatment. If they were royalty or dignitaries, the inn keeper would have somehow made a room for them. Moreover, the inn keeper did not know that the first -born son of Mary was the anticipated Messiah, the Saviour of the world. If he had that knowledge, he might have given a room in the inn or made arrangement with other inn keepers or home owners to give a room to a very important pregnant woman, at least on a compassionate ground. Because of these reasons, the inn keeper did not make provision of a room for Mary and her son.

The statement, which Mary laid Jesus in a manger, because there was no place for them in the inn (Luke 2:7), is a striking statement. It stated that the fact of having "no room" existed only at the birth of Jesus Christ; but it also foretold how Jesus Christ would not have room in the society and the people of His own race. St. John reflected on the life and career of Jesus Christ among His people, in the following words:

> The true light that enlightens every man was coming into the world. He was in the world, and the world was made through him, yet the world knew him not. He came to his own home, and his own people received him not. (Jn 1:9-11)

Jesus Christ had "no room" among the Jews, the chosen people of God, who were expecting the Messiah. They rejected Him from His birth to His death for various reasons. There are many events to confirm the fact that Jesus Christ was rejected by people. Let us refer to some events.

(1) When three wise men or Magis came from Persia to see the King of Jews in Bethlehem, they first went to inquire of the birth place of the King of the Jews, the Messiah, to the palace of King Herod

the Great (37- 4 B. C.) at Jerusalem. King Herod was not happy to receive the anticipated King of the Jews. He was troubled by the news. He thought of the Messiah as the threat to his throne. He secretly instructed the Magis to see the baby King, and to report him. But when they did not return to him, he ordered killing of male children of less than two years. King Herod the Great had no room for Jesus Christ, the Messiah, in his kingdom. Joseph, a parent of Jesus was instructed by an angel in a dream to flee to Egypt in order to save the life of Jesus. (Mt. 2:1-18)

(2) Jesus Christ was a wandering preacher. He had no money to own a room anywhere. Once a scribe approached Jesus Christ and said to him: "Teacher, I will follow you wherever you go." Then Jesus Christ said to him:

Foxes have holes, and birds of the air have nests; but the Son of man has nowhere to lay his head. (Mt. 8:19-20; Lk. 9:57-58)

The multitude used to gather to hear Jesus Christ preaching and healing their sick people. At evenings, everyone used to go to his home; but none of them invited Jesus to stay in their homes. When everyone left to his home, Jesus used to withdraw himself to the wilderness. (Lk. 5:16-17) There was no room for Jesus, a good teacher and healer of every disease, in any home.

(3) Jesus Christ went on healing the sick and casting out unclean spirit from the people. When Jesus Christ went to Gerascenes, he met a man with an unclean spirit. The man was living among the tombs. He was violent. He was chained many times; but he used to break fetters and no one was able to subdue him. His name was Legion, because he was possessed by many evil spirits. Jesus Christ ordered the evil spirits to leave the man. Then those spirits requested Jesus Christ to send them to the swine. Jesus Christ allowed them to do so. The herd of 2,000 swine was drowned in the sea by the evil spirits. The herdsmen saw how the herd was drowned, and the demonic sitting at the feet of Jesus, clothed in his right mind. The man was cured completely. Then the herdsmen requested Jesus

not to enter in their neighbourhood, namely Decapolis. (Mt. 8:28-34; Mk 5:1-20; Lk. 8:30-37) Jesus was not welcomed by the people of Decapolis; they refused him to enter their town. Jesus, who was healing people from the possession of evil spirits, had no room in Decapolis.

(4) Jesus Christ was a best teacher. He taught the people the word of God with an exceptional authority. He should have been recognized as an outstanding teacher or Rabbi by the scribes and Pharisees, religious teachers of the Jews. But the scribes and Pharisees did not like the preaching and teaching of Jesus Christ. They were filled with animosity and hostility toward Jesus Christ. They thought of Jesus Christ as a dangerous threat to their prestige and religious authority. They were the driving force seeking to kill Jesus Christ. Pontius Pilate (26-36), who was to judge and sentence Jesus to death, came to the conclusion that the chief priest and the Sanhedrim (religious council of Jews) handed over Jesus to him out of their envy toward Jesus. (Mk. 15:10) They stirred up the crowd against Jesus and forced Pontius Pilate to pass a sentence that Jesus be crucified. (Mk 15:15) Jesus Christ, who was an outstanding teacher among the religious scholars, had no room among the religious leadership.

An Application

One can argue that Jesus Christ was not given a room in the inn, in His own religious community, in His nation, because the people did not know that He would be the Saviour of the world. Having now known Him as the Saviour, can Jesus Christ and His teaching be given a central place in our community and nation? Can our civilized society accommodate Him in our legislative body, where the laws are made to maintain justice and fairness to all? It can be generally said that the laws are made by the members of Parliament to protect interest of the rich and to keep the revenue of the rich tax-free; and the taxes are imposed on the middle and poor classes. The tax system in unfair and unjust. Jesus Christ stands for economic justice and fairness; therefore, He would not have a room where such unfair laws are made.

Can Jesus Christ be accommodated in our economy? In our economic system, making profit, without any reasonable limit, is our aim. The profit is made at the cost of the life of the poor customers. Jesus Christ stands for the interest of the poor and the needy. Therefore, He would not have a room in the market economy.

Can Jesus Christ be accommodated in our social life? Our civilized society advocates human rights and freedoms of all kinds. Those rights and freedoms cannot be justified on the basis of the word of God. Jesus Christ stands for all moral laws and responsibilities. Therefore, He would not have a room in our modern and promiscuous society.

Can Jesus Christ be accommodated in our personal life? Our minds and thoughts are overcrowded with evil ideas; therefore, we may not obey His commands to be holy and righteous for God. We would reject Him for various reasons. Therefore, He would not have a room in our personal life.

Jesus Christ wants to enter in our hearts; He wants that we may give Him a room in our hearts. He always says to everyone: "Behold, I stand at the door and knock; if anyone hears my voice and opens the door, I will come in to him and eat with him, and he with me." (Rev. 3:20) If anyone accepts Jesus Christ as his / her personal Saviour, that person will be given power to become a child of God. (Jn 1:12) This change of life will bring joy to the sinner and to the Saviour. This is a meaning of celebrating Christmas.

Recommended Hymns from the Methodist Hymnal

117   'Hark! the herald-angels sing'

125   'O Little town of Bethlehem,'

126   'Give heed, my heart lift up thine eyes:'

127   'Cradled in a manger, meanly'

128   'A virgin most pure, as the'

150   'Thou didst leave Thy throne'

Recommended Responsive Reading from the Methodist Hymnal

5 (p.386),

Recommended Responsive Reading from A Worship Manual for Scriptural or Methodist Order of Service

79 (pp. 193-194).

Endnotes

[1] Paul Lee Tan, Encyclopedia of 7700 Illustrations: Signs of the Times, (Rockville, Maryland: Assurance Publishers, ninth printing, 1985), # 497.

[2] Idid., # 497.

Chapter - 8

Titles of the Sermon

'The Great Joy of Salvation,'

'The Great Joy Over Spiritual Salvation,'

'The Great Joy for Every Sinner,'

'Divine Proclamation of the Universal Joy.'

Scripture

Luke 2:1-18

Exodus 3:1-12

Judges 6:12; 13:2-7, 13-14

I Samuel 16:6-12

I Chronicles 21:16

Psalms 8:4-5; 16:8-11

Isaiah 7:13-14; 9:6-7

Daniel 9:3-19, 24-26

Micah 5:2

Habakkuk 3:17-18

Matthew 1:1, 6, 18

Luke 1:8-12, 19, 30-33; 15:4-7, 8-10, 11-31

John 3:16-17

Romans 5:10-11

Text: Luke 2:10

A Few Versions of the Text, Luke 2:10

Then the angel said to them, 'Do not be afraid, for behold, I bring you good tidings of great joy which will be to all people. *The New King James Version*

And the angel said to them, Fear not: for, behold, I bring you good tidings of great joy, which shall be to all people. *Explanatory Notes Upon the New Testament*

And the angel said to them, 'Be not afraid; for behold, I bring you good news of a great joy which will come to all the people; *Revised Standard Version*

But the angel said to them, 'Do not be afraid. I bring you good news of great joy that will be for all people. *New International Version*

But the angel said to them, 'Do not be afraid; I have good news for you: there is great joy coming to the whole people. *The New English Bible*

But the angel reassured them. 'Don't be afraid', he said. 'I bring you the most joyful news ever announced, and it is for everyone! *The Living Bible Illustrated*

The angel said to them, 'Don't be afraid! I have good news for you, a message that will fill everyone with joy. *God's Word*

Introduction

Students study hard in order to prepare themselves for examinations. They anxiously await the result of their performance; they hope to be rewarded for their toil. When the results are out, they celebrate their success, with joy and happiness in parties.

When women become pregnant, they have to go through pain and sufferings. They have to carry babies in wombs for about nine months. During the last months of their pregnancy, they suffer more than before. On the day of delivery, they suffer from childbearing pains. They bear the pains and sufferings with the hope that they will see their babies, delivered safely. As soon as mothers see their babies, they forget all their pains and sufferings, and they become joyful at the sight of their babies. The families celebrate birthdays of their children every year, with joy in parties.

Many nations in the world celebrate their independence days with pomp and joy. Those nations were ruled by the foreign powers, which were exploiting them economically. Those nations had to oppose the foreign rulers by various means of non-cooperation, including violent means. The patriots had to shed their blood and sacrificed many things for the freedom of their nations. They did those things with the hope that some day their struggle for independence would be fruitful. When they are given their political freedom, they celebrate their victory on the day of their independence. They continue celebrating the day with joy every year as the birthday of nations.

Introduction of the Text

The Jews lost their nationhood and political power to other nations. They were taken in captivity by Assyrian and Babylonian powers. The Persian power, through King Cyrus (539-530 B. C.), granted the permission to the Jews to return to Judah and Jerusalem, and to rebuild their holy city and the temple of God. They were given back their nationhood in part. They were ruled by the Roman power before and at the time of Jesus Christ. The Jews were praying to the LORD God that He may send them the Messiah to solve their problems. God promised them through the prophets that He would send them the Messiah, the Saviour. He told them where the anticipated Messiah would be born. He was to be born in the town of Bethlehem. When the Messiah, in the person of Jesus of Nazareth, was born, God sent an angel to the shepherds to announce the news of the birth of the Saviour. This fact is given in the words of the text, as follows:

> **And the angel said to them, 'Be not afraid; for behold, I bring you good news of a great joy which will come to all the people.** (Luke 2:7)

This is the text of our meditation now.

Context of the Text

When the anticipated Messiah, in the person of Jesus of Nazareth, was born in a manger in the town of Bethlehem, God sent an angel, His messenger, to proclaim the good news to the shepherds. Those shepherds were looking after their flock by night, when Jesus was born. When the angel, with his divine glory, appeared to them, they were afraid. It was expected of them to be afraid, because an angel is a supernatural being, similar to God. In the presence of some supernatural beings, man feels sense of awe and reverent fear. Even in the presence of kings and dignitaries we feel a sense of awe and reverence. Similarly, we will feel the sense of awe and worship stronger than we feel it in the presence of king and dignitaries. Their presence signifies authority and power.

The angel sensed that the shepherds were afraid; therefore, he wanted to give them an assurance that they should not be afraid of him, because he was going to give them good news of salvation, and not a bad news of judgment. The angel encouraged them to listen to the good news, saying:

> Be not afraid; for behold, I bring you good news of a great joy which will come to all the people; for to you is born this day in the city of David a Saviour, who is Christ the Lord. And this will be a sign for you: you will find a babe wrapped in swaddling cloths and laying in a manger. (Lk. 2:10-12)

These verses are intended to elaborate the text of our meditation (Lk. 2:7), which is quoted previously.

An Analysis of the Text

This text has two ideas. (A) The first idea is that when the angel appeared to the shepherds, he said to them, 'Be not afraid.'

(B) The second idea is that the angel announced to the shepherds the good news of a great joy, which will make all the people joyful.

Exposition of the Ideas of the Text

(A) The first idea is that when the angel appeared to the shepherds, he said to them, 'Be not afraid.' When the angel of the LORD God appeared to the shepherds, they saw the glory of God surrounding them. Their first reaction was that they were filled with reverent fear and awe. The scripture tells us that angels are supernatural beings. They are higher than man. A psalm writer wrote about where man stands in relation to God and His angels, in these words:

> what is man that thou art mindful of him, and the son of man thou dost care for him? Yet thou hast made him little less than God, and dost crown him with glory and honour. (Ps. 8:4-5)

Angels are the messengers of God. God sends them to pronounce His judgment and reveal His plan to man. Let us search the scripture to confirm the point.

(1) When Moses was keeping the flock, on the mountain Horeb, the mountain of God, an angle of the LORD God appeared to Moses in a flame of fire, out of the midst of a bush. Moses saw the bush on fire, but fire was not consuming the bush. It was an unusual phenomenon. He was curious to know the mystery. He approached the bush. Then the angel of the LORD said to Moses to remove his shoes, because he was standing on the holy ground. Then the angel told Moses why he appeared to Moses. He gave Moses the commission to liberate the people of Israel from the Egyptian bondage (Ex. 3:1-12).

(2) When Gideon was beating wheat in the wine press to hide it from Midianites, the angel of the LORD appeared to him and said to him, "The LORD is with you, you mighty man of valour." (Jud. 6:12) Gideon was given the mission to liberate the people of Israel from Midianites.

(3) When the people of Israel were subjected by the Philistines for forty years, God planned to liberate the people of Israel from the dominion of the Philistines. And an angel of the LORD appeared to a barren woman, the wife of Manoah; and he said to her that she would conceive and bear a son; and she should not drink wine or strong drink and eat nothing unclean; and she should not shave his head; and he would deliver the people of Israel from the Philistines (Jud. 13:2-7). The woman told about the appearing of

a man of God to her husband Manoah. He prayed to God to see the man of God, and be instructed how to raise their child. God heard his prayer. The same angel appeared to the woman; and she brought in her husband to meet the man of God (Jud. 13:13-14). The woman gave birth to Samson, who liberated the people of Israel from the Philistines.

(4) When King David (1002-962 B. C.) ordered to number the people of Israel, God was displeased with King David. God sent prophet Gad to King David to choose a kind of punishment for his wrong action. King David chose a pestilence upon Israel. Seventy thousand men of Israel were killed by an angel of God. Then God sent an angel to Jerusalem to destroy it. When the LORD God saw many people died of the pestilence, God changed His mind and stopped the angel destroying further. When David saw the angel of the LORD standing between earth and heaven, and in his hand a drawn sword stretched out over Jerusalem, David and elders repented. (I Chr. 21:16)

(5) When Daniel was praying to the LORD God and confessing his sin and the sin of the people of Israel, angel Gabriel appeared to him. He told Daniel what would take place during seventy weeks of years after the message. During first seven weeks, the people would return to Judah and would rebuild Jerusalem. The following sixty-two weeks, there would be rebuilding the city with squares and moat, but in a troubled time. After this period, an anointed one shall be cut off; and the city and the sanctuary would be destroyed thereafter, by a foreign power (Dan. 9:24-26).

Daniel prophesied about the anointed one and his being cut off. The anointed one was Jesus Christ.

(6) John the Baptist (ca. 5 B. C.-A. D. 28) was the forerunner of the Messiah, Jesus Christ. His parents were Zechariah and Elizabeth; they were righteous, but without a child. When Zechariah entered the sanctuary, he saw an angel of the LORD at the altar; he was troubled and fearful. (Lk. 1:8-12) The angel told him that his wife

would bear a son; and he should call him John. The name of the angel was Gabriel. (Lk. 1:19)

(7) The same angel, Gabriel, was sent by God to the virgin Mary at Nazareth to announce that she would be the mother of the Messiah. When Mary saw the angel and heard his greeting, she was greatly troubled at the saying. The angel told Mary:

> Do not be afraid, Mary, for you have found favour with God. And behold, you will conceive in your womb and bear a son, and you shall call his name Jesus. He will be great, and will be called the Son of the Most High; and the Lord God will give to him the throne of his father David, and he will reign over the house of Jacob for ever; and of his kingdom there will be no end. (Lk. 1: 30-33)

From the aforesaid evidences, one can come to a conclusion that the appearance of angels, the supernatural beings, creates reverent fear and awe in the hearts of those, who were privileged to see the angels and to hear their message. This was an expected reaction when an angel appeared to the shepherds, with his divine glory, to announce them the birth of the Lord Jesus Christ. When they were afraid, the angel told them, "Be not afraid," (Lk. 2:7) because he was there to give them good news of their salvation.

(B) The second idea is that the angel announced to the shepherds the good news of a great joy which would make all the people joyful. An angel was sent by the LORD God to the shepherds to announce the news of the birth of His Son, who is the Saviour of all people. It was the good news to the people, who were looking toward the coming of the Messiah, who would give them liberation from political and social oppression and from sin or spiritual darkness and despair. The coming of the Messiah, the King of the Jews, was prophesied by the prophets, human messengers of God. The ordinary, hard working people were looking toward the fulfilment of the prophecies.

The scripture has some prophecies regarding the Messiah- his lineage, virgin birth, the time of birth, and the place of birth. Those prophecies were made about eight centuries before the birth of the Messiah.

Prophet Isaiah (800 B. C.) prophesied that the Messiah would be born in the linage of David, when he wrote:

> For to us a child is born, to us a son is given; and the government will be upon his shoulder, and his name will be called 'Wonderful Counsellor, Mighty God, Everlasting Father, Prince of Peace.' Of the increase of his government and of peace there will be no end, upon the throne of David, and over his kingdom, to establish it, and to uphold it with justice and with righteousness from this time forth and for evermore. The zeal of the LORD of hosts will do this. (Is. 9:6-7)

The Messiah would be the King of Israel forever; and he would be born in the lineage of King David (1002-962 B. C.). This prophecy was fulfilled, when the Jesus Christ was born in the lineage of King David. (Mt. 1:1, 6)

The Messiah was to be born of a virgin. This was the promise and sign of the LORD God, given to King Ahaz (735-715 B. C.). Through prophet Isaiah, God said to King Ahaz:

> Hear then, O house of David! Is it too little for you to weary men, that you weary my God also? Therefore the LORD himself will give you a sign. Behold, a young woman shall conceive and bear a son, and shall call his name Immanuel. (Is. 7:13-14)

This prophecy was fulfilled, when Jesus Christ was born of the virgin Mary. (Mt. 1:18; Lk. 1:26-35)

The time of the birth of the Messiah was prophesied by prophet Daniel, when he prayed for his people and for Jerusalem (Dan. 9:3-19), in these words:

> Know therefore and understand that from the going forth of the word to restore and build Jerusalem to the coming of the anointed one, a prince, there shall be seven weeks. (Dan. 9:7)

The seven weeks in this verse are interpreted as 490 calendar years. The temple was rebuilt during the time of Darius I (522-486 B. C.); it was completed in 516 B. C. (Ezra 6:15). The walls of Jerusalem were restored during the time of Nehemiah, the governor of Judah (445-433 B. C.) This is roughly a period 500 years This calculation may suggest that Messiah, in the person of Jesus of Nazareth, was born before the death of Herod the Great (40-4 B. C.)

The place of birth of the Messiah was prophesied by prophet Micah (800 B. C.), when he wrote:

> But you, O Bethlehem Ephrathah, who are little to be among the clans of Judah, from you shall come forth for me one who is to be ruler in Israel, whose origin is from of old, from ancient days. (Mic.5: 2)

This prophecy was fulfilled, when Jesus Christ was born in the town of Bethlehem (Mt. 2:2; Lk. 2:4-7).

Then Jesus Christ, the anticipated King of Israel was born, the news was given by the angel of the LORD to the shepherds first. The shepherds were the ordinary, hard working people. They were not recognized as important people; they were easily forgotten people. This thought is implied in the event, when God rejected Saul as the king of Israel (1044-1004 B. C.) and asked prophet and priest Samuel to go to Bethlehem to the house of Jesse, and anoint one of the sons of Jesse as the next king of Israel. All the sons of Jesse passed before Samuel, and God did not choose any of them. Samuel then asked Jesse whether all his sons were there. Jesse replied that his youngest son was looking after sheep. Samuel asked Jesse to fetch him. When David was brought and passed before Samuel, God asked Samuel to anoint him. (I Sam. 16:6-12) Jesse forgot David, because he was the youngest and looking after sheep. Looking after sheep was not considered an important job; it could be given to anyone. Shepherding did not require skill or education. Therefore, the profession of shepherding was not valued as a great job. Because of this, shepherds were rejected and despised by the religious groups of Jews, namely, scribes and Pharisees.

The shepherds were simple minded and sincere people; they were not sophisticated or philosophical people. To these type of people, the angel appeared to give them good news, saying:

> for behold, I bring you good news of a great joy which will come to all the people; for to you is born this day in the city of David a Saviour, who is Christ the Lord. And this will be a sign for you: you will find a babe wrapped in swaddling cloths and laying in a manger. (Lk. 2:10-12)

The shepherds believed in the good news. They went in haste to look for the baby in the manger. They found Mary, Joseph, and the baby in the manger. They were happy that God's angels gave them the good news. The shepherds returned to their flock, glorifying and praising God for all they had heard and seen, as it had been told to them. (Lk. 2:15-20)

The shepherds were joyous, because they saw the prophesies about the coming of the Messiah were fulfilled in the baby Jesus. They saw the Messiah, the Saviour of them, in the baby Jesus. They were happy to see Jesus Christ, their Saviour. Their happiness was spiritual. The joy of salvation is not dependent upon abundance of material things; it is joy in itself. Prophet Habakkuk expressed his spiritual joy in the LORD, even in the face of material adversities, in the following words:

> Though the fig trees do not blossom, nor fruit be on the vines, the produce of the olive fail and the fields yield no food, the flock cut off from the fold and there be no herd in the stalls, yet I will rejoice in the LORD, I will joy in the God of my Salvation. (Hab. 3:17-18)

The believers are given the spiritual joy of salvation in the presence of God. King David (1002-962 B. C.) expressed this religious conviction in a psalm, in the following words:

> I keep the LORD always before me; because he is at my right hand, I shall not be moved. Therefore my heart is glad, and my soul rejoices; my body also dwells secure. For thou dost not give up me to Sheol or let thy godly one see the Pit....Thou dost show me the path of life; in thy presence there is fullness of joy, in thy right hand are pleasures for evermore. (Ps. 16:8-11)

This spiritual joy of salvation comes to the believers, when they are reconciled to God through Jesus Christ. St. Paul talked about this spiritual fact in the following words:

> For if while we were enemies we were reconciled to God by the death of his Son, much more, now that we are reconciled, shall we be saved by his life. Not only so, but we also rejoice in God through our Lord Jesus Christ, through whom we have now received our reconciliation. (Rom. 5:10-11)

The theological thought, contained in these verses, is simplified by the parables - the parable of the lost sheep (Lk. 15:4-7), of the lost coin (Lk.15:8-10), and of the prodigal son (Lk. 15: 11-31)- which

Jesus Christ used in his teaching about forgiving God. The intent of these parables is given in these words of the Lord Jesus Christ: "Just so, I tell you, there is joy before the angels of God over one sinner who repents." (Lk. 15:10)

In these parables, Jesus Christ spoke of God's joy over one sinner, who repents. God is the giver of salvation; and man is the receiver of salvation. Man also becomes happy, when he receives salvation. This is one of the striking events, recorded in the Bible, which talks about man's being happy because of his salvation. Zacchaueus was a sinner and a tax collector. He climbed on a tree to see Jesus Christ passing under. When Jesus Christ looked at Zacchaeus, He said to him, "Zacchaeus, make haste and come down; for I must stay at your house today." (Lk. 19:5) Zacchaeus made haste. He came down; and he received Jesus Christ joyfully. (Lk. 19:6) On their way to Zacchaeus' home, Zacchaeus said to Jesus Christ, "Behold Lord, the half of my goods I give to the poor; and if I have defrauded any one of anything, I restore it fourfold." (Lk. 19:8) Then Jesus Christ said to him:

> Today salvation has come to this house, since he also is a son of Abraham.
> For the Son of man came to seek and to save the lost. (Lk. 19:9-10)

The joy of salvation was not limited to the Jews; but it was to be given to every believer, irrespective of his / her creed, colour of skin, culture, and country. It was to be the joy for everyone in the world. St. John epitomized this good news of great joy to every believer, in these often cited verses:

> For God so loved the world that he gave his only Son, that whoever believes in him should not perish but have eternal life. For God sent the Son into the world, not to condemn the world, but that the world might be saved through him. (Jn 3:16-17)

Conclusion

The LORD God promised, through the prophets and saints, to send the Messiah to save the Jews and all people in the world from sin. When the anticipated Messiah was born in the person of Jesus Christ, the angel of the LORD God conveyed the good news of the birth of Jesus Christ to the shepherds, the ordinary and hard working people.

They believed in the good news. They hastily went to see the baby, the Saviour of the world. They were happy to receive the news; and they were happy to see the promise of God being fulfilled. They praised God. Their happiness was spiritual joy in the presence of God in Jesus Christ. Let all the believers have this spiritual joy in their hearts. This joy is joy in itself; it is not dependent on exchange of gifts during the Christmas festival. May this joy be multiplied on the day, when believers in Christ Jesus celebrate Christmas! Their joy will be multiplied, when they share it with others by their witness through words and deeds.

Recommended Hymns form the Methodist Hymnal

118   'O Come, all ye faithful,'

120   'Christians, awake, salute the happy morn,'

123   'Still the night, holy the night!'

125   'O Little town of Bethlehem,'

131   'The first Nowell the angel did say'

Recommended Responsive Reading from the Methodist Hymnal

5 (p. 486),

Recommended Responsive Reading from A Worship Manual for Scriptural or Methodist Order of Service

79 (pp. 193-194).

Chapter - 9

Titles of the Sermon

'Today, a Day of Salvation,'
'Saviour's Birth, a Good News,'
'Today's Good News.'

Scripture

Luke 2:1-20

Exodus 25:8; 29:45

Leviticus 26:12

I Samuel 16:12-13

II Samuel 7:12-14, 16

Psalms 110:1

Isaiah 11:2; 53:4-6; 63:1

Jeremiah 33:20-22

Ezekiel 37:24-28

Matthew 9:2, 5-6, 22; 15:21-28

Luke 5:12-13, 24; 7:47-50; 19:8-10

John 3:16,18

Philippians 2:5-11

Text: Luke 2:11

A Few Versions of the Text, Luke 2:11

For there is born for you this day in the city of David a Saviour, who is Christ the Lord. *The New King James Version*

For to you is born this day in the city of David a Saviour, who is Christ the Lord. *Explanatory Notes Upon the New Testament*

for to you is born this day in the city of David a Saviour, who is Christ the Lord. *Revised Standard Version*

Today in the town of David a Saviour has been born to you; he is Christ the Lord. *New International Version*

Today in the city of David a deliverer has been born to you- the Messiah, the Lord. *The New English Bible*

The Saviour- yes, the Messiah, the Lord- has been born tonight in Bethlehem! *The Living Bible Illustrated*

Today your Saviour, Christ the Lord, was born in David's city. *God's Word*

Introduction

We always anxiously wait for hearing good news, because they give us hope; and they provide solutions to our social, economic, and spiritual problems.

(1) United States of Soviet Russia was facing acute shortage of food and medicine in 1990, when the President Gorbachev was trying to implement economic and political reforms in the U. S. S. R. His reform policies became sceptical. President Gorbachev was instrumental to end the cold war between the east and the west hemispheres. His policies were favourable to the western countries; therefore, United States of America, Germany, and Canada decided to send economic aid to Russia. It was good news to the Russians that the western countries were going to help them in their economic and national crises.

(2) Ethiopia and Eritrea were facing civil wars and drought more than five years, till 1990. Millions of people and cattle had died of

hunger and thirst. In 1990 the world organization, called Oxfam, appealed to send aid to Ethiopia and Eritrea. Subsequently, the western countries decided to respond to their basic needs of food, water, and clothing. It was good news to the countries, which were anxiously waiting for relief.

(3) In Hamilton, Ontario, the workers of Stelco were on strike about three months in 1990. Many workers were anxiously waiting for good news that the demands of the workers would be met, and the strike would be over. The workers had to support their families and pay their regular bills; they had a hard time to meet their needs with their strike pay; they had to borrow money from banks. When a settlement was reached, and the strike was called off, and they had to go back to their jobs, they were very happy, because it was the good news to the workers. Other businesses were happy too, because their businesses were dependent on the Stelco workers.

These international and local events tell us that people became happy, when they received good news. There are some events in the Bible, emphasizing the same point.

(4) When Canaan was facing drought and famine, Jacob heard good news that grain was sold in Egypt; therefore, he sent his sons to bring grain from Egypt (Gen. 42:10; 43:1).

(5) King Hezekiah (715-687 B. C.) became seriously ill. God sent prophet Isaiah to King Hezekiah, with the following message: "Set your house in order; for you shall die, you shall not recover." (II Kg. 20:2) Then the king earnestly prayed to the LORD God and bitterly wept before God. God heard the cry of the king. He sent prophet Isaiah (800 B. C.) back with the message:

Thus says the LORD, the God of David your father, I have heard your prayer, I have seen your tears; behold, I will heal you; on the third day you shall go up to the house of the LORD. And I will add fifteen years to your life, I will deliver you and this city out of the hand of the king of Assyria, and I will defend this city for my own sake and for my servant David's sake. (II Kg. 20:5-6)

This was good news of protection against the enemy nation for the people of Jerusalem, and the good news of a physical recovery for the king himself.

(6) Jews were taken away as captives by the Assyrian and Babylonian powers. They were praying to the LORD God for return to their land. After forty years, God answered their prayer. Cyrus (539-530 B. C.), the king of Persia destroyed the Babylonian power; and ended the captivity of the Jews. God stirred up the spirit of King Cyrus to make the royal proclamation, as follows:

> The LORD, the God of heaven, has given me all the kingdoms of the earth, and he has charged me to build him a house at Jerusalem, which is in Judah. Whoever is among you of all his people, may his God be with him, and let him go up to Jerusalem, which is in Judah, and rebuild the house of the LORD, the God of Israel- he is the God who is in Jerusalem; and let each survivor, in whatever place he sojourns, be assisted by the men of his place with silver and gold, with goods and with beasts, besides freewill offerings for the house of God which is in Jerusalem. (Ezra 1:2-4)

This royal declaration encouraged the Jews to return to their land and to rebuild the temple of God. This royal decree gave them political and religious freedom. This was the good news which made the remnant of the Jews very happy.

Introduction of the Text

The people anxiously wait for good news, which would solve their economic, national, social, and personal problems. There were some people, who realized the absolute bondage of sin in life; and they prayed to God to send a Savour to redeem them from the spiritual bondage. God, in the due course of time, answered their prayers. God answered the prayers of the saints by sending Jesus Christ, the Saviour of the world. The day, Jesus was born, God sent angels to announce the good news to the shepherds, who were in fields, looking after their sheep. The angels said to the shepherds:

> **For to you is born this day in the city of David a Saviour who is Christ the Lord**. (Lk. 2:11)

This is the text of our mediation now.

The Context of the Text

After the virgin Mary gave birth to her first male child, Jesus, in a manger at Bethlehem, a city of King David (1002-962 B. C.), an angel of the LORD God appeared to the shepherds, who were keeping watch over their flock by night. He announced the good news, tiding, which would make all people joyous, saying:

> I bring you good news of a great joy which will come to all the people; for to you is born this day in the city of David, a Saviour, who is Christ the Lord. (Lk. 2:10-11)

This tiding was announced by the angel to the shepherds; and the good news was for all people. The good news was a heavenly declaration of the salvation of all people.

The news of salvation was specially good to the shepherds, who were the representatives of masses. What was a social and religious status of shepherds among the Jews? The shepherds were not able to keep the details of the ceremonial law of Moses; they could not observe all the meticulous rules and regulations concerning hand-washing and eating, because they had to meet constant demands of shepherding their flock. They were not trained in the Jewish rituals and theology; they were not sophisticated people; they were simple-minded people. Because they were not trained in a theology and they did not keep rituals literally, they were not respected by the upper or orthodox class of the Jews. They were despised by the orthodox people. They belonged to the low class of people. They were generally considered as sinners. As they were not religious in practice and concepts, they had no hope of being saved, because they could not earn their salvation by religious deeds. However, the shepherds were anxious to be saved. To these spiritually anxious people, the angel gave the good news of salvation. That good news made those shepherds joyous. This event was announced by the angel, saying to the shepherds:

> For to you is born this day in the city of David a Saviour who is Christ the Lord. (Lk. 2:11)

This is the text, within its historical background.

An Analysis of the Text

The text has four ideas. (A) The first idea is the divine announcement to the shepherds, "to you is born a Saviour."

(B) The second idea is the time of the birth of the Saviour, that is, "today."

(C) The third idea is the place where the Saviour was born, that is, he was born in the city of David.

(D) The fourth idea is the specific identification of the Saviour, that is, Christ the Lord.

Exposition of the Ideas of the Text

(A) The first idea of the text is the divine announcement to the shepherds, "to you is born a Saviour." God sent Jesus Christ into the world to redeem the world from sin; He was born to give salvation to all. The salvation in Jesus Christ is universal and all-inclusive. However, the salvation has to be personal, touching the life of individuals. In other words, salvation is a personal experience; everyone has to experience the grace and forgiveness of God in Jesus Christ. St. John brought out both these aspects of salvation, in the following words:

> For God so loved the world that he gave his only Son, that whoever believes in him should not perish but have eternal life.... He who believes in him is not condemned; he who does not believe is condemned already, because he has not believed in the name of the only Son of God. (Jn 3:16, 18)

These verses talk about the universality of salvation as well as acceptance and rejection of salvation by every individual. A person, who would accept to believe in the Son of God, will be saved; but a person, who rejects to believe in the name of Jesus Christ, would be condemned. In other words, salvation means to accept Jesus Christ as the personal Saviour. Why the salvation should become personal is confirmed by the examples, as follow.

(1) When Jesus Christ went to His own city [Bethlehem], some people brought to Him a paralytic, lying on his bed. Jesus Christ was convinced of their faith in Him; therefore, He said to the paralytic,

"Take heart, my son; your sins are forgiven." (Mt. 9:2) When the scribes heard the statement of Jesus Christ, they questioned the authority of Jesus to forgive sins; and they murmured against Him. Then Jesus Christ asked the scribes the question, "Which is easier, to say, 'Your sins are forgiven,' or to say, 'Rise and walk?'" (Mt.9: 5) He told the scribes that the Son of man has the divine authority to forgive sins. Then He said to the paralytic, "Rise, take your bed and go home." (Mt.9: 6; Lk. 5:24) The paralytic was healed instantly. This event tells us that forgiveness of sins precedes physical healing. Moreover, the spiritual and physical recovery were personal for the man, who was healed.

(2) A Pharisee, named Simon, invited Jesus Christ to dine in his house. When Jesus Christ sat at the table, a sinful woman stood behind Jesus Christ. She was weeping; she wetted feet of Jesus with tears, wiped them with her hair, and kissed them, and anointed them with alabaster ointment. Simon, in his mind, questioned the prophethood of Jesus, as Jesus Christ was allowing the woman to touch him. Jesus Christ then spoke with Simon in a parable, concluding with these words: "Therefore I tell you, her sins, which are many, are forgiven, for she loved much; but he who is forgiven little, loves little." (Lk. 7:47) Then Jesus Christ said to the sinful woman, "Your sins are forgiven.... Your faith has saved you; go in peace." (Lk. 7:48, 50) This event again confirms that the salvation of a person is personal.

Experiences of conversion of many believers affirm that conversion or salvation needs to be personal. Rev. Charles Wesley (December 18, 1702-1788), a brother of Rev. John Wesley (July 17,1703- March 2, 1791), was a founder of Methodist Church. He had an experience of conversion. Rev. Charles Wesley was very sick in April.1738. Peter Boehler (December 31, 1712-1775) stood by his bedside, and prayed for him. Peter Boehler was replaced by John Bray (June 1, 1794-May 25, 1868), who also prayed for recovery of Charles. A devout woman, who was seized with the conviction that she ought to speak some words of comfort to Charles, went in another room and said to Charles:

"In the name of Christ of Nazareth, arise! Thou shalt be healed of all thy infirmities." These words of comfort brought Rev. Charles Wesley spiritual deliverance; he was spiritually and physically recovered.[1]

(B) The second idea of the text is the time of the birth of the Saviour, that is, "today". The word 'today' implies instantaneity of time, and not the remoteness or future of time. It is very important word, because it does not ask the person, who anxiously waited to be saved, to wait further. It states that salvation can be experienced instantly. There are some examples to confirm the idea that in the presence of Jesus Christ sinners are saved instantly or immediately.

(1) A woman, who had suffered from a haemorrhage for twelve years, touched the fringe of Jesus' garment in faith; and she was made well instantly. (Mt. 9:22)

(2) When a Canaanite woman asked Jesus Christ to redeem her daughter from demonic possession, Jesus Christ said to her, "O woman, great is your faith! Be it done for you as you desire." Her daughter was healed instantly. (Mt. 15:21-28)

(3) At the word of Jesus Christ, a leper was made well instantly. (Lk. 5:12-13)

(4) Zacchaeus was a chief tax collector. He wished to see and meet Jesus Christ. As he was very short, he climbed up into a sycamore tree. Jesus Christ looked at him and told him that He was going to stay with Zacchaeus. On their way, Zacchaeus said to Jesus Christ, "Behold, Lord, the half of my goods I give to the poor; and if I have defrauded any one of anything, I restore it fourfold." (Lk. 19:8) Then Jesus Christ responded, "Today salvation has come to this house, since he also is a son of Abraham. For the Son of man came to seek and save the lost." (Lk. 19:9-10) Salvation of the household of Zacchaeus was instant; they did not have to wait for it tomorrow.

(C) The third idea of the text is the place where the Saviour was born, that is, He was born in the city of King David. It implies that the place and lineage of King David (1002-962 B. C.) was important as far the birth of the Saviour was concerned. History, culture, and religion of Judaism formed a meaningful background for the birth of the Lord Jesus Christ, the Saviour of the world.

God chose the people of Israel for the specific purpose. The LORD God said to Moses, "I will dwell among the people of Israel, and will be their God." (Ex. 29:45; 25:8) And the people of Israel will be God's people (Lev. 26:12). God established the nation of Israel; He chose David (I Sam. 16:12-13) to be a king for the purpose of establishing the kingdom of Israel. David (1002-962 B. C.) was an ideal king; he had fear of God in his heart. He wished to build a temple for the ark of the covenant of the LORD God. In response to King David's plan, God sent prophet Nathan to deliver the message, as follows:

> When your days are fulfilled and you lie down with your fathers, I will raise up your offspring after you, who shall come forth from your body, and I will establish his kingdom. He shall build a house for my name, and I will establish his kingdom for ever. I will be his father and he shall be my son. (II Sam. 7:12-14).... And your house and your kingdom shall be made sure forever before me; your throne shall be established for ever. (II Sam. 7:16)

God made this covenant with King David that his throne shall be established forever through the Messiah, an offspring of King David. King David, being filled with the spirit of God, addressed the Messiah, the Son of God, as his Lord (Ps. 110:1; Mt. 22:44; 26:44). God repeated the words of the covenant, which He made with King David, through prophet Ezekiel (Ezek. 37:24-28) and through prophet Jeremiah (Jer. 33:20-22), after passing away of King David.

God's promise of the covenant was fulfilled in Jesus Christ, who was born in the lineage of King David and in Bethlehem, a city of King David. God made Jesus Christ the Lord of all creation for ever. This idea is explained in the following pages.

(D) The fourth idea of the text is the specific identification of the Saviour, that is, Christ the Lord. The Saviour is distinguished from the rest of other leaders, who would act as redeemers of the people from difficult situations. The other leaders would not have the divine authority to forgive sins, and to save the people from sin and death. This authority is invested only in the Messiah, Jesus Christ, by God. This point was discussed in the explanation of the first idea of the text.

The title "Christ" means 'anointed of the LORD God.' Prophet Isaiah (800 B. C.) prophesied about the Messiah, in the following words:

> The Spirit of the LORD shall rest upon him, the spirit of wisdom and understanding, the spirit of counsel and might, the spirit of knowledge and the fear of the LORD. (Is. 11:2)

Then prophet Isaiah described how people would be saved by His vicarious sufferings, as follows:

> Surely he has borne our griefs and carried our sorrows; yet we esteemed him stricken, smitten by God, and afflicted. But he was wounded for our transgressions, he was bruised for our iniquities; upon him was the chastisement that made us whole, and with his stripes we are healed. All we like sheep have gone astray; we have turned everyone to his own way; and the LORD has laid on him the iniquity of us all. (Is. 53:4-6)

Then prophet Isaiah prophesied that Christ would be the mighty Saviour (Is. 63:1), because of His vicarious sufferings.

As the Messiah would save the people from their sin, God bestowed on Jesus Christ the best of all other names, that is, Lord. St. Paul spoke about this highest title of Jesus Christ to Christians at Philippi, as follows:

> Christ Jesus, who, though he was in the form of God, did not count equality with God a thing to be grasped, but emptied himself, taking the form of a servant, being born in the likeness of men. And being found in human form he humbled himself and became obedient unto death, even death on a cross. Therefore God has highly exalted him and bestowed on him the name which is above every name, that at the name of Jesus every knee should bow, in heaven and on earth and under the earth, and every tongue confess that Jesus Christ is Lord, to the glory of God the Father. (Phil. 2:5-11)

In other words, Christ Jesus bears the divine title, "Lord of all lords." He is the supreme Lord.

Conclusion

When Jesus was born of the virgin Mary, the angel of the LORD God appeared to the shepherds, who were keeping watch on their sheep in fields. He said to them that he brought for them a good news of a great joy to the people of the world; for to them was born that day in the city of David, a Saviour, who is Christ the Lord. This good news was for everyone in the world; it was the news of universal salvation. However, the shepherds had to accept Jesus Christ as their personal Saviour. That Saviour was born in the lineage and in the city of King David. His title is Christ the Lord; His title is the Messiah, the Lord of all. This was the good news of the first Christmas. The same message or the good news is delivered to the people in the world that for them Christ is born today or that their salvation is instant. Christ Jesus will save the people, who believe in His name. He will be their personal Saviour; and He will save them from sin and death; and He will give them eternal life.

Recommended Hymns form the Methodist Hymnal:

118   'O Come, all ye faithful,'

119   'Angels from the realms of glory,'

124   'See, amid the winter's snow,'

129   'While shepherds watched their'

130   'It came upon the midnight clear,'

131   'The first Nowell the angel did say'

143   'Good Christian men, rejoice'

150   'Thou didst leave Thy throne'

860   'Away in a manger, no crib for a bed,'

Recommended Responsive Reading from the Methodist Hymnal

5 (p. 386),

Recommended Responsive Reading from A Worship Manual for Scriptural or Methodist Order of Service

79 (pp.193-194).

Endnotes

[1] Rev. W. H. Fitchett, Wesley and His Century, A Study in Spiritual Forces (Toronto: The Ryerson Press, 1920), p. 120.

Chapter - 10

Titles of the Sermon

(Suitable for an Infant Baptism and for Sunday after Christmas)

'Circumcision of Jesus,'

'Naming of Jesus,'

'Preordained Naming of Jesus Christ',

'Mission Behind the Name Jesus,'

'Baptism the Substitute for Circumcision.'

Scripture

Luke 2:19-21

Genesis 17:9-14, 24-27; 21:4

Joshua 5:5

I Samuel 1:5, 10-11, 20, 23-27

Matthew 1:20-21

Luke 1: 5-7, 14-17, 19, 30-35

John 4:22

Acts 7:8; 15:8-11

Romans 4:1-12; 9:4-5

I Corinthians 7:17-20

Galatians 5:6; 6:15

Philippians 3:5

Text: Luke 2:21

A Few Versions of the Text, Luke 2:21

And when eight days were accomplished for the circumcising of the child, his name was called JESUS, which was so named of the angel before he was conceived in the womb. *King James Version*

And when eight days were fulfilled to circumcise the child, his name was called Jesus, which was named of the angel before he was conceived in the womb. *Explanatory Notes Upon the New Testament*

And at the end of eight days, when he was circumcised, he was called Jesus, the name given by the angel before he was conceived in the womb. *Revised Standard Version*

On the eight day, when it was time to circumcise him, he was named Jesus, the name the angel had given him before he was conceived. *New International Version*

Eight days later the time came to circumcise him, and he gave the name Jesus, the name given by the angel before he was conceived. *The New English Bible*

Eight days later, at the baby's circumcision ceremony, he was called Jesus, the name given him by the angel before he was even conceived. *The Living Bible Illustrated*

Eight days after his birth, the child was circumcised and named Jesus. This was the angel had given him before his mother became pregnant. *God's Word*

Introduction

In our time, followers of secularism demand that the state be separated from religion. In the democratic countries, like the U. S. A., Canada, and Britain the state is separated from religion, according to their constitutions. A person does not have to be religious in order to be a citizen of these lands. This policy is good in the sense that all people will be treated equally under the laws of the countries; and everyone has a right to practice and propagate his or her religious convictions. All religions will be respected equally and no religion will be preferred to other religions as far the national policies are concerned.

Followers of secularism also demand that children should not be taught religious values while they are infants; and let children have right to choose their religions when they are adults. In other words, children should not be raised by their parents, in accordance with their religions. In this demand, the followers of secularism have gone beyond the limits. They are violating the constitutional right to practice and propagate one's religion. How can the believers of religions perpetuate or continue to practice their faiths without bringing up their offspring in their religions? The parents have a natural responsibility to teach language and good habits and moral values. As learning begins at infancy, the parents have to teach social and moral values to their children. If infants are left to themselves to raise themselves, they would certainly learn bad and unacceptable manners and habits. If a garden is allowed to grow itself, without the supervision of a gardener, the garden will be filled with unwanted weeds and without green grass and beautiful flowers. Supervision of parents is a necessity to raise the children to be good persons. Therefore, the parents are given a bounden duty to raise their children in their cultural and moral values. A religion provides the cultural and moral values.

Introduction of the Text

The Hebrew parents are commanded by the LORD God to dedicate their infants to God by circumcising them. Jesus was a Hebrew infant. He had to undergo the act of circumcision at the end of his eight days. This event is recorded by an evangelist, in the following words:

> **And at the end of eight days, when he was circumcised, he was called Jesus, the name given by the angel before he was conceived in the womb.** (Luke 2:21)

This is the text of our meditation now.

The Context of the Text

Jesus Christ, the saviour of the world, was born in a Hebrew race. According to the laws and precepts of the Old Testament, He was to be raised in the religion of Hebrews. When Jesus became eight days old, his father and other relatives took him to the synagogue to be circumcised. At his circumcision, he was named Jesus. Circumcision is an initiation ceremony for the Jewish male children. Circumcision and naming the infant go together. These things took place in the life of Jesus Christ. These things provide us a context of the text, which is:

> And at the end of eight days, when he was circumcised, he was called Jesus, the name given by the angel before he was conceived in the womb. (Luke 2:21)

An Analysis of the Text

In this text, there are three ideas. (A) The first idea is that Jesus was circumcised when Jesus was eight days old.

(B) The second idea is that at his circumcision, the baby was named Jesus.

(C) The third idea is that the child was named Jesus before he was conceived in the womb.

An Exposition of the Ideas of the Text

(A) The first idea of the text is that Jesus was circumcised when he was eight days old. The rite of circumcision began with Abraham, when the LORD God made a covenant with Abraham, as follows:

> And God said to Abraham, As for you, you shall keep my covenant, you and your descendants after you throughout their generations. This is my covenant, which you shall keep, between me and you and your descendants after you: Every male among you shall be circumcised. You shall be circumcised in the flesh of your foreskins, and it shall be a sign of the covenant between me and you. He that is eight days old among you shall be circumcised; every male throughout your generation, whether born in your house, or bought with your money from any foreigner who is not of your offspring, both he that is born in your house and he that is bought with your money, shall be circumcised. So shall my covenant be in your flesh an everlasting covenant. Any uncircumcised male who is not circumcised in the flesh of his foreskin shall be cut off from his people; he has broken my covenant. (Gen. 17:9-14)

In keeping the words of the covenant, Abraham was circumcised when he was ninety-nine years old; Ishmael, his son, was circumcised when he was thirteen years old. All others in the family of Abraham were circumcised on the same day. (Gen. 17:24-27) Abraham circumcised his son Isaac when he was eight days old. (Gen. 21:4 cf. Acts 7:8)

Joshua circumcised all the males who were not circumcised, while they were in the wilderness. (Jos. 5:5)

There was a controversy over whether the Gentiles be circumcised before they become believers in Jesus Christ. The early church was facing the problem. Apostle Peter debated over the problem and said that the Holy Spirit was given to the uncircumcised Gentile as God gave it to the circumcised Jews. All are saved by the grace of the Lord Jesus. (Acts 15:8-11) By this argument the assembly was silenced.

St. Paul, who was circumcised on the eighth day (Phil. 3:5), preached the doctrine of justification by faith and not by works. He argued that Abraham was the father both of the uncircumcised and the circumcised because his faith was reckoned as righteousness. (Rom. 4:1-12) He made a ruling about this matter, when he wrote:

> Only, let every one lead the life which the Lord has assigned to him, and in which God has called him. This is my rule in all the churches. Was any one at the time of his call already circumcised? Let him not seek to remove the marks of circumcision. Was any one at the time of his call uncircumcised? Let him not seek circumcision. For neither circumcision counts for anything nor uncircumcision, but keeping the commandments of God. Every one should remain in the state in which he was called. (I Cor. 7:17-20)

In his Letter to the Galatians, he wrote:

> For neither circumcision counts for anything, nor uncircumcision, but a new creation. (Gal. 6: 15 cf. Gal. 5:6)

From these writings, we can conclude that Christians are exempted from the rite of circumcision. Circumcision was a means to be covenanted people of God. The baptism in the name of the Lord Jesus Christ is a means to enter into the kingdom of God and to be God's people. Therefore, circumcision was substituted by baptism.

(B) The second idea of the text is that at his circumcision, the baby was named Jesus. It is a Hebrew practice to name the male child when the infant was circumcised. Parents of the infants were given an authority to name the child at his circumcision. Let us find a few examples from the Bible.

(1) Isaac had two sons, Esau and Jacob. It is assumed that when his children were eight days old, he named them when they were circumcised. When Isaac became very old and blind, he wished to bless his son Esau. He asked Esau to go hunting and prepare a delicious meal for him so that he might bless him before his death. Rebekah, the wife of Jacob, heard this conversation. She encouraged her favourite son Jacob to steal the blessings from his father. Rebekah helped Jacob prepare a meal; and she also helped him to disguise him as Esau. Jacob was successful to receive the blessings of his father before Esau. When Esau went to serve the food to his father in order to receive his blessing, Isaac said to Esau that he had given those blessings to Jacob. Then Esau said:

> Is he not rightly named Jacob? For he has supplanted me these two times. He took away my birthright; and behold, he has taken away my blessing. (Gen. 27:36)

In other words, the name of Jacob implies cheating. He was named so, prophesying the future events of cheating.

(2) Philistines defeated the people of Israel in a battle. In that battle, sons of Eli, the priest, were killed; and Eli also died of shock when he heard that the Ark of the LORD God was taken away by the Philistines. At these crises, Eli's daughter-in-law gave birth to a son. She named him "Ichabod," saying 'the glory has departed from Israel' (I Sam. 4:21).

(3) Zechariah and his wife Elizabeth were very old. They were praying for a child for many years. Zachariah was a priest. His term to burn incense on the altar of the LORD God came. An angel appeared to him and told him that his wife Elizabeth will bear a son; and he should name him John. When an infant was eight days old, he was circumcised. The people asked Elizabeth what name

her child should be given. She replied saying 'John.' Then the people approached Zechariah, who had become dumb, because he did not believe the word of the angel that he would have a son. Zachariah asked for a writing tablet and wrote on it 'John.' Thus, both parents named the infant 'John,' at his circumcision. (Lk. 1:59-63)

Following the religious tradition of Judaism, Joseph named the infant 'Jesus,' when the infant was circumcised after he became eight days old.

(C) The third idea of the text is that the child was named Jesus before he was conceived in the womb. There is a possibility that the name Jesus was given to other Jewish children when they were circumcised. Nevertheless, they were not named so, before they were conceived in their mothers' womb. Jesus the Christ was given the name Jesus before He was conceived in the womb of His mother Mary. His birth was miraculous. He was conceived by the Holy Spirit and was born of a virgin. His birth was a supernatural birth. It was a prophecy that He, the Messiah, would be born not of a human seed but by the supernatural power, the Holy Spirit. He was the Son of God by His supernatural birth. (Lk. 1:35).

In the Bible, there are some male children, born by intervention of the LORD God to serve the purpose of God. Let us find a few examples.

(1) Elkanah had two wives, Peninnah and Hannah. Peninnah had children but Hannah had none, therefore, Elkanah would give her a portion because he thought that the LORD God had closed her womb (I Sam. 1:5). Peninnah used to tease and to provoke Hannah over the matter. Hannah used to cry every year when she went to the temple of God at Shiloh. One year she went into the temple; and poured out her heart to God and asked Him to give her a son; and she promised to dedicate her son to God for his entire life. (I Sam. 1:10-11) Eli the priest said to her that God may grant her prayer. When she gave birth to a son, she named him 'Samuel' meaning she had asked him of the LORD. (I Sam.1: 20) When

Samuel was weaned, his mother Hannah went to the temple to dedicate her son for God's service for his entire life. Samuel was lent to the LORD God. (I Sam. 1:23-27) Samuel became a prophet and a priest of the LORD God.

(2) Zechariah was a priest. He married a wife named Elizabeth, who was born in a family of Aaron. They both were religious. They had no child because Elizabeth was barren and Zechariah was very old. (Lk. 1:5-7) They were praying to the LORD God to give them a child.

Zachariah's term to burn incense on the altar of the LORD God came. When he entered to burn incense on the altar, the angel Gabriel (Lk. 1:19) appeared to him; and told him that his wife Elizabeth will bear a son; and he shall call his name John. The angel told the mission for his son John, in the following words:

> And you will have joy and gladness, and many will rejoice at his birth; for he will be great before the Lord, and he shall drink no wine nor strong drink, and he will be filled with the Holy Spirit, even from his mother's womb. And he will turn many of the sons of Israel to the Lord their God, and he will go before him in the spirit and power of Elijah, to turn the hearts of the fathers to the children, and the disobedient to the wisdom of the just, to make ready for the Lord a people prepared. (Lk. 1:14-17)

In other words, John would be a forerunner of the Messiah, whose mission was to prepare the way for the Lord.

In the birth of John the Baptist, we can see not only the divine intervention but also the purpose of God in order to prepare the way for Christ, the Messiah.

Six months after Elizabeth's pregnancy, God sent the angel Gabriel to Mary, who was a virgin, betrothed to Joseph. Gabriel said to the virgin Mary:

> Do not be afraid, Mary, for you have found favour with God. And behold, you will conceive in your womb and bear a son, and you shall call his name Jesus. He will be great, and will be called the Son of the Most High; and the Lord God will give to him the throne of his father David, and he will reign over the house of Jacob for ever; and of his kingdom there will be no end. (Lk. 1:30-33)

Jesus Christ was born of the virgin Mary and of the Holy Spirit. He is the Son of God and saviour of the world.

Mary was betrothed to Joseph before they came together. When Joseph found Mary pregnant, he decided to divorce her quietly. An angel of the LORD God appeared to Joseph in a dream and told him:

> Joseph, son of David, do not fear to take Mary your wife, for that which is conceived in her is of the Holy Spirit, she will bear a son, and you shall call his name Jesus, for he will save his people from their sins. (Mt. 1:20-21)

Both the parents of Jesus were told by the angel of the LORD God that Jesus would be born of the Holy Spirit; and He will be the saviour of world and everlasting ruler on the throne of King David. This was the purpose behind the birth of Jesus Christ.

Conclusion

From the event of the birth of Jesus Christ and His circumcision and naming, we can learn a few things.

(1) Jesus was born as a Hebrew or Jew. He had Jewish culture and heritage. It was a plan of God that the saviour of the world would come from His chosen people. Jesus Christ declared to the woman at Jacob's well: "we worship what we know, for salvation is from the Jews." (Jn 4:22) St. Paul elaborated this thought in Rom. 9: 4-5. In other words, there is no culture and religion from which comes the salvation of all, except Judaism. Therefore, we should not depict Jesus Christ any other way.

(2) Jesus as a Jewish male infant, was circumcised when he was eight days old. Circumcision was a rite to make the Hebrews as God's chosen people. After the circumcision, they were considered the people of the covenant, obeying the laws and rituals of Judaism. The apostles of the early church argued against the rite of the circumcision in case of the new believers in Jesus Christ. The rite of baptism by water and in the name of Jesus Christ make them the people of the new covenant, entering the kingdom of God. Thus, baptism substituted circumcision.

(3) The parents are given a right to name their infants at baptism. This implies that the parents have a right to raise up their children in Christian faith. No one should interfere with their right given by God. Parents should pray God what name they should give to their infant.

(4) The circumcision and naming of Jesus, when He was an infant, justifies infant baptism.

Recommended Hymns from the Methodist Hymnal

117   'Hark! The herald-angels sing'

118   'O Come, all ye faithful'

125   'O Little town of Bethlehem,'

128   'A virgin most pure, as the'

143   'Good Christian men, rejoice'

Recommended Responsive Reading from the Methodist Hymnal

5 (p. 336)

Recommended Responsive Reading from A Worship Manual for Scriptural or Methodist Order of Service

65 (pp. 170-171),

#79 (pp. 193-194).

Chapter - 11

Titles of the Sermon
'A Prophesied Controversy about Jesus Christ,'
'Simeon's Prophecy about Jesus Christ,'
Negative and Positive Responses to Jesus Christ.'

Scripture
Luke 2:22-35
Leviticus 12:3-4
Psalms 118:22
Isaiah 8:13-15; 28:16
Matthew 7:29; 9:11-13; 11:19; 21:11; 23:16-23, 27-28
Mark 1:22
Luke 7:16, 33-34, 39; 13:6-17; 14:1-6
John 1:9-13, 45-51; 3:16-21; 5:1-18;6:14; 7:17-18, 40; 8:26, 39-40
Acts 4:11-13
Romans 9:30-33; 10:11
I Peter 2:4-8

Text: Luke 2:34-35

A Few Versions of the Text, Luke 2:34-35
Behold, this child is destined for the fall and rising of many in Israel, and for a sign which will be spoken against "(yes, a sword will pierce through your own soul also), that the thoughts of many hearts may be revealed." *The New King James Version*

Behold, this child is set for the fall and rising again of many in Israel; and for a sign which shall be spoken against; (Yea, a sword will pierce through thy own soul also;) that the thoughts of many hearts may be revealed. *Explanatory Notes Upon the New Testament*

Behold, this child is set for fall and rising of many in Israel, and for a sign that is spoken against (and a sword will pierce through your own soul also), that thoughts out of many hearts may be revealed. *Revised Standard Version*

This child is destined to cause the falling and rising of many in Israel, and to be a sign that will be spoken against, so that the thoughts of many hearts may be revealed. And a sword will pierce your own soul too. *New International Version*

This child is destined to be a sign which men reject; and you too shall be pierced to the heart. Many in Israel will stand or fall because of him, and thus the secret thoughts of many will be laid bare. *The New English Bible*

A sword shall pierce your soul, for this child shall be rejected by many in Israel, and this to their undoing. And the deepest thought of many hearts shall be revealed. *The Living Bible Illustrated*

This child is the reason that many people in Israel will be condemned and many others will be saved. He will be a sign that will expose the thoughts of those who reject him. And a sword will pierce your heart. *God's Word*

Introduction

(1) In 1990, people of the world have witnessed the fall of the United Soviet States of Russia, and the declining popularity of the President Mikhail Gorbachev(March 2, 1931 -), as well as the rise of Russian Republic and its President Boris Yeltsin (February 1, 1931-April 23, 2007). President Yeltsin was in favour of political reforms and freedom. In order to show that President Yeltsin was supporting religious freedom movement in Russia, he went to a Russian Orthodox Church. Because of his support, some

established churches are growing rapidly in Russia. This is a radical change in the Russian society.

In many developed nations, religion has ceased to play a vital role in the lives of people. The place of religion was taken by fascism, Nazism, Communism, sexual liberation, race politics, and environmental politics. Nevertheless, religious zeal coexisted along with secularism, in the lives of many people. It was true in case of the Russian Christians. With reference to this phenomenon, John Henry Newman (February 21, 1801-August 11, 1890) said: "True religion is slow in growth and, when once planted, is difficult of dislodgement; but its intellectual counterfeit has no root in itself; it springs up suddenly, it suddenly withers." This observation is confirmed by the most spectacular testimony of what happened in Russia. In Russia, the communist ideology of Nicolai Lenin (1870-1924) collapsed in 1990-91, and both Orthodox and Catholic Christianity had survived all the assaults made upon them by the regime, and were strong and spreading.[1]

(2) Similar events took place in Poland. Adolf Hitler (April 20,1889-April 30, 1945) had closed schools, universities, and seminaries in Poland; and murdered a third of clergy class in Poland. When the Red Army imposed the Lublin government in 1945, they were confident that the church would disappear within a generation. The alien communist regime resisted Catholicism. But by 1960, the Catholic church gained its strength. The number of religious persons, i.e., priests, nuns, and monks grew to 36,500. Some 95% of children received Holy Communion. The movement of peasants into the towns re-evangelized the urban population. Sunday Mass attendance was more than 50%. The figures could be not matched anywhere in the world. Catholicism was the driving force behind the new Polish independent trade union, called Solidarity. Lech Walesa (September 29, 1943-)was its fervent Catholic leader. In 1989 the communist authority began to collapse in Poland. In August 1989, Poland became the first country in the Soviet block to appoint a non-Communist government, with Walesa's colleague, Tadeusz, as the Prime Minister. The destruction of communism was completed in 1990-91, when Walesa himself became the

President of Poland, and all remaining religious restraints were removed.[2]

(3) Not only the present ideologies, such as communism, positivism, liberalism, and race politics, oppose and reject Christianity, but also other religions do the same. For example, India is a secular State in principle; but she is governed by Hindus. Hindus believe in social hierarchy and idol worship. Hindus do not welcome Christian missionaries into India, because Christianity stands for spiritual equality of all, which is against Hindus' social hierarchy. Moreover, Christianity stands against idol worship, which is a Hindu practice of idol worship. For these reasons, Hindus oppose and reject Christianity.

Christianity is opposed by Islam and Buddhism. The countries, which are governed by these two religions, do not welcome Christian missionaries.

Introduction of the Text

Christianity had been rejected and opposed by various ideologies and other religions. It came out of Judaism. How the Jews would respond to the teaching of Jesus Christ was foretold by a devout Jew, named Simeon, to Mary, the mother of Jesus, in these words:

> Behold, this child is set for fall and rising of many in Israel, and for a sign that is spoken against (and a sword will pierce through your own soul also), that thoughts out of many hearts may be revealed. (Lk. 2:34-35)

This is the text of our meditation now.

The Context of the Text

Jesus (4 B. C. - A. D. 30) was born of virgin Mary, in Bethlehem. According to the laws of the Old Testament, Jesus was circumcised when He was eight days old. He was given name Jesus (Lk. 2:21). At the time of His circumcision, his mother Mary could not go to the temple, because she had to wait to complete her purifying for forty-one days. After this period of purification, she was allowed to enter the temple (Lev. 12:3-4). When Jesus was more than forty days old, His parents- Mary and Joseph- brought him up to Jerusalem in order to present Him to the LORD God.

As Jesus was to be presented to the LORD God, by his parents, Simeon entered the temple. Simeon was religious, devout, and old man from Jerusalem. The Holy Spirit revealed to him that he would not die until he sees God's anointed. Simeon approached the parents of Jesus and took Jesus in his arms and blessed God, saying:

> LORD, now lettest thou thy servant depart in peace, according to thy word; for mine eyes have seen thy salvation which thou hast prepared in the presence of all peoples, a light for revelation to the Gentiles, and for glory of thy people Israel. (Lk. 2:29-32)

Then Simeon addressed to the mother of Jesus, Mary; and said to her:

> Behold, this child is set for the fall and rising of many in Israel, and for a sign that is spoken against (and a sword will pierce through your own soul also), that thoughts out of many hearts may be revealed. (Lk. 2:34-35)

This is the text of our meditation, within its historical setting.

An Analysis of the Text

This text has four ideas. (A) The first idea is that baby Jesus was destined to cause many people to fall.

(B) The second idea is that baby Jesus was also destined to cause many to rise up.

(C) The third thought is that the baby Jesus would be the sign, revealing thoughts of many hearts.

(D) The fourth idea is that Mary would feel a pain as if a sword would pierce her own soul.

Exposition of the Ideas of the Text

(A) The first idea of the text is that baby Jesus was destined to cause many people to fall. This was the first part of the prophecy, which Simeon made to Mary, the mother of Jesus. Simon told her that many people would be offended by the teaching of Jesus Christ. This would be a negative way of responding to Jesus, who was a religious teacher and who is the Saviour of the world.

The baby Jesus, who was born in Bethlehem, would grow up into the man. His mission would be to give salvation to all people. But all people would not accept His teaching; many would accept, and many would reject His teaching. St. John had said about these ways of responding to Jesus' teaching by His own people, in the prologue of the gospel, as follows:

> The true light that enlightens every man was coming into the world. He was in the world, and the world was made through him, yet the world knew him not. He came to his own home, and his people received him not. But to all who received him, who believed in his name, he gave power to become children of God; who were born, not of blood nor of the will of the flesh nor of the will of man, but of God. (Jn 1:9-13)

St. John further explained these two ways, how the people would choose either salvation or condemnation, in the following words:

> For God so loved the world that he gave his only Son, that whoever believes in him should not perish but have eternal life. For God sent the Son into the world, not to condemn the world, but that the world might be saved through him. He who believes in him is not condemned; he who does not believe is condemned already, because he has not believed in the name of the only Son of God. And this is the judgment, that light has come into the world, and men loved darkness rather than light, because their deeds were evil. For every one who does evil hates the light, and does not come to the light, lest his deeds should be exposed. But he who does what is true comes to the light, that it may be clearly seen that his deeds have been wrought in God. (Jn 3:16-21

Jesus Christ was the Messiah, the anointed of God. God told that He would send the Messiah to save His chosen people, through His prophets. God also foretold how His people would respond to His Son. Eight centuries before the birth of the Messiah, prophet Isaiah (his period of prophecy 783-687 B.C.) wrote:

> But the LORD of hosts, him you shall regard as holy; let him be your fear, and let him be your dread. And he will become a sanctuary, and a stone of offence, and a rock of stumbling to both houses of Israel, a trap and a snare to the inhabitants of Jerusalem. And many shall stumble thereon; they shall fall and be broken; they shall be snared and taken. (Is. 8:13-15)

This prophecy was fulfilled in Jesus Christ. His teaching became a stumbling block to the leading men of the Jews and of the State. The scribes and pharisees, the religious leaders of the Jews, were offended by Jesus Christ, when He challenged their conventional teaching and positions.

Jesus Christ associated himself with the sinners, tax collectors, and ordinary people. He was, therefore, criticised as 'a friend of tax collectors and sinners.' (Lk. 7:33-34; Mt. 11:19) The Pharisees objected Jesus' association with sinners and tax collectors. They asked Jesus' disciples, 'Why does your teacher eat with tax collectors and sinners?' Jesus heard this and said to them:

> Those who are well have no need of a physician, but those who are sick. Go and learn what this means, 'I desire mercy, and not sacrifice.' For I came not to call the righteous, but sinners. (Mt. 9:11-13)

In short, Jesus' association with the sinners became a source of offence to the religious leaders of Jews.

Jesus Christ also challenged religious conventions of the Jews. He healed the sick on the many Sabbath days. (Lk. 13:6-17; 14:1-6; Jn 5:1-18). We should note Jesus' justification of healing the sick on the Sabbaths. When Jesus healed the sick, who was paralysed for thirty-eight (38) years, on the Sabbath, the Jews were offended; and began to persecute Jesus. Jesus Christ justified His healing on the Sabbath, saying, "My father is working still, and I am working." (Jn 5:17) His justification made them more angry, because He made Himself equal with God. (Jn 5:18)

(B) The second idea of the text is that baby Jesus was also destined to cause many to rise up. In other words, the teaching of Jesus Christ would cause many people to be saved from sin and spiritual destruction. Jesus Christ would be their personal Saviour. The people would become the children of God through Him. This is a positive way of responding to the teaching of Jesus Christ. The result of the positive way is the salvation of soul.

The teaching of Jesus Christ would be a stepping stone into the presence of God that the people would be justified by their faith in Jesus Christ. Prophet Isaiah prophesied about this positive response to the Messiah, in these words:

> Behold, I am laying in Zion for a foundation a stone, a tested stone, a precious cornerstone, of a sure foundation: He who believes will not be in haste. (Is. 28:16)

St. Paul (2 B. C.-67 A. D.) quoted this verse (Is. 28:16) with reference to the doctrine of salvation by faith; and he argued in his Letter to the Romans, as follows:

> That Gentiles who did not pursue righteousness have attained it, that is, righteousness through faith; but that Israel who pursued the righteousness which is based on law did not succeed in fulfilling that law. Why? Because they did not pursue it through faith, but as if it were based on works. They have stumbled over the stumbling stone, as it is written, 'Behold, I am laying in Zion a stone that will make men stumble, a rock that will make them fall; and he who believes in him will not be put to shame. (Rom. 9:30-33 cf. Rom. 10:11)

The apostles of Jesus Christ, and especially St. Peter, understood this and proclaimed the salvation of the mankind in Jesus Christ alone. St. Peter courageously said to the rulers and elders of the Jews:

> This is the stone which was rejected by you believers, but which has become the head of the corner. And there is salvation in no one else, for there is no other name under heaven given among men by which we must be saved. (Acts 4:11-13 cf. Ps. 118:22)

St. Peter wrote to Christians, exhorting them to believe in Jesus Christ as the Saviour of them, as they were destined to be saved. And he explained to them why many rejected Jesus Christ, because they were destined to reject him, in these words:

> Come to him, to that living stone, rejected by men but in God's sight chosen and precious;... For it stands in scripture: 'Behold, I am laying in Zion a stone, a cornerstone chosen and precious, and he who believes in him will not be put to shame.' To you therefore who believe, he is precious; but for those who do not believe, 'The very stone which the builders rejected has become the head of the corner,' and 'A stone that will make men stumble, a rock that will make them fall;' for they stumble because they disobey the word, as they were destined to do. (I Pet. 2:4-8)

The apostles of Jesus Christ made very clear to their listeners that they would be saved form sin and the final judgment, if they believe in Jesus Christ. Their positive response to the teaching of Jesus Christ would give them salvation.

(C) The third thought of the text is that the baby Jesus would be the sign, revealing thoughts of many hearts. In other words, the teaching of Jesus Christ would make the people realize the condition of their hearts. They would pass judgment upon themselves in the light of the teaching of Jesus Christ.

Jesus' way of teaching the people was different from the way of the scribes. He taught them with the divine authority; and His listeners noted the difference. This fact was noted down by the writers of the gospels. (Mt. 7: 29; Mk 1: 22) Jesus Christ taught them with authority, because He knew the will and intent of the LORD God. Jews marvelled at the teaching of Jesus Christ; and they wanted to know the source of His teaching. He said to them in the temple at Jerusalem:

> My teaching is not mine, but his who sent me; if any man's will is to do his will, he shall know whether the teaching is from God or whether I am speaking on my own authority. He who speaks on his own authority seeks his own glory; but he who seeks the glory of him who sent him is true, and in him there is no falsehood. (Jn 7:17-18)

By His teaching and the deeds of the miracles, Jesus proved to be the Messiah; and many began to believe in Jesus to be the Messiah, the Christ. (Lk. 7:16; Jn 6:14; 7:40; Mt. 21:11)

Jesus had the prophetic vision and insight to know the thoughts of the people. When Phillip told Nathaniel that he found the prophet from Nazareth, about whom Moses and the prophets wrote, Nathaniel questioned his statement. Phillip asked him to verify the fact; and brought him to Jesus. Jesus Christ spoke of Nathaniel as a man without guile; and told him that he was under a fig tree before Phillip met him. Then Nathaniel was convinced that Jesus was the Son of God, Christ. (Jn 1:45-51)

When a Pharisee, named Simeon, invited Jesus to dine at his home, and Simeon saw a sinful woman touching Jesus, Simeon thought in his heart, "If this man were a prophet, he would have known who and what sort of woman this is touching him, for she is a sinner." (Lk. 7:39) Then Jesus Christ spoke to him in the parable of the two debtors. Simeon then realized that Jesus was consciously allowing the sinful woman to touch him; he must have realized that Jesus had the ability to know inner thoughts of the people.

When Jesus claimed that His teaching was from God (Jn 7:17-18; 8:26), and the Jews claimed to be Abraham's descendants, Jesus Christ told them, "If you were Abraham's children, you would do what Abraham did, but now you seek to kill me, a man who has told you the truth which I heard from God; this is not what Abraham did." (Jn 8:39-40) Jesus Christ knew the inner thoughts of the people.

Jesus Christ set up the standard of right and wrong; He applied it against scribes and Pharisees, the religious leaders of the Jews. He exposed their hypocrisy several times. He boldly told them:

> Woe to you, scribes and Pharisees, hypocrites! For you tithe mint and dill and cummin, and have neglected the weightier matters of the law, justice and mercy and faith; these you ought to have done, without neglecting the others. (Mt. 23:23 cf. Mt. 23:16-22, 27-28).

In short, the religious leaders were offended whenever Jesus Christ questioned their religious precepts, and criticized them to be hypocrites.

(D) The fourth idea of the text is that Mary would feel a pain as if a sword would pierce her own soul. Mary was the woman, who gave birth to Jesus. She knew why God chose her to be the mother of His Son, Jesus Christ (Lk. 1:28-35). She had watched how the people were healed by His word and touch. She was watching then how the religious leaders were persecuting Jesus. When Jesus was arrested by the Jewish council and sentenced to be crucified, Mary learned about those events. She, with other women from Galilee, followed Jesus. When Jesus was on the cross, she stood beside His cross (Jn 19:25-27; Mt. 27:55-56). Her heart was filled with sorrow, when she saw the suffering of her innocent son. Her painful experience was as if a sword pierced through her soul. That was a prophecy of Simeon, which was fulfilled, when Jesus Christ was hung on the cross for the redemption of the world.

Conclusion

A devout Jew, Simeon, prophesied to Mary, the mother of Jesus, that her son could cause many people to stumble as well as many to be saved; He would reveal the inner thoughts of the people; and would judge them. When the people would reject His teaching and His divine claims, they would persecute Him and crucify Him; she would experience a severe pain as if her heart was pierced through by a sword.

Jesus Christ was born to be the Saviour of the world. People respond to His teaching and His divine claims either negatively or positively. Those, who respond Jesus Christ as their personal Saviour, would be saved from sin and the spiritual destruction. Therefore, the news of the birth of Jesus Christ brought hope of salvation to many; they were glad to receive the good news. May the same news, delivered on this Christmas day, bring us joy and happiness. Let us build our spiritual life on the spiritual rock, Jesus Christ Himself.

Recommended Hymns from the Methodist Hymnal

119   'Angels from the realm of glory,'

131   'The first Nowell the angel did say'

139   'The race that long in darkness pined'

242   'Come, Thou long-expected Jesus,'

Recommended Responsive Reading from A Worship Manual for a Scriptural or Methodist Order of Service

102 (pp.237-239).

Endnotes

[1] Paul Johnson, A History of the Modern World, from 1917 to 1990, (London: Weidenfeld and Nicolson, Revised Ed., 1991), pp. 700f.

[2] Ibid., pp. 701f.

Chapter - 12

Titles of the Sermon

'Jesus Christ the Word of God'

'Jesus Christ the Logos'

'Jesus Christ the Dabhar'

'Jesus Christ the Membra'

'Jesus Christ, God Personified'

Scripture

John 1:1-18

Psalms 145:15-16

Proverbs 8:22-31

Jeremiah 1:4-5

Amos 3:1

Matthew 9:7-8, 13; 12:7; 11:4-5; 15:30-31

Mark 2:5, 9-10; 9:2, 5; 12; 7:37

Luke 5: 20, 23, 25-26; 7:48

John 2:17; 11:45

Colossians 1:15-18; 2:2-3

Hebrews 1:1-3

I John 1:1-3

Text: John 1:14

A Few Versions of the Text, John 1:14

And the Word became flesh and dwelt among us, and we beheld His glory, the glory as of the only begotten of the Father, full of grace and truth. *The New King James Version*

And the Word was made flesh, and tabernacled among us, (and we beheld his glory, the glory as of the only begotten of the Father,) full of grace and truth. *Explanatory Notes Upon the New Testament*

And the Word became flesh and dwelt among us, full of grace and truth; we have beheld his glory, glory of the only son from the Father. *Revised Standard Version*

And the Word became flesh and lived for a while among us. We have seen his glory, the glory of the one and only Son, who came from the Father, full of grace and truth.*New International Version*

So the Word became flesh; he came to dwell among us, and we saw his glory, such glory as befits the Father's only Son, full of grace and truth. *The New English Bible*

And Christ became a human being and lived here on earth among us and was full of loving forgiveness and truth. And some of us have seen his glory- the glory of the only Son of the heavenly Father. *The Living Bible Illustrated*

The Word became human and lived among us. We saw his glory. It was the glory that the Father shares with his only Son, a glory full of kindness and truth. *God's Word*

Introduction

It is a well-known fact that Christmas is the celebration of the birth of Christ. Christians celebrate the festivities because they believe that Jesus Christ is the saviour of all the nations, cultures, creeds, and countries. Christianity is a universal religion in this sense.

During Christmas Season, Christians buy gifts to give to their relatives and friends and to their neighbours and to the needy. They give gifts to one another and make everyone happy because they believe that the LORD God, Yahweh gave them the most precious gift in the person of Jesus Christ, who saved them from sin and spiritual death. They know that God loved them first and they want to love their human brethren in response to God's love toward them.

As Christians buy gifts during the festival (or mass), this practice commercialized Christmas. Some of Christians forget the reason for the season which is the birth of Jesus Christ.

It is regrettable that Christmas greetings, "Merry Christmas" has become an offensive greetings to the nonbelievers, atheists, Jehovah Witness, Muslims, Jews, and Hindus. Our political climate makes Christians to celebrate the season without mentioning the reason, the name of Jesus the Christ. We are asked to make Christmas all-inclusive and non-offensive. Instead of saying "Merry Christmas" we should say "Happy Holidays." In the opinion of many Christians, this trend has passed the limit. Some of them said that the majority is marginalized. Christians are 80% of the population in Canada.

We should know the history of the U. S. A. and Canada that these free nations were created by the founders who were truly Christians; and who enshrined freedom of religions or conscience to anyone who lawfully enters the land. Christianity has elements of democracy. Those elements are apparently absent in Islam, Hinduism, Taoism, Shintoism, and other oriental religions.

Christians are not allowed to practise and propagate their faith in the countries where Islam, Hinduism, and Buddhism are predominant religions. Christians are persecuted and their educational and medical institutes are taken away. Other religions are not tolerant of Christian faith.

Christians, who have migrated to these lands, should enjoy their religious freedom and they should exercise their right to do so. They were and are tolerant of other religions in these lands.

Introduction of the Text

The reason of celebrating the Christmas festival is the birth of Jesus Christ, who is the saviour of the world. St. John, who wrote the gospel for the Jews and the Gentiles, stated the reason of the Christmas, in the following words:

> **And the Word became flesh and dwelt among us, full of grace and truth; we have beheld his glory, glory of the only Son from the Father.** (John 1:14)

This is the text of our meditation today.

The Context of the Text

St. John, an apostle of Jesus Christ, wanted to share the good news of salvation in Jesus Christ both to the Jews and the Gentiles. Therefore, he adopted a few concepts from Judaism and Hellenism and baptised those concepts to the people at large. He did not blindly adopt those concepts; but he intellectually or philosophically explained them with reference to the life and teaching of Jesus Christ, the only Son of God.

The Gospel according to St. John begins with the spiritual conviction that Jesus Christ is the WORD of God, He is the agent of creation, He was with God, and He is God.

In other words, the origin or birth of Jesus Christ is not from the earth but from the heaven, God the Father. Like other gospel writers (Mt. 1:1-17; Lk. 1:27), St. John did not mention the genealogy of Jesus Christ.

St. John's gospel begins with the statement:

> In the beginning was the Word, and the Word was with God, and the Word was God. (Jn 1:1)

We should note that in English translation Jesus Christ is said to be the WORD of God. The English term "WORD" has no philosophical background. It simply means a 'voice' which has a 'meaning' or which conveys a 'sense.' This term is inadequate to convey the message about

Jesus Christ, the WORD Of God. We have to go to the Hebrew and Hellenistic background of the WORD of God.

In the Hellenistic or Greek culture and philosophy, the term 'LOGOS' is used for the English term WORD of God. The Greek term LOGOS does not only mean meaningful or sensible voice; but it also means a sentence, a speech, a thought and even a whole book.

The Greek term LOGOS has very ancient Greek background. Heraclitus (500 B. C.), a pre-Socratic (469-399 B. C.) philosopher was the first one to use LOGOS in his philosophy. Thales (640-546 B. C.), Anaximander (611-546 B. C.), Anaximenes (mid 600-528 B. C.), Parmenides (515 B. C.-), Empedocles (490-430 B. C.), Anaxagorus (500-428 B. C.), Plato (427-347 B. C.), Aristotle (384-322 B. C.) and other Greek philosophers developed the concept of LOGOS.

LOGOS also has Roman background. Stoicism contributed much toward developing the LOGOS concept.

During the period of the diaspora, when Jews were scattered in Babylonian, Assyrians, and Persian Empires, Jews adopted Greek language and Hellenistic philosophy. The Old Testament, which was in Hebrew language, was translated by seventy Jewish scholars into Greek as early as the third century B. C. It is called the Hellenistic Bible. It is also known Septuagint (LXX). [1] Philo (20 B. C.-A. D. 50), a Jewish philosopher, used two Hebrew terms *dabhar* and *memra* as synonyms for LOGOS, in order to defend his religion. Thus, LOGOS obtained a Jewish philosophical implications.

During the first two centuries, Christianity became a popular religion among the non-Jews. St. John adopted the term LOGOS in order to explain the life and teaching of Jesus Christ. After St. John, St. Justin Martyr (A, D. 100-165) and Athenagorus (A. D. 133-190) used Greek philosophy in order to defend Christianity in the face of persecution.

In short, LOGOS has a very rich philosophical and theological background. However, we shall confine our explanation of LOGOS as it is found in the Bible.

An Analysis of the Text

This text has three ideas. (A) The first idea is that the WORD became flesh and dwelt among us.

(B) The second idea is that the WORD was full of grace and truth.

(C) The third idea is that we, the apostles of Jesus Christ, beheld the glory of Jesus Christ and His glory was of the only Son of God, the Father.

An Exposition of the Ideas of the Text

(A) The first idea of the text is that the WORD became flesh and dwelt among us. It was said before that Philo, a Jewish philosopher used two Hebrew words for *LOGOS*. The first word is *Dabhar* and the second, *Memra*.

(1) We should know the meanings of *Dabhar*. It means command, promise, speech, event, and act. This means that *Dabhar* combines both word and action. *Dabhar* is a manifestation of Yahweh and Yahweh is known through *Dabhar*. *Dabhar* has a dynamic force. The *Dabhar* of the word of God or Yahweh is powerful in itself. God argued through prophet Jeremiah, saying, "Do not my words scorch like fire? Are they not like a hammer that splinters rock? (Jer. 23:31) God created earth and heavens by His word (Gen. 1:1-231). This implies that *Dabhar* is not an abstract philosophical idea but it is the word of God, who is personal.

Dabhar is the means of Yahweh to communicate with people. God communicated with people through His prophets. Prophet Jeremiah bore a witness to this fact, when he said:

> The word of the LORD came to me: 'Before I formed you in the womb I knew you for my own; before you were born I consecrated you a prophet to the nations. (Jer. 1:4-5)

Similarly prophet Amos said:

> Listen, Israelites, to these words that the LORD addresses to you... (Am. 3:1)

Torah, or the books of the Old Testament' is regarded as the word of God, because God Yahweh spoke to the people of Israel through those sacred writings. Christians regard the Bible, which includes both the Old Testament and the New Testament, as the word of God. The whole Bible has sixty-six canonical books.

(2) Philo (20 B. C. −A. D. 50) used another Hebrew word '*Memra*' for *LOGOS*. *Memra* is connected with creation and providence. The wisdom literature of the Old Testament- Job, Psalms, Proverbs, and Ecclesiastes- spoke of *Memra* as existing before anything came into being, for example:

> The LORD created me at the beginning of his work, the first of his acts of old. Ages ago I was set up, at the first, before the beginning of the earth. When there were no depths I was brought forth, when there were no springs abounding with water. Before the mountains had been shaped, before the hills, I was brought forth; before he had made the earth with its fields, or the first of the dust of the world. When he established the heavens, I was there, when he drew a circle on the face of the deep, when he made firm the skies above, when he established the fountains of the deep, when he assigned to the sea its limit, so that the waters might not transgress his command, when he marked out the foundations of the earth, then I was beside him, like a master workman; and I was daily his delight, rejoicing before him always, rejoicing in his inhabited world and delighting in the sons of men. (Pr. 8:22-31)

In this passage *Memra* is described as the pre-existent being and the agent in the creation of the earth and heavens.

Secondly, *Memra* is connected with providence. A psalm writer wrote as follows:

> The eyes of all are lifted to thee, and thou givest them their food in due season. Thou openest thy hand, thou satisfiest the desire of every living thing. (Ps. 145:15-16)

It is presumed that apostle John was acquainted with Philo's Jewish philosophy, coming out of the wisdom literature of the Old Testament, that *Memra* and *Dabhar* were speaking of the Being who was pre-existent, coexistent with God Yahweh and the agent of the creation. He adopted these biblical ideas and applied to *LOGOS* in the prologue of his Gospel. He wrote, "In the beginning was the Word or *LOGOS*." (Jn 1:1) This means the *LOGOS* is pre-existent being. Then St. John added, "and the WORD or *LOGOS* was with God." (Jn 1:1) This means that *LOGOS* is coexistent being with God. Then St. John said, "all things were made through him, and without him was not anything made that was made." (Jn 1:3) This means *LOGOS* was the agent in creation. Then St. John said, "the WORD or *LOGOS* was God." (Jn 1:1) this means that *LOGOS* is identical with God. Identity between God and *LOGOS* is a unique concept of St. John. St. John's idea about *LOGOS* differed from Hellenistic, Greek, and Jewish philosophies. Further, St. John proclaimed that the *LOGOS* was incarnate in Jesus the Christ, when he said:

> And the Word became flesh and dwelt among us, full of grace and truth; we beheld his glory, the glory as of the only Son from the Father. (Jn 1:14)

Apostle Paul, who had a vision of Jesus Christ, believed Jesus Christ as the Son of God. He followed the trend of St. John about Jesus Christ. He spoke of Jesus Christ as the pre-existent Being and the agent in the creation, when he wrote the following words:

> He [Jesus Christ] is the image of the invisible God; the first-born of all creation; for in him all things were created, in heaven and on earth, visible and invisible, whether thrones or dominions or principalities or authorities— all things were created through him and for him. He is before all things, and in him all things hold together. (Col. 1:15-18 cf. Heb. 1:2)

Again, the writer of the Letter to the Hebrews wrote:

> But in these last days he has spoken to us by a Son, whom he appointed the heir of all things, through whom also he created the world. He reflects the glory of God and bears the very stamp of his nature upholding the universe by his word of power. (Heb. 1:2-3)

LOGOS in the writings of St. John and in St. Paul became distinct and unique when they put emphasis on personification or embodiment of *LOGOS*. St. John wrote, "And the Word became flesh and dwelt among us," (Jn 1:14). St. Paul similarly wrote: "to have all the riches of assured understanding and knowledge of God's mystery, of Christ, in whom are hid all the treasures of wisdom and knowledge." (Col. 2:2-3)

In short, both St. John and St. Paul proclaimed that the pre-existent *LOGOS* had become incarnate in Jesus Christ of Nazareth. Their *LOGOS* was different from Logos of Greek, Hellenistic and Jewish philosophers, because they made the divine *LOGOS* historical. L. W. Barnard (1924-) made the following observation on this point, saying:

> Rather, early Christian theologians begin with Jesus Christ as the fulfilment of God's purpose, the *logos* which God has spoken and who lived a historical life on earth. This was the line which divided Christian speculation from that of Hellenistic and Rabbinic Judaism and of Philo. [2]

According to the apostolic preaching, Jesus Christ was pre-existent of the creation, who was coexisting with God, and who was the agent in creation of the universe. All things were created for Him. He emptied Himself of the heavenly glory and became one of us in order to redeem us from sin and damnation, and for eternal life.

LOGOS became incarnate in the person of Jesus the Christ and He dwelt among the people. The apostles of Jesus Christ and other people saw Him, heard Him, and touched Him. The *LOGOS* was a real man and not a philosophical or speculative idea. Apostle John commented on dwelling of the Jesus Christ, the *LOGOS*, in his first letter, saying:

> That which was from the beginning, which we have heard, which we have seen with our eyes, which we have looked upon and touched with our hands, concerning the word of life- the life was made manifest, and we saw it, and testify to you, and proclaim to you the eternal life which was with the Father and was made manifest to you- that which we have seen and heard we proclaim also to you,.. (I Jn 1:1-3 cf. Jn 1:1, 4, 14)

The apostles of Jesus Christ wanted to bear eyewitness or first hand knowledge about Jesus Christ, the *LOGOS*.

(B) The second idea of the text is that the WORD was full of grace and truth. The apostles of Jesus Christ, who saw Him with their eyes, touched Him with their hands, heard Him with their ears, wanted to give authentic testimony about Jesus Christ to others. The twelve apostles and other followers of Jesus Christ were with Him during the short period of His ministry, which lasted about three years or more. They saw the mighty works or miracles He performed in their sight. He made blind to see, deaf to hear, lame to walk, dead to rise again (Mt. 9:7-8; 11:4-5; 15:30-31; Mk 2:12; 7:37; Lk. 5:25-26; Jn 11:45) When the people saw those miracles, they glorified God. Jesus Christ showed God's grace and forgiveness to the sinners and the people (Mt. 9:2, 5; Mk 2:5, 9-10; Lk. 5:20, 23; 7:48). He showed that He has the divine authority to forgive sins.

Jesus Christ revealed the true and challenging teaching about the word of God; and silenced and remonstrated Pharisees and the scribes (Mt. 9:13; 12:7). He revealed the truth of God to them and to others. In short, His life was full of truth and grace. Apostle John summarized about this, saying:

> For the law was given through Moses; grace and truth came through Jesus Christ. No one has ever seen God; the only Son, who is in the bosom of the Father, he has made him known. (Jn 1:17-18)

In other words, God's nature, and His grace and truth were revealed to the world by His Son, who is intimate with God the Father. In Jesus Christ we have the final and most trustworthy revelation of God. (Heb.1:2) There would be no one to do so after Him.

(C) The third idea of the text is that we, the apostles of Jesus Christ, beheld the glory of Jesus Christ and His glory was of the only Son of God, the Father. The apostles and other followers of Jesus Christ saw the mighty deeds and heard His challenging words of truth and grace. They saw His zeal for the work and word of God demonstrating His courage and authority (Jn 2:17). His words and works were glorious. They were surely evidences of the glory of the only Son of God.

Conclusion

Apostle John was acquainted with *LOGOS* of Hellenistic philosophy which was explained by a Jewish philosopher Philo, with reference to the Old Testament. *LOGOS*, the wisdom of God was existing before the creation and it coexisted with the LORD God Yahweh and it was the agent of creation. Apostle John thought of Jesus Christ as *LOGOS* of the Old Testament and he saw the characteristics of *LOGOS*, mentioned before, in Jesus Christ.

The uniqueness of the Gospel according to St. John, lies in the fact that it personified *LOGOS*, saying the *LOGOS* became man in the person of Jesus Christ. St. John witnessed that Jesus Christ dwelt among the people. People saw the glory of God in the words and works of Jesus Christ, the only Son of God.

Jesus Christ is the only saviour of the world. God in Jesus Christ came into the world to save us from our sins and damnation. This is the massage of Christmas for us today. Merry Christmas to everyone!

Recommended Hymns from the Methodist Hymnal

117   'Hark! The herald-angels sing'

118   'O Come, all ye faithful,'

124   'See, amid the winter's snow,'

220   'God is ascended up on high,'

Recommended Responsive Reading from the Methodist Hymnal

61 (p.411)

Recommended Responsive Reading from A Worship Manual for Scriptural or Methodist Order of Service

87 (pp. 208-209) or #118 (pp.273-273)

Endnotes

[1] The Interpreter's Bible, (New York: Abingdon Press; Nashville: Cokesbury Press, 1952), Vol. 1. p. 35.

[2] The Logos Theology of St. Justin Martyr 'Downside Review,' Vol. 89, p. 133

Chapter - 13
(A Pre-Christmas Sermon)

Titles of the Sermon

'John the Baptist a Forerunner of the Christ Jesus,'

'Attitude of John the Baptist toward Christ Jesus,'

'God's Servants Seeking No Importance.'

Scripture

John 3:22-30

Genesis 21:1-5

I Samuel 17:1-54; 18:7; 19:1-8; 20:35-42

I Kings 16:29-33; 18:40; 21:1-19

Isaiah 40:3; 53:1-6

Malachi 4:5-6

Matthew 3:7-12, 13-15; 4:18-25; 11:14, 16-19; 14: 3-4, 5-11; 17:9-13;

Mark 6:17-28; 9:11-13

Luke 1:5-80; 2:10-11; 7: 18-22, 29-30; 9:9

John 1: 23-34; 3:15, 26-30

Text: John 3:30

A Few Versions of the Text, John 3:30

He must increase, but I must decrease. *The New King James Version*

He must increase, but I must decrease. *Explanatory Notes Upon the New Testament*

He must increase, but I must decrease. *Revised Standard Version*

He must become greater, I must become less. *New International Version*

As he grows greater, I must grow less. *The New English Bible*

He must become greater and greater, and I must become less and less. *The Living Bible Illustrated*

He must increase in importance, while I must decrease in importance. *God's word*

Introduction

Jehovah Witness is considered to be a Christian sect rather than a denomination. This sect does not celebrate Christmas, the festivities surrounding the birth of Jesus the Christ or the Messiah. A theology of this sect is filled with many misunderstanigs about the scripture. It does not recognize the divinity of Jesus Christ; it does not consider that Jesus Christ is the Son of God; it fails to understand that Jesus Christ is the third person in the Holy Trinity. It cannot comprehend that Son of God is of the same substance of the God the Father and God the Holy Spirit. It is a dangerous and misguided sect. All those who believe in the word of God and who have attained spiritual maturity should be aware that Jehovah Witness is not a sect propagating the true gospel of Jesus Christ. How the believers in Jesus Christ should treat the believers of Jehovah Witness? I shall leave this matter for their discretion.

Christian denominations celebrate Christmas in accordance with the scripture, which recorded the words of an angel of the LORD to the shepherds in the field:

> Be not afraid; for behold, I bring you good news of a great joy which will
> come to all the people; for to you is born this day in the city of David a
> Saviour, who is Christ the Lord. (Lk. 2:10-11)

Christmas affirms good news of a great joy to the whole world. It is
good news of salvation of man from sin and death. It requires
celebration. We must celebrate the day of the birth of our Saviour.
Jehovah Witness is a wrong and misguided sect, which tells its followers
not to celebrate Christmas and even their own birthdays.

Introduction of the Text

We had been celebrating Christmas for centuries. Christmas is
the day when Jesus the Christ was born. Before Jesus Christ
was born, God sent John the Baptist, a forerunner to prepare
a way for Jesus Christ. John the Baptist was a humble servant of the
LORD God, Yahweh; he knew his life mission and his position in the
economy of God. When he heard that people were following Jesus
Christ and were abandoning him, he said:

He must increase, but I must decrease. (John 3:30)

This is the text of our meditation now.

The Context of the Text

Jesus Christ went from Galilee to the Jordan to John the Baptist (5 B.
C.-A. D. 28) to receive a baptism from him. John was hesitant to baptize
Jesus Christ, (Mt. 3:13-15) because he knew that Jesus was superior
to him, when he saw the Spirit descended on Jesus and remained on
Him (Jn 1:32). Having received the baptism from John the Baptist,
Jesus began to gather disciples and to start His ministry of preaching
and healing (Mt. 4:18-25). The crowds were following Jesus Christ
and His disciples.

Jesus Christ met Nicodemus in Jerusalem (Jn 3:1-15). Then He
and His disciples went from Jerusalem to Judea. His disciples were
baptising people in Judea. At the same time, John the Baptist was
baptizing the people at Aenon near Salim, before he was put in prison
by King Herod Antipas (4 B. C. – A. D.40).

The disciples of John the Baptist reported him that Jesus was baptizing in the neighbourhood and the people were following Jesus. (Jn 3:26) John the Baptist said to them:

> No one can receive anything except what is given him from heaven. You yourselves bear me witness, that I said, I am not the Christ, but have been sent before him. He who has the bride is the bridegroom; the friend of the bridegroom, who stands and hears him, rejoices greatly at the bridegroom's voice; therefore this joy of mine is now full. He must increase, but I must decrease. (Jn 3:27-30)

In this statement of John the Baptist, we can see that John believed in the plan of God that God gives certain position to man to fulfil an ordained mission. The servants of God should know this that they may not be jealous or envious of one another. John did not become envious of Jesus when he heard that the people were following Jesus and abandoning him. He believed it was an ordained way of his and of Jesus' ministry. He knew that he was not the Messiah or Christ; but he was sent before the Messiah to prepare a way for the Messiah. He gave an example of a relation that exists between the bridegroom and the friend of the bridegroom or the best man. The friend of a bridegroom rejoices over the voice of the bridegroom. He rejoices over the union of the bridegroom and the bride. John the Baptist meant by this illustration that he was a friend of the bridegroom, and the Messiah was the bridegroom, and the people of God was the bride. When he heard that the people were following Jesus, the Messiah, he was happy to see the union between the people of God and the Messiah. John the Baptist concluded his statement saying,

> He [the Messiah] must increase but I [John the Baptist] must decrease. (John 3:30)

This is the text, within its historical setting.

An Analysis of the Text

This text has one idea that the Messiah must increase and John the Baptist must decrease. Or the Messiah must become greater and John must become less. Or the Messiah must increase in importance and John must decrease in importance.

An Exposition of the Ideas of the Text

When John the Baptist heard from his disciples that Jesus was baptising the people and they were following Jesus, on one hand; but people were abandoning him, on the other hand. This would have upset a rabbi, if the rabbi was in competition with other rabbis. But John was not angry at and upset with Jesus; but he was happy by the good news. John the Baptist was happy to see that the ministry of Jesus Christ was becoming more popular and his ministry was fading away. Therefore, he said: "He [the Messiah] must increase but I [John the Baptist] must decrease." (John 3:30) Such humble attitude is rare. There is an example in the Old Testament, supporting such a noble attitude.

David, a bold but an untrained warrior, killed Goliath, a champion of the Philistines, and won victory for the people of Israel. (I Sam. 17:1-54). The court of King Saul (1044-1004 B. C.) recognized an importance of the victory of David. They praised David more than King Saul (I Sam. 18:7). King Saul was not happy with these things; he became envious of David. Jonathan was a son of the King Saul. Jonathan congratulated David. He foresaw that David would become the king of Israel after his father. He began to love David as his own soul. He was not jealous of David; and was not aspiring to be a king of Israel after his father. Jonathan made a covenant with David. In that covenant, Jonathan stripped himself of the robe that was upon him, and gave it to David. He also gave David his armour, sword, and girdle (I Sam. 18:4). Jonathan was ready to take a subordinate position to David. When King Saul advised his servants and Jonathan to kill David, yet Jonathan was delighted in David. He revealed the evil intention of his father to David to kill him. He advised David to hide in a place. Jonathan pleaded with King Saul not to kill innocent David. King Saul listened to Jonathan; and he swore not to kill David (I Sam. 19:1-8). When the evil spirit filled the mind of King Saul, he attempted to kill David with a spear. David fled and escaped from King Saul. David met Jonathan and told the event. Then Jonathan confirmed the evil intention of King Saul and helped David escape from his father (I Sam. 20:35-42).

John the Baptist was ready to take a subordinate position to Jesus Christ, because he knew the limits of his ministry; and he was to prepare a way for the Messiah. We should know more about the life and mission of John the Baptist shortly in this sermon.

It was a plan of God to send the prophet Elijah again on the earth in order to prepare a way for His Son, Jesus the Messiah. It was prophesied by Melachi, saying:

> Behold, I will send you Elijah the prophet before the terrible day of the LORD comes. (Mal. 4:5)

The birth and ministry of John the Baptist was preordained. He was born of Zechariah, a priest and of Elizabeth a daughter of Aaron. Both were righteous and very old, but without a child. They prayed to the LORD God to give them a child. When Zachariah's turn to burn incense to God came, an angel appeared to him in the temple. The angel told Zachariah that his wife would bear a son and he should call him John. Then the angel told him:

> And you will have joy and gladness, and many will rejoice at his birth; for he will be great before the Lord, and he shall drink no wine nor strong drink, and he will be filled with the Holy Spirit, even from his mother's womb. And he will turn many of the sons of Israel to the Lord their God, and he will go before him in the spirit of Elijah, to turn the hearts of the fathers to the children, and the disobedient to the wisdom of the just, to make ready for the Lord a people prepared. (Lk. 1:14-17)

The birth of John was miraculous as that of Isaac, the son of Abraham and Sarah who were very old to have a child. (Gen. 21:1-5)

The angel of the LORD God declared the mission of John that he would prepare the people to receive the Lord Jesus Christ.

When Eilizabeth was six months pregnant, an angle of the LORD appeared to the virgin Mary in Nazareth, a city of Galilee; and told her that Elizabeth her relative was pregnant. Mary went to see Elizabeth and stayed with the old couple three months in a city of Judah (Lk. 1:39, 56). Then she returned to Nazareth.

We should know about the ministry of Elijah. Elijah was a bold prophet, because he challenged the Baal worship, which was patronized by King Ahab (869-850 B. C.) and Queen Jezebel. (I Kg. 16:29-33) When the fire from heaven consumed the sacrifice, which Elijah offered to God Yahweh and thereby God proved Himself to be the true God, Elijah ordered the slaughter of the priests of Baal. (I Kg. 18:40) Secondly, Elijah confronted King Ahab when he took away the vineyard of Naboth and for the murder of Naboth by the conspiracy of Queen Jezebel (I Kg. 21:1-19). This was a very bold spirit of prophet Elijah. Was John the Baptist filled with the spirit of Elijah?

The mission of John the Baptist was to be forerunner or preparer of the kingdom of Christ. When some priests and Levites went from Jerusalem to Bethany, beyond Jordan (Jn 1:28) where John was serving God, to ask him questions: Are you the Christ? Are you Elijah? Are you the prophet? He denied being Christ, Elijah, and prophet. (Jn 1:25) He answered them, saying: "I am the voice of one crying in the wilderness, 'Make straight the way of the Lord,' as the prophet Isaiah said" {Is. 40:3] (Jn 1:23).

John the Baptist pointed toward the Messiah, who was to come after him, saying, "even he who comes after me, the thong of whose sandal I am not worthy to untie. (Jn 1:27) When Jesus went to John to be baptised, John said:

> Behold, the Lamb of God, who takes away the sins of the world! This is he of whom I said, 'After me comes a man who ranks before me, for he was before me. I myself did not know him; but for this I came baptizing with water, that he might be revealed to Israel.' (Jn 1:29-31)

After this, John the Baptist, gave a witness about Jesus, saying:

> I saw the Spirit descend as a dove from heaven, and it remained on him. I myself did not know him; but he who sent me to baptize with water said to me, 'He on whom you see the Spirit descend and remain, this is he who baptises with the Holy spirit.' And I have seen and have borne witness that this is the Son of God. (Jn 1:32-34)

John the Baptist was preaching the people to repent and to receive water baptism and turn to God. He was very courageous preacher and prophet. He denounced sins of the people. He asked them to confess their sins. He baptised them in the river Jordan.

When he saw the Pharisees and Sadducees coming for baptism, he said to them:

> You brood wipers! Who warned you to flee from the wrath to come? Bear fruit that befits repentance, and do not presume to say to yourselves, 'We have Abraham as our father; 'for I tell you, God is able from these stones to raise up children to Abraham. Even now the axe is laid to the root of the tree; every tree therefore that does not bear good fruit is cut down and thrown into the fire. (Mt. 3:7-10).

John the Baptist pointed out toward the Messiah; and he spoke about how his position and baptism were inferior to the position and baptism of the Messiah. He declared to the people, saying:

> I baptize you with water for repentance, but he who is coming after me is mightier than I, whose sandals I am not worthy to carry; he will baptize you with the Holy Spirit and with fire. His winnowing fork is in his hand, and he will clear his threshing floor and gather his wheat into the granary, but the chaff he will burn with unquenchable fire. (Mt. 3:11-12)

His message was for repentance, and for declairing the judgment of the Lord, coming after him.

John the Baptist did not spare the king of the Jews. He condemned Herod the tetrarch for his unethical relationship with Herodias, the wife of his brother Philip. Herod took away his brother's wife and unlawfully made her his wife or concubine. When King Herod Antipas heard the judgment, he arrested John and put him in a prison. (Mt. 14:3-4) Herod wanted to put John the Baptist to death; but he was afraid that the people would revolt against him because the people honoured John as a prophet. Herodius also wanted to kill John the Baptist because he condemned her relationship with King Herod. (Mk 6:19)

When John the Baptist was in the prison of Herod, he sent his two disciples to Jesus in order to verify that He was the Messiah. Jesus sent a message through the disciples of John Baptist that He was the Messiah and that He was performing the miracles, demonstrating His divine power, and the disciples of John the Baptist had seen those miracles. (Lk. 7:18-22)

When the messengers of John had gone, Jesus gave a tribute to John the Baptist, saying to the crowd:

> What then did you go out to see? A prophet? Yes, I tell you, and more than a prophet. This is he of whom it is written, 'Behold, I send my messenger before thy face, who shall prepare thy way before thee.' I tell you, among those born of women none is greater than John; yet he who is least in the kingdom of God is greater than he. (Lk. 7:26-28)

Jesus Christ declared John the Baptist as Elijah. He said concerning the rejection of the message of John by the people:

> But to what shall I compare this generation? It is like children sitting in the market places and calling to their playmates, 'We piped to you, and you did not dance; we wailed, and you did not mourn.'

> For John came neither eating nor drinking, and they say, 'He has a demon;' the Son of man came eating and drinking, and they say, 'Behold, a glutton and a drunkard, a friend of tax collectors and sinners!' Yet wisdom is justified by her deeds. (Mt. 11:16-19)

In other words, the message of John the Baptist and of Jesus Christ were rejected by the people, who acted like whimsical children, and who had no wisdom to look at the words and works of both John the Baptist and Jesus Christ.

King Herod was waiting for an opportunity to kill John. At his birthday, King Herod was pleased with the dance of the daughter of Herodias. He promised to give any thing for her performance. Herodias, through her daughter asked for the head of John the Baptist. King Herod complied with her demand; and beheaded innocent John, for his royal prestige and keeping his promise. (Mt. 14:5-11; Mk 6:21-28; Lk. 9:9) Thus,there was a conspiracy to kill John the Baptist.

John the Baptist was beheaded by King Herod Antipas. After this event, Jesus took Peter, James and John on a mountain. He was transfigured before them. They saw Moses and Elijah with Jesus. When they came down the mountain, Jesus told them not to tell about the event, until the Son of Man or Jesus Christ was resurrected from the dead (Mt. 17:9). The disciples of Jesus Christ were aware of the prophecy that Elijah would return before the Messiah. They asked

Jesus Christ the question, Why do the scribes say that first Elijah must come? (Mt. 17:10) Jesus Christ explained to them saying:

> Elijah does come, and he is to restore all things; but I tell you that Elijah has already come, and they did not know him, but did to him whatever they pleased. So also the Son of man will suffer at their hands. (Mt. 17:11-12)

The disciples understood that Jesus was speaking to them of John the Baptist. (Mt. 17:13)

The preaching and baptism of John the Baptist were accepted by the ordinary people and tax collectors; but the scribes and Pharisees rejected the purpose of God and the baptism of John (Lk. 7: 29-30) Jesus then prophesied that He was going to suffer at the hands of the scribes and the Pharisees (Mt. 17:12). The suffering of the Messiah were preordained. Through His vicarious sufferings, the sinners in the world are saved for eternal life (Is. 53:1-6).

Conclusion

What can we learn from the work and attitude of John the Baptist?

(1) John the Baptist accepted his subordinate position to that of Jesus the Christ or Messiah. He understood his mission in terms of preparing the way for the Messiah that the people may be ready to hear from the Messiah.

John the Baptist represents the true spirit of servantship of God. This is a right spirit in the ministry. Let there be no professional rivalry among the leaders, teachers, and preachers of Jesus Christ. As John the Baptist pointed toward the Messiah, all the servants of God should point toward Jesus Christ, the Lord and Saviour of mankind. May God grant this spirit to all Christian leaders that they may not seek impotance in the kingdom of God; and that they give glory and honour to their Lord, the Lord of the lords, and the King of kings.

(2) Secondly, how do you receive the message of God's servants? Unless we have the spiritual maturity to perceive the biblical content of the message, we may reject the message and justify the rejection as mentioned in the parable of the children in market

places. Study the parable and know the right way of looking at preaching the word of God anywhere and anytime.

Recommended Hymns from the Methodist Hymnal

117   'Hark! The herald-angels sing'

119   'Angels from the realms of glory,'

120   'Christians, awake, salute the happy morn,'

124   'See, amid the winter's snow,'

125   'O Little town of Bethlehem,'

Recommended Responsive Reading from the Methodist Hymnal

5 (p. 386),

Recommended Responsive Reading from A Worship Manual for Scriptural or Methodist Order of Service

79 (pp. 193-194).

Chapter - 14

Titles of the Sermon

'The Dimensions of God's Love in Jesus Christ,'

'All-inclusive and Everlasting Love of God in Jesus Christ,'

Scripture

Ephesians 3:14-21

Genesis 18:17-19

I Samuel 3:11-14

Isaiah 9:2-7; 53

Jeremiah 31:2-6

Amos 3:7

Daniel 2:12-19, 31-45

Matthew 7:7; 18:18-20; 21:21-22

Luke 2:10-11

John 1:14; 3:16; 14:13-14

Romans 5:6-8

Ephesians 3:2-3,6

Philippians 2:6-8

Hebrews 6:24-25

James 1:5-7

I John 2:9-11; 5:14

Text: Ephesians 3:17-18

A Few Versions of the Text, Ephesians 3:17-18

that Christ may dwell in your hearts through faith; that you, being rooted and grounded in love, may be able to comprehend with all the saints what is the width and length and depth and height- *The New King James Version*

That Christ may dwell in your hearts by faith; that being rooted and grounded in love, Ye may be able to comprehend with all the saints, what is the breadth, and length, and depth, and height; *Explanatory Notes Upon the New Testament*

That you, being rooted and grounded in love, may have power to comprehend with all saints what is the breadth and length and height and depth and to know the love of Christ which surpasses knowledge, that you may be filled with all the fullness of God. *Revised Standard Version*

So that Christ may dwell in your hearts through faith. And I pray that you, being rooted and established in love, together with all the saints, to grasp how wide and long and high and deep is the love of Christ, *New International Version*

That through faith Christ may dwell in your hearts in love. With deep roots and firm foundations, may you be strong to grasp, with all God's people, what is the breadth and length and height and depth of the love of Christ, *The New English Bible*

And I pray that Christ will be more and more at home in your hearts, living within you as you trust in Him. May your roots go down deep into the soil of God's marvellous love; and you may be able to feel and understand, as all God's children should, how long, how wide, how deep, and how high is love really is; *The Living Bible Illustrated*

Then Christ will live in you through faith. I also pray that love may be the ground into which you sink your roots and on which you have your foundation. This way, with all of God's people you will be able to understand how wide, long, high, and deep his love is. *God's Word*

Introduction

(1) A gentleman was a professed Christian. He regularly attended Sunday services and generously supported his church financially. He used to take the Holy communion without failure. He used to read the Bible daily and pray every day. He was an active member of the church. He was apparently a devout Christian.

He was taken seriously ill; therefore, he was admitted in a hospital for recovery. He was lying down on his bed and was searching his heart. He realized that he had a little love for God in his heart, though he was outwardly devout and professed Christian. He was troubled about having little love for God in his heart.

People of his church were asked to pray for him and to visit him. One of his friends went to see him in the hospital. He confessed to his friend that he had little love for God in his heart. His friend did not give him a short sermon. But he told his sick friend about his own personal experience in the following words:

> When I go home from here, I expect to take my baby on my knee, look into her sweet eyes, listen to her charming prattle, and tired as I am, her presence will rest me; for I love that child with unutterable tenderness. But she loves me little. If my heart were breaking it would not disturb her sleep. If my body were racked with pain, it would not interrupt her play. If I were dead, she would forget me in a few days. Beside this, she had never brought me a penny, but was a constant expense to me. I am not rich, but there is not money enough in the world to buy my baby. How is it? Does she love me, or do I love her? Do I withhold my love until I know she loves me? Am I waiting for her to do something worthy of my love before extending it?

The gentleman heard his friend attentively and realized the point made. Tears began to roll down on the sick man's face and he exclaimed, "Oh, I see, 'it is not my love to God, but God's love for me, that I should be thinking of.' And I do love him now as I never loved him before." [1]

(2) All Christians know the gospel in a short form, given in the verse John 3:16, which they recite often: "For God so loved the world that he gave his only Son, that whoever believes in him should not perish but have eternal life." In this verse we can clearly see three

dimensions of God's love, as follows. The breadth of God's love in these words, "God so loved the world." The length of God's love in these words, "that He gave His only begotten Son." The depth of God's love, in these words, "that whosoever believeth on Him shall not perish." The height of God's love in these words, "But shall have everlasting life." ²

Introduction of the Text

When St. John in 3:16 was talking about God's love, he did not explicitly talk about the dimensions of God's love, with deliberate emphasis. It was St. Paul, who mentioned the dimensions of God's love, and how believers should be able to comprehend them, in the following words of the text:

> **That you, being rooted and grounded in love, may have power to comprehend with all saints what is the breadth and length and height and depth and to know the love of Christ which surpasses knowledge, that you may be filled with all the fullness of God**. (Ephesians 3:17b-19)

This is the text of our meditation now.

The Context of the Text

The text is taken from the prayer of St. Paul for the Christians at Ephesus. The church at Ephesus was formed by the Christians, who were Gentiles previously. St. Paul was specially called to be the preacher to the Gentiles. He was chosen of God in Jesus Christ to reveal the divine mystery to the Gentiles. The hidden and divine mystery was that the Gentiles become heirs with Israel or they be joined to the body of Israel, the people of God, and they be eligible to share together in the promise in Jesus Christ (Eph. 3:6). This revelation was given to St. Paul by the grace of God (Eph. 3:2-3). He was to preach unsearchable riches of Christ to the Gentiles. He prayed for the Ephesians that Christ may dwell in their hearts through their faith; and they be rooted and grounded in love of God in Jesus Christ. When this would happen, the Ephesians, with the rest of the believers, would be able to know the dimensions - width, length, height, and depth- of the love of God in Christ Jesus.

An Analysis of the Text

The text has four ideas. (A) The first idea is to understand four dimensions of the love of Jesus Christ namely, (i) breadth, (ii) length, (iii) height, and (iv) depth.

(B) The second idea is the condition of being able to understand these four dimension, which is to be rooted and grounded in love.

(C) The third idea is that the Ephesians would comprehend the dimensions with other saints or with other devoted Christians. This is a second condition of comprehension of the dimensions.

(D) The fourth idea is the knowledge of the dimensions would surpass their knowledge; and the Ephesians would be filled with the fullness of God.

Exposition of the Ideas of the Text

(A) The first idea of the text is to understand four dimensions of the love of Jesus Christ namely, (i) breadth, (ii) length, (iii) height, and (iv) depth.

(i) Let us reflect upon the depth of God's love in Jesus Christ. The depth of God's love in Jesus Christ is demonstrated in the descent of God and in humility of Christ Jesus. The Son of God, Jesus Christ, renounced His heavenly glory and splendour; and He became a man. The WORD, which was God, became flesh and dwelt among us, the sinners (Jn 1:14). St. Paul described the descent of God in Christ, in these following words:

> [Christ], though he was in the form of God, did not count equality with God a thing to be grasped, but emptied himself, taking the form of a servant, being born in the likeness of men. And being found in human form he humbled himself and became obedient unto death, even death on a cross. (Phil. 2:6-8)

Rev. Charles Wesley (December 18, 1707- March 29, 1788), a founder and a hymn-writer of Methodist Church, saw the depth and height of God's love in Christ Jesus. He poetically expressed his thought in a hymn as follows:

I long to know, and to make known,

The heights and depths of love divine,

The kindness Thou to me hast shown,

Whose sin was counted Thine;

My God for me resigned His breath;

He died to save my soul from death. [3]

It appears that this hymn of Rev. C. Wesley was based on Rom.5:6-8.

Further, the depth of God's love in Christ Jesus becomes humanly comprehensible, when we think of the parentage and place of the birth of the Lord Jesus Christ. Jesus was not born in a ruling and wealthy family. He was born of poor, hard-working, ordinary parents. He was born in a carpenter's family. Carpenters had no high social status; labour class had the lowest status in the Jewish society. His birth place brings out significance of God's humility. He was not born in a palace; he was not born in his own parents' home; he was not born in a comfortable hospital; he was not born in a rented house or an inn. He was not born in his neighbour's house or anybody's house. He was born in a manger where animals live. He was born in the lowest place of birth.

The death of Christ Jesus adds to His divine humility. When Son of God was born as a man, He humbled Himself, and became a servant of all, including His disciples, He washed their feet in humility. He accepted human death; the immortal became a mortal. Further, He accepted a humiliated death of the cross. This is how the depth of God's love in Jesus Christ was demonstrated.

(ii) Let us reflect on the height of God's love in Christ Jesus. As the depth of God's love in Christ Jesus is the descent of God from heaven to the earth, the height of God's love would then be the ascent of Christ Jesus from the earth to the heaven.

The scripture tells us that when God raised Jesus Christ from the dead; God made Him sit in the highest position in the heaven. Christ Jesus is sitting at the right hand of God (Mk 16:18; Lk. 22:69; Acts 7:55; Rom. 8:34; Col. 3:1). A question should then be asked: Does Christ Jesus, the exalted Lord, continue His love towards the believers? This is a divine mystery. This would remain a divine mystery until God reveals this to someone like St. Paul. St. Paul, whom God revealed, told the believers about this mystery in these words:

> Christ holds his priesthood permanently, because he continued for ever. Consequently he is able for all time to save those who draw near to God through him, since he always lives to make intercession for them. (Heb. 6:24-25)

William Cowper (November 26. 1731- April 25, 1800) a hymn writer, makes Jesus talk about Jesus's love, in this verse:

> Mine is an unchangeable love,
>
> higher than the heights above,
>
> deeper than the depths beneath,
>
> Free and faithful, strong as death.[4]

(iii) Let us reflect on the width of God's love in Christ Jesus. The width stands for extent or inclusion.

(a) When Jesus Christ was born as the Saviour of the people, this good news was first proclaimed by an angel to the shepherds. An angel of the LORD said to the shepherds:

> Do not be afraid! For I am here with good news for you, which will bring great joy to all the people. This very night in David's town your Saviour was born-Christ the Lord! (Lk. 2:10-11)

The shepherds represented the simple, ordinary, hard-working people. They might have a little education. They were neglected and despised by educated and religious class of Jews.

(b) The news of the birth of Jesus Christ reached to the farthest east. Three Magis, or wise and intellectual astrologists, saw the star of Jesus' birth. They followed the star and went to worship the anticipated King of the Jews, the Messiah. Those Magis were enlightened by the science of astrology; they were looking for the spiritual enlightenment; therefore, they went to see and honour the Messiah.

(c) Three wise men went to King Herod the Great (37- 4 B. C.), inquiring about the birth-place of the Messiah, the heavenly king of the Jews. King Herod was upset by the news of the birth of the king of the Jews. King Herod was a wealthy and powerful man. He had employed the Scribes to interpret the scripture. King Herod the Great felt threatened by the news; and he became hostile to the Messiah. He ordered killing of male infants below two years in order to eliminate another rival king to him.

The news about the birth of Jesus Christ, the anticipated Messiah, the spiritual King of the Jews, the Saviour of the world, reached to the illiterate, uneducated, ordinary shepherds. It reached to the wise and intellectual people, the three Magis. It reached to the poor and the wealthy, to the weak and powerful, to the masses, to the leaders, to the ordinary people and to the king, to the people near and far. It reached to the friendly people and hostile people. It reached everywhere and everyone. This indicates that God's love in Christ Jesus is widest, all-inclusive, and universal. God' s love is irrespective of social differences caused by education, mental ability, wealth, age, profession, colour, culture, and country. This is the scope of the width or breadth of God's love in Christ Jesus.

(iv) Let us reflect on the length of God's love in Christ Jesus. How does the love of God in Christ Jesus last? Is it short lived or is it everlasting love? The scripture tells us the God is eternal, He is without beginning and endless Spirit; therefore, His love endures from generation to generation; it is never ending love. God spoke about His love, through prophet Jeremiah in a verse: " I have loved you with an everlasting love; therefore I have continued my faithfulness to you." (Jer. 31:3) Further this divine love is very costly. Jesus said to His disciples about this love towards them in these words:

This is my commandment, that you love one another as I have loved you. Greater love has no man than this, that a man lay down his life for his friends. (Jn 15:12-13)

Christ Jesus paid the fullest price of His love towards His followers by sacrificing His life on the cross. God's love in Christ Jesus is priceless and immeasurable.

(B) The second idea of the text is the first condition of being able to understand these four dimensions, which is to be rooted and grounded in love. In other words, without being rooted and grounded in love, a believer cannot comprehend these four dimensions. A believer must love God in return and he / she has to love his / her brethren as an expression his / her love towards God. Loving brethren of faith is an evidence of loving God; hating brethren of faith is contrary to loving and knowing God. Apostle John brought this spiritual thought very vigorously, in these words:

> He who says he is in the light and hates his brother is in the darkness still. He who loves his brother abides in the light, and in it there is no cause for stumbling. But he who hates his brother is in the darkness and walks in the darkness, and does not know where he is going, because the darkness has blinded his eyes. (I Jn 2:9-11)

God always reveals His plans and intentions to His devoted servants, e.g. prophets and seers, who walk in the righteous path of God. Prophet Amos (800 B. C.) bore witness to this spiritual fact when he wrote: "Surely the LORD God does nothing, without revealing his secret to his servants the prophets.' (Am. 3:7) There are many evidences in the Bible to prove the point. God revealed His plan to destroy Sodom and Gomorrah to Abraham (Gen. 18:17-19). God revealed His intention to punish the sons of Eli to Samuel (I Sam. 3:11-14). God revealed His plan of redemption to prophet Isaiah several times (Is. 9:2-7; 53).

(C) The third idea of the text is that the Ephesians would comprehend the dimensions with other saints or with other devoted Christians. This is a second condition of comprehension of the dimensions. God does not reveal Himself to the prophets or saints as individuals in isolation; but He reveals Himself when the saints gather themselves together and seek God's guidance; He reveals Himself in the community of faithful believers. There are a few examples to illustrate the point.

King Nebuchadnezzar (605-562 B. C.) had a disturbing dream. He ordered the wise men of Babylon to tell him the dream he had, and its interpretation. The king decided to slay the wise men, if they could do what he ordered. Daniel, Hananiah, Mishael, and Azariah were among those wise men. Daniel asked his companions to seek God's mercy concerning this mystery. When they sought God's mercy together, Daniel had a vision at night about the mystery. (Dan. 2:12-19) He then told King Nebuchadnezzar the dream and its interpretation (Dan. 2:31-45).

Jesus Christ put emphasis on the togetherness of the believers in seeking God's direction, in these words:

> Truly, I say to you, whatever you bind on earth shall be bound in heaven, and whatever you loose on earth shall be loosed in heaven. Again I say to you, if two of you agree on earth about anything they ask, it will be done for them by my Father in heaven. For where two or three are gathered in my name, there am I in the midst of them. (Mt. 18:18-20 cf. Mt. 7:7; 21:21-22; Jn 14:13-14).

The apostles experienced this truth; and they encouraged the believers to ask for wisdom and other things in the name of Christ Jesus; and He would grant them (Jas. 1:5-7; I Jn 5:14). They emphasized the collective way of worship and service of the Lord Jesus Chris in the churches.

(D) The fourth idea of the text is the knowledge of the dimensions would surpass their knowledge; and the Ephesians would be filled with the fullness of God. In other words, when the Ephesians would comprehend the four dimensions of the love of God in Christ Jesus, they would realize that their former knowledge of the love of God was very much limited; and their present knowledge surpassed their previous knowledge. The spiritual knowledge of the Ephesians would be deeper than before. The spiritual knowledge of believers increases, as God would teach them. Jesus Christ made this point when He said:

> It is written in the prophets, 'And they shall all be taught by God.' Every one who has heard and learned from the Father comes to me. Not that any one has seen the Father except him who is from God; he has seen the Father. Truly, truly, I say to you, he who believes has eternal life. (Jn 6:45-47)

Jesus Christ said this on the basis of a prophecy of Isaiah (800 B. C.) (Is. 54:13) and the experience of a psalm writer (Ps. 71:17). Apostle Paul wrote to the Thessalonians that they were taught of God to love one another (I Thes. 4:9). He also prophesied that the knowledge of the believers will increase, when they would see God face to face. He wrote to the Corinthians:

> For our knowledge is imperfect and our prophecy is imperfect; but when the perfect comes, the imperfect will pass away.... For now we see in a mirror dimly, but then face to face. Now I know in part; then I shall understand fully, even as I have been understood. (I Cor. 13:9-10, 12)

The knowledge of believers increases day by day; this gradual spiritual growth would lead to the complete knowledge of God. The believers are expected to be filled with the fullness of God. This is an eschatological hope for Christian believers. This hope was given by St. Paul to the Ephesians, when he wrote this text to them.

Conclusion

St. Paul prayed for the Ephesians that they be rooted and grounded in the love of God. Then they would be able to comprehend the depth, height, width, and length of God's love in Jesus Christ. Their growing in the knowledge of the dimensions of the love of God would lead them to the fullness of God, abiding in them. This was a prayer of St. Paul for the Ephesians. Let this be our prayer at Christmas:

> Higher than the highest heaven,
>
> Deeper than the deepest sea,
>
> Lord, Thy love at last hath conquered;
>
> Grant me now my supplication:
>
> None of self, and of Thee.[5]

Recommended Hymns from the Methodist Hymnal

62   'O Love, how deep, how broad, how high!'

117   'Hark! the herald-angles sing'

125   'O Little town of Bethlehem,'

129   'While shepherds watched their '

131   'The first Nowell the angle did say'

170   'O The bitter shame and sorrow,'

257   'O Come, O come, Immanuel,'

432   'Hark, my soul! it is the Lord;'

452   'What shall I do my God to love,'

556   'Deepen the would Thy hands have made'

584   'Thou, Jesu, Thou my breast inspire,'

Recommended Responsive Reading from the Methodist Hymnal
5 (p.386).

Recommended Responsive Reading from A Worship Manual for Scriptural or Methodist Order of Service
79 (pp.193-194).

Recommended Invocation from the Methodist Hymnal
Methodist Hymnal, hymn # 135:1-3.

Endnotes
[1] Paul Lee Tan, Encyclopedia of 7700 Illustrations: Signs of the Time, # 1941.

[2] Ibid., # 1949

[3] Methodist Hymnal # 452.2.

[4] Ibid., # 432.4.

[5] Methodist Hymnal, Hymn # 70.4.

Chapter - 15
(A Pre-Christmas Sermon)

Titles of the Sermon

'Christians Are Light in the Lord Jesus Christ,'

'Christians Walking as Children of Light,'

'Fruit of the Light-Goodness, Righteousness, and Truth.'

Scripture

Ephesians 5:1-20

Genesis 1:3-5

Job 29:3

Psalms 27:1; 119:105-106

Proverbs 6:22-23

Isaiah 2:2-5; 9:2, 6-7; 60:19

Micah 7:8

Matthew 5:14-16

John 1:4, 9-12; 8:2; 12:46

Acts 13:46-47; 26:22-23

Ephesians 2:1-7

Colossians 1:13

I Peter 2:12

I John 1: 5-7

Text: Ephesians 5:8-9

A Few Versions of the Text, Ephesians 5:8-9

For you were once darkness, but now you are light in the Lord. Walk as children of light (for the fruit of the Spirit is in all goodness, righteousness, and truth), *The New King James_Version*

For ye were once darkness, but now ye are light in the Lord: walk as children of light: (The fruit of light is in all goodness and righteousness and truth): *Explanatory Notes Upon the New Testament*

For once you were darkness, but now you are light in the Lord; walk as children of light (for the fruit of light is found in all that is good and right and true); *Revised Standard Version*

For you were once darkness,but now you are light in the Lord. Live as children of light (for the fruit of light consists in all goodness, righteousness and truth)... *New International Version*

For though you were once all darkness, now as Christians you are light. Live like men who are at home in daylight, for where light is, there are goodness springing up, all justice and truth. *The New English Bible*

For though once your heart was full of darkness, now it is full of light from the Lord, and your behaviour should show it! Because of this light within you, you should do only what is good and right and true. *The Living Bible Illustrated*

Once you lived in the dark, but now the Lord has filled you with light. Live as children who have light. Light produces everything that is good, that has God's approval, and that is true. *God's Word*

Introduction

When an individual is given new identity, the person has to act in accordance with his new identity. He cannot keep his former ways, when he is given new identity. This fact of life can be easily understood, when a person is adopted by another family, and when a person migrates to another land. An adopted person has to adhere to the new life style of the family, which adopted him or her. An immigrant has to adopt the new laws and customs of the new country, which accepted him or her as an immigrant.

Introduction of the Text

The principle of adoption is applicable to persons who convert to another religion or faith. Converted persons cannot keep the system of belief and practices of their former religion. They have to give up their former system of belief and religious practices; and have to adhere to the new system of belief and practices of their new religion. The same principle is extended and applied to spiritual life of persons. St. Paul expected of the Christians at Ephesus to act as children of light of the Lord Jesus Christ, because they embraced the new faith, and gave up their former style of life, when he wrote to them:

> **for once you were darkness, but now you are light in the Lord; walk as children of light (for the fruit of light is found in all that is good and right and true); (Ephesians 5:8-9)**

This is the text of our meditation now.

The Context of the Text

St. Paul had to remind Christians at Ephesus that as they had embraced the gospel of Jesus Christ by giving up their former life style, they had to prove that they were then the children of the light in Jesus Christ; therefore, he exhorted them, saying:

> for once you were darkness, but now you are light in the Lord; walk as children of light (for the fruit of light is found in all that is good and right and true); (Ephesians 5:8-9)

This is the text, within its possible historical setting.

An Analysis of the Text

This text has three ideas. (A) The first idea is that the believers are now the light in the Lord Jesus Christ.

(B) The second idea is an exhortation to Christians to walk as children of light.

(C) The third idea is the fruit of light: goodness, righteousness, and truth.

An Exposition of the Ideas of the Text

(A) The first idea of the text is that the believers are now the light in the Lord Jesus Christ. The believers at Ephesus were formerly living in darkness. Living in darkness would mean they were living in wickedness or in a sinful life. St. Paul had told them in the previous chapter of the letter, how God in Jesus Christ saved them and brought a change in their life, when he wrote them:

> And you he made alive, when you were dead through the trespasses and sins in which you once walked, following the course of this world, following the prince of the power of the air, the spirit that is now at work in the sons of disobedience. Among these we all once lived in the passion of our flesh, following the desires of body and mind, and so were by nature children of wrath, like the rest of mankind. But God, who is rich in mercy, out of the great love with which he loved us, even when we were dead through our trespasses, made us alive together with Christ (by grace you have been saved), and raised us up with him, and made us sit with him in the heavenly places in Christ Jesus, that in the coming ages he might show the immeasurable riches of his grace in kindness towards us in Christ Jesus. (Eph. 2:1-7)

In other words, the Ephesians were saved by the grace of God in Jesus Christ; they were saved from sins and condemnation, and were saved for the everlasting presence with Jesus Christ in heaven. There was a radical change in their spiritual status; they were no longer the children of wrath; but they had become the children of God in Jesus Christ. They were not following the worldly life of satisfying desires of flesh and mind; but they were following the dictates of the Spirit of God.

Because of this change, the believers in Jesus Christ, have become the light in the Lord Jesus Christ. The phrase 'the light in the Lord Jesus Christ,' should be understood with reference to the word of God, the Bible.

The first thing the LORD God created was light (Gen. 1:3). Before God created light, there was darkness upon the earth; and the earth was without form. The darkness stood for primeval chaos, before the creative power of God set to work on it. God separated the light from the darkness; He called the light Day and the darkness Night (Gen. 1:4-5). After creating the light, other things were created and formed.

The writers of the Bible associated God and His laws with the light, as far spiritual life of man was concerned. King David (1002-962 B. C.) in his psalm, said:

> The LORD is my light and salvation; whom should I fear? (Ps. 27:1 cf. Is. 60:19; Job 29:3, Mic.7:8)

The laws and precepts, which were given by the LORD God to His people Israel, were compared with the light. A psalm writer said:

> Thy word is a lamp to guide my feet and a light on my path. I have sworn an oath and confirmed it, to observe thy righteous ordinances. (Ps. 119:105-106)

Prophet Isaiah prophesied that many nations would go to the nation of Israel to learn about the righteous path, when he wrote:

> It shall come to pass in the latter days that the mountain of the house of the LORD shall be established as the highest of the mountains, and shall be raised above the hills; and all the nations shall flow to it, and many peoples shall come, and say: "Come, let us go to the mountain of the LORD, to the house of the God of Jacob; that he may teach us his ways and that we may walk in his paths." For out of Zion shall go forth the law, and the word of the LORD from Jerusalem. He shall judge between the nations, and shall decide for many peoples; and they shall beat their swords into ploughshares, and their spears into pruning hooks; nations shall not lift up sword against nations, neither shall they learn war any more. O house of Jacob, come, let us walk in the light of the LORD. (Is. 2:2-5)

King Solomon (962-942 B. C.), the writer of the Proverbs, said:

> For the commandment is a lamp, and teaching a light, and the reproofs of discipline are the way of life, to preserve you from the evil woman, from the smooth tongue of the adventuress. (Pr. 6:22-23)

The word of God and His wisdom was to be revealed to all people, including the Gentiles and the Jews, who were deprived of learning the word of God. God's messenger, the Messiah was to appear to fulfil this universal task. Prophet Isaiah prophesied saying:

The people who walked in darkness have seen a great light; those who dwelt in a land of deep darkness, on them has light shined..... For to us a child is born, to us a son is given; and the government will be upon his shoulder, and his name will be called "Wonderful Counsellor, Mighty God, Everlasting Father, Prince of Peace." Of the increase of his government and of peace there will be no end, upon the throne of David, and over his kingdom, to establish it, and to uphold it with justice and with righteousness from this time forth and for evermore. The zeal of the LORD of hosts will do this. (Is. 9:2, 6-7)

Jesus Christ was the anticipated Messiah. He came into the world to give the light of salvation to all. He once said to the people, "I am the light of the world; he who follows me will not walk in darkness, but will have the light of life."(Jn 8:2) Again, He asserted His spiritual claim, saying, "I have come as light into the world, that whoever believes in me may not remain in the darkness." (Jn 12:46)

The apostles bore a witness to Jesus Christ as the light of the salvation to the people. St. John wrote:

In him was life, and the life was the light of men... The true light that enlightens every man was coming into the world. He was in the world, and the world was made through him, yet the world knew him not. He came to his own home, and his own people received him not. But to all who received him, who believed in his name, he gave power to become children of God; (Jn 1:4, 9-12)

Another apostle, St. Paul, bore the witness to Jesus Christ, saying to King Agrippa II (A. D. 54/5-93):

To this day I have had the help that comes from God, and so I stand here testifying both to small and great, saying nothing but what the prophets and Moses said would come to pass: that the Christ must suffer, and that, by being the first to rise from the dead, he would proclaim light both to the people and to the Gentiles. (Acts 26:22-23)

St. Paul and Barnabas spoke to the Jews and the Gentiles at Antioch of Pisidia, in the following words:

It was necessary that the word of God should be spoken first to you. Since you thrust it from you, and judge yourselves unworthy of eternal life, behold, we turn to the Gentiles. For so the Lord has commanded us, saying, 'I have set you to be a light for the Gentiles, that you may bring salvation to the uttermost parts of the earth." (Acts 13:46-47)

This paragraph explains why the apostles began to preach the gospel, the good news, of salvation to the Gentiles. The apostles were prescribed to spread the good news to all people, both Jews and the Gentiles.

Jesus of Nazareth (4 B. C.- A. D.30) or Jesus Christ did not only give the believers the commission to spread the good news, but He compared them with the light of the world, as He Himself is the light of the world. He said to the people who would be His believers:

> You are the light of the world. A city set on a hill cannot be hid. Nor do men light a lamp and put it under a bushel, but on a stand, and it gives light to all in the house. Let your light so shine before men, that they may see your good works and give glory to your Father who is in heaven. (Mt. 5:14-16)

St. Paul adopted this idea from Jesus Christ and applied to the believers, exhorting them in the words of the first part of the text of our meditation:

> for once you were darkness, but now you are light in the Lord; (Eph. 5:8)

(B) The second idea of the text is an exhortation to Christians to walk as children of light. As Christians have taken up new identity in terms of being children of God or children of the light in the Lord Jesus Christ, they have to fulfil the expectations of their identity. Jesus Christ told His followers to let their light be shown through their good deeds (Mt. 5:16). St. Paul adopted this teaching. He exhorted the church at Ephesus, saying, "walk as children of light," in the text of our meditation. The concept of walking in the light was taken seriously by apostle John. He challenged Christians to lead a morally pure life, when he said:

> This is the message we have heard from him and proclaim to you, that God is light and in him is no darkness at all. If we say we have fellowship with him while we walk in darkness, we lie and do not live according to the truth; but if we walk in the light, as he is in the light, we have fellowship with one another, and the blood of Jesus his Son cleanses us from all sin. (I Jn 1:5-7)

Leading pure or sinless life implies having fellowship with God, who is the light, and right relationship with fellow brethren. As God is the spiritual light for mankind, human beings have to act as reflectors of God's light. As Christians are the children of the light, they have to reflect the righteous character of God through their moral conduct. They have to disseminate the spiritual light of God in the world.

St. Peter similarly exhorted Christians, saying: "Maintain good conduct among the Gentiles, so that in case they speak against you as wrongdoers, they may see your good deeds and glorify God on the day of visitation." (I Pet. 2:12)

(C) The third idea of the text is the fruit of light: goodness, righteousness, and truth. The fruit or outcomes of walking in the light in the Lord Jesus Christ are to practise goodness, righteousness, and truth. These fruits of light are against the fruit of darkness, such as, wickedness, unrighteousness, and falsehood. The people, who walk in darkness, do the evil deeds always. They act against what is right and just. They do not follow truth; but they practise dishonesty and deception. They are the children of the devil.As far Christians are concerned, they are freed from the dominion of spiritual darkness; and are transferred to the kingdom of the Lord Jesus Christ, by God (Col. 1:13). They have to prove that they are free from moral darkness, on one hand. And on the other hand, they have to manifest the fruit of light, which are goodness, righteousness, and truth.

Conclusion

The exhortation of St. Paul to Christians at Ephesus is still applicable to our Christian life. We should bear in mind that we were liberated from spiritual darkness and transferred to the spiritual light in the Lord Jesus Christ; therefore, we have to examine our attitudes and deeds whether they reflect the divine light. God wants us to be His children, doing good deeds and glorifying Him. Being the children of God is our privilege. Therefore, we have to fulfil the obligations, which go with the spiritual privilege.

Recommended Hymns from the Methodist Hymnal

132   'As with gladness men of old'

154   'I heard the voice of Jesus say: '

238   'My faith looks up to Thee'

516   'When we walk with the Lord'

582   'Brightly beams our father's mercy'

631   'Walk in the light: so shalt thou know'

Recommended Responsive Reading from the Methodist Hymnal

71 (p. 414),

Recommended Responsive Reading from A Worship Manual for Scriptural or Methodist Order of Service

72 (pp.180-182).

Chapter - 16

Titles of the Sermon
'Common Origin of Christ and of Christians,'
'Brethren of Jesus Christ,'
'One Origin of the Sanctifier and the Sanctified.'

Scripture
Hebrews 2:1-18
Genesis 1:26-27, 30; 5:1
Psalms 8:3-8
Proverbs 15:8-9
Isaiah 1:12-17
Amos 5:21-24
Matthew 9:12-13
Mark 2:15-17
Luke 5:30-32; 15:3-7, 8-10,11-32
John 1:3, 12-13
Galatians 3:26-28
Philippians 2:5-11
Collosians 3:10-11
James 3:9

Text: Hebrews 2:11

A Few Versions of the Text, Hebrews 2:11

For both He who sanctifies and those who are being sanctified are all of one, for which reason He is not ashamed to call them brethren, *The New King James Version*

For both He who sanctifieth, and all that are being sanctified, are of one, for which cause he is not ashamed to call them brethren, *Explanatory Notes Upon the New Testament*

For he who sanctifies and those who are sanctified have all one origin. That is why he is not ashamed to call them brethren. *Revised Standard Version*

Both the one who makes men holy and those who are made holy are of the same family. So Jesus is not ashamed to call them brothers. *New International Version*

For a consecrating priest and those whom he consecrated are all of one stock; and that is why the Son does not shrink calling men his brothers. *The New English Bible*

We who have been made holy by Jesus, now have the same Father he has. That is why Jesus is not ashamed to call his brothers. *The Living Bible Illustrated*

Jesus, who makes people holy, and all those who are made holy have the same Father. That is why Jesus isn't ashamed to call them brothers and sisters. *God's Word*

Introduction

Every one of us is born in a society, which has an ancestral history and code of ethics. The code of ethics sets a moral standard for our conduct. The moral standard judges who are our good or bad ancestors. We are proud of our good ancestors; and we should be ashamed of our bad ancestors. Our ancestral background can be either noble or ignoble; there are both light and shade in our ancestral heritage. When we talk about our ancestral background, we would find both ups and downs in that history; and we should know strength and weakness of our human nature, in our ancestors.

We have no control over choosing our ancestors; we are born in family, which has both good and bad ancestors. Nevertheless, we can choose to influence our descendants. Bad ancestors have bad influence on their following generation in general. Ada Take was born in A. D. 1740. As far her name, she took every bad thing. She was a pervert or promiscuous woman. She practised everything which was permissible. She died as an alcoholic. She had seven hundred descendants. Among them were 100 [a hundred] children, born out of wedlock, 181 [one hundred eighty one] women of the street, 142 [one hundred forty two] beggars, 46 [forty-six] work house inmates, 76 [seventy-six] criminals; total 445 [five hundred forty-five] bad persons out of 700 [seven hundred]. Ada Take cost the country an estimated $ 1,200,000. 00 [1] The society had to pay such a high cost for such an immoral woman, and for her bad descendants.

On the other hand, good ancestors have good influence on their descendants. Gilbert Seldon (June 19, 1598-November 9, 1677) was a reporter of Reuter, a newspaper of Parish. He described Rothschild family in Parish, in the following words:

> From the top of a 10 [ten] story ultramodern building at 21 Rue Laffitte, three generations of Rothschild look down on a fourth generation which is already paving the way for the fourth to run the family's immense fortune and worldwide interests.

'God willing, the sons of our sons will become bankers and businessmen,' says Baron Guy de Rothschild, head of the most famous international banking families. Every day at 10:20 a.m. sharp, the fourth generation of the family, headed by Baron Guy, confers in the mahogany panelled board room in the heart of the Parish banking area, watching from the walls are the portraits of their powerful ancestors.[2]

These illustrations tell us that bad ancestors and good ancestors have influence on their following generations. The descendants would be proud of their good ancestors; and they would be ashamed of their bad ancestors.

Introduction of the Text

Jesus Christ, the Saviour of the world, was born in a Jewish family, which had both good and bad ancestors. There are two genealogies in the New Testament (Mt. 1:1-17; Lk. 3:23-38) tracing the lineage of Jesus. In St. Matthew's account, four women are named in the genealogy: Tamar (Gen. 38:7, 10, 18), Rehab (Jos. 6:17, 25), Ruth, a Moabite (Gen. 19:30-38), Bathsheba (II Sam. 11). Tamar's story is a tale of incest and prostitution, and deception. Rehab was a harlot. Ruth was a Moabite, the entire race of incest. David had a secret sexual relationship with Bathsheba. These four women were outcast. St. Matthew mentioned these four women in the genealogy of Jesus in order to point out that the Messianic line was populated with Gentiles, fornicators, adulteresses, liars, cursed kings. In this genealogy, the people in the Messianic genealogy are not on the display; but God's grace is on display. [3]

In the genealogy of Jesus, there are both good and bad ancestors. However, Jesus did not show His pride over His good ancestors or His shame over His bad ancestors. He showed His indifference to His genealogy, because He was more than man. He was God, who became man. He was with God in creating earth and heaven (Jn 1:1-3) and all things exist for Him (Heb. 2:10). He, being God himself, is the ultimate standard of morality. He entered the world to restore the fallen humanity to its godly image. For this purpose He sanctified man. The writer of the Letter to the Hebrews made this point, in these words:

> For he who sanctifies and those who are sanctified have all one origin. That is why he is not ashamed to call them brethren. (Hebrews 2:11)

This is the text of our meditation now.

The Context of the Text

The writer of the Letter to the Hebrews was talking about the great salvation with the following characteristics. First, the salvation was divine in terms that it was declared by the Lord Jesus Christ; it was attested by those who heard about it; and which was supported by the divine miracles and by the gifts of the Holy Spirit.

Secondly, the great salvation was given to man by Jesus Christ through His sufferings on the cross for everyone.

Thirdly, Jesus Christ was the pioneer of the salvation. He became the pioneer, the head or source of salvation, because of His sufferings and death on the cross. His sufferings made Jesus Christ fit or adequate for the task.[4]

Fourthly, the merit of the sufferings of Jesus Christ is the source of sanctification of believers. The sanctification of man made Jesus call His followers 'brethren,' without being ashamed of the sanctified believers. These thoughts are expressed in the words of the text:

> For he who sanctifies and those who are sanctified have all one origin. That is why he is not ashamed to call them brethren. (Hebrews 2:11)

This is the text, within its theological setting.

An Analysis of the Text

This text has two ideas. (A) The first idea is that Jesus Christ, who sanctifies, and the believers, who are sanctified by Jesus Christ, have one origin, that is, God the Father. God is the Father of Jesus Christ and His followers.

(B) The second idea is the result of the common spiritual origin of Jesus Christ and His followers, that is, Jesus is not ashamed to call His followers His brethren.

Exposition of the Ideas of the Text

(A) The first idea of the text is that Jesus Christ, who sanctifies through His blood, and the believers, who are sanctified by Jesus Christ, have one origin, that is, God the Father. God is the Father of Jesus Christ and His followers.

Jesus Christ, the Messiah, is the Son of God, coexisting with God (Jn 1:1); He created all things on the earth and in heaven (Jn 1:3; Heb. 2:10). He volunteered to empty Himself of the heavenly glory and to accept a humiliating death on the cross for the redemption of mankind. Concerning this spiritual mystery and truth, St. Paul wrote to the Philippians:

> Have this mind among yourselves, which is yours in Christ Jesus, who, though he was in the form of God, did not count equality with God a thing to be grasped, but emptied himself, taking the form of a servant, being born in the likeness of men. And being found in human form he humbled himself and became obedient unto death, even death on a cross. Therefore God has highly exalted him and bestowed on him the name which is above every name, that at the name of Jesus every knee should bow, in heaven and on earth and under earth, and every tongue confess that Jesus Christ is Lord, to the glory of God the Father. (Phil. 2:5-11)

God made Jesus Christ the Lord of all, because of His sacrifice on the cross, for the redemption of man.

The word of God tells us that man is a special creature of God; God made man the crown of creation. At the creation of man God said to the Son of God and to the Holy spirit:

> Let us make man in our image, after our likeness; and let them have dominion over the fish of the sea, and over the birds of the air, and over the cattle, and over all the earth, and over every creeping thing that creeps upon the earth. (Gen. 1:26 cf. Gen. 1:27-30; 5:1; Jas. 3:9)

Keeping in mind this original plan of God for man's dominion, King David (1002-962 B. C.) in the Psalm said:

> When I look at thy heavens, the work of thy fingers, the moon and the stars which thou hast established; what is man that thou art mindful of him, and the son of man that thou dost care for him? Yet thou hast made him little less than God, and dost crown him with glory and honour. Thou hast given him dominion over the works of thy hands; thou hast put all things under his feet, all sheep and oxen, and also the beasts of the field, the birds of the air, and the fish of the sea, whatever passes along the paths of the sea. (Ps. 8:3-8)

Some of these verses are quoted by the writer of the Letter to the Hebrews in 2: 6-8. These verses talk about the glory, which man was destined to obtain. But man sinned, and failed to attain the glory.

As man failed to attain the glory and dominion, God wanted to restore man in His image. Therefore, God sent His Son, Jesus Christ, to be our redeemer. Jesus Christ was fully aware of His divine mission. He came to save and sanctify sinners. He identified Himself with sinners, the outcasts of the society. He was not ashamed of eating, walking, talking, and staying with sinners. When Jesus Christ heard the objection of the Pharisees over Jesus' fellowship with sinners and tax collectors, Jesus Christ said to them:

> Those who are well have no need of a physician, but those who are sick. Go and learn what this means, 'I desire mercy, and not sacrifice.' For I came not to call the righteous, but sinners. (Mt. 9:12-13; Mk 2:15-17; Lk. 5:30-32)

On another occasion, Jesus Christ justified His association with sinners, through three parables- the parable of a lost sheep (Lk. 15:3-7), the parable of a lost coin (Lk. 15:8-10) and the parable of a prodigal son (Lk. 15:11-32).

Jesus Christ came to the world to sanctify man and to make people the children of God. St. John testified this spiritual fact, realized in Jesus Christ, in these words:

> But to all who received him, who believed in his name, he gave power to become children of God; who were born, not of the blood nor of the will of the flesh nor of the will of man, but of God. (Jn 1:12-13)

St. Paul wrote to Christians about this new and all-inclusive creation in Jesus Christ. He wrote to the Galatians:

> For in Christ Jesus you are all sons of God, through faith. For as many of you as were baptized into Christ have put on Christ. There is neither Jew nor Greek, there is neither male nor female; for you are all one in Christ Jesus. (Gal. 3:26-28)

Through the blood of Jesus Christ, believers are sanctified and thereby they are restored to the original image. St. Paul wrote to the Colossians about this new creation in Christ Jesus, thus:

> and have put on the new nature, which is being renewed in knowledge after the image of its creator. Here there cannot be Greek and Jew, circumcised and uncircumcised, barbarian, Scythian, slave, free man, but Christ is all, and in all. (Col. 3:10-11)

Jesus Christ removed our sins, the spiritual filth, from us and made us God's children once again; He made us daughters and sons of God as He is the Son of God. Therefore, Jesus Christ, who sanctifies, and the believers, who are sanctified, have become the children of God; God is their Father; He is the common source of their divine origin.

(B) The second idea of the text is the result of the common spiritual origin of Jesus Christ and His followers, that is, Jesus Christ is not ashamed to call His followers His brethren. When believers are accepted or adopted as children of God, Jesus Christ would not be ashamed to accept them as His brethren.

God in Jesus Christ would not accept or adopt those people, who are spiritually filthy, because such an acceptance would be repugnant to God, who is pure, holy, and righteous. It is the sin or iniquity of man which causes God to reject man and his religious deeds. This thought has been emphasized by prophets and other inspired writers. The compiler of the Proverbs wrote:

> The sacrifice of the wicked is an abomination to the LORD, but the prayer of the upright is his delight. The way of the wicked is an abomination to the LORD, but he loves him who pursues righteousness. (Pr. 15:8-9)

Prophet Isaiah (period of his prophecy 783-687 B.C.) elaborated this idea when God spoke to the people of Sodom and Gomorrah:

> When you come to appear before me, who requires of you this trampling of my court? Bring no more vain offerings; incense is an abomination to me. New moon and Sabbath and the calling of assemblies - I cannot endure iniquity and solemn assembly. Your new moons and your appointed feasts my soul hates; they have become a burden to me, I am weary of bearing them. When you spread forth your hands, I will hide my eyes from you; even though you make many prayers, I will not listen; your hands are full of blood. Wash yourselves; make yourselves clean; remove the evil of your doings from before my eyes; cease to do evil, learn to do good; seek justice, correct oppression; defend the fatherless, plead for the widow. (Is.1:12-17)

God sent a similar message to the people of Israel, through prophet Amos (Am. 1:1, period of his prophecy 786-742 B.C.), saying:

> I hate, I despise your feasts, and I take no delight in your solemn assemblies. Even though you offer me your burnt offerings and cereal offerings, I will not accept them, and the peace offerings of your fatted beasts I will not look upon. Take away from me the noise of your songs; to the melody of your harps I will not listen. But let justice roll down like waters, and righteousness like an everflowing stream. (Am. 5:21-24)

These scriptural passages make it very clear that God would not accept man's religious deeds, when man's heart is filled with wickedness and sin. God commands man to be holy as He is holy and pure. The means of cleansing man's heart is the belief in the sacrificial blood of Jesus Christ. God forgives man's sin and sanctifies man, because of the blood of Jesus Christ. How God forgives and accepts a sinful man was told by Jesus Christ in the parable of the prodigal son. When the prodigal son repented of his sins before his father, the father asked his servants to cleanse his son and to put on him the best robe, a ring on his hand, shoes on his feet. (Lk. 15:22) Thus the son was restored by his father to his sonship. The father was not ashamed of his son any more, because the son was bodily and spiritually cleansed.

Conclusion

Jesus Christ was born to sanctify the people and to make them His brethren or children of God. God in Jesus Christ was born to give us the second or spiritual birth or to make God our spiritual Father. The believers and Jesus Christ have God as their common Father. Jesus Christ shed His blood on the cross to sanctify us and to make us acceptable to God. When Jesus Christ sanctifies us to present us to God as His children, He would not be ashamed to call the believers His brethren in God.

Every Christmas is the reminder of the birthday of our Saviour Jesus Christ. This reminder is connected with our spiritual destiny, which is to become the children of God. Let us aspire to be the children of God and brethren of Jesus Christ, because the way for our salvation is prepared for us. Let us rejoice and be glad in this day of our salvation.

Recommended Hymns from the Methodist Hymnal

117   'Hark! the herald-angels sing'

118   'O Come, all ye faithful,'

124   'See, amid the winter's snow,'

125   'O Little town of Bethlehem,'

133   'From the eastern mountains'

134   'Glory be to God on high,'

136   'The Maker of the sun and moon,'

140   'God from on high hath heard;'

Endnotes

[1] Paul Lee Tan, Encyclopedia of 7700 Illustrations: Signs of the Times, # 3701.

[2] Ibid., # 5123.

[3] John F. MacArthur, Jr., The Miracle of Christmas, (Grand Rapids, Michigan: Zondervan Publishing House, 1995), pp. 28-34.

[4] W. Barclay, The Letter to the Hebrews, p. 19.

PART - II

Jesus as the Messiah at the First Palm Sunday:
The Trimphal Entry of Jesus Christ
into Jerusalem:
Seven Textual Sermons on the Palm Sunday

Chapter - 17

Titles of the Sermon

'Cost of Royally Welcoming the Lord,'
'Serving the Lord with Precious things,
'Serving the Lord with Enthusiasm.'

Scripture

Matthew 21:1-11
Exodus 23:16
Leviticus 23:5
Numbers 28:16-17
Deuteronomy 16:1-8
II Kings 9:1-37
I Chronicles 16:31-36
Isaiah 44:23; 49:12-13; 55:12
Zechariah 9:9
Matthew 16:20; 21:10; 26:63
Mark 8:30; 11:1-4; 14:61
Luke 4:41; 9:21; 18-22;
John 7:26; 10:24

Text: Matthew 21:8

A Few Versions of the Text, Matthew 21:8

And a very great multitude spread their clothes on the road; others cut down branches from the trees and spread them on the road. *New King James Version*

And a very great multitude spread their garments in the way; and others cut down branches from the trees, and strewed them in the way. *Explanatory Notes Upon the New Testament*

Most of the crowd spread their garments on the road and others cut down branches from the trees and spread them on the road. *Revised Standard Version*

And a very large crowd spread their cloaks on the road, while others cut down branches from the trees and spread them on the road. *New International Version*

Crowds of the people carpeted the road with their cloaks, and some cut branches from the tress to spread in his path. *The New English Bible*

And some in the crowd threw down their coats along the road ahead of him, and others cut branches from the trees and spread them out before him. *The Living Bible Illustrated*

Most of the people spread their coats on the road. Others cut branches from the trees and spread them on the road. *God's Word*

Introduction

During April 1987, President Reagan (February 6, 1911- June 5, 2004; in office January 20, 1981- January 20, 1989) the fortieth President of the U. S. A. had a summit meeting with the Prime Minister Brian Mulrony (in office 1984-1993). When the President Reagan arrived at Ottawa Airport, the Canadian government, represented by the Prime Minister, Governor General, and other dignitaries went to the airport to extend a royal welcome to President Reagan. This practice of royal welcome or the treatment of royal welcome is extended to all Presidents and Prime Ministers of all nations. This is a universal practice. When Prince Charles came to Hamilton in order to open aeroplane museum and air-show in March 1996, he was extended a royal welcome by the Canadian government. We should note that a red carpet is spread before the dignitaries when they are welcomed. The red carpet is beautiful and costly. The phrase 'red carpet treatment' seems to be originated from the use of a red carpet in welcoming the dignitaries.

When the people, represented by political dignitaries, welcome dignitaries of the nations, they welcome them with pomp and zeal. As they are excited to welcome the dignitaries, they do not count the cost of welcoming dignitaries.

The people who welcome the dignitaries make preparation to welcome their guests. They also publicize the event through media, such as news papers, radios, and televisions. Giving publicity to the event is a form of proclamation about the dignitaries. As the Government welcomes dignitaries and royal persons, with pomp and ceremony, ordinary people welcome their dear relatives and friends with similar zeal and ceremony. In India, there is a practice of welcoming the dear ones by offering them garlands. Those garlands are generally costly; but the welcoming party does not count the cost of welcoming their dear ones. The welcoming parties publicize the event by telling others who is going to visit them.

Introduction of the Text

During the last week of the life of Jesus Christ, He was given a royal welcome by His disciples, followers, and other people. At the words of Jesus Christ, two disciples brought a colt; the disciples of Jesus Christ put their outer garments on the donkey. They made Jesus Christ sit on it. They were filled with zeal to welcome Jesus Christ in Jerusalem from Bethany. They gave Him a royal welcome. How the crowd welcomed Jesus Christ is described in the following words:

> **Most of the crowd spread their garments on the road and others cut down branches from the trees and spread them on the road.** (Matthew 21:8)

This is the text of our meditation now.

The Context of the Text

Jews were wondering whether Jesus was the Christ or the Messiah for many days (Mt. 26:63; Mk 14:61; Jn 7:26; 10:24). Jesus Christ rebuked the evil spirits when they began to declare Him to be the Son of God (Lk. 4:41; Mk 1: 34). Jesus Christ also commanded His disciples not to reveal that He was the anticipated Messiah (Lk.9:21; Mt. 16:20; Mk. 8:30). He did these things because such proclamations would have become premature. He wanted to proclaim His Messiahship on an appointed day. He was waiting for the day to proclaim His Messiahship.

Jesus Christ made a preparation for the day. He spoke to His follower, who was living in Bethaphage, to lend Him his colt for a day. The follower had agreed to do so. When Jesus Christ and His disciples came to Bethany, on their way to Jerusalem, Jesus Christ sent His two disciples to Bethaphage to fetch a colt. He told them:

> Go into the village opposite you, and immediately you will find an ass tied, and a colt with her; untie them and bring to me. If any one says anything to you, you shall say, 'The Lord has need of them and he will send them immediately.' (Mt. 21:2-3)

The disciples brought the donkey and her colt. They put their garments on them; and they made Jesus Christ sit on the colt, on which no one had ever yet sat (Lk. 19:30). The crowd was filled with zeal and joy to take Jesus Christ from Bethany to Jerusalem in procession and proclaiming Him to be the Christ, the King of Israel. How the crowd gave the royal welcome or treatment is described in the words of the text:

> Most of the crowd spread their garments on the road and others cut down branches from the trees and spread them on the road (Mt. 21:8)

This is the text within its historical setting.

An Analysis of the Text

This text tells us about two ways how the crowd gave royal welcome to Jesus Christ.

(A) The first way of the crowd was that they spread their garments on the road.

(B) The second way of the crowd was to cut branches from the trees and spread them on the road.

An Exposition of the Ideas of the Text

(A) The first way of the crowd was that they spread their garments on the road. The crowd noticed what the disciples did for Jesus Christ when two disciples fetched a colt for Jesus Christ. The disciples put their outer garments on the colt; and made Jesus Christ sit on the colt. The crowd took notice of this; and the crowd took a lead or direction from the action of the disciples. The crowd spread their garments on the road.

The crowd knew how to treat a king from their ancient custom of honouring their king. Prophet Elisha asked one of the sons of the prophets to go to Ramoth-gilead; and look for Jehu and take him in the inner chamber and pour oil on his head and say, 'Thus says the LORD, I anoint you king over Israel.' (II Kg. 9:1-3)

When the young prophet went to Ramoth-gilead, he saw the commanders of the army of the King of Joram (849-842 B. C.), the king of Israel, holding a council. Jehu was one of the commanders. The young prophet led Jehu in the inner chamber; and poured the oil on his head and said to Jehu:

> Thus says the LORD the God of Israel, I anoint you king over the people of the LORD, over Israel. And you shall strike down the house of Ahab your master, that I may avenge on Jezebel the blood of my servants the prophets, and the blood of all the servants of the LORD. For the whole house of Ahab shall perish; and I will cut off from Ahab every male, bond and free, in Israel..... And the dogs shall eat Jezebel in the territory of Jezreel, and none shall bury her. (II Kg. 9:6-10)

After this, the young prophet fled from the house. Jehu then joined the council of the commanders. They asked him what the young man said to him. Jehu told them saying, "Thus says the LORD, I anoint you king over Israel." (II Kg. 9:12) Then every commander of the council took his outer garment, and put it under Jehu on the bare steps, and blew the trumpet and proclaimed Jehu as the king of Israel. (II Kg. 9:13)

Jehu (842-815 B. C.) conspired against King Joram (849-842 B. C.), the king of Israel. King Joram was wounded in a war against King Hazael, the king of Syria; he went to be healed in Jezreel. King Ahaziah, the king of Judah (783-742 B. C.), went to see King Joram at Jezreel. Jehu went to Jezreel and killed King Joram; and threw his body on the plot of ground, belonging to Naboth the Jezereelite. Then Jehu went to the house where Queen Jezebel was residing. Jehu commanded the eunuchs to throw Queen Jezebel from a window down; and they did. Dogs ate her flesh. (II Kg. 9:14-37) This is how King Jehu fulfilled a divine commission of righteous judgment and justice.

We go back to the point how the other commanders made Jehu the king of Israel and how they treated him royally. In that fashion, Jesus Christ was treated by His disciples, followers, and the other people.

(B) The second way of the crowd was to cut branches from the trees and spread them on the road. This action of honouring Jesus Christ as the King was an extension of their first action namely, spreading their outer garments on the road.

There is no parallel event in the Old Testament when the people cut branches to honour a king or dignitary. The branches of trees are the outer garments of the trees. There are some references in the Old Testament, indicating that trees would be happy when the LORD God would come to the earth; and give them the joy of salvation.

King David (1002-961 B. C.) and the elders of Israel brought the ark of the covenant of the LORD from the house of Obededom to the tent in Jerusalem. King David appointed Asaph and his sons to sing thanksgiving songs to the LORD. The psalm of the thanksgiving has the following verses:

> Let the heavens be glad, and let the earth rejoice, and let them say among the nations, "The LORD reigns!" Let the sea roar, and all that fills it, let the field exult, and everything in it! Then shall the tress of the wood sing for joy before the LORD, for he comes to judge the earth. O Give thanks to the

LORD, for he is good; for his steadfast love endures for ever! Say also: "Deliver us, O God of our salvation, and gather and save us from among the nations, that we may give thanks to thy holy name, and glory in thy praise. Blessed be the LORD, the God of Israel, from everlasting to everlasting!" (I Chr. 16:31-36)

This psalm of thanksgiving was composed by Asaph. He referred to everything in the field rejoicing at the coming of the LORD God. He also prayed to God for deliverance from other nations and thanked God for His salvation.

When the LORD would come to reign all the nations, there will be joy all over. A psalm writer expressed his feelings in the following words:

Say among the nations, "The LORD reigns! Yea, the world is established, it shall never be moved; he will judge the peoples with equity." Let the heavens be glad, and let the earth rejoice; let the sea roar, and all that fills it; let the field exult, and everything in it! Then shall all the trees of the wood sing for joy before the LORD, for he comes, for he comes to judge the earth. He will judge the world with righteousness, and the peoples with truth. (Ps. 96:10-13)

Prophet Isaiah prophesied the return of the exiles to the promised land. He praised God for His mercy and thanked God for deliverance. He wrote:

Lo, these shall come from afar, and lo, these from the north and from the west, and these from the land of Syene. Sing for joy, O heavens, and exult, O earth; break forth, O mountains, into singing! For the Lord has comforted his people, and will have compassion on his afflicted. (Is. 49:12-13)

Isaiah prophesied that there would be joy among the people of Israel, when they would be redeemed by God. He wrote:

Sing, O heaven, for the LORD has done it; shout, O depths of the earth; break forth into singing, O mountains, O forest, and every tree in it! For the LORD has redeemed Jacob, and will be glorified in Israel. (Is. 44:23)

Isaiah spoke of the joy of salvation, effecting people and the trees, in these words:

For you shall go out in joy, and be led forth in peace; the mountains and the hills before you shall break forth into singing and all the trees of the field shall clap their hands. (Is. 55:12)

The disciples, followers, and the other people put their outer garments on the road. Some of them cut the branches of trees and put them on the road. The crowd did these two things when they gave a royal welcome to the Lord Jesus Christ. The people took Jesus Christ from Bethany to Jerusalem in procession; and they were shouting very loudly: "Hosanna to the Son of David! Blessed is he who comes in the name of LORD! Hosanna in the highest!" (Mt. 21:10)

They welcomed Jesus Christ as the Messiah, the King of Israel.

Jesus Christ wanted to proclaim His Messiahship at an appointed time. He planned the day to declare His Messiahship on the Sunday, the Palm Sunday.

Jews were commanded by God to observe the Passover feast every year. The Passover feast was linked with a national freedom of Israel. Therefore, every Jew was expected to be in Jerusalem, during the Passover feast (Ex. 23:15; Lev. 23:5; Num. 28:16-17; Deut. 16:1-8). The Jews, who were scattered all over the world, would plan to be in Jerusalem during the Passover feast. Subsequently, Jerusalem used to be overcrowded during the season. Jesus of Nazareth (4 B. C. – A. D. 30) decided to proclaim His Messiahship to the world through the Jews coming to Jerusalem as pilgrims and returning to the countries after the Passover feast. He also decided the day of His entry in Jerusalem. It was Sunday after the Passover feast began.

Jesus Christ also planned to have a colt to ride on in the procession (Mk 11:1-4). He chose the colt, symbolizing His kingship of peace, and also to fulfil the prophesy of Zachariah:

> Rejoice greatly, O daughter of Zion! Shout aloud, O daughter of Jerusalem! Lo, your king comes to you; triumphant and victorious is he, humble and ridding on an ass, on a colt, the foal of an ass. (Zech. 9:9)

Now, we should reflect on how the disciples, followers, and the crowd royally treated the Lord Jesus Christ as the King of Israel.

The crowd was filled with enthusiasm and happiness. They were ready to sacrifice anything and to do anything in their power to give a royal treatment to the Lord Jesus Christ. They spread their garments on the road. Their outer garments were good, clean, and even costly. They were so much filled with the spirit of joy of welcoming the Lord Jesus Christ that they did not care whether their cloaks be dirty, crushed, trampled, and torn. They showed that they were ready to pay the price of treating Jesus Christ royally.

The crowd was filled with joy and zeal when they were giving the royal treatment to the Lord Jesus Christ. In the presence of the Lord, they experienced the joy of salvation. They forgot themselves; and they were not mindful of what sophisticated Scribes and Pharisees would think of their expressing joy. They were filled with 'ecstasy' or 'intense delight.' When king David and the elders of Israel were bringing the ark of God from the household of Obededom to Jerusalem, King David danced before the LORD God with all his might and without much clothes on. King David and the people of Israel were shouting with joy; and they were blowing horns. (II Sam. 6:12-15) They were filled with ecstasy. Similarly, the crowd was filled with ecstasy when they accorded the royal welcome to the Lord Jesus Christ.

The crowd cut branches of trees and spread them on the road. They were ready to do work in enhancing the royal treatment, which was given to the Lord Jesus Christ. The crowd used the branches of trees to indicate their joy and the joy of the nature in welcoming the Lord as the King of Israel, the Saviour of all the people.

An Application and Conclusion:

The crowd on the Palm Sunday proclaimed Jesus Christ as the Messiah or the King of Israel; and they spread their outer garments and the branches of trees on the road. The crowd took Jesus Christ in procession from Bethany to Jerusalem. The crowd was ready to sacrifice and do anything to proclaim the Messiahship of Jesus Christ. The proclamation of the Messiahship is a form of evangelism. The work of evangelism requires talents, money, time, and resources of the followers of Jesus Christ. The believers have to ask a question to themselves such as, are they ready to sacrifice and to toil in order to evangelize the world? Or are they ready to spread anything costly before the Lord Jesus Christ? Or are they prepared to give more than minimum required for evangelism?

The crowd was so much filled with overwhelming zeal that it lost in ecstasy in the presence of God. The believers have to ask a question to themselves such as, do they forget themselves and their interests in serving the Lord Jesus Christ?

The Palm Sunday service should spiritually and mentally lead the believers to participate in the procession, which took Jesus from Bethany to Jerusalem, and joyfully say "Hosanna" to our King.

Recommended Hymns from the Methodist Hymnal:

84   'All glory, loud, and honour'

192   'Ride on, ride on in majesty'

836   'Hosanna, loud hosanna'

837   'Children of Jerusalem'

Recommended Responsive Readings from the Methodist Hymnal:

34 (pp. 397f.) or

45 (pp. 403f.).

Recommended Responsive Reading from A Worship Manual for Scriptural or Methodist Order of Service

27 (p.114) or

39 (pp.133-134).

Chapter - 18

Titles of the Sermon

'A Royal Welcome to Jesus Christ,'

'Joyous Shout to the Lord Jesus Christ,'

'Threefold Shout to the Lord Jesus Christ,'

'Jubilant Spirit to Welcome the Lord,'

'Zealous Spirit at the Palm Sunday.'

Scripture

Matthew 21:1-11

Psalms 2:7-8

Isaiah 9:6-7; 11:4; 32:1; 42:3

Jeremiah 23:5-6

Daniel 7:14

Zechariah 9:9

Matthew 7:28; 8:16-17; 16:13, 20; 21:6

Mark 1:22, 32-34; 2:1-10; 5:35-42; 8:28,30; 11:10, 14

Luke 4:32, 41; 5:18-26; 9:21; 19:40

John 6:38, 40; 11:1-15; 12:13; 14:10-11; 18:37

Romans 13:1-7

Colossians 1:15-18

Text: Matthew 21:9

A Few Versions of the Text, Matthew 21:9

Then the multitude who went before and those who followed cried out, saying: "Hosanna to the Son of David! Blessed is He who comes in the name of the LORD! Hosanna in the highest! *The New King James Version*

And the multitude that went before, and that followed after, cried, saying, Hosanna to the Son of David; Blessed in the name of the Lord is he that cometh: Hosanna in the highest. *Explanatory Notes Upon the New Testament*

The crowds that went before Jesus and that followed him shouted, 'Hosanna to the Son of David! Blessed is he who comes in the name of the Lord! Hosanna in the highest! *Revised Standard Version*

The crowd that went ahead of him and those that followed shouted, "Hosanna to the Son of David!" "Blessed is he who comes in the name of the Lord!" "Hosanna in the highest!" *New International Version*

Then the crowd that went and the others that came behind raised the shout: 'Hosanna to the Son of David! Blessings son him who comes in the name of the Lord! Hosanna in the heavens! *The New English Bible*

the crowds surged on ahead and pressed along behind, shouting, "God bless King David's Son!"... "God's Man is here!... Bless him, Lord!"... Praise God in highest heaven!" *The Living Bible Illustrated*

The crowd that went ahead of him and that followed him was shouting "Hosanna to the Son of David! Blessed is the one who comes in the name of the Lord! Hosanna in the highest heaven!" *God's Word*

Introduction

Palm Sunday is celebrated by all Christian churches in the world, in remembrance that the Lord Jesus Christ was welcomed by the crowd as the Messiah in the city of Jerusalem. Jesus Christ was given a royal treatment by His disciples, followers, and others; and they joyfully shouted, "Hosanna to the Son of David."

It is a universal manner to honour heroes, royalties, and dignitaries and to welcome them with joyous shouts and pomps. In 1983, Hollywood produced a movie on the life of Mahatma Gandhi (October 20,1869- January 12, 1948). In that movie, there is a memorable event, depicting how Indians gave heroic welcome to Mr. Mohandas Karmachand Gandhi, when he returned to India from South Africa. The crowd was filled with joy and was shouting, *"Mahatma, Mahatma"* (i.e. great soul) to him.

Mr. Mohandas K. Gandhi was a great Indian leader. He was born on October 20, 1869. He went to London, England in 1888 to study law. He returned to India to practise law at the Bombay High Court in 1891. He went to South Africa in 1893 on a business trip. He witnessed and personally experienced the severe discrimination against Indians there. He decided to stay in South Africa to combat racism. In a few years, he became widely known as a lawyer and a public figure. In 1894 he organized the Natal Indian Congress and in 1903, the Transvaal Indian Association. He started a weekly newspaper, "Indian Opinion" in 1904. He gave up his law career in 1908 in order to completely devote himself to the Indian cause. Two years later, the Transvaal Government approved an anti-Asiatic law, making discrimination against Indians legal. Mr. Gandhi invented a new approach to fight against the evil administration. He called the new way *"Satyagraha,"* a passive, non-violent resistance to the Government. Mr. Gandhi achieved his first success in 1914 when the minister of defence of the Union of South Africa, General Jan Christiaan. Smuts (May 24,1870-September 11,1950), made an agreement with Mr. Gandhi; and lifted some of the restrictions that had been imposed on Indians.

In 1915 Mr. Gandhi returned to India. This was the time when he was given a heroic welcome by Indians, calling him *"Mahatma"*. He then became an advocate of *"Swaraj"* ("home rule") for India. He was the father of independent India. He was assassinated on January 12, 1948.[1]

In the oriental countries, like Japan and China, the emperor was believed to be a god, who rules over the land and its people. Japan had no constitution and no legal system until 1946, when the Emperor of Japan publicly declared that he was not a god.[2] When an emperor is thought to be a god, it is needless to say that he was treated royally and reverently.

Canada has maintained its link with the Great Britain. The Queen of the Great Britain is the head of the state in Canada. Whenever the Queen and other members of the royal family visit Canada, the Canadians and their Government welcome them with joy; and give them red carpet treatment. This practice is in keeping with the scripture, which prescribes how to be subject to the governing authority, for the authority is given by God (Rom. 13:1-7).

Introduction of the Text

Jesus Christ established His authority by teaching and performing miracles. People were astonished at His teaching because He taught them as one who had authority, and not as the scribes did. (Mt. 7:28; Mk 1:22; Lk. 4:32). People recognized Jesus Christ to be a prophet (Mk 8:28). He exercised His authority to forgive sins; and He told thus to the people, when He cured a paralytic in Capernaum (Mk 2:1-10; Lk. 5:18-26). He exercised His authority on death. He brought a few persons, like Lazarus and daughter of a ruler, back to life (Mk 5:35-42; Jn 11:1-15).

People recognized the divine authority of Jesus Christ; but they did not know that Jesus Christ was the Messiah, the everlasting King sitting on the throne of King David. Jesus Christ had to proclaim His Messiahship or the divine kingship to the people at a right time. He planned His triumphal entry into Jerusalem. The disciples and followers of Jesus Christ and others formed a procession at Bethany and took Jesus Christ to Jerusalem. When some people heard that Jesus Christ was coming to Jerusalem, they took branches of tress and went out to meet Him (Jn 12:13). This event is described by St. Matthew in the following words:

The crowds that went before Jesus and that followed him shouted, 'Hosanna to the Son of David! Blessed is he who comes in the name of the Lord! Hosanna in the highest! (Mt. 21:9)

This is the text of our meditation now.

The Context of the Text

The crowd formed a procession to take Jesus Christ from Bethany to Jerusalem in order to proclaim Him as the Messiah or the everlasting King enthroned on King David's throne. Jesus Christ approved the shout of the crowd: "Hosanna to the Son of David! Blessed is he who comes in the name of the Lord! Hosanna in the highest!", because the shout was at the appropriate time.

Jesus Christ did not wish to publicly proclaim His Messiahship before that Sunday. He wanted to keep His Messiahship secret from the public for a few years. When Jesus Christ drove out demons from many persons, the demons were crying, "You are the Son of God!" Jesus Christ rebuked the demons; and did not allow them to speak, telling He was the Christ (Lk. 4:41; Mt. 8:16-17; Mk 1:32-34), because it was not an appropriate time to declare His Messiahship.

Having performed many miracles and taught with authority, Jesus Christ knew that the people and His disciples had some opinions about Him. When Jesus Christ and His disciples went in the district of Caesarea Philippi, Jesus Christ asked His disciples, "Who do men say that the Son of Man is?" (Mt. 16:13) They gave Him a few answers. Then Jesus Christ asked them, "But who do you say that I am?" Simon Peter replied, "You are the Christ, the Son of the Living God." As His disciples realized Him to be the Messiah or Christ, Jesus Christ strictly charged them to tell no one that He was the Christ. (Lk. 9:21; Mt. 16:20; Mk 8:30)

Jesus Christ wanted to keep His Messiahship secret for a time being. Jesus Christ was waiting for the appropriate time to proclaim His Messiahship. That appropriate time to proclaim His Messiahship publicly was a few days away from His crucifixion. It was the Sunday before the Good Friday.

Jesus Christ knew the prophecy how the Christ would enter Jerusalem. Prophet Zachariah had prophesied about the entrance of the Messiah in Jerusalem, when he wrote these words:

> Rejoice greatly, O daughter of Zion! Shout aloud, O daughter of Jerusalem! Lo, your king comes to you; triumphant and victorious is he, humble and ridding on an ass, on a colt, the foal of an ass. (Zech. 9: 9)

This prophecy was fulfilled when Jesus Christ chose a colt to ride on it in the procession. It seems that Jesus Christ made an arrangement of borrowing a colt from His follower, residing in Bethphage. When Jesus Christ and His twelve disciples approached Bethphage, on their way to Jerusalem, Jesus Christ instructed His two disciples:

> Go into the village opposite you, and as soon as you enter it you will find a colt, on which no one has ever sat; untie it and bring it. If any one says to you, 'Why are you doing this? Say, 'The Lord has need of it, and will send it back here immediately.' (Mk. 11:4)

'The Lord has need of it' was the password. The owner understood it; and allowed the disciples of Jesus Christ to take away the colt.

When the colt was brought, the procession was formed. In that procession, there were some Pharisees. They did not like the joyous shout of the crowd; they asked Jesus Christ to silence the crowd from shouting "Hosanna". Jesus Christ did not silence the crowd; but He approved the shout, proclaiming His Messiahship. He responded to the request of the Pharisees, saying, "If they keep quiet, I tell you, the stones themselves will shout." (Lk. 19:40) In other words, it was impossible to silence any one from proclaiming His Messiahship. Jesus Christ fully approved the joyous shout of the crowd. In the procession, the crowd shouted:

> "Hosanna to the Son of David! Blessed is he who comes in the name of the Lord! Hosanna in the highest! (Mt. 21:9)

This is the historical setting of the text of our meditation.

An Analysis of the Text

In this text, there are four ideas. (A) The first idea is that the crowd went before and behind Jesus, putting Jesus at the centre of the procession.

(B) The second idea is the first part of the shout of the crowd, "Hosanna to the Son of David!"

(C) The third idea is the second part of the shout of the crowd, "Blessed is he who comes in the name of the Lord!"

(D) The fourth idea is the third part of the shout of the crowd, "Hosanna in the highest!"

An Exposition of the Ideas of the Text

(A) The first idea of the text is that the crowd went before and behind Jesus Christ, putting Jesus Christ at the centre of the procession. The crowd put Jesus Christ at the centre of the procession; they made the procession Christ-centred; they made Christ the centre of their activities or the focus of their procession. Jesus Christ must be given central position or pre-eminence in the life of the Church. St. Paul exhorted the Colossians, in these words:

> He is the image of the invisible God, the first-born of all creation; for in him all things were created, in heaven and on earth, visible and invisible,... all things were created through him and for him. He is before all things, and in him all things hold together. He is the head of the body, the Church; he is the beginning, the first-born from the dead, that in everything he might be pre-eminent. (Col. 1:15-18)

We should note what the crowd did for Jesus Christ when they put Him in the centre of the procession. They were ready to sacrifice everything in order to proclaim the Messiahship of Jesus. They put their garments on the colt and made Jesus Christ sit thereon (Mt. 21:6). They spread their garments on the road. Some of them cut branches of the trees and spread on the road. Their outer garments were good, clean, and even costly. When they were filled with a religious zeal, they did not care whether their cloaks be dirty, crushed, trampled, and torn. They were ready to pay the price of proclaiming Jesus' Messiahship. They cut branches of the trees and spread them on the way of Jesus Christ. They were willing to do hard work, including cutting the branches of the tress. They did not mind of toiling for the Lord when they proclaimed the Messiahship of Jesus.

(B) The second idea of the text is the first part of the shout of the crowd, "Hosanna to the Son of David!" The crowd acknowledged the royalty of Jesus Christ as He was born in the family of King David. According to the gospel of St. Mark, the crowd shouted, saying: "Blessed is the kingdom of our father David that is coming!" (Mk 11:10) It means that the future kingdom of King David would be a blessed kingdom. When the crowd shouted thus with reference to Jesus Christ, it meant that King David's kingdom would be a blessed one, as Jesus Christ was going to be enthroned on it.

Kingship of Jesus Christ is divine and everlasting kingship. God had promised King David that there would be a ruler, born in his house, whose kingdom would be everlasting, in the following words:

> I will tell you of the decree of the LORD: He said to me, "You are my son; today I have begotten you. Ask of me, and I will make the nations your heritage, and the ends of the earth your possession." (Ps. 2:7-8)

When the Babylonian power destroyed the kingdom of King David, God promised to Daniel, saying:

> And to him was given dominion and glory and kingdom, that all peoples, nations, and languages should serve him; his dominion is an everlasting dominion, which shall not pass away, and his kingdom one that shall not be destroyed. (Dan. 7:14)

God repeated the promise through prophet Isaiah, saying:

> For to us a child is born, to us a son is given; and the government will be upon his shoulder, and his name will be called "Wonderful Counsellor, Mighty God, Everlasting Father, Prince of Peace." Of the increase of his government and of peace there will no end, upon the throne of David, and over his kingdom, to establish it, and to uphold it with justice and with righteousness from this time forth and for evermore. The zeal of the LORD of host will do this. (Is. 9:6-7 cf. Is. 11:4; 32:1; 42:3)

The same promise was again repeated by God through prophet Jeremiah (Jer. 23:5-6). How the Messiah would enter Jerusalem was prophesied by prophet Zachariah (Zech. 9:9); the prophecy is referred early. All these prophecies were fulfilled when the crowd shouted saying, "Hosanna to the Son of David!"

Jesus Christ knew His kingship to be of this kind. When Pontius Pilate (A. D. 26-36) asked Jesus Christ of His kingship, Jesus Christ confirmed it, saying:

> You say that I am a king. For this I was born, and for this I have come into the world, to bear witness to the truth. (Jn 18:37)

(C) The third idea of the text is the second part of the shout of the crowd, "Blessed is he who comes in the name of the Lord!" According to the gospel of St. John, the crowd shouted, "Blessed is he who comes in the name of the Lord, even the king of Israel." (Jn 12:13) It means that Jesus Christ came as the Messiah or everlasting King of Israel and also in the name of the LORD God. Jesus Christ argued with His disciples and the Jews on many occasions that He came into the world in the name of the LORD God, the true King of Israel. Jesus Christ said to the Jews:

> For I have come down from heaven, not to do my own will, but the will of him who sent me....For this is the will of my Father that every one who sees the Son and believes in him should have eternal life; and I will raise him up at the last day. (Jn 6: 38, 40)

Jesus Christ said to Philip, one of His disciples, these words:

> The words that I say to you I do not speak on my own authority; but the Father who dwells in me does his works. Believe me that I am in the Father and the Father in me; or else believe me for the sake of the works themselves. (Jn 14:10-11)

(D) The fourth idea of the text is the third part of the shout of the crowd, "Hosanna in the highest!" This shout must mean, "Let even the angles in the highest height of heaven cry unto God, Save now!" [3] In other words, all heavenly beings cry to God, asking Him to save them. It was going to be a heavenly as well as cosmic cry for salvation.

Conclusion

The crowd put Jesus Christ at the centre of the procession. They were filled with enthusiasm to welcome Jesus Christ, the Messiah. They sacrificed whatever they could in order to proclaim the Messiahship to the people. They boldly proclaimed Jesus Christ as the everlasting King to be enthroned on the throne of King David. They proclaimed

Him to be the King from above. The believers have to ask the questions as follow: Are they going to put Jesus Christ at the centre of their life and of their church activities? Are they going to be zealous about the evangelism? Are they ready to sacrifice all possible things for the glory and honour of God in Jesus Christ?

Recommended Hymns from the Methodist Hymnal:

84   'All glory, laud, and honour'

91   'All hail the power of Jesus' name'

116   'Sing we the King who is coming'

192   'Ride on, ride on in majesty!'

836   'Hosanna, loud hosanna'

837   'Children of Jerusalem'

Recommended Responsive Reading from A Worship Manual for Scriptural or Methodist Order of Service

90 (pp. 214-215).

Endnotes

[1] The New American Encyclopedia, Vol. 9, pp. 3198-3199.

[2] P. Johnson, A History of the Modern World, from 1917 to the 1990, pp. 177-179).

[3] W. Barclay, Gospel of Matthew, Vol. II, p. 264.

Chapter - 19

Titles of the Sermon

'Children's Perfect Praise of the Messiah,'

'Perfect Praise of God by the Innocents,'

'Perfect Praise of the Messiah in the Temple by Children,'

'A Fulfilment of Never Read Prophecy about the Messiah.'

Scripture

Matthew 21:1-17

Psalms 8:1-2

Matthew 13:3, 13-14; 18:5-6; 19:13-14)

Mark 10:15

Luke 18:17; 19:39-40

John 18:3-37

Text: Matthew 21:16

A Few Versions of the Text, Matthew 21:16

And said to Him, "do You hear what these are saying?" And Jesus said to them, "Yes, Have you never read, 'Out of the mouth of babes and nursing infants You have perfected praise? *New King James Version*

And said to him, Hearest thou what these say? And Jesus saith to them, Yes; have you never read, Out of the mouth of babes and sucklings thou hast perfected praise? *Explanatory Notes Upon the New Testament* and they said to him, "do you hear what these are saying?" And Jesus said to them, "Yes; have you never read, 'Out of the mouth of babes and sucklings thou hast brought perfect praise'?" *Revised Standard Version*

"Do you hear what these children are saying?" They asked him. "Yes," replied Jesus, "have you never read, "From the lips of children and infants you have ordained praise?" *New International Version*

and they asked him indignantly, 'do you hear what they are saying?' Jesus answered, 'I do; have you never read that text, "Thou hast made children and babes at the breast sound aloud thy praise?"' *The New English Bible*

they were disturbed and indignant and asked him, "Do you hear what these children are saying?" "Yes," Jesus replied. "Didn't you ever read the Scriptures? For they say, 'Even little babies shall praise him!" *The Living Bible Illustrated*

They said to him, "do you hear what these children are saying?" Jesus replied, "Yes, I do. Have you never read, 'From the mouths of little children and infants, you have created praise?"' *God's Word*

Introduction

(1) This is a story about a European king. The king was very much mindful of his appearance. He had many tailors, preparing for him fashionable royal dresses or robes. He used to send tailors to various parts of the world to find elegant dresses for him. He wanted to wear most expensive and very impressive dresses on all occasions. The king was spending his wealth on new dresses. The tailors were always busy with preparing and inventing new fashionable royal dresses. They were exhausted of doing these things. The king was demanding so much of them. They did not know what to do.

Those tailors ran out of new ideas. The king told them that he wanted a new dress to wear in the royal procession. He ordered them that a new dress should be ready for the procession. The tailors told the price of the new dress. They hired a weaver to prepare a cloth for the dress. The king was anxious to see the cloth, after a few weeks. The king saw the weavers busy with making a cloth. They were running back and forth as if they were making a cloth. The tailors were praising how beautiful the cloth was. The king did not see the cloth and he did not say anything about the invisible cloth. The tailors asked the king to come to take a new measurement. The king went to see them; and they took measurements to prepare a new dress for the king. The tailors then began to cut the cloth and used sewing machines to put pieces of the cloth to make a dress for the king. The king watched the movements and actions of the tailors. They praised much about the new royal dress.

On the day of procession, they removed all clothes from the body of the king. Then they put a new invisible dress on the king. The king was impressed by their praise of the new dress.

The procession started. Everyone was praising the new dress of the king. Everybody was afraid to say anything against the king and the people. There was a child in the procession. When he saw the king, he said to his father, "Dad, the king is wearing nothing; he is naked. Where is his new royal dress?" The king and the people heard the child. The father of the child tried to silence his son. The child was laughing; and was repeating the same words.

The child spoke without fear and with innocence. He told the truth plainly. The king realized his excessive obsession for new dresses, which made people not to tell the truth. He realized that his foolishness was responsible for his going in the procession nude. He came to his senses, because an innocent child told the truth plainly and openly.

(2) Bertel Thorwaldsen (ca. 1770-24 March 1844) was a great sculptor. He once carved a statue of Jesus Christ. He wished to see if the statue would cause the right reaction of heart in those who would see it. Many adults spoke highly of the statue. But Thorwaldsen was questioning the comments of the people, who saw the statue. Then he brought a little child to see the statue and asked him, "What do you think that is?" The child innocently and plainly replied, "It is a great man." Thorwaldsen then realized that he failed to make the statue. So he scraped his first statue; and began

again to carve another statue. When he had finished making the statue, he brought the same child; and asked him to look at the statue; and asked him the same question, "What do you think that is?" The child smiled and said, "That is Jesus, who said: 'Let the children come to me.'" Then Thorwaldsen knew that this time he was successful in making the statue.[1]

(3) George Macdonald (December 10, 1824- September 18, 1905) formed a principle of judging whether a person is Christian. He said that if a child thinks of a person good person, then all the likelihood is that the person is good; and if a child shrinks away, a man may be great, but very certainly he is not Christlike.[2] It is very true that children always avoid bad neighbours and bad relatives.

From the aforesaid stories, we can conclude that when children are innocent, they tell the truth without fear. Their judgments and testimonies are truthful because of their innocence.

Introduction of the Text

How innocent children bear testimonies to the truth is told to us in a brief conversation between religious leaders and Jesus Christ, as follows:

And they [chief priests and the scribes] said to him [Jesus Christ], 'Do you hear what these are saying?' And Jesus said to them, 'Yes; have you never read, 'Out of the mouth of babes and sucklings thou hast brought perfect praise?' (Matthew 21:16)

This is the text of our meditation today.

The Context of the Text

The crowd brought Jesus Christ in procession from Bethany to Jerusalem on the Sunday, which Christians call it Palm Sunday. The crowd was enthusiastic in giving royal welcome to Jesus. The crowd was shouting, "Hosanna to the Son of David! Blessed is he who comes in the name of the LORD! Hosanna in the highest!" (Mt. 21:9) This was how Jesus was welcome as the Messiah, the Christ, by the crowd.

On Monday after entering Jerusalem, Jesus Christ went to the temple. People were selling pigeons at high cost; money-changers were making high profits. The people turned the holy temple into a centre of commerce. The cheating and profiting in the holy temple became acceptable. Jesus did not approve the immoral practice of trade, done in the temple of the LORD God. He boldly condemned the people, saying: It is written, 'My house shall be called a house of prayer'; but you make it a den of robbers.'(Mt. 21:13) Then Jesus vigorously or zealously cleansed the temple of the LORD God. He restored the sacredness of the temple by challenging vested interests of the ungodly people.

On the following day, Tuesday Jesus Christ healed the blind and lame. The children saw the wonderful things which Jesus Christ did. Then the children began to cry out in the temple, "Hosanna to the Son of David!" The children recognized that Jesus was the Messiah, or the Christ. They were proclaiming Jesus as the King, who was born in the lineage of King David (1002-962 B.C.), and who was to be the everlasting King, the Messiah, in their innocence, were proclaiming Jesus as the Messiah, the anticipated King of Israel. When the chief priests and the scribes heard the shout of the children, they became jealous of Jesus Christ; they were angry at the children and at Jesus Christ. They approached Jesus Christ with a question:

> "Do you hear what these [children] are saying?" And Jesus said to them, "Yes; have you never read, 'Out of the mouth of babes and sucklings thou hast brought perfect praise'? (Mt. 21:16)

This is the text of our meditation with its historical setting.

An Analysis of the Text

This text has three ideas. (A) The first idea is the question which the chief priests and the scribes asked Jesus Christ, "Do you hear what they are saying?"

(B) The second idea is the answer of Jesus Christ, saying, "Yes."

(C) The third idea is the question which Jesus Christ asked the chief priests and the scribes, "Have you never read, 'Out of the mouth of babes and sucklings thou hast brought perfect praise?'"

Exposition of the Ideas of the Text

(A) The first idea of the text is the question which the chief priests and the scribes asked Jesus Christ, "Do you hear what they are saying?" The children were shouting to Jesus Christ, "Hosanna to the Son of David!" Everyone was able to hear the shout of the children; and yet the chief priests and the scribes asked Jesus Christ the question, "do you hear what these [children] are saying?" They asked this question not because of their doubting Jesus' capacity to hear; they knew Jesus was not deaf. They asked this question, because they were angry at the children and at Jesus Christ. They were jealous of the reputation of Jesus Christ. They were respectable leaders; and they did not wish anyone surpassing them; they were offended by the claim, which the shout of the children ascribed to Jesus Christ.

The second reason of putting this question to Jesus Christ was that the chief priests and the scribes wanted to make sure that Jesus Christ understood the implications of being the Son of David or the anticipated and everlasting King to be enthroned on the throne of King David, or the Messiah. In other words, they wanted to know whether Jesus Christ wished to be proclaimed and endorsed as His spiritual Kingship by the children.

(B) The second idea of the text is the answer of Jesus Christ, saying, "Yes." When the high priests and the scribes asked Jesus Christ the question, "Do you hear what they [children] are saying?" Jesus Christ answered them positively, saying, "Yes." Jesus Christ was not hiding His spiritual Kingship any longer as He did in the past, because the time was right to proclaim and endorse it. He knew the right time had arrived, when He had to profess and proclaim His Messiahship publicly. This was the reason why He arranged for an ass and a colt for His procession on the Sunday, the Palm Sunday. Jesus was ready to profess and proclaim His Messiahship, or His spiritual Kingship, if anyone would have asked Him.

When Jesus Christ heard the question of the chief priests and scribes, He was not going to silence the children because they were proclaiming His Messiahship at the right time. Jesus Christ did not rebuke His disciples, followers, and the crowd, when some Pharisees from the crowd asked Jesus Christ, "Teacher, rebuke your disciples." In reply to this request, Jesus Christ said: "I tell you if these were silent, the very stones would cry out." (Lk. 19:39-40). As Jesus Christ approved the shout of His disciples and the crowd on the Palm Sunday, He approved the same shout of the children on Tuesday.

Jesus continued to proclaim His spiritual Kingship after His arrest. When Pontius Pilate (A. D. 26-36) interrogated Jesus Christ about His Kingship of Israel, Jesus Christ answered him:

> You say that I am a king. For this I was born, and for this I have come into the world, to bear witness to the truth. Everyone who is of the truth hears my voice. (Jn 18:37)

(C) The third idea of the text is the question, which Jesus Christ asked the chief priests and the scribes, "Have you never read, 'Out of the mouth of babes and sucklings thou hast brought perfect praise?'" Jesus Christ did not only approve the shout of the children, but He also told the religious leaders as to why the children were thus shouting. He explained to them shouts of the children as the fulfilment of a prophecy, given in the scripture. Jesus quoted the prophecy:

> Thou whose glory above the heavens is chanted by the mouth of babes and infants. (Ps. 8:1-2)

King David (1002-962 B. C.) wrote this psalm # 8. He praised God for His creation of the earth, heavens, and of man. He mentioned that when children see the heaven above, they praise God perfectly. Children praise God perfectly, because they are innocent; and God abides in them. Adults are different from children; they develop a sense of embarrassment out of their social upbringing; they prevent others from shouting or expressing loudly; they learn to suppress natural expression.

When the children saw Jesus Christ performing the miracles of healing in the temple, they instinctively knew that Jesus was the

Messiah; therefore, they naturally and innocently offered perfect praise to Jesus Christ. (Mt. 21:14-15)

Jesus Christ loved the children for their innocence. When parents brought their children to be blessed by Jesus Christ, some of His disciples did not like parents taking their children to Him; therefore, they rebuked the parents for doing this. Then Jesus Christ said to His disciples:

> Let the children come to me, and do not hinder them; for to such belongs the kingdom of heaven. (Mt. 19:13-14)

Then Jesus Christ added:

> Truly, I say to you, whoever does not receive the kingdom of God like a child shall not enter it. (Mk 10:15; Lk. 18:17)

Jesus Christ set an example of children before His disciples. Once His disciples were discussing, "Who is the greatest in the kingdom of heaven?" Jesus Christ called a child and put him in the midst of His disciples; and said to them:

> Truly, I say to you, unless you turn and become like children, you will never enter the kingdom of heaven. Whoever humbles himself like this child, he is the greatest in the kingdom of heaven. (Mt. 19:3)

In this verse, Jesus Christ placed emphasis on the innocence of children in terms of a requirement for entering the kingdom of God. He also praised the humility of children, which would make them greatest in the kingdom of heaven. Jesus Christ loved the children, because they have the virtues of innocence and humility. Then Jesus added:

> Whoever receives one such child in my name receives me; but whoever causes one of these little ones who believe in me to sin, it would be better for him to have a great millstone fastened around his neck and to be drowned in the depth of the sea. (Mt. 18:5-6)

In these verses, Jesus Christ exhorted people to treat the children as very important; and asked to receive them as they would receive the Lord Jesus Christ Himself. A person, who makes children sin, is condemned by the Lord Jesus, for such wicked person deserves to be punished by death.

Conclusion

Jesus Christ approved the shout of the children, who instinctively recognized His Messiahship and proclaimed His spiritual Kingship to the people. Their witness to His spiritual Kingship was sincere or honest and reliable, because children were innocent and humble. Their praise of Jesus Christ came from their hearts. Because of these values, children have a very important place in the kingdom of God and in the Church of Jesus Christ.

Recommended Hymns from the Methodist Hymnal

84   'All glory, laud, and honour'

192   'Ride on, ride on in majesty'

836   'Hosanna, loud Hosanna'

837   'Children of Jerusalem'

Recommended Responsive Reading from A Worship Manual for Scriptural or Methodist Order of Service

90 (pp. 214-215).

Endnotes

[1] William Barclay, Gospel of Matthew, Vol. II, p. 275.

[2] Ibid., p. 275.

Chapter - 20

Titles of the Sermon

'Jesus Christ's Coming in the Name of the LORD God,'

'Blessed King,'

'Blessed Messiah,'

'A Blessed Kingdom of David.'

Scripture

Mark 11: 1-11

II Kings 9:4-9

I Chronicles 17:11-14

Psalms 2:7-8; 72:5-8

Isaiah 9:6-7; 11:4; 32:1; 35:5-6; 42:1-4

Jeremiah 23:5-6

Daniel 7:14

Zechariah 9:9-10

Matthew 11:2-6; 12:9-14, 18-21; 21:1-9

Mark 3:11; 8:27-30; 11:1-10

Luke 19:28-40

John 5:19-24; 6:14-15, 35, 38, 40; 8:12, 14-16; 10:22-26; 12:12-13; 14:9-11; 18:37

Acts 13:33

Hebrews 1:5; 5:5

Text: Mark 11:9-10

A Few Versions of the Text, Mark 11:9-10

Then those who went before and those who followed cried out, saying: "Hosanna! 'Blessed is He who comes in the name of the LORD!' Blessed is the kingdom of our father David That comes in the name of the LORD! Hosanna in the highest!" *The New King James Version*

And they that went before, and they that followed after, cried, saying, Hosanna: Blessed in the name of the Lord is he that cometh: Blessed be the kingdom of our father David that cometh: Hosanna in the highest. *Explanatory Notes Upon the New Testament*

And those who went before and those who followed cried out, "Hosanna! 'Blessed is he who comes in the name of the Lord!' Blessed is the kingdom of our father David that is coming! Hosanna in the highest!" *Revised Standard Version*

Those who went ahead and those who followed shouted, "Hosanna!" "Blessed is he who comes in the name of the Lord!" "Blessed is the coming kingdom of our father David!" "Hosanna in the highest!" *New International Version*

and those who went ahead and the others who came behind shouted, 'Hosanna! Blessings on him who comes in the name of the Lord! Blessings on the coming kingdom of our father David! Hosanna in the highest!' *The New English Bible*

He was in the centre of the procession with crowds ahead and behind, and all of them shouting, "Hail to the King!" "Praise God for him who comes in the name of the Lord" Praise God for the return of our father David's kingdom..." Hail to the King of the universe!" *The Living Bible Illustrated*

Those who went ahead and those who followed him were shouting, "Hosanna! 'Blessed is the one who comes in the name of the Lord!' Blessed is our ancestor David's kingdom that is coming! Hosanna in the highest heaven!" *God's Word*

Introduction

All Christian denominations in the world celebrate Palm Sunday every year in remembrance of the day, when the crowd accorded the royal welcome to Jesus Christ in the city of Jerusalem. The crowd was shouting: "Hosanna! 'Blessed is he who comes in the name of the Lord!' Blessed is the kingdom of our father David that is coming! Hosanna in the highest!" (Mk. 11:10; Mt. 21:10) The people honoured the Lord Jesus Christ as the King who came in the name of the LORD God, and to be enthroned on the throne of King David forever.

This joyous and triumphal event made George Frederick Handel (February 23, 1687- April 14,1759) to compose his great 'Messiah.' He composed it under an unfavourable condition. His right hand was paralysed; he became poor; his creditors seized him, and threatened to imprison him. Handel was so much disheartened by these tragic experiences that he had no desire to live longer. Yet he still had a little faith, which helped him to compose "The Hallelujah Chorus" which is a part of his great 'Messiah'.[1]

Six years after the death of George Handel, on March 23, 1743, 'The Messiah' was first performed in London, England, when the king was present in the great audience. All the people were deeply moved by the 'Hallelujah Chorus' that with the impressive words, 'For the Lord God omnipotent reigneth,' the whole audience, including the king, sprang to its feet, and remained standing throughout the chorus. From that time to this day, it has been the custom to stand during the chorus whenever it is performed.[2]

When Queen Victoria (May 24,1819- January 22, 1901) had just ascended her throne, as it was the custom of Royalty to hear 'The Messiah' rendered. The Queen was instructed not to rise when the others stood at the hallelujah chorus. When that magnificent chorus was being sung and the singers were shouting 'Hallelujah! Hallelujah! For the Lord God omnipotent reigneth" she sat with great difficulty. It seemed as if she would rise in spite of the custom of kings and queens; but finally when they came to that part of the chorus where with a shout they proclaim Him the King of kings, suddenly the young

Queen rose and stood with bowed head, as if she would take her own crown from off her head and cast it at His feet. [3]

Jesus Christ is the King of kings, and the Lord of lords (Phil. 2:9-10). Let us honour Him and prise Him, because He came in the name of the LORD God.

Introduction of the Text

On the first Palm Sunday, the crowd enthusiastically welcomed Jesus Christ as the Messiah, the King of the Jews. This event was so much important to the gospel writers that every one of them had recorded it (Mt. 21: 1-9; Mk 11:1-10; Lk.19:28-40; Jn 12:12-13). St. Mark described the event, telling how the crowd welcomed Jesus Christ into Jerusalem, in these words:

> And those who went before and those who followed cried out, "Hosanna! 'Blessed is he who comes in the name of the Lord!' Blessed is the kingdom of our father David that is coming! Hosanna in the highest!" (Mk. 11:9-10)

This is the text of our meditation today.

The Context of the Text

Jesus Christ was fully aware of His Messiahship from the very beginning of His ministry. He knew that He was the Christ, the anointed one of God. His mission was to liberate the people from sin and death, and to give them the spiritual salvation. He did not wish to mix up His divine Messiahship with the political leadership. The Jews were ruled by the Roman power at the time of Jesus of Nazareth (ca 4 B. C-A. D. 30); and they were expecting the Messiah to liberate them from the political oppression, and He would make them a free nation once again. Jesus Christ performed many miracles in the presence of His disciples and the crowd, indicating that He was the Messiah. When Jesus Christ fed five thousand people, people began to think of Jesus as the prophet, who was to come into the world (Jn 6:14). They planned to take Jesus Christ by force in order to make Him a king; but Jesus Christ, knowing the intention of the crowd, withdrew again to the mountain by Himself (Jn 6:15). Jesus Christ did not wish to be a king of the Jews, giving them hope of political freedom from the Roman power.

When Jesus Christ healed a man with a withered hand on a Sabbath, the Pharisees took counsel against Jesus, how to destroy Him (Mt. 12:9-14). Jesus Christ withdrew from the synagogue. Many people followed him; and He healed them all. He ordered them not to make Him known as God's anointed one. This He said to fulfil the prophecy of Isaiah (Is. 42:1-4; Mt. 12:18-21).

When Jesus Christ healed many and removed the evil spirits from them, the evil spirits cried out, "You are the Son of God." (Mk. 3:11), Jesus Christ strictly ordered the evil spirits not to make Him known as the Son of God or Christ.

The disciples of Jesus Christ saw the miracles, which Jesus performed, and they heard the comments of the crowd as to who Jesus could be. On their way to Caesarea Philippi, Jesus Christ asked His disciples, "Who do men say that I am?" The disciples gave different answers such as, "John the Baptist, Elijah, and a prophet." Then Jesus Christ asked them, 'But who do you say that I am?' Simon Peter answered Jesus, "You are the Christ." Then Jesus Christ charged them not to tell anyone about Him that He was the Messiah (Mk 8:27-30). Jesus Christ charged them so, because that their proclamation would have become premature; and His Messiahship would have been misunderstood.

Jesus Christ was waiting for a right time to proclaim His Messiahship publicly. The earthly ministry of Jesus Christ was coming to the end, after three years or more. He made an arrangement with His follower to lend Him a colt. When Jesus Christ and His disciples came to Bethphage, Jesus Christ sent His two disciples to His follower in Bethphage, saying:

> Go into the village opposite you, and as soon as you enter it you will find a colt tied, on which no one has ever sat; untie it and bring it. If any one says to you, 'Why are you doing this?' Say, 'The Lord has need of it and will send it back here immediately. (Mk 11:1-4)

The disciples fetched the colt. The crowd threw their cloaks on the colt; and they made Jesus Christ ride on it. Then the crowd spread their cloaks on the road. Spreading garments on the road was an oriental way of extending royal treatment (II Kg. 9:4-9). Jesus Christ approved this royal treatment, given by His followers and the crowd. Some persons cut branches of trees, and spread them on the road.

The crowd formed a procession. They put Jesus Christ at the centre of the procession. Some people went ahead and others followed Jesus Christ. They were enthusiastically taking Jesus Christ in procession from Bethany to Jerusalem; and they were joyfully shouting for Jesus Christ, saying:

> Hosanna! 'Blessed is he who comes in the name of the Lord!' Blessed is the kingdom of our father David that is coming! Hosanna in the highest! (Mk 11:9-10)

This is the text of our meditation, within its historical setting.

An Analysis of the Text

In this text there are three ideas. (A) The first idea is how the crowd addressed Jesus Christ. The crowd said, 'Blessed is he who comes in the name of the LORD.'

(B) The second idea is how the crowd linked Jesus Christ, the Messiah, with their ideal king, King David. The crowd said, 'Blessed is the kingdom of our father David that is coming.'

(C) The third idea is how the crowd expressed their enthusiasm and zeal in welcoming Jesus Christ. The crowd said, 'Hosanna in the highest!'

Exposition of the Ideas of the Text

(A) The first idea of the text is how the crowd addressed Jesus Christ. The crowd said, 'Blessed is he who comes in the name of the LORD.' Jesus Christ came into the world in the name of the LORD God. The scripture bears witnesses to this fact.

(1) Jesus Christ performed many miracles, as the signs indicating that God sent Him as the Messiah. Prophet Isaiah prophesied about the miraculous works of the Messiah, in the following words:

> Then the eyes of the blind shall be opened, and the ears of the deaf unstopped; then shall the lame man leap like a hart, and the tongue of the dumb sing for joy. (Is. 35:5-6)

Jesus Christ was performing these kinds of miracles. John the Baptist heard about those miracles, while he was in prison of King Herod Antipas (4 B. C.- A. D. 40). He sent a word by his disciples to Jesus Christ, asking Him, "Are you he who is to come, or shall we look for another?" Jesus Christ answered the inquirer, saying:

> Go and tell John what you hear and see: the blind receive their sight and the lame walk, lepers are cleansed and the deaf hear, and the dead are raised up, and the poor have good news preached to them. And blessed is he who takes no offence at me. (Mt. 11:2-6)

The reply of Jesus Christ to John the Baptist (ca. 5 B. C. –A. D. 28) was that he should know that Jesus was the Christ, the anticipated Messiah, because He had been doing the miracles that the Messiah was expected to do, and which were prophesied by prophet Isaiah.

(2) Jesus Christ argued with the Jews on many occasions that He was sent by God to do His will and work. When Jesus healed a man, who was sick for thirty-eight years, on a Sabbath, the Jews accused Jesus Christ of breaking the Sabbath. Jesus Christ justified His act of healing, saying to the Jews:

> Truly, truly, I say to you, the Son can do nothing of his own accord, but only what he sees the Father doing; for whatever he does, that the Son does likewise. For the Father loves the Son, and shows him all that he himself is doing; and greater works than these will he show him, that you may marvel. For as the Father raises the dead and gives them life, so also the Son gives life to whom he will... He who does not honour the Son does not honour the Father who sent him. Truly, truly, I say to you, he who hears my word and believes him who sent me, has eternal life,... (Jn 5:19-24)

After feeding the five thousand, Jesus said to the Jews, "I am the bread of life; he who comes to me shall not hunger, and he who believes in me shall never thirst." (Jn 6:35) Then He added:

For I have come down from heaven, not to do my own will, but the will of him who sent me... For this is the will of my Father, that every one who sees the Son and believes in him should have eternal life; and I will raise him up at the last day. (Jn 6:38, 40)

Jesus Christ went to the temple at Jerusalem during a Passover feast. He said to the Jews in the treasury of the temple:

I am the light of the world; he who follows me will not walk in darkness, but will have the light of life. (Jn 8:12)

Then the Pharisees questioned His claim, saying, "You are bearing witness to yourself; your testimony is not true. Jesus Christ answered them, saying:

Even if I do bear witness to myself, my testimony is true, for I know whence I have come and whither I am going, but you do not know whence I come or whither I am going... Yet even if I do judge, my judgment is true, for it is not I alone that judge, but I and he who sent me. (Jn 8:14-16)

At the feast of the Dedication at Jerusalem, the Jews asked Jesus Christ, "How long will you keep us in suspense? If you are the Christ, tell us plainly (Jn 10:22-24). Jesus Christ answered them, saying:

I told you, and you do not believe. The works that I do in my Father's name, they bear witness to me; but you do not believe, because you do not belong to my sheep. (Jn 10: 25-26)

When Phillip, a disciple of Jesus Christ, asked Jesus Christ to show them His Father, Jesus Christ answered Phillip, saying:

Have I been with you so long, and yet you do not know me, Phillip? He who has seen me has seen the Father; how can you say, 'show us the Father? Do you not believe that I am in the Father and the Father in me? The words that I say to you I do not speak on my own authority; but the Father who dwells in me and does his works. Believe me that I am in the Father and the Father in me; or else believe me for the sake of the works themselves. (Jn 14:9-11)

By these arguments with the Jews and His disciples, Jesus Christ asserted that He had come in the name of the LORD God.

(B) The second idea of the text is how the crowd linked Jesus Christ, the Messiah, with their ideal king, King David (1002-962 B. C.) The crowd said, 'Blessed is the kingdom of our father David that is coming.' The crowd first proclaimed that Jesus Christ came in the name of the LORD God. The crowd secondly proclaimed that the future kingdom of King David would be the blessed kingdom. The crowd thought of the future kingdom of King David as the blessed kingdom, because the Messiah, who was born in the lineage of King David, would be enthroned forever; and He would be the prince of peace and righteousness.

God was pleased with King David, when King David thought to build a temple for the LORD God. God sent prophet Nathan to King David with the message:

> When your days are fulfilled to go to be with your fathers, I will raise up your offspring after you, one of your own sons, and I will establish his kingdom. He shall build a house for me, and I will establish his throne for ever. I will be his father, and he shall be my son; I will not take my steadfast love from him, as I took it from him who was before you, but I will confirm him in my house and in my kingdom for ever and his throne shall be established for ever. (I Chr. 17:11-14)

God promised King David that He would raise up a son in his lineage; and He would make him an everlasting King. King David, being inspired by the Spirit of God, wrote in a psalm about this promise:

> I will tell of the decree of the LORD: He said to me, "You are my son, today I have begotten you. Ask of me, and I will make the nations your heritage, and the ends of the earth your possession." (Ps. 2:7-8; Acts 13:33; Heb. 1:5, 5:5)

King David spoke of the universal kingdom in this psalm. Similarly, King Solomon (962-922 B. C.) in a psalm spoke of the everlasting and peaceful kingdom of the King in these words:

> May he live while the sun endures, and as long as the moon, throughout all generations! May he be like the rain that falls on the mown grass, like showers that water the earth! In his days may righteousness flourish, and peace abound, till the moon be no more! May he have dominion from sea to sea, and from the River to the ends of the earth! (Ps. 72:5-8)

When the kingdom of Judah was destroyed, and the Jews were taken into captivity to Babylon in 588 B. C., God revealed His future plan to prophet Daniel about the everlasting kingdom of the Messiah. Daniel wrote about it, in these words:

> And to him was given dominion and glory and kingdom that all peoples, nations, and languages should serve him; his dominion is an everlasting dominion, which shall not pass away, and his kingdom one that shall not be destroyed. (Dan. 7:14)

God repeated the promise through prophet Isaiah, when he wrote:

> For to us a child is born, to us a son is given; and the government will be upon his shoulder, and his name will be called 'Wonderful Counsellor, Mighty God, Everlasting Father, Prince of Peace.' Of the increase of his government and of peace there will be no end, upon the throne of David, and over his kingdom, to establish it, and to uphold it with justice and with righteousness from this time forth and for evermore. The zeal of the LORD of hosts will do this. (Is. 9:6-7 cf. Is. 11:4; 32:1; 42:3)

God reaffirmed His promise through prophet Jeremiah (Jer. 1:2-3; his period of prophecy 642-583 B.C.), when he prophesied thus:

> Behold, the days are coming, says the LORD, when I will raise up for David a righteous Branch, and he shall reign as king and deal wisely, and shall execute justice and righteousness in the land. In his days Judah will be saved, and Israel will dwell securely. And this the name by which he will be called: 'The LORD is our righteousness. (Jer. 23:5-6)

Prophet Zechariah (Zec. 1:2-3; his period of prophecy 520-486 B.C.) prophesied how the Messiah would enter Jerusalem and how his kingdom will be universal and peaceful, in the following words:

> Rejoice greatly, O daughter of Zion! Shout aloud, O daughter of Jerusalem! Lo, your king comes to you; triumphant and victorious is he, humble and riding on an ass, on a colt the foal of an ass. I will cut off the chariot from Ephraim and the war horse from Jerusalem; and the battle bow shall be cut off, and he shall command peace to the nations; his dominion shall be from sea to sea, and from the River to the ends of the earth. (Zec. 9:9-10)

When Jesus Christ entered Jerusalem triumphantly in order to proclaim His Messiahship publicly, He used a colt to ride on, as the symbol of peace. He fulfilled the prophecy of Zechariah.

When Pontius Pilate (A. D. 26-36) questioned His kingship, Jesus Christ said to him:

> You say that I am a king. For this I was born, and for this I have come into the world, to bear witness to the truth. Every one who is of the truth hears my voice. (Jn 18:37)

Jesus Christ proclaimed His Messiahship publicly; and He approved the shout of the crowd, saying, "Blessed is the kingdom of our father David that is coming."

(C) The third idea of the text is how the crowd expressed their enthusiasm and zeal in welcoming Jesus Christ. The crowd said, 'Hosanna in the highest!' The word 'Hosanna' at the time of Jesus Christ was used to express good wishes and admiration. It was used to express a hearty acclamation. It was similar to our present word 'hurrah'. Its original meaning was changed before the time of Jesus Christ. The words do change their meanings in the course of time, e. g. kids, rocks, pot, grass, etc.

The original meaning of the word 'Hosanna' would make better sense than the secondary or acquired meaning. The original meaning of 'Hosanna' was 'save now or help us, we pray.' It meant 'Help Israel, O God.' It was a distress call of man to God. It was like our present S. O. S. call. This original meaning of 'Hosanna' would put other ideas of the text namely, Jesus Christ came in the name of the LORD God and the kingdom of the Messiah would be universal and eternal, in their proper perspective.

'Hosanna in the highest' means Hosanna in the highest heaven. It meant that the sound of Hosanna may fill all heaven. It was the jubilant cry of the crowd to welcome Jesus Christy as the King of kings and the Lord of lords.

Conclusion

The crowd welcomed Jesus Christ as the Messiah, who came in the name of the LORD God. They welcomed Him as the King of Israel to govern the kingdom of King David, with peace and righteousness, and for ever, and all over the world. They shouted Hosanna to Jesus Christ, as the jubilant loud cry, even to be filled in all heaven.

Let the hearts of the believers be filled with the zeal and enthusiasm to welcome the Lord Jesus Christ; and they themselves proclaim that the Lord Jesus Christ came into the world in the name of God; and He is enthroned on the throne of King David to rule the world and heaven, forever, with peace and righteousness.

Recommended Hymns from the Methodist Hymnal

84   'All glory, laud, and honour'

91   'All hail the power of Jesus' name'

116   'Sing we the King who is coming'

192   'Ride on, ride on in majesty!'

836   'Hosanna, loud hosanna'

837   'Children of Jerusalem'

Recommended Responsive Reading from A Worship Manual for Scriptural or Methodist Order of Service

90 (pp. 214-215).

Endnotes

[1] Paul Lee Tan, Encyclopedia of 7700 Illustrations: Signs of the Time, # 4173.

[2] Ibid., # 1872.

[3] Ibid., # 75876.

Chapter - 21

Titles of the Sermon
'Zeal of the Lord Jesus Christ'
'The Cost of the Righteous Zeal of the Lord Jesus Christ.'

Scripture
John 2:13-22
Psalms 67:7-9
Isaiah 56:7
Matthew 11: 12, 17; 12: 9-12, 14; 19: 3-9; 21:13, 43-46;
22:16-21; 23:13, 23-24, 27-28
Mark 1:17; 3:1-6; 11:15-19, 28, 30, 33
Luke 6:6-10; 14:2-6; 19:45-46; 20:21-22, 25
John 1:11; 2:17, 19, 22; 9:13-16

Text: John 2:17

A Few Versions of the Text, John 2:17
Then His disciples remembered that it was written, "Zeal for Your house has eaten Me up." *The New King James Version*

And his disciples remembered that it is written, The zeal of thine house eateh me up. *Explanatory Notes Upon the New Testament*

His disciples remembered that it was written, "Zeal for thy house will consume me." *Revised Standard Version*

His disciples remembered that it is written: "Zeal for your house will consume me." *New International Version*

His disciples recalled the words of the scripture, 'Zeal for thy house will destroy me.' *The New English Bible*

Then his disciples remembered this prophecy from the Scripture: "Concern for God's House will be my undoing." *The Living Bible Illustrated*

His disciples remembered that Scripture said, "Devotion for your house will consume me." *God's Word*

Introduction

The persons who introduced and stood for religious reforms had to face persecution and even death. Let us find a few examples from a history of the church in Europe.

(1) John Wycliffe (c.1328- December 31, 1384) studied at Balliol College, Oxford; and earned M. A. and doctorate in a theology. He was sympathetic to the Franciscan ideal of apostolic poverty. He entered the service of the English crown. King Edward III (1312-1377) presented him with the parish of Lutterworth. He wrote two books: *On Divine Lordship* in 1375 and *On Civil Lordship* in 1376. He argued that "divine lordship is the basis of any lordship of the creature." Man serves as a steward, who holds his power in trust from God. Man can hold the power as long as he is in a state of grace. When churchmen act wickedly they are not in the state of grace; therefore, secular authority should deprive them of their property. He took a stand against paying tribute to a pope; and he advocated confiscation of ecclesiastical property by the State under certain conditions.

Wycliffe had an Augustinian view of the church as the body of predestined believers; and he described church as militant on earth, and triumphant in heaven. He wrote a book *On the Power of the Pope* in 1379. In this book he denied the divine origin of the papal office;

and identified pope as the Antichrist and his followers as the "twelve daughters of the diabolical leech."

Wycliffe was a reformer of the fourteenth century. His reform was based upon the supreme authority of the Scriptures, which is the standard of faith for every Christian and the standard of all human perfection. He was busy with training poor preachers to preach the gospel in the language of the people. The preachers were nicknamed 'Lollards,' because of their style of preaching.[1]

After Wycliffe's death, Lollards continued to be popular in England. King Richard II (January 6, 1367- February 14, 1400) tolerated Lollards. Despite their condemnation by ecclesiastical courts, the Lollards sent a petition in 1395 to the parliament for help in reforming religion according to the ideas of the Scripture. King Henry IV (1399-1413), as he was in need of the support from the hierarchy, passed a statue in 1401 against Lollards to suppress their movement. There was a dynastic tie between England and Bohemia, for King Richard II had married Anne, a daughter of King Wenceslaus (November 29, 1358- August 16, 1419) of Bohemia. This political connection increased traffic and transfer of ideas between the two lands. Wycliffe's ideas of reform entered into Bohemia.

(2) There was an independent Czech reform movement in Bohemia. It was led by Matthew of Janov (ca. 1335-1393). Jan Hus (ca. 1372- July 6,1415) became the leader of the native movement after 1402, when he was appointed a preacher in Bethlehem Chapel, near the University in the heart of Prague. Jan Hus studied at the Charles University in Prague; and he became a lecturer in 1398. He was deeply pious. His preaching had a moral impact on the people. He quickly gained a reputation as a popular lecturer and powerful preacher. He was preaching in Czech. He became a national hero. Fearing the implications of Hus's teachings, the local clergy urged Archbishop Zbynek of Prague (1592-1606) to proceed against Hus; and the curia condemned Hus's teachings. Hus was forbidden to preach in Bethlehem Chapel. When this happened, Hus declared that "in the things pertaining to salvation God is to

be obeyed than man." In March 1411 the ban was pronounced against Hus as a disobedient son of the church. Afterwards the whole city was put under the interdict for protecting a heretic. In May 1412 a papal emissary went to Prague to proclaim papal bulls, authorizing sale of indulgences. People paraded throughout the streets of Prague; and they burned papal bulls. King Wenceslaus (26 February 1361-16 August 1419) intervened in the interest of public order; and three young men were sentenced to death for declaring the indulgences unlawful. The king Wenceslaus asked Hus to leave Prague. Hus spent a year and half to write expositions on the faith. His book "*On the Church*" presented a spiritual conception of a church of believers under the headship of Christ. His ideas were similar to Wycliffe's ideas.

The Council of Constance was facing the problem of Bohemia. Hus was summoned to appear before the Council. Emperor Sigismund of Germany (15 February 1361- 9 December 1437) provided a safe-conduct, promising his safe return to Bohemia, no matter what the Council thought of his teaching. His case was heard by the Council on June 5, 1415. The charges were laid against him on the basis of his book "*On the Church.*" He was asked to say his writing was false, and to denounce his teaching. He was given a month to change his position. He wrote to his supporters in Prague: "I write this in prison and in chains, expecting tomorrow to receive a sentence of death, full of hope in God that I shall not sware from the truth, nor adjure errors imputed to me by false witnesses."

On July 6, 1451, the Council condemned Jan Hus to death in the presence of Emperor Sigismund, who did nothing to keep his promise to give safe return to Hus to Bohemia.

When Jan Hus was prepared for execution and to be burned, he was asked to recant, he answered:

> God is my witness that I have never taught or preached that which false witnesses have testified against me. He knows that the great object of all my preaching and writing was to convert men from sin. In the truth of that gospel which hitherto I have written, taught, and preached, I now joyfully die.[2]

Jan Hus was burned alive for taking a stand against the papal teaching and practices. He was filled with the biblical conviction; and he was ready to sacrifice his life for God.

(3) Marin Luther (November 10, 1483-February 18,1546) was born on November 10, 1483 in Eisleben, Germany. He entered the University of Erfurt in 1501 and received B. A. in 1502, and M. A. in 1505. He entered the Augustinian monastery in 1505, for his spiritual struggle for religious certainty and assurance. In 1506 he was admitted to the order of monks. He was ordained into the priesthood in 1507. Martin Luther went to the University of Wittenberg in 1508 as an instructor of philosophy. He received B. D. in 1509. He returned to teach at Erfurt from 1509 to 1511. He was reassigned to Wittenberg, where he remained for the rest of his life. He received his doctorate on October 18, 1512; and he assumed the chair for biblical studies, taking an oath to protect and expound the word of God to the best of his ability. He began to expound Paul's Epistle to the Romans in 1515-1516. He achieved an evangelical breakthrough, when he was expounding Rom. 1:17: "For therein is the righteousness of God revealed from faith to faith: as it is written, The just shall live by faith." He understood this verse with reference to Rom. 3:24. Then he understood the righteousness of God as a passive, imputed righteousness that God gives freely to man through Christ. This helped him to form the doctrine of salvation by God's grace alone, received as a gift through faith and without dependence upon human merit. With reference to this doctrine, he examined church doctrines and practices; and he found them wanting.

Luther was against abuse of the sale of indulgence; and he questioned their validity. In April 1571 John Tetzel, supersalesman of indulgence, went to Wittenberg to sale indulgences, Luther urged bishops to intervene. When the bishops failed to act, Luther prepared his ninety-five theses on indulgence; and he sent copies to Bishop Jerome of Brandenburg. He posted them on the north door of the Castle Church on All Saint's Day, challenging anyone to an academic disputation.

His theses were carried to the farthest corners of Europe. Martin Luther had ruined the sale of indulgences; and he unknowingly launched the Reformation.

Dominican John Tetzel threatened to have Luther the heretic in fire within three weeks. Tetzels' fellow Dominican in Saxony preached that Martin Luther be burned. Dominicans in Germany officially denounced Martin Luther to the pope on February 3, 1518.

Martin Luther was a prolific writer; he produced more than four hundred books between 1516 and 1546. In 1520, he wrote three famous books: *Address to the Christian Nobility of the German Nation, The Babylonian Captivity of the Church,* and *On the Liberty of the Christian Man.*

He translated the New Testament in Germany from Greek in 1522; and his Sanhedrin translated the Old Testament in German from Hebrew. The entire work was completed in 1534.

Pope Leo, on June 15, 1520, published the bull, citing forty-one heresies in Martin Luther's writings, and giving him sixty days in which to recant and to demand his books be burned. In retaliation the Wittenberg University faculty and students gathered on December 10, 1520, outside the Elster gate to build a bonfire and burn copies of scholastic writings and the cannon law. On January 3, 1521, the pope issued the bull excommunicating Martin Luther as a heretic outside the law, meaning death to the heretic. He was summoned on March 6, 1521 to appear before the emperor and the diet of the Holy Roman Empire meeting in Worms. Luther went and took his stand. On April 18, 1521, he answered:

> Since then your serene majesty and your lordships seek a simple answer, I will give in this manner, neither horned nor toothed: Unless I am convinced by the testimony of the Scripture or by clear reason (for I do not trust either in the pope or in the councils alone, since it is well known that they have often erred and contradicted themselves), I am bound by the Scriptures I have quoted and my conscience is captive to the word of God. I cannot and I will not retract anything, since it is neither safe nor right to go against conscience. I cannot do otherwise, here I stand, may God help me. Amen.[3]

Martin Luther had asked Elector III of Saxony, Frederick the Wise (1463-1525) for protection. When Martin Luther and his party were returning from Worm to Wittenberg, Elector Frederick sent a troop of armed horsemen to kidnap Martin Luther in order to hide him somewhere. Marin Luther was taken to Wartburg Castle; and he stayed there ten months. He escaped a death penalty, because of royal protection and popular support. After restless activities of the reforms, he died on February 18, 1546 at Eisleben.

John Wycliffee, Jan Hus, and Martin Luther were the zealous reformers, basing their religious reforms on the Scripture. They were persecuted and condemned by the Roman Catholic Church. Jan Hus was burned alive. They had to pay the price for religious reforms.

Introduction of the Text

God in Jesus Christ came into the world to redeem the mankind from sin and death. He was the promised Messiah of the Jews, the redeemer of the people. He was given a royal and zealous welcome by the crowds in Jerusalem on the Palm Sunday. He declared His Messiahship to the pilgrims and to all people, who came to Jerusalem to celebrate the Passover. On the following day, He returned to the temple in Jerusalem; and cleansed the temple from corrupt trades; and He restored it to be the house of God. Jesus Christ demonstrated His zeal in doing this God's work. The disciples did not understand why Jesus Christ was doing this. After His death and resurrection, the disciples of Jesus Christ reflected on the event of cleansing the temple. This observation is given to us in the following words:

> **His disciples remembered that it was written, "Zeal for thy house will consume me."** (John 2:17)

This is the text of our meditation now.

The Context of the Text

According to the Gospel of John, the cleansing of the temple at Jerusalem by Jesus Christ took place at the beginning of the ministry of Jesus Christ. This may not be true chronologically. Biblical scholars have given some explanations about this. One of the explanations is that St. John had concentrated on the ministry of Jesus Christ at Jerusalem; and the synoptic Gospel writers had concentrated on the ministry of Jesus Christ in Galilee. St. John was concerned about proclaiming Jesus Christ as the promised Messiah at every point of his writing; and he was not mindful of chronological order of events. However, all four Gospels are complementary to one another.

According to the chronological order of the synoptic Gospel writers, Jesus Christ entered Jerusalem to proclaim that He was the promised Messiah, the King of Israel, on the Palm Sunday. On the following day (Mk 11:12), He entered Jerusalem. He was angry at the activities, which were taking place in the temple, the house of God, at Jerusalem. He saw some people selling oxen, sheep, and pigeons, which were the victims of sacrifice; He also saw the moneychangers at their business. The business was carried in the name of religion; but it was a corrupt business. Jesus Christ was upset with the corruption that was behind the business. He made a whip of cord; and He drove away all oxen and sheep out of the temple. He overturned the seats of those, who were selling pigeons; and He said to them, "Take these things away; you shall not make my Father's house a house of trade." (Jn 2:17) He overturned the tables of the moneychangers. He said to the business owners, "Is it not written, 'My house shall be called a house of prayer for all the nations?' But you have made it a den of robbers." (Mk 11:17 cf. Mt. 21:13; Lk. 19:46)

Jesus Christ demonstrated His spiritual authority, vested in the Messiah, to the people in the temple. The Pharisees and scribes questioned the authority of Jesus Christ in cleansing the temple. The disciples of Jesus Christ saw the zeal in cleansing the temple. St. John reflected on the event and wrote:

> His disciples remembered that it was written, "Zeal for thy house will consume me." (John 2:17)

This is the text of our meditation, within its historical setting.

Analysis of the Text

This text has one idea that the disciples remembered the fulfilment of the prophecy that the Messiah would be consumed by the zeal in cleansing the temple, the house of God. This idea can be divided into two parts.

(A) The first part of the idea would be that Jesus Christ demonstrated His zeal for God's work and word, in the presence of His disciples.

(B) The second part of the idea would be that the zeal of Jesus Christ was culminated in cleansing the temple, the house of God. This was a prophecy about the work of the Messiah.

Exposition of the Ideas of the Text

(A) The first part of the idea is that Jesus Christ demonstrated His zeal for God's work and word, in the presence of His disciples. Jesus Christ had been zealous in doing God's work and teaching His word. He was not afraid of offending anyone, when He was doing right and just things in the sight of God. Let us see some of the evidences, which augment the boldness of Jesus Christ in doing and saying right things.

(1) Jesus Christ entered a synagogue on a Sabbath day. In the synagogue, there was a man with a withered hand. Pharisees asked Jesus Christ a question, "Is it lawful to heal on the sabbath?" (Mt. 12:9) They asked this question in order to accuse Him of breaking the Sabbath. Jesus Christ in His reply to them said:

> What a man of you, if he has one sheep and it falls into a pit on the sabbath, will not lay hold of it and lift it out? Of how much more value is a man than a sheep! So it is lawful to do good on the sabbath. (Mt. 12:11-12)

Jesus Christ healed the man on the Sabbath, against the wishes of the Pharisees. He taught them to do good things on the Sabbath. But the Pharisees were offended by what Jesus Christ said and did; they took a counsel to destroy Jesus Christ (Mt. 12:14). Similar events have been recorded by other gospel writers (Lk.6:6-10; 14:2-6; Mk 3:1-6; Jn 9:13-16).

(2) A Pharisee asked Jesus Christ a question, "Is it lawful to divorce one's wife for any cause?" (Mt. 19:3) They asked this question to test His understanding of the scripture. Jesus Christ replied them that God has joined together man and woman; therefore, man should not put them asunder. (Mt, 19:5-6) Then the Pharisees asked Jesus Christ, "Why then Moses command one to give a certificate of divorce, and put her away?" (Mt. 19:7) Then Jesus Christ answered them:

> For your hardness of heart Moses allowed you to divorce your wives, but from the beginning it was not so. And I say to you: whoever divorces his wife, except for unchastity, and marries another, commits adultery. (Mt. 19:8-9)

Jesus Christ explained to the Pharisees that Moses permitted divorce, because of hardness of heart of the people; but divorce is not in the mind of God, when He joins man and woman in matrimony. Moreover, Jesus Christ exercised His authority in telling them when divorce would be justifiable.

The Pharisees might have been offended by His explanation and by the use of His spiritual authority.

(3) Jesus Christ spoke to Pharisees in parables. One of those parables was the parable of a householder, who planted a vineyard and rented it to tenants. The householder sent his servants and his son to collect his fruit; but the wicked tenants killed them. Jesus Christ concluded the parable saying to the Pharisees:

> Therefore I tell you, the kingdom of God will be taken from you and given to a nation producing the fruits of it. (Mt. 21:43)

The chief priest and the Pharisees understood that Jesus Christ was talking about them through the parable. They were offended by the parable; and they were planning to arrest Jesus Christ (Mt. 21:45-46).

(4) The Pharisees took counsel how to catch Jesus in His talk. They sent their disciples along with Herodians. They cunningly complemented Jesus Christ; and asked Him a difficult question:

> Teacher, we know that you are true, and teach the way of God truthfully, and care for no man; for you do not regard the position of men. Tell us, then, what you think. Is it lawful to pay taxes to Caesar, or not? (Mt. 22:16-17;Lk. 20:21-22)

Jesus Christ knew that they were malicious and crafty. He knew their intention. He replied to them saying: "Why put me to the test, you hypocrites? Show me the money for the tax." When they gave Him a coin, Jesus asked them a question, "Whose likeness and inscription is this?" They said, "Caesar's." Then Jesus replied:

> "Render therefore to Caesar the things that are Caesar's, and to God the things that are God's." (Mt. 22:18-21; Lk. 20:25)

(5) During the last days of His ministry, Jesus Christ openly and boldly condemned the scribes and Pharisees for their hypocrisy, and misguiding the people in religious matters, saying:

> But woe to you, scribes and Pharisees, hypocrites! because you shut the kingdom of heaven against men; for you neither enter yourselves, nor allow those who would enter to go in. (Mt. 23:13)

> Woe to you, scribes and Pharisees, hypocrites! for you tithe mint and dill and cummin, and have neglected the weightier matters of the law, justice and mercy and faith; these you ought to have done, without neglecting the others. You blind guides, straining out a gnat and swallowing a camel! (Mt. 23:23-24)

> Woe to you, scribes and Pharisees, hypocrites! for you are like white-washed tombs, which outwardly appear beautiful, but within they are full of dead men's bones and all uncleanness. So you also outwardly appear righteous to men, but within you are full of hypocrisy and iniquity. (Mt. 23:27-28)

Jesus Christ showed His boldness and truthfulness in doing godly things, and teaching the word of God. He was not afraid of the religious leaders, scribes and the Pharisees. He did these things, because He was filled with godly zeal and enthusiasm.

(B) The second part of the idea is that the zeal of Jesus Christ was culminated in cleansing the temple, the house of God. This was a prophesy about the work of the Messiah.

Jesus Christ demonstrated the same zeal when He entered the temple in Jerusalem to proclaim His Messiahship to the people. The declaration of His Messiahship or Christhood involved a fulfilment of the prophecy that the Messiah would cleanse the temple, the house of God. King David, being inspired by the spirit of God, wrote the following words:

> For it is for thy sake that I have borne reproach, that shame has covered my face. I have become a stranger to my brethren, and alien to my mother's sons. For the zeal of thy house has consumed me and the insults of those who insult thee have fallen on me. (Ps. 69:7-9)

These words of the psalm imply that the Messiah would have to pay the price, when He would cleanse the temple, the house of God, in terms of being considered as a stranger by His own people, and being punished by His own race. Jesus Christ was not received by His own people as the Messiah (Jn 1:11). When He cleansed the temple, He made scribes, the Pharisees, and high priests furious; and they plotted to crucify him.

When Jesus Christ entered the temple, during the last week of His earthly life, He found merchants selling oxen, sheep, and pigeons in the temple. Those animals were prescribed for sacrifices; the pilgrims had to buy those animals from the merchants, at any price. The prices of the animals were unreasonable. The merchants were making exorbitant profit. Those merchants were sharing their profit with the religious authority of the temple; therefore, the merchants were allowed to carry their business even in the temple. Subsequently, the temple was turned into a noisy marketplace; it did not remain the holy place, where people could worship God in peace and truth. Jesus Christ was annoyed to see that the holy temple of God, the place of worshipping God for the people and the pilgrims, turned into a marketplace. He was also angry at the businessmen that they were carrying out the corrupt business in the temple, the house of God, in the name of religion. Jesus Christ had the prophetic spirit and courage to tell the people to stop the corrupt business, and to tell them the only purpose of having the temple of the LORD God. Therefore, Jesus made a whip of cords, and drove these animals out of the temple.

Secondly, the animals for sacrifices were to be bought with the currency, which was approved by the temple authority. The secular currency was not allowed to be used in the temple. In order to exchange the secular currency into the temple currency, there were moneychangers in the temple. They were making top profit by exchanging the currency. They were thus exploiting the pilgrims and other worshippers. Jesus Christ was angry by the corrupt business. He wanted to stop this kind business. Therefore, He poured out the coins of the moneychangers; and He overturned their tables. He said to those who were selling pigeons, "Take these things away; you shall not make my Father's house a house of trade." (Jn 2:16) This saying of Jesus Christ was also applicable to the businessmen. St. Mark recorded the event, describing that Jesus Christ did not allow anyone to carry anything through the temple. He said to the businessmen and others: "Is it not written, 'My house shall be called a house of prayer for all the nations'? But you have made it a den of robbers." (Mk 11:17 cf. Mt. 21:13; Lk.19: 46) When Jesus Christ addressed the people in these words, He precisely quoted the words of God, which prophet Jeremiah had written (Jer. 7:11), and which prophet Isaiah had also written (Is. 56:7).

When Jesus Christ began to cleanse the temple, He attacked the vested interest of the businessmen and of the scribes and the priests. The chief priests and the scribes heard the words of Jesus Christ; they sought a way to destroy Him. But they were afraid of Jesus Christ, because the multitude was surprised at the teaching of Jesus Christ (Mk 11:18). When Jesus Christ entered the temple next day, on Monday, the chief priests, scribes, and elders approached Jesus Christ; and they asked Him, "By what authority are you doing these things, or who gave you this authority to do them?" (Mk 11:28) The temple authority questioned the authority of Jesus Christ to carry out the religious reforms. In reply, Jesus Christ asked them the question: "Was the baptism of John from heaven or from men?" (Mk 11:30) As they did not answer the question, Jesus Christ told them, "Neither will I tell you by what authority I do these things." (Mk 11:33)

According to St. John, when Jesus Christ was cleansing the temple, some Jews asked Jesus Christ: "What sign have you to show us for doing this?" Jesus Christ answered them, "Destroy this temple and in three days I will raise it up." (Jn 2:19) After the resurrection of Jesus Christ, the disciples understood that He allegorically spoke of the temple in terms of His own body (Jn 2:22). This saying of Jesus Christ implied that He knew the price He had to pay in order to cleanse the temple. He paid the price of cleansing the temple by His blood on the cross.

Conclusion

The gospel writers wrote the works and words of Jesus Christ, about fifty years after His death on the cross, and after His physical resurrection on the Easter Sunday. They reflected on the cleansing of the temple; and they saw in Jesus Christ how He was consumed by the zeal for God's work and for God's temple. They remembered what was prophesied about the Messiah was fulfilled in the words and works of Jesus Christ.

Recommended Hymns from the Methodist Hymnal

84   'All glory, laud, and honour'

192   'Ride on, ride on in majesty!'

836   'Hosanna, loud hosanna,'

837   'Children of Jerusalem'

Recommended Responsive Reading from A Worship Manual for Scriptural or Methodist Order of Service

90 (pp. 214-215).

Endnotes

[1] Lewis W. Spitz, The Renaissance and Reformation Movements, (Chicago: Rand McNally & Company, 1971) pp. 27-28.

[2] Lewis W. Spitz, op. cit., pp. 33-35.

[3] Lewis W. Spitz op. cit., pp. 328-340.

Chapter - 22

Titles of the Sermon

'Unpreventable Following of Jesus Christ'

'Fulfilment of God's Plan in spite of Human Barriers.'

Scripture

John 12:1-19

Exodus 23:14-17; 34:23

Deuteronomy 16:16

Matthew 12:1-14, 26-28; 13:53-56; 15:2-6; 21:10; 22:16-17, 22:21-28, 34-40

Mark 3:1-6

Luke 6:6-11; 10:25-28, 30-37; 19:38-40

John 11:48; 12:13, 19, 20, 23-24

Text: John 12:19

A Few Versions of the Text, John 12:19

The Pharisees therefore said among themselves, "You see that you are accomplishing nothing, Look, the world has gone after him!" *The New King James Version*

The Pharisees therefore said to each other, Perceive ye how ye prevail nothing? Behold, the world is gone after him. *Explanatory Notes upon the New Testament*

The Pharisees then said to one another, "You see that you can do nothing; look, the world has gone after him. " *Revised Standard Version*

So the Pharisees said to one another, "See, this is getting us nowhere. Look how the whole world has gone after him!" *New International Version*

The Pharisees said to one another, 'You see you are doing no good at all; why, all the world has gone after him!' *The New English Bible*

Then the Pharisees said to each other, "We've lost. Look - the whole world has gone after him!" *The Living Bible Illustrated*

The Pharisees said to each other, "This is getting us nowhere. Look! The whole world is following him!" *God's Word*

Introduction

It is a historical fact that Christianity became a universal faith through the evangelical work of the missionaries, who were foreigners. St. Paul was a Jew, converted to Christian faith; he became a missionary to the Gentiles or non-Jews. He established many churches at various cities such as Corinth, Rome, Philippie, Galatia, Colossae, and Thessalonica. He was taken as a prisoner to Rome. David Livingstone (19 March 1813-1 May1873), who was white by race, went to Africa as a missionary; and blacks embraced Christianity. R. G. Wilder (unknown dates), and William Carey (17 August 1769- 9June1834), who were white, went to India as missionary; and browns embraced Christianity. James Hudson Taylor (21 May1832-3 June 1905), who was white, went to China as a missionary; and yellows embraced Christianity. These outstanding missionaries and other missionaries were the foreigners, propagating the gospel to all races of humanity.

Missionaries, being foreigners, were not received well by the natives. The missionaries had to face many difficulties. People were not ready to hear them, and receive a faith of the foreigners. The missionaries had to be patient and courageous in spreading the gospel. Once a person was converted to Christianity, he or she was able to bring his immediate family, relatives, and friends to learn about Christian faith. This is how the number of the converts grew. But it was a very slow process.

The missionary work brought social, religious, and political changes in various lands. The missionaries were the spiritual leaders. Their leadership was initially rejected by the natives. But their leadership and contributions to the well-being of the people were recognized by native Christians and other people of the lands, because of the missionary works in the fields of education, medicine, and charity.

Introduction of the Text

At the initial stage, the spiritual leadership of Jesus Christ was not accepted by His people, the Jews. The Pharisees, the religious leaders of the Jews, opposed Jesus Christ at all times. They did not wish the people to be followers of Jesus Christ. But there came a time, when the Pharisees could do nothing to prevent people from following Jesus Christ. They said to each other, saying:

> **You see that you can do nothing; look, the world has gone after him.**
> (Jn 12:19)

This is the text of our meditation now.

The Context of the Text

When Lazarus died, many Jews had come to Bethany to console Martha and Mary, sisters of Lazarus. The body of Lazarus was kept in a tomb. On the fourth day, after the death of Lazarus, Jesus Christ went to see the bereaved family. He met Martha first. Martha went to call her Sister Mary, telling her that Jesus, the teacher, had arrived. Mary went to see Jesus Christ. She was weeping; and many Jews were also weeping with her. Jesus Christ was deeply moved by their weeping. Jesus Christ went to the tomb, following Martha, Mary, and other Jews. He raised Lazarus from the dead, in the presence of the people.

Many Jews believed in Jesus Christ because of this miracle. Some of the Jews went to the Pharisees; and told them about the miracle. They were concerned about the safety of the temple and of their nation. They thought, "If we let him go on thus, everyone will believe in Jesus, and the Romans will come and destroy both our holy place and our nation." (Jn 11:48) The Romans were ruling Palestine. They thought of the Jews as fanatics. If they would come to know that people were following their leader Jesus Christ in order to revolt against the Roman power, the Roman authority would destroy the temple at Jerusalem and the Jews of Palestine. In order to avoid that political crisis, the Pharisees thought to kill Jesus. Jesus Christ somehow suspected a plot against His life; He, therefore, did not go openly among the Jews thence.

Jesus Christ and His disciples went to Ephraim; they went back to Bethany, six days before the Passover. When the Jews learned that Jesus Christ returned to Bethany, they went to see Jesus Christ and Lazarus. Because of Lazarus being raised from the dead, many Jews believed in Jesus as a prophet of God.

On the Sabbath day, a crowd from Bethany learned that Jesus Christ was going to Jerusalem; they wanted to recognize the Messiahship or spiritual Kingship of Jesus Christ. They formed a procession; and put Jesus at the centre of the procession. The crowd broke the branches of trees; and spread them on the way of Jesus Christ. The crowd was shouting in honour of Jesus Christ, saying:

> Blessed is the King who comes in the name of the Lord! Peace in heaven and glory in the highest! (Lk. 19:38)

There was another crowd at Jerusalem. The crowd learned that Jesus Christ raised Lazarus from the dead; and that Jesus Christ was entering Jerusalem on the Sabbath day. They wished to welcome Jesus Christ in Jerusalem. They took branches of palm trees; and went to meet Jesus Christ, shouting:

> Hosanna! Blessed is he who comes in the name of the Lord, even the king of Israel. (Jn 12:13)

These two crowds brought Jesus Christ from Bethany to Jerusalem. They were shouting Hosanna to Jesus Christ. When the Pharisees came to know about the triumphal entry of Jesus Christ into Jerusalem, they said to one another:

> You see that you can do nothing; look, the world has gone after him. (Jn 12:19)

This is the text of our meditation, within its historical setting.

An Analysis of the Text

This text has two ideas. (A) The first idea is that the Pharisees said to one another, "You see that you can do nothing."

(B) The second idea is that the Pharisees saw the world had gone after Jesus Christ.

Exposition of the Ideas of the Text

(A) The first idea of the text is that the Pharisees said to one another, "You see that you can do nothing." It means that the Pharisees were blaming and criticising one another that they were incapable of doing anything to prevent the people from following Jesus Christ. They became helpless at this time. This implies that the Pharisees used many devices to prevent the people from following Jesus Christ. Let us study their devices.

(a) The Pharisees and Sadducees, who were the religious leaders of the Jews, devised many ways to prevent the people following Jesus Christ. Their first method was to ask intricate questions to Jesus Christ in the presence of the people in order to test His knowledge about the scripture and to prove the people that Jesus Christ was not knowledgeable about the scripture. Sadducees did not believe in the physical resurrection. They asked Jesus Christ a question:

> Teacher, Moses said, 'If a man dies, having no children, his brother must marry the widow, and raise up children for his brother.' Now there were seven brothers among us; the first married, and died, and having no children left his wife to his brother. So too the second and third, down to the seventh. In the resurrection, therefore, to which seven will she be wife? For they all had her. (Mt. 22:23-28)

Jesus Christ told the Sadducees that they did not know the scripture nor the power of God. He told them that after resurrection, nobody marries; and God is the God of the living. The crowd was impressed by the teaching of Jesus. (Mt. 22:23)

After this event, one of the Pharisees asked Jesus Christ a question in order to test the knowledge of Jesus Christ. He asked, "Teacher, which is the great commandment in the law?" Jesus Christ answered him correctly (Mt. 22:34-40).

On another occasion, with the same intention, a Pharisee asked a question to Jesus Christ, "Teacher, what shall I do to inherit eternal life? Jesus Christ asked two questions to him and he answered his own questions (Lk. 10:25-28). The same lawyer asked Jesus Christ, "And who is my neighbour?" (Lk. 10:30). Jesus Christ made him to answer his own question (Lk. 10:30-37)

(b) Secondly, the Pharisees and Sadducees were asking Jesus Christ the questions in order to trap him in religio-political dilemmas. The Pharisees sent their disciples to Jesus Christ, with Herodians. They said to Jesus Christ:

> Teacher, we know that you are true, and teach the way of God truthfully, and care for no man; for you do not regard the position of men. Tell us, then, what you think. Is it lawful to pay taxes to Caesar, or not? (Mt. 22:16-17)

Jesus Christ said to them, "Why put me to the test, you hypocrites? Show me the money for the tax?" When they showed him a coin, he asked them a question, "Whose likeness and inscription is this?" They answered, "Caesar's." Jesus Christ then told them:

> Render therefore to Caesar the things that are Caesar's, and to God the things that are God's. (Mt. 22:21)

They were impressed by His answer.

(c) Thirdly, the Pharisees were not ready to give proper credit to Jesus Christ for the miracles, which He performed in the presence of the people. They thought of Him using demonic power to take away evil spirits from the sick. When Jesus Christ healed dumb demoniac, people were amazed; and they said, "Can this be the Son of David? Or the Messiah?" But the Pharisees replied, "It is only Beelzebub, the prince of demons, that this man casts out demons." Jesus Christ heard this comment; and He responded to the Pharisees, in the following words:

> If Satan casts out Satan, he is divided against himself; how then will his kingdom stand? And if I cast out demons by Beelzebub, by whom do your sons cast them out?.. But if it is by the Spirit of God that I cast out demons, then the kingdom of God has come upon you. (Mt. 12:26-28)

(d) Fourthly, the Pharisees and Sadducees accused Jesus Christ of breaking the Sabbath when He healed the people on the Sabbaths. (Mt. 12:9-14; Mk 3:1-6; Lk. 6:6-11) They ignored the divine power that was working at the word of Jesus Christ. They wished to put Jesus Christ on trial for breaking the Sabbath.

(e) Fifthly, the Pharisees and Sadducees were watching Jesus Christ and His disciples very closely in order to accuse them for breaking the religious traditions of Jews (Mt. 15:2-6; 12:1-8) and to mobilize the crowd against Jesus Christ and His disciples.

(f) Finally, they tried to belittle the teaching and miracles of Jesus Christ by pointing out His humble origin. The Pharisees and Sadducees said to the people:

> Where did this man get this wisdom and these mighty works? Is not this the carpenter's son? Is not his mother called Mary? And are not his brothers James and Joseph and Simon and Judas? Are not all his sisters with us? Where then did this man get all this? (Mt. 13:53-56)

In short, the Pharisees and Sadducees did everything to prevent the people from following Jesus Christ. But they were not successful. Therefore, they said one another, "You see that you can do nothing." (Jn 12:19)

(B) The second idea of the text is that the Pharisees saw the world had gone after Jesus. The Pharisees admitted their failure to prevent the people from following Jesus Christ, on one hand; they witnessed that the world had gone after Jesus Christ, on the other hand.

We have to understand how the two crowds, one from Bethany, and another from Jerusalem, represented the world. God told the Jews to observe the Passover feast every year (Ex. 23:14-17; 34:23; Deut. 16:16). Therefore, it became a tradition that every adult male Jew, who lived within twenty miles of Jerusalem, was going to Jerusalem to celebrate the Passover feast, which was their national religious festival. At the time of the celebration of the Passover, Jews from every corner of the world made their way to Jerusalem. Those pilgrims, who came to Jerusalem from various parts of the world, heard about Jesus Christ raising Lazarus from the dead. Some of those pilgrims formed a crowd and went to see Jesus Christ. In this sense, the world had gone after Jesus Christ.

Jesus Christ was welcome by the crowd in the temple at Jerusalem on Sunday (i.e., Palm Sunday), five days before His crucifixion and a week before His physical resurrection. He was given a triumphant welcome by the crowd. He was welcome as the Messiah or the Son of David; and He approved the welcome given by the people. At the feast of the Passover feast, many Greeks were gathered in Jerusalem. Some of those Greeks wished to see Jesus Christ (Jn 12:20). When Jesus Christ heard about this request of the Greeks, He said to His disciples:

> The hour has come for the Son of man to be glorified. Truly, truly, I say to you, unless a grain of wheat falls into the earth and dies, it remains alone; but if it dies, it bears much fruit. (Jn 12:23-24)

Those Greeks, who wished to see Jesus Christ, were likely to be the Gentiles. They wanted to recognize the Messiahship or spiritual Kingship of Jesus Christ. Their going to see Jesus Christ was symbolic that the world was going after Jesus Christ. This is another meaning of the expression of the Pharisees that the world had gone after Jesus Christ.

Jesus Christ finally and publicly proclaimed His Messiahship in terms of being the spiritual King of Israel, who would be enthroned on the throne of King David (1002-962 B. C.) for ever. He played His part in arranging His triumphal entry into Jerusalem. People were filled with enthusiasm to proclaim Jesus as the anticipated Messiah. They were shouting: "Hosanna to the Son of David! Blessed is he who comes in the name of the Lord! Hosanna in the highest! " (Mt. 21:10) In that procession, there were some Pharisees; they did not approve the zealous shout of the crowd; they asked Jesus Christ to silence the crowd. Jesus Christ approved the shout; and He said to the Pharisees, "If they keep quiet, I tell you, these stones themselves will shout."

(Lk. 19:40) In other words, Jesus Christ told the Pharisees that no one could silence the people; no one could dampen their zeal; any effort to repress the proclamation of His spiritual Kingship would be futile. The Pharisees could do nothing to prevent the people from following Jesus Christ. They had to watch the whole world going after Jesus Christ.

Conclusion

The Pharisees and Sadducees did everything to prevent the people from following Jesus as the Messiah; but they were not successful. It was the will of God in Jesus Christ to proclaim His Messiahship or Saviourship to the world at the appropriate time. No human effort was going to stop the event which was planned by God. The will of the Lord God gets fulfilled under any circumstance.

Recommended Hymns from the Methodist Hymnal

84   'All glory, laud, and honour'

91   'All hail the power of Jesus' name'

116   'Sing we the King who is coming '

192   'Ride on, ride on in majesty'

836   'Hosanna, loud hosanna'

837   'Children of Jerusalem'

Recommended Responsive Reading from the Methodist Hymnal

45 (pp. 403f.).

Recommended Responsive Reading from A Worship Manual for Scriptural or Methodist Order of Service

39 (pp. 133-134).

Chapter - 23

Titles of the Sermon
'An Assurance to the People of God,'
'Prophesied Humility of the Messiah,'
'Humility of the Messiah in Jesus Christ.'

Scripture

John 12:12-18
Numbers 22:21-34
Psalms 89:35-36; 110:1
Isaiah 9:6-7
Zechariah 9:5-10
Matthew 9:20-23; 17:1-9; 21:1-11
Mark 1: 34; 5:25-38; 11:1-10; 10:42
Luke 4:41; 7:36-50; 8:43-48; 19:29-38; 22:25-27
John 12: 14-15; 13:1-15;
I Timothy 6:15
I Pet. 5:1-5
Revelation 3:21; 17:14; 19:16

Text: John 12:14-15

A Few Versions of the Text, John 12:14-15

Then Jesus, when He had found a young donkey, sat on it; as it is written, "Fear not, daughter of Zion; Behold, your King is coming, Sitting on a donkey's colt!" *The New King James Version*

And Jesus, having found a young ass, rode thereon; as is written, Fear not, daughter of Zion: behold, thy King cometh, sitting on as ass's colt. *Explanatory Notes Upon the New Testament*

And Jesus found a young ass and sat upon it; as it is written, "Fear not, daughter of Zion; behold, your king is coming, sitting on an ass's colt!" *Revised Standard Version*

And Jesus found a young donkey and sat upon it, as it is written, "Do not be afraid, O Daughter of Zion; see, your king is coming, seated on a donkey's colt!" *New International Version*

And Jesus found a donkey and mounted it, in accordance with the text of Scripture: 'Fear no more, daughter of Zion; see, your king is coming, mounted on as ass's colt!' *The New English Bible*

Jesus rode along on young donkey fulfilling the prophecy that said: "Don't be afraid of your King, people of Israel, for he will come to you meekly, sitting on a donkey's colt!" *The Living Bible Illustrated*

Jesus obtained a donkey and sat upon it, as Scripture says: "Don't be afraid, people of Zion! Your King is coming. He is riding on a donkey's colt!" *God's Word*

Introduction

The scripture tells us that Jesus Christ was not a man, a common man; but He was more than any man. He was the Messiah, the Son of God, and the saviour of the world. After His resurrection, He was acknowledged as the Lord of lords and King of kings, by the apostles of the Church. St. Paul wrote to Timothy, saying that Jesus Christ is the only Sovereign, the King of kings and Lord of lords. (I Tim. 6:15)

St Paul had used the title Lord to Jesus Christ in his letters to the churches (Rom. 4:24, 5:11, 6:23, 8:39, 13:14, 14:8; I Cor. 6:14, 8:6;

II Cor. 4:5; Gal. 6:14; Phil.2:11,3:8). St. Peter similarly addressed Jesus Christ "chief Shepherd" (I Pet. 5:4). This implies that Jesus Christ is the Lord of lords (II Pet. 1:11, 2:1). Apostle John also addressed Jesus Christ as Lord of lords and King of kings (Rev. 17:14; 19:16).

Introduction of the Text

The title "King" was used for the Messiah by the prophets. The Messiah would be the spiritual King of the Jews. He would be enthroned on the throne of King David forever (Ps. 89:35-36; Is. 9:7). He would also be enthroned with the LORD God (Ps. 110:1; Rev. 3:21). Prophet Zechariah (his period of prophecy 520-486 B.C.) had prophesied how the spiritual King of the Jews would enter Jerusalem, in the following words:

> Rejoice greatly, O daughter of Zion! Shout aloud, O daughter of Jerusalem! Lo, your king comes to you; triumphant and victorious is he, humble and riding on an ass, on a colt the foal of an ass. (Zec. 9:9)

The LORD God revealed to prophet Zechariah how the Messiah would enter Jerusalem with humility; and that the Messiah would use a colt, a young donkey to ride. Jesus Christ knew about the prophecy about Him, which was remained to be fulfilled. This prophecy about the Messiah was fulfilled, when Jesus Christ used a young donkey to enter Jerusalem and to proclaim His heavenly kingship to the people in Jerusalem. Concerning this event, St. John wrote as follows:

> **And Jesus found a young ass and sat upon it; as it is written, "Fear not, daughter of Zion; behold, your king is coming, sitting on an ass's colt!"** (John 12:14-15)

This is the text of our meditation today.

The Context of the Text

Jesus Christ was the Messiah, the Christ, or the anointed one of the LORD God. It was the plan of God to send Jesus Christ into the world to work out salvation for mankind.

When Jesus Christ came into the world to do the appointed work of the Messiah, He did not wish to declare that He was the Messiah, at the beginning of His ministry. He forbade evil spirits to say that He was the Son of God. (Lk. 4:41; Mk 1: 34) He forbade His disciples, Peter, John, and James not to declare His Messiahship to anyone, after He was transfigured on a mountain. (Mt. 17:1-9; Lk. 9:28-36). He kept this secret during His preaching and healing ministry.

Jesus Christ was waiting for an appropriate time to declare that He was the Messiah. He made an arrangement for a colt with one of His followers. When Jesus Christ and His disciples reached Bethphage, the Mount of Olives, He sent two disciples to the village and told them that they would find a colt with a donkey, untie them and bring them to Him. If anybody would ask them an explanation for their action, they should tell them that the Lord had need of them; and He would return them immediately. (Mt. 21:2-3) His disciples found a cold and a donkey. They brought them to Jesus Christ. He used the colt to carry Him to Jerusalem in order to declare His heavenly kingship or Messiahship to the people in Jerusalem.

The disciples of Jesus Christ put their garment on the colt and Jesus Christ sat on the colt. The people formed a procession. They spread their garments on the road; and they cut branches of trees and spread on the road. They were shouting, "Hosanna to the son of David! Blessed is he who comes in the name of the Lord! Hosanna in the highest! (Mt. 21:9) Jesus Christ approved the shout of the people. As far this arrangement was concerned, St. John commented on it, saying:

> And Jesus found a young ass and sat upon it; as it is written, "Fear not, daughter of Zion; behold, your king is coming, sitting on an ass's colt!" (John 12:14-15)

This is the text, within its historical background.

An Analysis of the Text

This text has three ideas. (A) The first idea is that Jesus Christ found a young donkey and He sat upon it.

(B) The second idea is a caution issued to the people of Jerusalem that they should not be afraid because their King was coming to them.

(C) The third idea is that their King would come to them, seated on a donkey's colt.

An Exposition of the Ideas of the Text:

(A) The first idea of the text is that Jesus Christ found a young donkey; and He sat upon it. Two disciples of Jesus Christ went to a town and found a colt with a donkey; and they brought them to Jesus Christ. Other disciples put their clothes on the colt and made Jesus Christ sit on the colt, on which no man had sat before.

Jesus Christ knew that He was the Messiah, the everlasting spiritual King of the Jews. In the ancient world, kings used to ride on horses and carry swords with them. They were the supreme commanders of the armies. They had all powers; and the people were subjected to them. They were ruling the people with authority and power. The kings of the Jews were similar with the rest of the kings of other nations. As the Messiah was the spiritual King of the Jews, He would be different from all other kings. He would not be proud and arrogant, unduly demonstrating His power and authority. On the contrary, He would be humble and serving the people. He would not act like a warrior, ready to kill his opponents and subdue them. He would be the prince of peace. Prophet Isaiah prophesied about the Messiah, saying:

> For to us a child is born, to us a son is given; and the government will be upon his shoulders, and his name will be called 'Wonderful Counsellor, Mighty God, Everlasting Father, Prince of Peace. (Is. 9:6)

The Messiah would be called the Prince of Peace. He would not be a king of wars and destruction. His kingdom would be everlasting. His kingdom would not be temporary. He would rule the people with justice and righteousness. He would not rule the people with disregard toward justice and righteousness.

Jesus Christ was humble. His disciples respected Him as a great teacher and the Messiah. Nevertheless, He washed the feet of His disciples and taught them humility by His own example (Jn 13:1-12). After washing the feet of His disciples, Jesus Christ said to them:

> You call me Teacher and Lord; and you are right, for so I am. If I then, your Lord and Teacher, have washed your feet, you ought to wash one another's feet. For I have given you an example, that you also should do as I have done to you. (Jn 13:13-15)

Jesus Christ wanted His disciples to be humble as He was. He once exhorted them, saying:

> The kings of the Gentiles exercise lordship over them; and those in authority over them are called benefactors. But not so with you; rather let the greatest among you become as the youngest, and the leader as one who serves. For which is greater, one who sits at table, or one who serves? Is it not the one who sits at table? But I am among you as one who serves. (Lk. 22:25-27)

A colt symbolizes humility of the rider. Jesus Christ used the colt to express His humility.

(B) The second idea the text is a caution issued to the people of Jerusalem that they should not be afraid because their King was coming to them. Kings represented power and authority; and all people were subjected to them. Kings were the absolute authority on the people. They were highly respected by the people. Therefore, it had been a practice to issue a warning about the coming of the king so that all vehicles and pedestrians move away from the way of the king. If anyone would disobey the order, he or she would be punished, even by death penalty. People were afraid of their kings. Messiah was the King of kings and Lord of lords. If people were afraid to come into the presence of the worldly kings, they should be more afraid of the King of kings. But Messiah was not like other kings. He was always with the people. People of all kinds, such as Sadducees, Pharisees, the pious leaders of the Jews, tax collectors, sinners, and Heathens surrounded Him. He was touched by everyone. Recall an event when a sinful woman touched the feet of Jesus Christ, while He was eating at Simon's house. (Lk. 7:36-50) Recall another event when a woman, with an issue of blood, who made a way through a crowd, touched the hem of Jesus' garment; and was healed instantly. (Mt. 9:20-23; Mk 5:25-34; Lk. 8:43-48) He did not shun the touch of ordinary people and sinners. He talked with them and ate with them. He showed them love and affection. He was the friend of sinners and every sick person. Jesus

Christ, the Messiah, was the loving and caring King; therefore, the people should not to be afraid of Him. Because of His close contact with the people, they should rejoice and shout aloud when they would welcome their King of kings or the Messiah. Jesus Christ was accorded a royal welcome when the crowd and children were shouting Hosanna to the Lord Jesus. The event of welcoming Jesus Christ was filled with zeal and enthusiasm. This was the first palm Sunday.

(C) The third idea of the text is that their King would come to them, seated on a donkey's colt. Jesus Christ used the colt in order to fulfil the prophecy of prophet Zachariah, which was quoted before and we refer it again:

> Rejoice greatly, O daughter of Zion! Shout aloud, O daughter of Jerusalem!
> Lo, your king comes to you; triumphant and victorious is he, humble and
> riding on an ass, on a colt the foal of an ass. (Zec. 9:9)

The anticipated Messiah would not use a horse but rather use a colt. There are some differences between a horse and a donkey. Horses run faster than donkeys, therefore they were used in the battle-field in the olden days. Donkeys are stronger than horses, therefore they are used to transfer goods and people. Recall an event when Balaam saddled his donkey and went to see the princes of Moab, against the will of God. God sent an angel to strike Balaam. The donkey saw the angel; and avoided the angel. Balaam struck the ass third time; and the ass spoke to Balaam. (Num. 22:21-34) Horses represent war and pride; and donkeys represent peace and humility. The Messiah, who was the prince of peace and humility, used a colt to declare His kingship for peace and humility.

Jesus Christ was the anticipated Messiah; people were waiting for His coming that He may restore peace and righteousness to Jews and the Gentiles. According the prophecy of Zechariah, the Messiah or the Christ would use a colt of donkey. Therefore Jesus Christ used a colt of a donkey in order to fulfil the prophecy.

Conclusion

When Jesus Christ entered Jerusalem to declare His Messiahship or Christhood, He used a colt of donkey to declare that He was the prince of peace and righteousness. The crowd and children welcomed the Jesus Christ as the King; and they shouted hosanna to welcome Him. They were filled with zeal. We, the followers of Jesus Christ, should have the similar zeal and enthusiasm to declare the supreme Kingship of Jesus Christ.

Recommended Hymns from the Methodist Hymnal

84   'All glory, laud, and honour'

91   'All hail the power of Jesus' name'

116   'Sing we the King who is coming'

192   'Ride on, ride on in majesty!'

836   'Hosanna, loud hosanna'

Recommended Responsive Reading from A Worship Manual for Scriptural or Methodist Order of Service

90 (pp. 214-215).

PART - III

Jesus as the Messiah at His Resurrection:
The Ressurection of Jesus Christ and its
Implications for Believers:
Eight Textual Sermons on the Easter Sunday

Chapter - 24

Titles of the Sermon
'Removal of a Big Stone,'
"Removal of a Heavy Stone,'
'Knowing Life Beyond the Grave,'
'Questions About Resurrection,'
'Questions About the Resurrection of the Lord Jesus Christ,'
'Entering the Empty Tomb.'

Scripture
Mark 16:1-8
Psalms 16:9-10; 49:14-15; 71:20-21
Hosea 13:4
Matthew 17:20-21; 28:2, 5-10
Mark 8:30-31; 16:40-47
Luke 9:22; 18:27; 24:5-6
John 20:19
I Corinthians 15:12-13
I Thessalonians 4:13-14

Text: Mark 16:3

A Few Versions of the Text, Mark 16:3
And they said among themselves, 'Who will roll away the stone from the door of the tomb for us?' *The New King James Version*

And they said one to another, Who shall roll us away the stone from the door of the sepulchre? (for it was very great.) *Explanatory Notes Upon the New Testament*

And they were saying to one another, 'Who will roll away the stone for us from the door of the tomb?' *Revised Standard Version*

and they asked each other, 'Who will roll the stone away from the entrance of the tomb?' *New International Version*

They were wondering among themselves who would roll away the stone for them from the entrance of the tomb, *The New English Bible*

On the way they were discussing how they could ever roll aside the huge stone from the entrance. *The Living Bible Illustrated*

They said to one another, 'Who will roll away the stone for us from the entrance of the tomb?' *God's Word*

Introduction

Easter Sunday is observed by all Christians in the world, because it is very significant Sunday in the life of the believers and in the life of Jesus Christ. The observance of this Sunday reminds the believers of the victory of Jesus Christ over death and sin. It gives them the assurance of their bodily resurrection at the second coming of the Lord Jesus Christ. The belief in the physical resurrection is very vital for the spiritual life of the believers. Concerning this important matter, St. Paul wrote to the Corinthians:

> Now if Christ is preached as raised from the dead, how can some of you say that there is no resurrection of the dead? But if there is no resurrection of the dead, then Christ has not been raised; if Christ has not been raised, then our preaching is in vain and your faith is in vain. We are even found to be misrepresenting God, because we testified of God that he raised Christ, whom he did not raise if it is true that the dead are not raised. For if the dead are not raised, then Christ has not been raised. If Christ has not been raised, your faith is futile and you are still in your sins. Then those also who have fallen asleep in Christ have perished. If for this life only we have hoped in Christ, we are of all men most to be pitied. But in fact Christ has been raised from the dead, the first fruits of those who have fallen asleep. For as by a man came death, by a man has come also the resurrection of the dead.

> For as in Adam all die, so also in Christ shall all be made alive. But each in his own order: Christ the first fruits, then at his coming those who belong to Christ. (I Cor. 15:12-23)

The belief of Christians in their bodily resurrection is linked with the physical resurrection of Christ, the Messiah. The LORD God had foretold about the bodily resurrection of the Messiah through King David (1002-962 B. C.), His servant, when he was inspired by the divine Spirit to write these words:

> Therefore my heart is glad, and my soul rejoices, my body also dwells secure. For thou dost not give me up to Sheol, or let thy godly one see the Pit. (Ps. 16:9-10)

Again, King David wrote these words concerning the resurrection of the Messiah:

> Like the sheep they are appointed for Sheol; Death shall be their shepherd; straight to the grave they descend, and their form shall waste away; Sheol shall be their home. But God will ransom my soul from the power of Sheol, for he will receive me. (Ps. 49:14-15 cf. Ps. 71:2-21; Hos. 13:4)

When Peter, a disciple of Jesus Christ, told Jesus, "You are the Christ." (Mk 8:30), Jesus Christ began to tell them about His destiny, saying:

> The Son of man must suffer many things, and be rejected by the elders and the chief priests and the scribes, and be killed, and after three days rise again. (Mk 8:31 cf. Lk. 9:22)

Jesus Christ foretold about His bodily resurrection to His disciples very plainly. But they forgot about it. It was difficult for them to believe in the bodily resurrection of Jesus Christ.

Introduction of the Text

As the disciples and followers of Jesus Christ did not believe in the bodily resurrection of Jesus Christ, the Messiah, they went to see His dead body or corpse, resting in the tomb, on the third day after His death. Mary Magdalene, Mary the mother of James, and Salome bought the spices when the Sabbath was passed, after 6:00 p. m. on Saturday. They went to the tomb on the Sunday morning. They went very early at the sun rise (Mk 16:2). They wanted to anoint the dead body of Jesus with the spices. As they were going toward the tomb, they said to one another:

> **Who will roll away the stone for us from the door of the tomb?**
> (Mk 16:3)

This is the text of our meditation now.

The Context of the Text

The aforesaid ladies saw the death of Jesus on the cross on the past Friday (Mk 16:40-41). Christians call that Friday, "Good Friday." They also saw Joseph Arimathea, a respected member of the Jewish council, wrapped dead body of Jesus Christ in the linen shroud; and kept in the tomb in the garden; and then he rolled a heavy stone on the door of the tomb (Mk 16: 43-47). Those ladies, who were eyewitnesses to the death and burial of Jesus Christ, went to the tomb on the Sunday morning to do the final rite to the corpse of Jesus Christ. As they had seen the heavy stone rolled on the door of the tomb, they asked a question among themselves:

> Who will roll away the stone for us from the door of the tomb? (Mk 16:3)

They asked this question among themselves, because they were not that much physically strong to roll away the heavy stone from the door of the tomb. Without removing the stone they would not enter the tomb to put spices on the body of Jesus Christ. This is the context of the text.

An Analysis of the Text

This text has two ideas. (A) The first idea is that the ladies asked the question among themselves as to who would roll away the stone for them from the door of the tomb, because they were expecting somebody to remove the stone.

(B) The second idea implied that the ladies were expecting to see the dead body of Jesus Christ in the tomb.

Exposition of the Ideas of the Text

(A) The first idea is that the ladies asked the question among themselves as to who would roll away the stone for them from the door of the tomb, because they were expecting somebody to remove the stone. The ladies raised the question, "Who will roll away the stone for us from the door of the tomb?" among themselves, before they reached the tomb, wherein the body of Jesus Christ was kept.

The stones, which were rolled over the doors of tombs, were generally heavy, weighing about four tons. Those ladies knew that they would not be able to roll back the stone even though they would apply their strength collectively; they needed extra help to roll away the stone from the door of the tomb. Nevertheless, they did not turn back in order to get somebody to help them; they continued their journey toward the tomb. They might have thought that they would wait at the tomb till the disciples or followers of Jesus Christ would show at the tomb in order to do the final service to the dead body of Jesus. They might have prayed in their minds, asking God to send someone to help them remove the stone.

When they reached the tomb, they were surprised to see that the stone was already rolled away from the door of the tomb. St. Matthew explained how that took place, in these words:

> There was a great earthquake; for an angel of the LORD descended from heaven and came and rolled back the stone, and sat upon it. (Mt. 28:2)

It was a miracle; it was a divine or supernatural act. Jesus Christ once said, "What is impossible with men is possible with God." (Lk.18:27) God is always ready and able to remove heavy obstacles in the path of His children, when they earnestly pray to Him for removal of the obstacles. There is a power in the prayers of the righteous. Jesus Christ taught to His disciples about the power of prayer when He said:

> For truly, I say to you, if you have faith as a grain of mustard seed, you will say to this mountain, 'Move from here to there', and it will move; and nothing will be impossible to you. (Mt. 17:20-21)

The angel or angels of the LORD removed the stone away from the door of the tomb. The angels did not do for Jesus Christ. There was no need of it for Jesus Christ, because God had raised Him from the dead. The resurrected Lord Jesus Christ had no more physical limitations; He could go through thick barriers. For an example, when the disciples were sitting in a room, behind a closed door, the resurrected Lord Jesus Christ appeared to them in the room (Jn 20:19).

The angels rolled away the stone for the sake of the faithful ladies, who could not enter the tomb, if the stone had remained at the door. The stone was rolled away for the sake of the ladies that they could enter the tomb and see what had happened to the body of Jesus Christ. God wanted to show the ladies the evidence of His power in raising His Son from the dead. He wanted to show them His faithfulness in keeping His promise to raise the Messiah, the Christ, from the dead. He wanted to show them how He ultimately made His Son victorious over death and sins of the world.

The resurrection of Jesus Christ is the most unique historical phenomenon. The founders of all other religions are dead. Only Jesus Christ was raised from the dead and to be the ever living Lord of all. This is a uniqueness of Jesus Christ and of the Christian faith. There are other distinctiveness of these. The empty tomb of Jesus Christ is a historical evidence of the resurrection of the Lord Jesus Christ. As a pilgrim to the holy land, I bear a witness to the empty tomb where the dead body of Jesus Christ was kept.

This historical fact has a bearing on the belief in the bodily resurrection of the believers. About this issue, St. Paul wrote to the Thessalonians:

> But we would not have you ignorant, brethren, concerning those who are asleep, that you may not grieve as others do who have no hope. For since we believe that Jesus died and rose again, even so, through Jesus, God will bring with him those who have fallen asleep. (I Thes. 4:13-14)

The stone at the door of the tomb of Jesus Christ stood for a thick barrier between lifeless existence in grave and the eternal life beyond the grave. People had no knowledge about what would happen after their physical death. Atheistic and agnostics believe that there is no life beyond the grave; for them death is the final destiny of life.

But thanks be to God the Almighty, who showed us that there is the everlasting life beyond the grave, by raising Jesus Christ from the dead. Removal of the stone from the door of Jesus' tomb was meant to remove our ignorance about the life beyond the grave. It was highly impossible for man to know this divine mystery. But God then revealed to mankind the knowledge about our final destiny. The stone was removed by the will of God. It was God's command to His angels to help the mankind know the eternal life beyond the grave.

(B) The second idea implied that the ladies were expecting to see the dead body of Jesus Christ in the tomb. The ladies entered the tomb to look for the dead body of Jesus Christ. They did not find the body of Jesus Christ in the tomb; therefore, they were perplexed with the questions such as: What did happen to His body? Who did take His body away? Where could they find His body? And who could help them find the body of Jesus Christ? While they were in that mental frame of questioning, two men stood by them in dazzling apparel. The ladies were frightened by the sudden appearance of those two angels. They bowed their faces to the ground so that they could avoid looking at the two angels. One of the angels said to them:

> Do not be afraid; for I know that you seek Jesus who was crucified. He is not here; for he has risen, as he said. Come, see the place where he lay. (Mt. 28:5-6)

Then the second angel said to them:

> Why do you seek the living among the dead? Remember how he told you, while he was still in Galilee, that the Son of man must be delivered into the hands of sinful men, and be crucified, and on the third day rise. (Lk. 24:5-6)

The angel asked the question, "Why do you seek the living among the dead?" to the ladies in order that they might remember what Jesus Christ told them about His physical resurrection. The angel asked this question; and repeated the words of Jesus Christ to them; and made it easy for them to remember the words of Jesus Christ. Then they believed in the resurrection of Jesus Christ, as announced by the angels.

The question, "why do you seek the living among the dead?" implies that there is no need to seek the living among the dead. That kind of search would be foolish from a human point of view, because living and dead are opposite realities. Moreover, that kind of search would question God's promises, His power, and His faithfulness to raise Messiah from the dead, from a spiritual point of view.

Having announced the good news of the resurrection of Jesus Christ, the angel asked them to do the following thing:

> Then go quickly and tell his disciples that he has been risen from the dead, and behold, he is going before you to Galilee; there you will see him. Lo, I have told you. (Mt. 28:7)

The ladies quickly departed from the tomb with fear and joy; and they were running to tell the good news to the disciples of Jesus Christ. On their way, Jesus Christ met them and said, "Hail!" or victory or triumph. Then they worshipped the risen Lord (Mt. 28:9-10). Jesus said to them:

> Do not be afraid; go and tell my brethren to go to Galilee, and they will see me. (Mt.28:10)

Conclusion

The good news of the resurrection of Jesus Christ was announced by the angels. Jesus Christ confirmed the news of His resurrection when He appeared to the ladies. He asked the ladies to go and tell the other disciples that they should go to Galilee and see Jesus Christ there. The ladies were commissioned to witness the resurrection of the Lord Jesus Christ and to prepare His disciples to meet the resurrected Lord in Galilee.

The resurrection of Jesus Christ is a historical event. It is incredible but true. His resurrection is the evidence that Jesus Christ won victory over death and sin. As His physical resurrection was real, it gives hope to the believers that they would be resurrected at His second coming, and they will have victory over death and sin. Moreover, the believers have a hope in life beyond the grave; their spiritual destiny is to be with the ever living Lord Jesus Christ for ever.

Recommended Hymns from the Methodist Hymnal

204 'Christ the Lord is risen today;'

206 'Christ is risen! Hallelujah!'

210 'Christ Jesus lay in death's'

211 'Low in the grave He lay'

213 'Thine be the glory, risen, conquering'

230 'Rejoice and be glad! the '

235 'I know that my Redeemer lives-'

238 'My faith looks up to Thee;'

661 'Come, let us with our Lord arise'

Recommended Responsive Reading from A Worship Manual for Scriptural or Methodist Order of Service

100 (pp.234-235).

Chapter - 25

Titles of the Sermon
'Search of the Living Among the Dead,'
'The Living Presence of Jesus Christ Among the Believers,'
'The Resurrection of Jesus Christ as an Act of God,'
'Supernatural Faith and Hope in the Resurrection of the Believers.'

Scripture
Luke 24:1-12
Genesis 17:8
Exodus 3:1-12; 29:45
Leviticus 26:12
Joshua 3:10
Psalms 16:9-11
Isaiah 53:3-5
Hosea 6:1-2
Matthew 16:15-16, 20; 27:57-61
Mark 15:43-47
Luke 1:8-22, 26-34; 2:8-14; 23:50-56; 24:6-7
John 20:2,15
II Corinthians 5:16-17
Acts 1:3; 7:5
Romans 8:9-14
I Corinthians 3:16-17; 6:19; 15:4

II Corinthians 6:16

Philippians 2:7-8

Hebrews 9:24

Text: Luke 24:5

A Few Versions of the Text, Luke 24:5

Then, as they were afraid and bowed their faces to the earth, they said to them, 'Why do you seek the living among the dead?' *The New King James Version*

And as they afraid, and bowed their faces to the earth, they said to them, Why seek ye the living among the dead? *Explanatory Notes Upon the New Testament*

And as they were frightened and bowed their faces to the ground, the men said to them, 'Why do you seek the living among the dead?' *Revised Standard Version*

In their fright the women bowed with their faces to the ground, but the men said to them, 'Why do you look for the living among the dead?' *New International Version*

They were terrified, and stood with eyes cast down, but the men said, 'Why search among the dead for one who lives?' *New English Bible*

The women were terrified and bowed low before them. Then the men asked, 'Why are you looking in a tomb for someone who is alive?' *The Living Bible Illustrated*

The women were terrified and bowed to the ground. The men asked the women, 'Why are you looking among the dead for the living one?' *God's Word*

Introduction

I was listening to the radio talk show on the radio station 'C. H. M. L.' in Hamilton, Ontario, in April 1994. The host of the talk show was asking questions to the listeners in order to get their opinions on the celebration of Easter. He asked the following questions: Why do all have holidays on the Good Friday and Easter Sunday? Is not this practice of observing Christian holidays discriminatory? Are we not giving preference to Christian holidays over holidays of other religions? Some listeners said that they would like to enjoy those Christian holidays without giving them any religious significance. They associate Easter holiday with Easter Bunny and not with Jesus Christ. Some Christian listeners said that this is a Christian country; and we should maintain our religious holidays. Some Christian listeners predicted that all Christian holidays will be taken away; and they will be substituted by holidays of other religions. Some Christians told that Christians should get involved in secular politics in order to maintain Christian holidays and Christian values in this country.

Canada and the U. S. A. are countries where people are given a right of religious expression. In these two countries, people have a right to choose their faiths and practise them; there is the policy of religious tolerance. It is a well-known fact that Christians are not allowed to propagate, preach, and practise their religion where Hindus and Muslims are ruling the countries. Observance of Christian holidays in these two countries cannot be considered discriminatory, where other religions are allowed their free expression. Christians should maintain Christian holidays and biblical values in these two countries even through political involvement.

Easter Bunny and Easter eggs are parts of commercialization of Easter; but they do not convey the real meaning of Easter. Easter is not a holiday just for enjoyment and rest. It has a unique religious significance for Christians. It is a happy or joyous celebration for Christians, because it reminds them of the spiritual victory of the Lord Jesus Christ over death and sin, due to His physical resurrection from the dead. Belief in the resurrection of Jesus Christ from the dead makes Christianity a unique faith among other religions. This doctrine also challenges Christians to lead a victorious life over sin and temptations and to aspire for the first event of resurrection.

Introduction of the Text

The resurrection of Jesus Christ had given boldness to the apostles to teach and practise Christian faith, when there was fierce opposition to proclaim the gospel of Jesus Christ. The apostles and the followers had seen the resurrected Lord Jesus Christ. Angels bore a witness to the fact of the resurrection of Jesus Christ. They encouraged the followers of Jesus Christ to tell about the incredible and unique fact of the resurrection of Jesus Christ. The ladies, who went to the tomb to do final service to the dead body of Jesus Christ, saw angels. How those ladies responded to the very impressive appearance of the angels; and what an angel said to them is given in the words as follow:

> **and as they were frightened and bowed their faces to the ground, the men said to them, 'Why do you seek the living among the dead?**
> (Luke 24:5)

This is the text of our meditation now.

The Context of the Text

Jesus Christ (4B. C. -A. D.30) was crucified and dead on Friday. This event was witnessed by some of the followers and disciples of Jesus Christ. Mary Magdalene, Mary, the mother of James the younger and of Joseph (Mt. 55-56), Salome (Mk 16:1; Lk. 24:10), and Joanna (Lk. 24:10), who ministered Jesus Christ in Galilee, came from Galilee to Jerusalem. They saw Jesus Christ crucified and dead on the cross. After the death of Jesus Christ, Joseph of Arimathea went to Pontius Pilate (in the office, A. D.26-36) and asked for the body of Jesus. He wrapped the body of Jesus Christ in a linen shroud; and put it in a tomb and rolled a stone against the door of the tomb. The ladies saw where the body of Jesus Christ kept by Joseph of Arimathea (Mt. 27:57-61; Mk 15:43-47; Lk. 23:50-56).

According to a Jewish custom, those ladies went to the tomb very early on Sunday to apply spices to the dead body of Jesus Christ. When they reached the tomb, they were surprised to notice that the stone was removed from the door of the tomb. They entered the tomb, looking for the dead body of Jesus Christ. They did not find the body; and they were wondering as to what happened to the body of Jesus Christ.

While the ladies were looking for the body of Jesus Christ, two men, wearing dazzling dresses, appeared to them in the tomb. They were the angels. The sudden and unexpected appearance of the two angles made the ladies bewildered; they were not able to look at the faces of the angels. They were looking at the ground. One of the angels asked them this question: "Why do you seek the living among the dead?" This is a part of the text. The whole text is given within its historical setting.

An Analysis of the Text

This text has two ideas. (A) The first idea is how the ladies responded to the sudden appearance of the angles. They were frightened and bowed their faces to the ground.

(B) The second idea is the question, which the angel asked them, "Why do you seek the living among the dead?"

Exposition of the Ideas of the Text

(A) The first idea of the text is how the ladies responded to the sudden appearance of the angles. They were frightened and bowed their faces to the ground. When the ladies did not find the dead body of Jesus Christ, they were perplexed. In that confused frame of mind, they saw two men standing by them in dazzling apparel. The dazzling apparel means shining clothes; and the tomb became lighted by the appearance of the two men, who were angels or supernatural beings. The ladies were doubly frightened. They had no courage to look into the faces of the two men. They bowed their faces to the ground. This gesture stands for reverence and awe to the superior, and especially to the heavenly beings or angels. This was a way how the ladies responded to the sudden appearance of the angels.

The angels are the supernatural beings; they are the messengers of the LORD God. God sent His messages through His angels. There are some events, recorded in the Bible, to tell us how persons responded to the appearance of angels.

(1) The angel of the LORD God appeared to Moses in the burning bush on the mountain of God, mount Sinai or mount Horeb (Ex. 3:1; 19:18). Moses was asked by the angel to remove his shoes, because he was standing on a holy ground; he was asked to be respectful in the presence of the servant of God (Ex. 3:1-12).

(2) An angel of the LORD God appeared to Zechariah to announce that his wife, Elizabeth, would be the mother of John the Baptist, the forerunner of the Messiah, he was fearful (Lk. 1:8-22).

(3) When an angel appeared to Mary to announce that she would be the mother of the Messiah, she was afraid (Lk. 1:26-34).

(4) When an angel appeared to the shepherds to give them a good news of the birth of the Messiah, they were filled with fear (Lk. 2:8-14).

These events confirm the reaction of the ladies who saw the angels in the tomb; they were fearful by the presence of the angels.

(B) The second idea of the text is the question, which the angel asked them, "Why do you seek the living among the dead?" In other words, the angel asked the ladies the reasons as to why they were seeking the body of Jesus Christ among the dead?

The ladies never thought of the resurrection of their Lord Jesus Christ. They saw that Lord Jesus Christ was dead on the cross; and his lifeless body was kept in the tomb. They did not give any reason in their reply to the question of the angel. We have to speculate those reasons.

(1) First, The ladies had a common knowledge that all beings on the earth, including human beings, are mortal; all human beings are subject to death; and no one is exempted from death; death is sure and inevitable to all beings. They thought of Jesus Christ as a man, subject to death in general. Some of the apostles thought of

Jesus Christ only as a man for a long time. Only after the death and resurrection of the Lord Jesus Christ, apostles thought of Him from a different point of view. St. Paul wrote to the Corinthians about how they once regarded Jesus Christ from a human point of view:

> From now on, therefore, we regard no one from a human point of view; even though we once regarded Christ from a human point of view, we regard him thus no longer. Therefore, if anyone is in Christ, he is a new creation; the old has passed away, behold the new has come. (II Cor. 5:16-17)

St. Paul's way of evaluating other Christians from a human point of view was changed, because he saw the divinity of Jesus Christ in Christians. He discovered the depth of divine humility in the death of the Son of God on the cross. Concerning this, he wrote to the Philippians:

> [Christ Jesus] emptied himself, taking the form of a servant, being born in the likeness of men. And being found in human form he humbled himself and became obedient unto death, even death on a cross. (Phi. 2:7-8)

(2) Secondly, the ladies had a common sense that a dead body is lifeless and motionless; a corpse does not move by itself, it stays permanently where it is laid. The ladies were expecting that the dead body of Jesus Christ would remain where it was placed; it was placed in the tomb, behind a huge stone. When they did not find the dead body of Jesus Christ in the tomb, they were perplexed. They were thinking that someone must have removed the body of their Lord and hid it somewhere (Jn 20:2). When Mary Magdalene was weeping outside the tomb, Jesus Christ appeared to her; but she mistook Him to be a gardener and said to Him, "Sir, if you have carried him away, tell me where you have laid him, and I will take him away." (Jn 20:15) Mary at this point did not believe that Jesus Christ would be raised from the dead. When Jesus Christ called her by her name, she recognized the voice of her teacher; and then she was convinced that Lord Jesus Christ was raised from the dead.

(3) Thirdly, the ladies had a common sense or perspective at the worldly events. The worldly events happen in terms of cause and effect sequence. The common sense philosophy of life does not look for miracles or supernatural intervention in the life-system; therefore, the ladies did not anticipate any miracle or extraordinary event as far the dead body of Jesus Christ was concerned. They were pleasantly surprised to see and know that Jesus Christ was raised from the dead.

(4) Fourthly, the common perspective of the ladies at the life caused them to forget what Jesus Christ had told them and other disciples about His suffering, death, and resurrection. Their common sense philosophy doubted the prophecy of Jesus Christ that He would be resurrected. The angel had to remind them of the words of Jesus Christ, saying:

> Remember how he told you, while he was still in Galilee, that the Son of man must be delivered into the hands of sinful men, and be crucified and on the third day rise. (Lk. 24:6-7)

This reminder of the two angel to the ladies should take us into a historical background why Jesus Christ had to prophesy about His crucifixion and resurrection to His disciples. The disciples of Jesus Christ watched Jesus Christ performing many miracles and teaching people with the divine authority. Jesus Christ once asked His disciples a question, "who do men say that the Son of man is?" The disciples gave various answers to Jesus Christ (Mt. 16:13-16). Then Jesus Christ asked them very important and personal question, "But who do say that I am?" (Mt. 16:15) Peter answered him, "You are the Christ, the Son of the living God." (Mt. 16:16) The disciples realized Jesus to be the Messiah. Then Jesus told them not to tell others that He was the Messiah.

The Old Testament has many prophesies about the Messiah. One of those prophesies is:

> Therefore my heart is glad, and my soul rejoices; my body also dwells secure. For thou dost not give me up to Sheol, or let thy godly one see the Pit. Thou

dost show me the path of life; in thy presence is fulness of joy, in the right hand are pleasures for evermore. (Ps. 16:9-11)

The words, Sheol and Pit, in this quotation stand for hell or the place of the eternal punishment. The Messiah would not have eternal punishment in Sheol; but He would enjoy everlasting pleasures in the sight of the LORD God. In other words, the Messiah would be resurrected from the dead. According to this prophesy, Jesus Christ was raised from the dead, because He was the real Messiah (I Cor. 15:4)

Prophet Isaiah prophesied that the Messiah would suffer for sins of the world; and by His sufferings the people would be healed. He wrote:

He was despised and rejected by men; a man of sorrows, and acquainted with grief; and as one from whom men hide their faces and he was despised, and we esteemed him not. Surely he has borne our griefs and carried our sorrows; yet we esteemed him stricken, smitten by God, and afflicted. But he was wounded for our transgressions, he was bruised for our iniquities; upon him was the chastisement that made us whole, and with his stripes we are healed. (Is. 53:3-5)

Prophet Isaiah did not speak about the resurrection of the Messiah. It was left for the prophet Hosea (Hos. 1:1; his period of his prophecy 783-687 B.C.), who spoke of the people of God as the Messiah, who would be healed and resurrected by God, in the following words:

Come, let us return to the LORD, for has torn, that he may heal us; he has stricken, and he will bind us up. After two days he will revive us; on the third day he will raise us up, that we may live before him. (Hos. 6:1-2)

This prophesy is primarily applicable to the resurrection of the Messiah, Jesus Christ, on the third day, after His sufferings and death on the cross. This prophesy also implies the resurrection of all believers in the LORD God.

Jesus Christ knew that these prophesies would be fulfilled in His life. When the disciples realized Jesus to be the Messiah, Jesus Christ began to tell them that He was destined to suffer many things from the elders and chief priest, including death; and then be resurrected on the third day (Mt. 16:20).

The ladies then understood the prophecies about Christ; and they believed in the resurrection of Jesus Christ. They were asked to release the good news to the disciples of Jesus Christ. When those ladies told the news to other disciples about the resurrection of Jesus Christ, they found it difficult to believe.

After the physical resurrection, Jesus Christ appeared to the eleven apostles and other disciples many times, for forty days (Acts 1:3). They were fully convinced of the resurrection of the Lord Jesus Christ. Some of those apostles wrote about the life and teaching of Jesus Christ with reference to the resurrection of their Lord Jesus Christ. They changed their perspective about Jesus Christ, after they experienced the living presence of their Lord among them.

The question of the angel to the ladies, "why do you seek the living among the dead?"implied that Jesus Christ was resurrected from the dead and He is alive forever; therefore, the followers of Jesus Christ should look for the ever-living Christ among the living, such as human beings. The ever-living Christ is in heaven and in presence of God. St. Paul wrote about it:

> For Christ has entered not into a sanctuary made with hands,.. But into heaven itself, now to appear in the presence of God on our behalf. (Heb. 9:24)

Secondly, the presence of the living Lord is in God's people. St. Paul wrote to the Corinthians about it again and again, as follows:

> Do you not know that you are God's temple and that God's Spirit dwells in you?. For God's temple is holy, and that temple you are. (I Cor. 3:16-17 cf. I Cor. 6:19)

Again he wrote to them:

> For we are the temple of the living God; as God said: 'I will live in them and move among them, and I will be their God, and they shall be my people. (II Cor. 6:16)

That God will the God of His people and He would live among them is the very old promise of God, given to the people of Israel (Gen. 17:8; Ex. 29:45; Lev. 26:12; Jos. 3:10). The Church is the new Israel, therefore, the same promise is given to the Church (Acts 7:5; II Cor. 6:16).

The presence of God in Jesus Christ among His people makes them different people here and now. St. Paul wrote to the Romans concerning this spiritual matter, in these words:

> But you are not in the flesh, you are in the Spirit, if in fact the Spirit of God dwells in you. Anyone who does not have the Spirit of Christ does not belong to him. But if Christ is in you, although your bodies are dead because of sin, your spirits are alive because of righteousness. If the Spirit of him who raised Jesus from the dead dwells in you, he who raised Christ Jesus from the dead will give life to your mortal bodies also through his Spirit which dwells in you. So then, brethren, we are debtors, not to the flesh, to live according to the flesh - for if you live according to the flesh you will die, but if by the Spirit you put to death the deeds of the body you will live. For all who are led by the Spirit of God are the sons of God. (Rom. 8:9-14)

Conclusion

Easter is the joyous and victorious celebration, because Jesus Christ was raised by God from the dead on the Sunday. His physical resurrection is the evidence of His victory over sin and death. His followers were happy to see their Lord resurrected. The resurrected Lord lives among His people; He could be found in them. It is the responsibility of the believers to show to the world that God in Jesus Christ lives among them; and He causes them to be different for His sake. This is the meaning of the Easter and challenge for the believers.

Recommended Hymns from the Methodist Hymnal

204   'Christ the Lord is risen to-day; Hallelujah!'

206   'Christ is risen! Hallelujah!'

208   'The day of resurrection!'

210   'Christ Jesus lay in death's '

565   'I know that my Redeemer lives,'

Responsive Reading from the Methodist Hymnal

#46 (p. 404),

Recommended Responsive Reading from A Worship Manual for Scriptural or Methodist Order of Service

92 (pp.217-219) or

40 (pp. 135-136).

Invocation: Methodist Hymn # 684

Benediction: Hebrews 13:20-21.

Chapter - 26

Titles of the Sermon
'Feeding Christ's Flock,'

'Tending Christ's Sheep,'

'Loving Jesus Christ in terms of Feeding Christ's Flock.'

Scripture
John 21:2-18

Genesis 22:12

I Chronicles 28:9

Psalms 44:21

Job 1:21

Ezekiel 34:2-5,19

Matthew 16:17-18; 19:16,21; 28:2, 13-14, 16, 19-20

Mark 8:27-30; 16:1, 6-7, 9, 12, 14, 16-19

Luke 9:18-21; 24:10, 18, 30-35, 38-40, 42-43

John 1:49; 20:2, 7, 18, 27; 21:2

Acts 1:9, 12

Text: John 21:15

A Few Versions of the Text, John 21:15
So when they had eaten breakfast, Jesus said to Simon Peter, 'Simon, son of Jonah, do you love Me more than theses? He said to him, 'Yes,

Lord; You know that I love You.' He said to him, 'Feed My lambs.' *The New King James Version*

When they had dined, Jesus saith to Simon Peter, Simon, son of Jonah, lovest thou me more than these do? He saith to him, Yea. Lord; thou knowest that I love thee. He saith to him, Feed my lambs. *Explanatory Notes Upon the New Testament*

When they had finished breakfast, Jesus said to Simon Peter, 'Simon, son of John, do you love me more than these?' He said to him, 'Yes, Lord; you know that I love you.' He said to him, 'Feed my lambs.' *Revised Standard Version*

When they had finished eating, Jesus said to Simon Peter, 'Simon, son of John, do you truly love me more than these?' 'Yes, Lord;' he said, 'you know that I love you.' Jesus said, 'Feed my lambs.' *New International Version*

After breakfast, Jesus said to Simon Peter, 'Simon son of John, do you love me more than all else?' 'Yes, Lord,' he answered, 'you know that I love you.' 'Then feed my lambs' he said. *The New English Bible*

After breakfast Jesus said to Simon Peter, 'Simon, son of John, do you love me more than these others?' 'Yes,' Peter replied, 'You know I am your friend.' 'Then feed my lambs,' Jesus told him. *The Living Bible Illustrated*

After they had eaten breakfast, Jesus asked Simon Peter, 'Simon, son of John, do you love me more than the other disciples do?' Peter answered him, 'Yes, Lord, you know that I love you.' Jesus told him, 'Feed my lambs.' *God's Word*

Introduction

Easter Sunday is observed by all churches in the world, because it affirms the Christian belief in the physical resurrection of the Lord Jesus Christ, and in the resurrection of all believers at the second coming of the Lord. The gospel of the Lord Jesus Christ was written by four writers, who were the disciples of Jesus Christ, and who witnessed the resurrected Lord. These writers had given us the accounts of Jesus' appearances to the followers and to the apostles, after the Easter morning. These accounts differ in details; therefore, it is possible that readers might be confused about the sequence of the appearances of Jesus. Therefore, one should make an attempt to give a possible sequence of those appearances of Jesus Christ.

All four writers of the gospel mentioned Mary Magdalene, who went to anoint the dead body of Jesus before the sunrise on Sunday. St. Matthew recorded that Mary Magdalene went with other Mary (Mt. 28:2). St. Mark further identified Mary as the lady, from whom Jesus had cast out seven demons (Mk 16:9). St. Mark identified the other Mary as the mother of James (Mk 16:1). St. Luke agreed with the report (Lk. 24:10). St. Mark mentioned Salome (Mk 16:1) as a third woman; and St. Luke identified the third woman as Joanna. St. Luke added that there were other women (Lk. 24:10). This means that a group of women, either of two, or of three, or more than three, went to the tomb to anoint the body of Jesus Christ. Among those ladies, Mary Magdalene was a most devout follower of Jesus Christ.

According to St. Mark, when the three women reached the tomb, they saw the stone rolled away from the door of the tomb. They entered the tomb. They saw a young man, dressed in a white robe; he was an angel. He said to them:

> Do not be amazed; you seek Jesus of Nazareth, who was crucified. He has risen, he is not here; see the place where they laid him. But go, tell his disciples and Peter that he is going before you to Galilee; there you will see him, as he told you. (Mk 16:6-7)

The ladies fled from the tomb. They were so much afraid that they said nothing about the event to anyone.

Mary Magdalene somehow overcame fear. She went to Simon Peter and John; and said to them:

> They have taken the Lord out of the tomb, and we do not know where they have laid him. (Jn 20:2)

Mary Magdalene's statement implied that she and other ladies saw the empty tomb; and they had no idea about where the body was taken away. Peter and John rushed toward the tomb. They saw the linen cloths lying, and the napkin rolled up (Jn 20:7). John believed in the resurrection of the Lord Jesus Christ. John and Peter went back to their homes.

Mary Magdalene followed John and Peter. She did not see John and Peter at the tomb, because they had left for their homes. Mary stood outside the tomb weeping. She stooped to look into the tomb again. She saw two angels, sitting where the body of Jesus had lain. They asked her, "Woman, why are you weeping?" She replied, "Because they have taken away my Lord, and I do not know where they have laid him." (Jn 20:13-14) Then she turned around; and she saw a man. She supposed him to be a gardener. It was Jesus Christ. When Jesus Christ called her 'Mary,' she recognized his voice; and she said to Him 'Rabboni' (teacher). Jesus Christ told Mary Magdalene to tell His disciples that He would ascend to God the Father (Jn 20:18). She told the disciples that she had seen the Lord, and what He said to her. This is how Jesus Christ first appeared to Mary Magdalene (Mk 16:9). When she told the disciples that Jesus Christ is alive and she had seen him, they would not believe her report (Mk 16:11).

On that Sunday, in the afternoon, two men were going from Jerusalem to Emmaus. Emmaus is seven miles away from Jerusalem. One of them was Cleopas (Lk. 24:18). They were talking about the ladies, who went to the tomb of Jesus. They had a vision of angels, who told the ladies that Jesus was resurrected. The disciples went to see the tomb; and found their report correct. A stranger joined them in their discussion. When they reached Emmaus, it was dark; therefore, they asked the stranger to stay with them over night. When the stranger broke the bread, and blessed it, and gave it to them, their eyes were opened. Then they recognized Him to be Jesus, the resurrected Lord. Then Jesus Christ vanished out of their sight (Lk 24:30-31). At the same hour, Cleopas and other disciple left Emmaus for Jerusalem in order to tell other disciples how Jesus Christ appeared to them (Lk 24:33; Mk 16:12).

The disciples were meeting behind the closed doors, for the fear of the Jews. It might be about 11:00 p. m., when the two disciples returned from Emmaus to Jerusalem. They saw the ten disciples of Jesus Christ and others gathered together. They told the disciples, who returned from Emmaus to Jerusalem, that the Lord has risen indeed, and He has appeared to Simon (Lk. 24:34). Then the two disciples told them what had happened on their road to Emmaus and how Jesus Christ appeared to them (Lk. 24:35).

As they were telling about the appearance of Jesus Christ, He Himself stood among them. They were frightened. When Jesus Christ appeared to the group of His disciples for the first time, He said to them, 'Peace be with you.' According to St. Mark, Jesus Christ scolded them, because they did not believe those, who saw Him after He had risen (Mk 16:14). He said to them, "Why are you troubled, and why do questionings rise in your hearts? See my hands and my feet, that it is I myself; handle me, and see; for a spirit has not flesh and bones as you see that I have." (Lk. 24:38-40). He then asked them, "Have you anything here to eat?" They gave Him a piece of broiled fish; He took it and ate before them (Lk. 24:42-43).

When Jesus Christ appeared to the group of the disciples, Thomas was not with them. He did not believe that they had seen the Lord. He wanted to place his finger in the mark of nails, and put his hand in the side of the resurrected Lord. He expressed his doubts about the resurrection of Jesus Christ. Eight days later, when the disciples and Thomas were in the house and doors were shut, Jesus Christ appeared to them second time. He asked Thomas to put his finger and hand on His hands and the side. He said to Thomas, 'Do not be faithless, but believing.' (Jn 20:27)

Jesus Christ appeared to Simon Peter, and Thomas (called the Twin), Nathaniel, who were the sons of Zebedee, and John, and two other disciples by the Sea of Tiberias, third time (Jn 21:2), when they went fishing.

Jesus Christ finally appeared to the eleven disciples and others, whey they gathered on the mountain in Galilee (Mt. 28:16), called the

Mount of Olivet (Acts 1:12). They worshipped Him. The Lord Jesus Christ gave them the mandate, saying:

> All authority in heaven and on earth has been given to me. Go therefore and make disciples of all nations, baptizing them in the name of the Father and of the Son and of the Holy Spirit, teaching them to observe all that I have commanded you; and lo, I am with you always, to the close of the age. (Mt. 18-20)

Then Jesus Christ was lifted up, and a cloud took Him out of their sight (Acts 1:9). He was taken up into heaven. After this event of ascension, the disciples returned to Jerusalem from the Monunt Olivet (Acts 1:12; Mk 16:19).

This rearranging the sequence of the appearances of Jesus Christ, after His physical resurrection, might help us to understand the text of our meditation today.

Introduction of the Text

When Jesus Christ appeared to the eleven disciples and other followers on the Mount of Olivet, He gave them the commission to preach the gospel and to convert the people to Christian faith. This commission was given to all followers, but there should be someone to implement the commission; there should a person in charge of the followers. After the leadership of Jesus Christ, St. Peter was chosen to be the first leader of the ten disciples and other followers. When Jesus Christ gave the chief office to St. Peter, Jesus said to him:

> **Simon, son of John, do you love me more than these? He said to him, 'Yes, Lord; you know that I love you.' He said to him, 'Feed my lambs.'** (Jn 21:15)

This is the text of our meditation today.

The Context of the Text

The conversation, given in the text, took place between the risen Lord Jesus Christ and Peter, after they finished breakfast. The resurrected Lord had the breakfast with Peter, Thomas, Nathaniel (who were the sons of Zebedee), and other disciples at the seashore of the Sea of

Tiberias (Jn 21:1-2), when Jesus Christ appeared to them third time (Jn 21:14).

Peter and other disciples went fishing, but they caught nothing throughout night. Before the daybreak, Jesus Christ stood on the beach and asked them, "Children, have you any fish?" (Jn 21:5) They replied, "No." Then Jesus Christ asked them, "Cast the net on the right side of the boat, and you will find some." (Jn 21:6) When they did so, they caught the large quantity of fish. When Peter hauled the net ashore, Jesus Christ said to the disciples, 'Come and have breakfast.' (Jn 21:12)

Everybody knew that it was the risen Lord Jesus Christ, who asked them to have a breakfast with them. When they had finished breakfast, Jesus said to Simon Peter:

> Simon, son of John, do you love me more than these? He said to him, 'Yes, Lord; you know that I love you.' He said to him, 'Feed my lambs.' (Jn 21:15)

This is the background of the text.

An Analysis of the Text

In this text, there are three ideas. (A) The first idea is the question, which the risen Lord Jesus Christ asked Simon Peter, 'Simon, son of John, do you love me more than these?'

(B) The second idea is the answer, Peter gave to the risen Lord, which was, 'Yes, Lord; you know that I love you.'

(C) The third idea is a command of the Lord Jesus to Peter, which was, 'Feed my lambs.'

Exposition of the Ideas of the Text

(A) The first idea of the text is the question, which the risen Lord Jesus Christ asked Simon Peter, 'Simon, son of John, do you love me more than these?' In other words, the risen Lord Jesus Christ asked Simon Peter did he love more than other disciples did. This was a very important and heart- searching question, because Jesus Christ had told Peter before that he would build His Church on Peter, the Rock (*petros* in Greek) (Mt.16:18).

We should recall how Simon Peter became a disciple of Jesus Christ. St. Luke recorded the event thus. People asked Jesus Christ to preach the word of God, when He was standing by the lake of Gennesaret. Jesus saw two boats by the lake. He entered the boat of Simon and asked him to put his boat out a little from the land. Jesus sat in the boat and taught the people. After his preaching, Jesus Christ asked Simon, 'Put out into the deep and let down your nets for a catch.' (Lk. 5:4) Simon answered Jesus Christ, 'Master, we toiled all night and took nothing! But at your word I will let down the nets.' (Lk.5:5) When they had done this, they caught a large quantity of fish; therefore, Simon had to call other fishermen to help them. Simon was astonished at the catch, which filled two boats. James and John, the son of Zebedee, were Simon's partners. Simon saw the miracle. He said to Jesus, 'Depart from me, for I am a sinful man, O Lord.' (Lk. 5:8) But Jesus said to Simon, 'Do not be afraid; henceforth you will be catching men.' (Lk. 5:10 cf. Mt. 4:18-20; Mk 1:16-20; Jn 1:35-40) Simon and his partners left everything and followed Jesus Christ.

This event is similar to the event of the third appearance of Jesus Christ when they caught a large quantity of fish, when Jesus Christ directed them to let down the nets for a catch.

Simon Peter had a special gift of revelation, which was to be used in building the Church. Recall an event. When Jesus went into the district of Caesarea Philippi, He asked His disciples, 'What do men say that the Son of man is?' The disciples replied Him, saying, "Some say John the Baptist, others say Elijah, and others Jeremiah or one of the prophets." (Mt. 16:14) Then Jesus Christ asked them, "But what do you say that I am?" Simon Peter replied, "You are the Christ, the Son of the living God." Then Jesus said to Simon Peter:

Blessed are you, Simon Bar-Jona! For flesh and blood has not revealed this to you, but my Father who is in heaven. And I tell you, you are Peter, and on this rock I will build my church, and the powers of death shall not prevail against it. (Mt. 16:17-18 cf. Lk. 9:18-21; Mk 8:27-30; Jn 1:49)

Jesus Christ had a plan to build His church on the leadership of Simon Peter. Jesus Christ chose Peter to lay the foundation of His church. Peter was chosen as the leader of disciples and followers of Jesus Christ, after the resurrection of Jesus Christ. Peter and other disciples were expected to preach the gospel immediately, after they saw the resurrected Lord Jesus Christ. But Simon Peter and other disciples went back to fishing rather than preaching the gospel and the teaching the word of God. This was a potential threat to laying the foundation of the Church of Jesus Christ. Therefore, the risen Lord Jesus Christ had to appear to Peter third time, and to give him the unavoidable commission to build His Church. As Simon left everything and followed Jesus Christ, when he became a disciple of Jesus, he had to leave again everything to build the Church of Jesus Christ (Jn 21:19).

The question, 'Do you love me more than these?' was asked three times as Peter denied Jesus Christ thrice. The question was asked three times to test his firm faithfulness. God had tested faithfulness of His servants several times. Let us refer to a few such events.

(1) God wanted to test Abraham's faith; therefore, God asked Abraham to sacrifice his only son Isaac. Abraham took his son on a mountain to offer him to God. As Abraham took knife to slay his son, LORD God said to Abraham:

> Do not lay your hand on the lad or do anything to him; for now I know that you fear God. Seeing you have not withheld your son, your only son, from me. (Gen. 22:12)

Abraham demonstrated by his action that he loved God more than his only son. This is a reason why Abraham became the father of faith for both the Jews and the Gentiles.

(2) Job was a very rich man. He was blameless and righteous man in the sight of God. Satan argued with God that Job was righteous, because God protected him; but if God would remove His protection from Job, Job would curse God. God allowed Satan to bring all calamities on Job. Children of Job were murdered; his servants were killed; his everything was destroyed. When everything was gone, Job arose and worshipped God, saying:

> Naked I came from my mother's womb, and naked shall I return; the LORD gave, and the LORD has taken away; blessed be the name of the LORD. (Job 1:21)

Job demonstrated his love and faithfulness to God, when he lost everything. He loved God more than anything in the world.

In contrast to Abraham and Job, there is a story in the New Testament, telling how a rich man loved his riches more than God. The young rich man, who was keeping God's commandments, asked Jesus Christ, "Teacher, what good deed must I do, to have eternal life?" (Mt. 19:16) When he told Jesus Christ that he was keeping all commandments and he asked Jesus what did he lack still. Jesus Christ told him:

> If you would be perfect, go, and sell what you possess and give to the poor, and you will have treasure in heaven; and come, follow me. (Mt. 19:21)

When that young man heard this, he went away sorrowfully; for he had great possession. That young rich man loved his wealth more than God.

(B) The second idea of the text is the answer, Peter gave to the risen Lord, which was, 'Yes, Lord; you know that I love you.' Simon Peter answered positively to the risen Lord Jesus Christ that he loved the Lord and the Lord knew that Peter was sincere about his answer. Peter knew that the risen Lord is indeed God, who knows all inner thoughts of man and nothing could be hidden from His sight. God is omniscient; He knows all things. A psalm writer wrote that God knows the secrets of our hearts (Ps. 44:21). King David (1002-962 B. C.) said to his son Solomon (962-922 B. C.):

> And you, Solomon, my son, know the God of your father, and serve him with a whole heart and with a willing mind; for the LORD searches all hearts, and understands every plan and thought. If you seek him, he will be found by you; but if you forsake him, he will cast you off for ever. (I Chr. 28:9)

God cannot be deceived by hypocrisy of His servants. Simon Peter knew about it. He told the risen Lord Jesus Christ that He knows and judges every human heart.

(C) The third idea of the text is a command of the Lord Jesus to Peter, which was, 'Feed my lambs.' Jesus Christ commanded Simon Peter to express his love to Jesus Christ by action. In other words, love is not an artificial sentiment; but it is the care through actions. Peter was asked to demonstrate his love to the Lord by feeding His lambs. Lambs represent the people who are helpless, who need help of others, who need protection from others. Jesus Christ asked Peter to look after His followers or people who are helpless, who are in want, who need protection. Peter was compared with a good shepherd, who would take care of the Lord's lambs. Peter was asked to care for the spiritual welfare of the Church of God in Jesus Christ.

God appreciates good shepherds or leaders; but God condemns bad shepherds or leaders. God said through prophet Ezekiel (Ezek. 1:1-3; period of his prophecy 627-587 B.C.) these words:

> Thus says the LORD God: Ho, shepherds of Israel who have been feeding yourselves! Should not shepherds feed the sheep? You eat the fat, you clothe yourselves with wool, you slaughter the fatlings; but you do not feed the sheep. The weak you have not strengthened, the sick you have not healed, the crippled you have not bound up, the strayed you have not brought back, the lost you have not sought, and with force and harshness you have ruled them. So they were scattered, because there was no shepherd; and they became food for all the wild beasts...I am against the shepherd; and I will require my sheep at their hand, and put a stop to their feeding the sheep; no longer shall the shepherds feed themselves. I will rescue my sheep from their mouths, that they may not be food for them. (Ezek.34:2-5, 10)

God expects of His servants to feed the lambs and to feed His flock.

Conclusion

The risen Lord Jesus Christ asked Simon Peter, 'Do you love more than these?' He is asking the same question to the pastors, leaders, and members of His Church. What will be your and my answer to Him? Do we love our Lord more than our colleagues love the Lord? Do we feed His followers, who are in needs? Do we feed His flock, the Church? We are accountable to God. God knows our hearts. Love the Lord God with all your hearts, minds, and souls and obey His command. God certainly will bless us when we obey His mandate.

Recommended Hymns from the Methodist Hymnal

50   'The Lord's my Shepherd, I'll not'

51   'The God of love my shepherd is'

76   'The King of love my shepherd is'

400   'Take my life, and let it be'

432   'Hark, my soul! It is the Lord'

524   'My God, I thank Thee, who hast'

600   'O Master, let me walk with Thee'

770   'Jesus, to Thy table led'

Recommended Responsive Reading from A Worship Manual for Scriptural or Methodist Order of Service

92 (pp. 217-219) or

100 (pp. 234-235).

Chapter - 27

The Titles of the Sermon

'The Significance of the Third Appearance of Jesus Christ,'

'Commission to St. Peter,
after the Third Appearance of Jesus Christ,'

'Following the Lord Jesus Christ,
after His Third Appearance.'

Scripture

John 21:1-19

Isaiah 53:1, 3-5

Hosea 6:1-2

Mark 16:6-7, 11-15, 19

Luke 5:1-11; 24:12, 18, 33-35

John 1:41-42; 20:2, 7, 13-15, 18, 21-22, 27; 24:38-40, 42-43

I Corinthians 15:3-8

Text: John 21:18-19

A Few Versions of the Text, John 21:18-19

Most assuredly, I say to you, when you were younger, you girded yourself and walked where you wished; but when you are old, you will stretch out your hands, and another will gird you and carry you where you do not wish. This He spoke, signifying by what death he would glorify God. And when He had spoken this, He said to him, 'Follow Me.' *The New King James Version*

Verily, verily, I say unto thee, When thou wast young, thou didst gird thyself, and walk whither thou wouldest; but when thou shalt be old, thou shalt stretch out thy hands, and another shall gird thee, and carry thee whither thou wouldest not. This he said, signifying by what death he would glorify God. And having said this, he saith to him, Follow me. *Explanatory Notes Upon the New Testament*

Truly, truly, I say to you, when you were young, you girded yourself and walked where you would; but when you are old, you will stretch out your hands, and another will gird you and carry you where you do not wish to go. (This he said to show by what death he was to glorify God.) And after this he said to him, 'Follow me.' *Revised Standard Version*

I will tell you the truth, when you were younger you dressed yourself and went where you wanted; but when you are old you will stretch out your hands, and someone else will dress you and lead you where you do not want to go. Jesus said this to indicate the kind of death by which Peter would glorify God. Then he said to him, "Follow me!" *New International Version*

And further, I tell you this in very truth: when you were young you fastened your belt about you and walked where you chose; but when you are old you will stretch out your arms, and a stranger will bind you fast, and carry you where you have no wish to go. He said this to indicate the manner of death by which Peter was to glorify God. Then he added, 'Follow me.' *New English Bible*

When you were young, you were able to do as you liked and go wherever you wanted to, but when you are old, you will stretch your hands and other will direct you and take you where you don't want to go. Jesus said this tell him know what kind of death he would die to glorify God. Then Jesus told him, 'Follow me.' *The Living Bible Illustrated*

I can guarantee this truth: When you were young, you would get ready to go where you wanted. But when you're old, you will stretch your hands and someone else will get you ready to take where you don't want to go. Jesus said this to show by what kind of death Peter would bring glory to God. After saying this, Jesus told Peter, 'Follow me!' *God's Word*

Introduction

All Christian churches in the world celebrate Easter Sunday. This celebration reminds Christians of the physical resurrection of the Lord Jesus Christ. Resurrection from the dead is not a common fact of human life; the common fact of life is death; therefore, it would be difficult to believe in the resurrection of Jesus Christ.

The sufferings of Jesus Christ on the cross and His physical resurrection from the dead were preordained events. The word of God i. e. the Bible, has prophecies about the vicarious sufferings of the Messiah on the cross on behalf of the sinners and for the redemption of sinners (Is. 53: 3-5). This notion of vicarious sufferings of Jesus Christ cannot be generally accepted from a human point of view. It is difficult to believe it as prophet Isaiah had said (Is. 53:1); human reason or intellect cannot easily accept the notion of the vicarious suffering. It needs a heart of faith to accept it and experience the efficacy of the vicarious sufferings of Jesus Christ for the sinful world. It is a matter of faith which is based on the word of God. We have to accept what the word of God tells us, even though it might be difficult to digest intellectually.

The physical resurrection of the Lord Jesus Christ is the most unique event in the history of mankind. It is difficult to comprehend this incredible event in the face of the fact that all have died and none has been raised from the dead. The ordinary mind cannot fathom it. However, prophets prophesied about the physical resurrection of the Messiah (Hos. 6:1-2). It needs a faith to accept this fact. We have to believe in the testimonies of the apostles, who had seen the resurrected Lord Jesus Christ in the word of God. St. Paul looked at the life of Jesus Christ from the scriptural point of view, when he wrote to the Corinthians these words:

> For I delivered to you as of first importance what I also received, that Christ died for our sins in accordance with the scripture, that he was buried, and that he was raised on the third day in accordance with the scripture, and he appeared to Cephas [Simon Peter], then to the twelve. Then he appeared to more than five hundred brethren at one time. Most of whom are still alive, though some have fallen asleep. Then he appeared to James, then to all the apostles. Last of all, as to one untimely born, he appeared also to me. (I Cor. 15:3-8)

The resurrection of Jesus Christ was the outstanding act of God in the history of mankind. The early believers saw the resurrected Lord; and they bore witnesses that God raised Him from the dead and He is with God the Father, sitting at His right hand (Mt. 26:64; Mk 12:36; 14:62; 16:19; Lk. 20:42; 22:69; Acts 2:33 -35; 7:55-65; Rom. 8:34; Eph. 1:20; Col. 3:1; Heb.1:13; I Pet. 3:22).

Introduction of the Text

Jesus Christ appeared to the apostles three times in order to fully convince them that He was risen from the dead. Having proved them of His physical resurrection, He gave them the commission or mandate to preach His gospel and to convert the world to the Christian faith. He had to appoint a leader for the apostles and the believers. Therefore, He appeared to the apostles third time and spoke with Simon Peter and gave him the task of shepherding His Church. When Peter accepted the task, the risen Lord Jesus Christ foretold him what kind of death he would suffer. Then He asked Simon Peter to follow Him. This discourse is given in the following words:

> **Truly, truly, I say to you, when you were young, you girded yourself and walked where you would; but when you are old, you will stretch out your hands, and another will gird you and carry you where you do not wish to go. (This he said to show by what death he was to glorify God.) And after this he said to him, 'Follow me.'** (Jn 21:18-19)

This is the text of our meditation now.

The Context of the Text

Jesus Christ appeared to the disciples third time by the sea of Tiberias for the specific purpose of choosing Simon Peter to lead other apostles to evangelize the world. Thomas called the Twin, Nathanael, the sons of Zebedee, John, and two other disciples went fishing at the invitation of Simon Peter. They worked hard over a night and caught nothing. At the daybreak, someone stood on the beach; He asked them ' have you any fish?' They answered Him, 'No.' Then He said to them to cast the net on the right side of the boat. When they cast the net, they caught a great quantity of fish. John recognized that someone was the Lord Jesus Christ. When Simon Peter heard John saying, 'It is the Lord!', he jumped into the sea.

Other disciples dragged the net to the shore. They saw a charcoal fire, with fish laying on it, and bread. Jesus asked them to bring some of the fish. Simon Peter went aboard and hauled the net ashore. There were a hundred and fifty-three fish in the net. Then Jesus Christ invited them to have breakfast.

After the breakfast, Jesus Christ said to Simon Peter, 'Simon, son of John, do you love me more than these? Peter answered, Yes, Lord; you know that I love you.' Then Jesus Christ gave him a commission, saying, "Feed my lambs." Jesus Christ asked the same question to Peter second time and Peter gave the same answer. Then Jesus Christ gave him a more serious part of the commission saying, "Tend my sheep." Jesus Christ asked Peter the same question third time. Peter was grievous, he replied to Jesus Christ, "Lord, you know everything; you know that I love you." Then Jesus Christ gave him a higher commission saying, "Feed my sheep." (Jn 21:15-17) Thus Jesus Christ gave the all-inclusive task of shepherding His flock to Simon Peter. Jesus Christ, the Son of God, knew Simon Peter's commitment to His work. Jesus Christ foretold that Peter would be crucified in order to glorify God through his faithful service to the Lord Jesus Christ. After this Jesus Christ said to Peter, "Follow me."

An Analysis of the Text

The text has only one idea which is the command of the risen Lord Jesus Christ to Simon Peter, to follow Him.

Exposition of the Idea of the Text

When the risen Lord Jesus Christ appeared to the disciples third time, He chose to speak with Simon Peter and assigned him the complete task of shepherding His flock or to take care of the followers of Jesus Christ, who were helpless and who were in need of a leader looking after the spiritual needs of the mature followers. The risen Lord assigned these duties to Simon Peter. Assigning the complete spiritual supervision of the followers of Jesus Christ to Simon Peter by the risen Lord. Jesus Christ made the third appearance of Jesus Christ more significant than His previous two appearances to the disciples. We have to understand this importance of the third appearance of the Lord Jesus Christ. Let us do it from various perspectives. First let us try to construct the sequence of the events from the four gospels.

According to the gospel of St. Mark, when the three women reached the tomb, they saw the stone from the door of the tomb rolled away. They entered the tomb, they saw a young man, dressed in a white robe; he was an angel. He said to them:

> Do not be amazed; you seek Jesus of Nazareth, who was crucified. He has risen, he is not here; see the place where they laid him. But go, tell his disciples and Peter that he is going before you to Galilee; there you will see him, as he told you. (Mk 16:6-7)

The ladies fled from the tomb; they were so much afraid that they said nothing about the event to anyone. Mary Magdalane was one of those ladies.

Mary Magdalane overcame fear. She went to Simon Peter and John; and said to them, "They have taken the Lord out of the tomb, and we do not know where they have laid him. " (Jn 20:2) Mary Magdalene's statement implies that she and other ladies saw the empty tomb and they had no idea about where the body of Jesus Christ was taken away. Peter and John rushed toward the tomb; they saw the linen cloths lying and the napkin rolled up (Jn 20:7). John believed in the resurrection of the Lord Jesus Christ. John and Peter went back to their homes.

Mary Magdalene followed Simon Peter and John; she did not see Simon Peter and John at the tomb because they had left for their homes. Mary stood outside the tomb weeping; she stooped to look into the tomb again; she saw two angels, sitting where the body of Jesus had lain. They asked her, "Woman, why are you weeping? She replied, "Because they have taken away my Lord, and I do not know where they have laid him." (Jn 20:13-14) Then she turned around and saw a man standing by her. It was the risen Lord Jesus, but she did not know that He was Jesus. Jesus asked her, "Woman, why are you weeping? Whom do you seek?" Mary supposed him to be a gardener and said to him, "Sir, if you have carried him away, tell me where you have laid him, and I will take him away." (Jn 20:15) Then Jesus called her 'Mary,' she recognized his voice and said to him '*Rabboni*' (teacher). Jesus Christ told Mary to tell His disciples that He would ascend to God the Father (Jn 20:18). She told the disciples that she had seen the Lord and what He said to her. This is how Jesus first appeared to Mary Magdalene (Mk 16:9). When she told the disciples that Jesus Christ is alive and she had seen Him, they would not believe her report (Mk 16:11). The apostles thought of the news as an idle tale (Lk. 24:12).

On that Sunday, in the afternoon, two men were going from Jerusalem to Emmaus; Emmaus is seven miles away from Jerusalem. One of them was Cleopas (Lk. 24:18). They were talking about the ladies, who went to the tomb of Jesus. They had a vision of angels, who told the ladies that Jesus was resurrected. The disciples went to see the tomb and found their report correct. A stranger joined them in their discussion. When they reached Emmaus, it was dark; therefore, they asked the stranger to stay over night with them. When the stranger broke the bread and blessed it and gave it to them, their eyes were opened; and then they recognized him to be Jesus, the resurrected Lord. Then Jesus Christ vanished out of their sight (Lk 24:30-31). At the same hour, Cleopas and other disciple left Emmaus for Jerusalem in order to tell other disciples how Jesus Christ appeared to them (Lk 24:33; Mk 16:12).

The disciples were meeting behind the closed doors, for the fear of the Jews. It might be about 11:00 p. m., when the two disciples returned from Emmaus to Jerusalem; they saw the ten disciples of Jesus and others gathered together. They told the disciples, who had returned from Emmaus to Jerusalem, that the Lord had risen indeed, and had appeared to Simon! (Lk. 24:34) Then the two disciples told them what had happened on their road to Emmaus and how Jesus Christ appeared to them (Lk. 24:35).

(1) As they were telling about the appearance of Jesus, Jesus Christ Himself stood among them. They were frightened. When Jesus Christ appeared to the group of His disciples for the first time, He said to them, 'Peace be with you. As the Father has sent me, even so I send you.' Jesus Christ breathed on them and said to them, 'Receive the Holy Spirit.' (Jn 20:21-22) According to Mark, Jesus Christ scolded them because they did not believe those who saw Him after He had risen (Mk 16:14). He said to them, "Why are you troubled, and why do questionings rise in your hearts? See my hands and my feet, that it is I myself; handle me, and see; for a spirit has not flesh and bones as you see that I have." (Lk. 24:38-40). The risen Lord was attempting to prove that His resurrection was real and it was not docetic or ghostlike appearance. To reaffirm his point, He asked them, "Have you anything here to eat?" They gave Him a piece of broiled fish; He took it and ate before them (Lk. 24:42-43). This was the first appearance of the risen Lord to His disciples.

(2) When Jesus Christ first appeared to the group of the disciples, Thomas was not with them. He did not believe that they had seen the Lord. He might have argued with other disciples that they were hallucinated; and they failed to touch the wounds in the hands and side of Jesus Christ. He could not believe that Jesus Christ was resurrected unless he would place his finger in the mark of nails, and put his hand in His side. He expressed his doubts about the resurrection of Jesus Christ. His sceptic thinking created a room of doubt in the heart of some disciples. Eight days later,

when the disciples and Thomas were in the house and doors were shut, Jesus Christ appeared to them second time. He asked Thomas to put his finger and hand on His hands and the side. He said to Thomas, 'Do not be faithless, but believing.' (Jn 20:27)   Then Jesus Christ told them, "Go into the world and preach the gospel to the whole creation." (Mk 16:15) This was the second appearance of the risen Lord to His disciples.

(3) Jesus appeared to Simon Peter, Thomas, Nathanael, sons of Zebedee, John, and two other disciples by the Sea of Tiberias third time (Jn 21:2), when they went fishing. What was the significance of the third appearance of the risen Lord? Let us think of its reasons.

(a) The Lord Jesus Christ appeared twice to His disciples that they should believe, without any doubt, that He was physically resurrected from the dead. When Jesus Christ appeared first to Mary Magdalene and sent a message through her to His disciples, they did not believe in her testimony, therefore, the resurrected Lord appeared to the disciples for the first time. Thomas was absent at the first appearance of Jesus Christ and he questioned the testimony of other disciples that they saw the resurrected Lord. Jesus, therefore, appeared to them second time. The main reason for His two appearances was that they should believe that He was risen from the dead and that they should believe in His resurrection without any doubt. The second reason was that He asked them to preach the gospel to the world.

(b) The disciples of Jesus Christ were convinced that Jesus Christ was raised from the dead. Their belief remained personal and inactive; they did not start preaching the gospel; they did not take the commission of the risen Lord seriously. They were afraid of the Jews, who would treat them with harshness and persecute them, if they dare to bear witness that Jesus of Nazareth was raised from the dead and they were preaching His gospel to others. They were on the point of giving up preaching and going up to resume their former profession namely, fishing. When Simon Peter told them that he was going fishing, they followed him and they engaged in fishing. It was a wise move from a human point of view. But it was a crisis of great importance to the commission which Jesus Christ gave twice to His disciples in two appearances. Therefore the risen Lord had to appear to His disciples third time in order to encourage them doing His assignment.

(c) The risen Lord gave the commission to preach His gospel to the whole world. But there was no leader to lead the disciples and to organize the work of the disciples. Therefore, Jesus Christ had to appear third time to make Simon Peter to be the leader of the group. After the breakfast, Jesus exclusively spoke to Simon Peter and asked him whether Peter loved Him. The risen Lord asked this question to Peter three times. At every answer of Simon Peter, Jesus gave him the commission in successive stages namely, feeding the lambs, tending the sheep, and feeding the sheep. Simon Peter accepted the all-comprehensive work of leadership of the Church of Jesus Christ or shepherding His flock.

(d) The risen Lord Jesus Christ chose Simon Peter to be the leader of His disciples and followers because Jesus Christ knew the courageous spirit of Simon. When Simon Peter accepted the task of shepherding, Jesus Christ foretold the way Peter would be killed while he was doing his God-given work. Then Jesus Christ said to Peter, "Follow Me."

When Jesus Christ began His teaching and healing ministry, some persons were impressed by His teaching and they desired to follow Him. Jesus asked them 'to follow Him.' Jesus Christ saw Matthew, sitting at tax office, Jesus said to Matthew, 'Follow Me'; and he followed Jesus (Mt. 9:9). Jesus saw Levi the son of Alphaeus, sitting at the tax office, Jesus asked Him to follow him and Levi followed Jesus (Mk 2:14) Jesus asked Philip to follow Him (Jn 1:43). This was a common way of Jesus calling others to be His disciples. He used the same words when He, the risen Lord, called Simon Peter to follow Him when He appeared third time to His disciples.

There is a special story in the gospel according to St. Luke, narrating how Simon Peter was called to be a follower of Jesus. This story is similar to the event when Jesus Christ appeared to the disciples third time. Let us briefly recall the event.

While the people pressed upon Jesus of Nazareth to preach the word of God, He was standing by the lake of Gennesaret. He saw two boats. He got into the boat of Simon and asked Simon to put the boat a little away from the land. Jesus sat in the boat and taught the people from the boat. After He finished preaching, He said to Simon "Put out into the deep and let down your nets for a catch." Simon said to Jesus that they toiled at night and caught nothing but at His word Simon let down the nets. Simon caught a great quantity of fish. He asked his partners to help to put fish into boats. Both the boats were filled. Simon understood the great catch of fish as a miracle. Simon fell down at Jesus' feet and said, "Depart from me, for I am a sinful man., O Lord." Then Jesus Christ said to Simon, "Do not be afraid; henceforth you will be catching men." Simon and his partners brought their boats to land; they left everything and followed Jesus Christ. (Lk. 5:1-11)

Jesus Christ was with His disciples for three years or more. He taught them and prepared them to catch men. Simon Peter was a distinctive disciple of Jesus Christ. According to the gospel of St. John, Andrew brought his brother Simon to Jesus Christ. Jesus looked at Simon and said, "So you are Simon the son of John? You shall be called Cephas" (which means Peter). (Jn. 1:41-42)

Simon Peter had a special gift of revelation which was to be used in building the church. When Jesus Christ went into the district of Caesarea Philippi, He asked His disciples, "What do men say that the Son of man is?" The disciples replied saying, "Some say John the Baptist, other say Elijah, and other Jeremiah or one of the prophets." (Mt. 16:14) Then Jesus Christ asked them, "But what do you say that I am?" Simon Peter replied, "You are the Christ, the Son of the living God." Then Jesus said to Simon Peter:

> Blessed are you, Simon Bar-Jona! For flesh and blood has not revealed this to you, but my Father who is in heaven. And I tell you, you are Peter, and on this rock I will build my church, and the powers of death shall not prevail against it. (Mt. 16:17-18 cf. Lk. 9:18-21; Mk 8:27-30, Jn 1:49)

Jesus Christ chose Simon Peter to be the leader to lay the foundation of His church. Peter had to assume the role of leadership, after the resurrection of Jesus Christ. Jesus Christ asked His disciples to preach the gospel to the world when He appeared them twice. They were expected to preach the gospel immediately; but they went back to fishing rather than preaching the gospel. This was a potential threat to laying foundation of the church. Therefore, Jesus Christ appeared to the disciples third time. He chose Peter to speak after the breakfast. He gave Peter the task of shepherding the church. Then the risen Lord asked Simon Peter to follow Him.

Simon Peter was the first disciple to see the risen Lord Jesus Christ. He saw the risen Lord in three appearances when Jesus Christ appeared to the group of disciples. He, therefore, was fully convinced that Jesus Christ was raised from the dead; he had no doubt that he was following the command of God in Christ Jesus. Knowing the renewed faithfulness of Simon Peter, the risen Lord Christ Jesus foretold Simon Peter that he would be crucified as He was crucified. Jesus gave Simon Peter the full commission of shepherding His Church and commanded him to follow Him.

Conclusion

The third appearance of the Lord Jesus Christ to His disciples was very significant because He had to appear to them and select Simon Peter to be the leader of His disciples and the followers and through him to implement His common commission of evangelizing the world.

Recommended Hymns from the Methodist Hymnal

110   'Jesu, Lover of my soul,'

235   'I know that my Redeemer '

238   'My faith looks up to thee'

241   'O Son of Man, our hero strong and tender'

391   'Thy life was given for me'

Recommended Responsive Reading from the Methodist Hymnal

56 (p. 409),

Recommended Responsive Reading from A Worship Manual for Scriptural or Methodist Order of Service

53 (pp.153-154).

Chapter - 28

The Titles of the Sermon

'Resurrected Life in Jesus Christ,'

'Spiritual Implications of Christian Belief
in the Resurrection of Jesus Christ,'

'Moral Life in Christ Jesus.'

Scripture

I Corinthians 15:1-29

Genesis 3:19

Psalms 6:5; 16:6-11; 30:9; 39:13; 88:10-12; 115:17; 132:11

Isaiah 38:18

John 3:6-8; 14:1-3

Acts 2:22-32; 3:13-16; 13:26-37

Romans 5:12, 18-19; 6:5-11, 14, 23

I Corinthians 15:20-23

Galatians 6:7-8

Colossians 2:12-15; 3:1-4

II Timothy 2:8-13; 3:1-7

Hebrews 11:1-7

I Timothy 2:8-13; 3:1-7

I Peter 2:24

Text: I Corinthians 15:17

A Few Versions of the Text, I Corinthians 15:17

And if Christ is not risen, your faith is futile; you are still in your sins! *New King James Version*

And if Christ be not raised, your faith is vain; ye are still in your sins. *Explanatory Notes Upon the New Testament*

If Christ has not been raised, your faith is futile and you are still in your sins. *Revised Standard Version*

And if Christ has not been raised, your faith is futile; you are still in your sins. *New International Version*

And if Christ was not raised, your faith has nothing in it and you are still in your old state of sin. *The New English Bibles*

And you are very foolish to keep on trusting God to save you, and you are still under condemnation of your sins; *The Living Bible Illustrated*

If Christ hasn't come back to life, your faith is nonsense and sin still has you in its power. *God's Word*

Introduction

In the month of March 2007, some T. V. Stations, like CNN and TV Ontario, presented a documentary, questioning the resurrection of Jesus Christ. A Jewish reporter from the U. S. A., named James Cameron, wanted to reveal a secret before the Easter of 2007. He referred to two limestone ossuaries, found in a 2000 year old tomb in Jerusalem in 1980. He heard some archeologists that they had discovered the tomb of Jesus and his bones in the tomb. He believed the tomb might have once held the remains of Jesus of Nazareth and his family. On the tombs it was written "Jesus, son of Joseph." James Cameron thought that after death of Jesus, he was buried by his disciples in his family tomb. [1] He wanted to expose that Jesus Christ was never resurrected; and the belief in the resurrection of Jesus Christ is false. The reporter ignored these facts that names of Jesus and Joseph were popular names. These tombs were at two or three places. Therefore, his conclusion is questionable.   The tomb, where the body of Jesus Christ was kept by His followers, became empty when Jesus

Christ was raised from the dead by God. His apostles and the followers had seen the resurrected Lord Jesus about forty days after His resurrection and before His ascension to heaven. (Acts 1:1-3) They saw many undeniable proofs of the resurrection of Jesus Christ. None of the apostles spoke of the spiritual resurrection of the body of Jesus Christ; but they boldly spoke of the bodily resurrection of Jesus Christ. Moreover, none of the Jewish and Roman authorities were able to present the dead body or skeleton of Jesus Christ to disprove the witness of the apostles about the historical fact of the bodily resurrection of Jesus Christ. The believers in our time and in the future must know the implications of the belief in the resurrection of Jesus Christ.

We live in a scientific and technological world. We reason out many things, and make our conclusions rational or logical. We would not accept any conclusion drawn from any person unless we verify it. Rules of the science are universal and verifiable. The rules of science operate in the phenomenal world or world of matter. We have to recognize that there is a reality which transcends the world of matter; it is called the spiritual world. The spiritual world has its rules; the comprehension of those rules or principles is beyond our human comprehension. We can see the results of the operation of the spiritual rules in our human life; but we cannot know how they operate in our life. We have to believe that there is the spiritual world. Immanuel Kant (April 22,1724- February 12. 1804), a modern philosopher, distinguished these two worlds. He called this world the phenomenal world and other world, a noumenal world. This distinction between the phenomenal and noumenal world was maintained by Jesus Christ when He said to Nicodemus:

> That which is born of the flesh is flesh, and that which is born of the Spirit is spirit. Do not marvel that I said to you, 'You must be born anew.' The wind blows where it wills, and you hear the sound of it, but you do not know whence it comes or whither it goes; so it is with every one who is born of the Spirit. (Jn 3:6-8)

We must be born of the Spirit in order to understand the spiritual world. We have to believe that there is the spiritual world, which affects our life; and yet we cannot understand the principles of the spiritual world. Our belief in God forms the basis to accept the truth or reality of miracles. The divine miracles are the factual events, which take place when the supernatural laws mysteriously operate in this world. The resurrection of Jesus Christ is a greatest miracle, which took place in the human world. There is an empty tomb as an evidence to infer the fact of the resurrection of Jesus Christ. But our scientific laws are not able to explain this miracle. Nevertheless, we should not doubt the incredible event of the resurrection of Jesus Christ, only because phenomenal science cannot explain it.

Faith had been playing a very important role in the spiritual life of the believers. St. Paul defined faith as 'the assurance of things hoped for, the conviction of things not seen.' (Heb. 11:1) He made this definition of faith from the biblical events. He argued in the following words:

> For by it [faith] the men of old received divine approval. By faith we understand that the world was created by the word of God, so that what is seen was made out of things which do not appear... By faith Enoch was taken up so that he should not see death; and he was not found because God had taken him. Now before he was taken he was attested as having pleased God. And without faith it is impossible to please him. For whoever would draw near to God must believe that he exists and that he rewards those who seek him. By faith Noah, being warned by God concerning events as yet unseen, took heed and constructed an ark for the saving of his household; by this he condemned the world and became an heir of the righteousness which comes by faith. (Heb. 11:2-7)

Christians believe that the world was created by the word of God (Gen. 1:3-24; Heb. 11:2). They believe that the word of God has the power to create and to destroy the world. It is a matter of faith. Charles R. Darwin (February 12, 1809- April 19. 1882) put forward a theory of evolution in the name of science; it is an interpretation of the fossils and physiological developments in beings; this theory is a speculation. Those who have studied the theory of evolution would know the flaws of the theory. However, the theory of evolution makes someone to question the belief in the creation theology.

Introduction of the Text

As the mundane or scientific knowledge makes some persons question the belief in the creation of the world by the word of God, the common sense knowledge made some Christian believers to question their belief in the resurrection of Jesus Christ, and in their resurrection, during the time of St. Paul, even though they accepted the gospel of Jesus Christ and embraced Christian faith. St. Paul had to deal with this problem. He wrote to the Christians at Corinth, arguing with them the necessity of belief in the resurrection of the Lord Jesus Christ and the implications of this belief to their spiritual life, in these words:

> **If Christ has not been raised, your faith is futile and you are still in your sins.** (I Cor. 15:17)

This is the text of our mediation now.

The Context of the Text

St. Paul wrote to the Christians, who were not believing in the resurrection of the dead. They questioned the resurrection of Jesus Christ and the Christian faith of the resurrection of the dead, because their reasoning was based on their scientific observation of the facts of life that no human being was resurrected from the dead. Subsequently, they questioned the life beyond the grave. Their reasoning was similar to the philosophy of materialism. According to materialism, matter is the ultimate reality; and there are no soul and spirit in man; life starts at a cradle and ends at grave; and there is no life beyond the grave. Some Christians at Corinth were influenced by the materialism; therefore, they did not believe in the resurrection of the dead.

Some of those Christians were the Jews previously. Sadducees, who were religious teachers of the Jews denied both immortality of the spirit and the resurrection of the body (Acts 23:8). The Old Testament contains some verses, which give a bleak, grim pessimistic picture of life beyond grave. Let us quote a few of those verses:

> Dost thou work wonders for the dead? Do the shades rise up to praise thee?
> Is thy steadfast love declared in the grave, or thy faithfulness in Abanddon?
> Are thy wonders known in the darkness, or thy saving help in the land of
> forgetfulness? (Ps. 88:10-12 cf. Ps. 6:5; 30:9; 39:13; 115:17).

Again

> For Sheol cannot thank thee, death cannot praise thee; those who go down
> to the pit cannot hope for thy faithfulness. (Is. 38:18)

In general, the Old Testament does not give an optimistic picture of
the life that is to come. Nevertheless, there are some verses, which
give glimpses of the life to come.

Because of these reasons, some Christians at Corinth, who had a
background of Judaism and of materialism, did not believe in the
Christian doctrine of the resurrection of the dead; they questioned
the belief in the resurrection of the Lord Jesus Christ; and they did
not believe in the resurrection of the believers and the resurrection
of the dead in general. As the Corinthians did not know the spiritual
implications of the doctrine of the resurrection of the Lord Jesus
Christ, St. Paul had to tell them why they should believe in the doctrine
of the resurrection of the dead. Therefore, in his argument, he wrote
the words of the text:

> If Christ has not been raised, your faith is futile and you are still in your
> sins. (I Cor. 15:17)

This is the text within its historical background.

An Analysis of the Text

This text has two arguments. (A) The first argument is that if Jesus
Christ had not been raised, the faith of the Christians at Corinth was
futile or nonsense.

(B) The second argument is that if Jesus Christ had not been raised,
the Christians at Corinth were still in their sins.

Exposition of the Ideas of the Text

(A) The first argument of the text is that if Jesus Christ had not been
raised, the faith of the Christians at Corinth was futile or nonsense.

In other words, the belief in the resurrection of the Lord Jesus Christ makes the faith of Christians powerful and solid. If there is a denomination in Christianity, which does not believe in the resurrection of the Lord Jesus Christ, its faith becomes trivial, futile, or nonsense. A denomination may be carrying out its charitable activities in terms of serving the needy and poor; but if it does not believe in the resurrection of Jesus Christ, it becomes a humanitarian and social organization. It can carry out its social and charitable activities without recognizing the presence and power of God in Jesus Christ. Therefore, it ceases to be a Christian denomination with Christian conviction. St. Paul prophesied about this, when he wrote to Timothy these words:

> But understand this, that in the last days there will come times of stress. For men will be lovers of self, lovers of money, proud, arrogant, abusive,...unholy, treacherous, reckless, swollen with conceit, lovers of pleasure than lovers of God, holding the form of religion but denying the power of it. Avoid such people. For among them are those who make their way into the households...who will listen to anybody and can never arrive at a knowledge of the truth. (II Tim. 3:1-7)

The early or the apostolic church put a great emphasis on the belief in the resurrection of the Lord Jesus Christ; therefore, its witness was powerful. St. Peter, who became the leader of the early church, spoke about the power of God in the miracles of Jesus Christ and in the resurrection of Jesus Christ Himself. It was the central doctrine of preaching the gospel to the people. On the day of the Pentecost, St. Peter addressed the critics of Christians in these words:

> Men of Israel, hear these words: Jesus of Nazareth, a man attested to you by God with mighty works and wonders and signs which God did through him in your midst, as you yourselves know- this Jesus, delivered up according to definite plan and foreknowledge of God, you crucified and killed by the hands of lawless men. But God raised him up, having loosed the pangs of death, because it was not possible for him to be held by it. For David says concerning him,
>
> *'I saw the Lord always before me, for he is at my right hand that I may not be shaken; therefore my heart was glad, and my tongue rejoiced; moreover my flesh will dwell in hope. For thou wilt not abandon my soul to Hades, nor let thy Holy One see corruption. Thou hast made known to me the way of life; thou wilt make me full of gladness with thy presence.'*

Brethren, I may say to you confidently of the patriarch David that he both died and was buried, and his tomb is with us to this day. Being therefore a prophet, and knowing that God had sworn with an oath to him that he would set one of his descendants upon his throne, he foresaw and spoke of the resurrection of the Christ, that he was not abandoned to Hades, nor did his flesh see corruption. This Jesus God raised up, and of that we all are witnesses. (Acts 2:22-32)

In his address or preaching, St. Peter argued that the resurrection of Jesus Christ was prophesied by prophet David in the scripture (Ps. 16:8-11; 132:11); and early Christians were witnesses of the resurrection of Jesus Christ.

St. Peter and St. John went to the temple at Jerusalem; and they cured a crippled man in the name of Jesus Christ. The man clung to them; and people gathered together in Solomon's portico. Then St. Peter said to the people:

> The God of Abraham and of Isaac and of Jacob, the God of our fathers, glorified his servant Jesus, whom you delivered up and denied in the presence of Pilate, when he had decided to release him. But you denied the Holy and Righteous One, and asked for a murderer to be granted to you, and killed the Author of life whom God raised from the dead. To this we are witness. And his name, by faith in his name, has made this man strong whom you see and know; the faith which is through Jesus has given the man this perfect health in the presence you all. (Acts 3:13-16)

St. Peter continued emphasizing the resurrection of Jesus Christ, when he wrote to various churches, because it was a central doctrine of preaching the gospel of Jesus Christ. He wrote the following words:

> He [Jesus Christ] was destined before the foundation of the world but was made manifest at the end of the times for your sake. Through him you have confidence in God, who raised him from the dead and gave him glory, so that your faith and hope are in God. (I Pet. 1:20-21)

Alike St. Peter, St. Paul put the central emphasis on the belief in the resurrection of Jesus Christ from the beginning of his ministry. When he went with others to the synagogue at Antioch, he grasped an opportunity to talk about Jesus Christ to the Jews. He said to them:

> Brethren, sons of the family of Abraham, and those among you that fear God, to us has been sent the message of this salvation. For those who live in Jerusalem and their rulers, because they did not recognise him nor

understand the utterances of the prophets which are read every sabbath, fulfilled these by condemning him. Though they could not charge him with nothing deserving death, yet they asked Pilate to have him killed. And when they had fulfilled all that was written of him, they took him down from the tree, and laid him in a tomb. But God raised him from the dead; and for many days he appeared to those who came up with him from Galilee to Jerusalem, who are now his witnesses to the people. And we bring you the good news that God promised to the fathers, this he has fulfilled to us their children by raising Jesus; as also it is written in the second psalm,

'Thou art my Son, today I have begotten thee.'

And as for the fact that he raised him from the dead, no more to return to corruption, he spoke in this way,

'I will give you the holy and sure blessings of David.'

Therefore he says also in another psalm,

'Thou wilt not let they Holy One see corruption.'

For David, after he had served the counsel of God in his own generation, fell asleep, and saw corruption; but he whom God raised up saw no corruption. (Acts 13:26-37)

St. Paul in his letters always talked about Jesus Christ being raised by God from the dead (Rom. 6:4, 8; 7:4; 8:11; 10:9; Gal. 1:1; Eph. 1:20; 2:5; Col. 2:12; I Thes. 1:10; II Tim 2:8). St. Paul preached the gospel of the resurrected Lord Jesus Christ; and for this task he was imprisoned. He bore all kinds of sufferings for the sake of God's people that they may have everlasting life. He wrote to St. Timothy:

Remember Jesus Christ, risen from the dead, descended from David, as preached in my gospel, the gospel for which I am suffering and wearing fetters like a criminal. But the word of God is not fettered. Therefore I endure everything for the sake of the elect, that they may also obtain salvation in Christ Jesus with its eternal glory. The saying is sure: If we have died with him, we shall also live with him; if we endure, we shall also reign with him; if we deny him, he also will deny us; if we are faithless, he remains faithful - for he cannot deny himself. (II Tim. 2:8-13)

From all these scriptural evidences, we can conclude that the belief in the resurrection of Jesus Christ was central doctrine in the preaching of the apostles. This is a biblical teaching. This is the sure position about the resurrection of the Lord Jesus Christ, upheld by the word of God, the Bible.

The physical resurrection of the Lord Jesus Christ is a greatest evidence of God's might and power. He is omnipotent God. He performed many miracles through His servants, the prophets, and Jesus Christ to demonstrate His power. But the greatest miracle of God is manifested in the resurrection of the Lord Jesus Christ. Therefore, questioning the resurrection of Jesus Christ or denying it amounts to questioning the power of God. This type of questioning makes Christianity a religion of powerless God; it reduces Christianity to nothing.

The belief in the resurrection of the Lord Jesus Christ is the foundation of the resurrection of the believers in Christ Jesus. Jesus Christ gave this hope and assurance, when He said to His disciples:

> Let not your hearts be troubled; believe in God, believe also in me. In my Father's house are many rooms; if it were not so, would I have told you that I go and prepare a place for you? And when I go and prepare a place for you, I will come again, and will take you to myself; that where I am you may be also. (Jn 14:1-3)

The apostles also taught Christians to believe in their resurrection, as God raised Jesus Christ from the dead, and they would live with Him forever. St. Paul wrote to the Romans:

> For if we have been united with him in a death like his, we shall certainly be united with him in a resurrection like his....But if we have died with Christ, we believe that we shall also live with him. (Rom. 6:5, 8)

He repeated the same conviction with other churches (I Cor. 15:20-23; Col. 2:12). He spoke of God as giving Christians the hope and assurance of being raised from the dead, as God raised Jesus Christ from the dead (Acts 17:31).

It is the teaching of the apostle that Christians should believe in the resurrection of the Lord Jesus Christ and also in their resurrection. This belief makes Christian faith unique and powerful among other religions. All Christians, therefore, must have faith in the resurrection of Christ Jesus, and subsequently in their own resurrection at the second coming of the Lord Jesus Christ to judge the world.

(B) The second argument of the text is that if Christ had not been raised the Christians at Corinth were still in their sins. The resurrection of the Lord Jesus Christ indicates the victory of Jesus Christ over death and sins of the world. The death is the result of our sins. St. Paul wrote to the Romans saying, "For the wages of sin is death." (Rom. 6:23) He had spoken to them before about the cause and effect of relationship between sin and death, when he wrote these words:

> Therefore as sin came into the world through one man and death through
> sin, and death spread to all men because all men sinned. (Rom. 5:12)

St. Paul referred to Adam, the first man, who sinned against the command of the LORD God; and the offsprings of Adam had been subjected to death (Gen. 3:19 cf. Rom. 5:12, 18-19). He reaffirmed the spiritual fact, when he wrote to the Romans (Rom. 5:12).

Prophet Ezekiel (Ezek. 1:2; 40:1, his period of prophecy ca. 598-573 B.C.) said it very plainly, 'the soul that sins shall die.' (Ezek. 18:4, 20) Each soul will have to reap the consequences of his deed; God will hold every person accountable for his or her actions, both good and evil. Bearing the relationship between sin and death in mind, St. Paul exhorted the Galatians to do the spiritual deeds to have the eternal life, when he wrote these words:

> Do not be deceived; God is not mocked, for whatever a man sows, that he
> will also reap. For he who sows to his own flesh will from the flesh reap
> corruption; but he who sows to the Spirit will from the Spirit reap eternal
> life. (Gal. 6:7-8)

God sent the Messiah, Christ Jesus, into the world, to destroy death and its cause. The cause of death is sin. The resurrection of Jesus Christ is not only His victory over death; but it is also His victory over sin, which is the root cause of death. Therefore, Christian believers will have victory over sin and its result, death. The resurrection of the Lord Jesus Christ assures them this type of victory, especially the victory over sin in this world. St. Paul wrote to the Roman about this triumph and assurance in the following words:

> For if we have been united with him in a death like his, we shall certainly be united with in a resurrection like his. We know that our old self was crucified with him so that the sinful body might be destroyed, and we might no longer be enslaved to sin. For he who has died is freed from sin. But if we have died with Christ, we believe that we shall also live with him. For we know that Christ being raised from the dead will never die again; death no longer has dominion over him. The death he died he died to sin, once for all, but the life he lives he lives to God. So you also must consider yourselves dead to sin and alive to God in Christ Jesus. (Rom. 6:5-11 cf. Col. 2:12-15)

St. Paul again told the Romans that sin would not have dominion over them (Rom. 6:14). The believers are expected to lead a spiritual life, because it indicates victory over sin. St. Paul exhorted to the Colossians in these words:

> If then you have been raised with Christ, seek the things that are above, where Christ is, seated at the right hand of God. Set you minds on things that are above, not on things that are on earth. For you have died, and your life is hid with Christ in God. When Christ who is our life appears, then you also will appear with him in glory. (Col. 3:1-4)

St. Peter similarly exhorted Christians to lead a righteous life. He wrote them, saying:

> Christ himself bore our sins in his body on the tree, that we might die to sin and live to righteousness. (I Pet. 2:24)

Conclusion

The resurrection of the Lord Jesus Christ is the evidence of the victory of God in Jesus Christ over death and the root cause of death namely, sins of the world. Christians believe that as they share in the suffering and death of their Lord, they would be resurrected from the dead; and they will be with the Lord forever. They are given victory over sin in the world; therefore, they have to lead a moral and spiritual life here and now; and await for their resurrection. They have to bear witness to the resurrection of Jesus Christ and make their faith strong.

Recommended Hymns from the Methodist Hymnal

206   'Christ is risen! Hallelujah!'

211   ' Low in the grave He lay'

213   'Thine be the glory, risen, conquering Son'

230   'Rejoice and be glad! '

Recommended Responsive Reading from the Methodist Hymnal

74 (pp. 416),

Recommended Responsive Reading from A Worship Manual for Scriptural or Methodist Order of Service

76 (pp.189-190).

Endnotes

[1] The Hamilton Spectator, April 7, 2007, p. D7.

Chapter - 29

The Titles of the Sermon

'Knowing the Power of Christ's Resurrection,'

'Sharing Christ's Sufferings,'

'Attaining the Resurrection from the Dead,'

'Christ-like Sufferings and Resurrection.'

Scripture

Philippians 3:2-21

John 6:40,44, 54; 14:2-3

Romans 7:17; 8:9-11

I Corinthians 15:20-23

II Corinthians 4:10-12; 11:23-28

Galatians 2:20

Ephesians 2:5-6

Colossians 3:1-2

I Thessalonians 4:16

II Timothy 2:10-13

Revelation 20:6

Text: Philippians 3:10-11

A Few Versions of the Text, Philippians 3:10-11

That I may know Him and the power of His resurrection, and the fellowship of His sufferings, being conformed to His death. If, by any means, I may attain to the resurrection from the dead. *The New King James Version*

That I may know him, and the power of his resurrection, and the fellowship of his sufferings, being made conformable to his death. If by any means I may attain to the resurrection of the dead. *Explanatory Notes Upon the New Testament*

That I may know him and the power of his resurrection, and may share his sufferings, becoming like him in his death, that if possible I may attain to the resurrection from the dead. *Revised Standard Version*

I want to know Christ and the power of his resurrection and the fellowship of sharing in his sufferings, becoming like him in his death, and so, somehow, to attain to the resurrection from the dead. *New International Version*

All I care for is to know Christ, to experience the power of his resurrection, and to share his sufferings, in growing conformity with his death, if only I may finally arrive at the resurrection from the dead. *New English Bible*

Now I have given up everything else- I have found it to be the only way to really know Christ and to experience the mighty power that brought back to life again, and to find out what it means to suffer and to die with him. So, whatever it takes, I will be one who lives in the flesh newness of life of those who are alive from the dead. *The Living Bible Illustrated*

Faith knows the power that his coming back to life gives and what it means to share his suffering. In this way I'm becoming like him in his death, with the confidence that I'll come back to life from the dead. *God's Word*

Introduction

When Christians recite the Nicene Creed, they say, "And I look for the Resurrection of the dead." The Christian belief in the resurrection of the dead is unique or outstanding with reference to other world religions. This belief is based on the historical event of the resurrection of Jesus Christ. That historical fact and the promise of Jesus Christ have given assurance to the Christians that they too will be resurrected on the last day or at the second coming of the Lord Jesus Christ (Jn 6:40, 44, 54) and then they will be with their Lord for ever (Jn 14:2-3 cf. I Cor. 15:20-23).

Easter Sunday is the day of remembrance of the physical resurrection of the Lord Jesus Christ and also the day of the assurance of the resurrection of the Christian believers at the second coming of the Lord Jesus Christ.

The Christian belief in their bodily resurrection is their spiritual hope. It is a kind of reward to the Christians, if they work for their Lord.

William Trewartha Bray known as Preacher Billy Bray (June 1, 1794-May 25,1818) was serving a large congregation in a city. In the neighbourhood of the city, there were two mines. One mine was prosperous. The management of the mine was giving good wages to the miners. The work at this mine was not hard. The other mine was poor; the work at that mine was hard; the management of the mine was giving lower wages. A worker, who was working for the second mine, where wages were poor, showed himself at the first mine, where wages were good, on the pay-day. The manager inquired of the worker and found out that the worker was working at the other mine. The worker pleaded very earnestly that he should be paid by this mine, where wages were better. His pleading was dismissed. The manager told the worker that he must come there to work, if he expects this management pay for his wages.

The preacher Billy Bray applied this illustration to the congregation and exhorted his congregation that they must serve Jesus Christ, if they would share His glory hereafter, but if they would serve the devil now, they must go to the devil for their wages. [1]

Introduction of the Text

It is a common sense that where we work we should ask for wages and other benefits. Where we affiliate ourselves, we go for benefits. It is wrong to get benefits or to expect benefits from where we did not affiliate with and work for. This common principle is applied to our spiritual life. This is evident in what St. Paul wrote to the Philippians, saying:

> that I may know him and the power of his resurrection, and may share his sufferings, becoming like him in his death, that if possible I may attain to the resurrection from the dead. (Phil. 3:10-11)

This is the text of our meditation now.

The Context of the Text

In the congregation at Philippie, there were some Jews who were converted to Christian faith. Those Jewish Christians were called 'Judaizers' or 'Circumcision Party'. The Judaizers were advocating that before a person becomes a true Christian he must become a Jew; he must be circumcised and he must keep the Mosaic law. They were teaching legalism and subsequently making Christianity a sect of Judaism. Those Judaizers gave hard time to St. Paul. St. Paul knew that Judaizers were the opponents of the gospel of Jesus Christ, which is 'salvation by faith and not by works'. St. Paul warned the Philippians to be aware of those evil doers or the "dogs"(Phil.3:2). He took a firm stand against the Circumcision Party, because the said party was jeopardising the gospel of the Lord Jesus Christ.

The Circumcision Party was proud of its Jewish heritage; and it was looking down upon the Gentile Christians. The said party was explicitly advocating the confidence in flesh, which has no place in the Christian faith. St. Paul had to tell the Judaizers how he looked upon his Jewish heritage, when he said these words:

> If any other man thinks he has reason for confidence in the flesh, I have more: Circumcised on the eighth day, of the people of Israel, of the tribe of Benjamin, a Hebrew born of Hebrews; as to the law a Pharisee, as to zeal a persecutor of the church, as to righteousness under the law blameless. (Phil. 3:4-6)

Having stated the reasons of his pride of the flesh, St. Paul told the Judaizers what he did with those points of pride, when he wrote:

> But whatever gain I had, I counted as loss for the sake of Christ. Indeed I count everything as loss because of the surpassing worth of knowing Christ Jesus my Lord. For his sake I have suffered the loss of all things, and count them as refuse, in order that I may gain Christ and be found in him, not having a righteousness of my own, based on law, but that which is through faith in Christ, the righteousness from God that depends on faith. (Phil. 3:7-9)

St. Paul gave up all his claims of heritage for another reason which was to attain the resurrection from the dead. He wrote:

> that I may know him and the power of his resurrection, and may share his sufferings, becoming like him in his death, that if possible I may attain to the resurrection from the dead. (Phi. 3:10-11)

This is the text within its historical and theological setting.

An Analysis of the Text

This text has three ideas. (A) The first idea is that St. Paul wished to know the Lord Jesus Christ and the power of His resurrection.

(B) The second idea is that St. Paul wished to share the sufferings of the Lord Jesus Christ and become like Jesus Christ in his death.

(C) The third idea is that if it would be possible that he wished to attain the resurrection from the dead.

Exposition of the Ideas of the Text

(A) The first idea of the text is that St. Paul wished to know the Lord Jesus Christ and the power of His resurrection. What did it mean to know Jesus Christ for St. Paul? He had the vision of Jesus Christ on his way to Damascus, before he was converted to Christian faith. He had heard the teaching of Jesus Christ from the apostles of Jesus Christ; he also had heard the testimonies about Jesus Christ from the apostles and followers of Jesus Christ. This knowledge about Jesus Christ was a secondary knowledge to St. Paul. He did not wish to know more about Jesus Christ from the testimonies of others. Further, he did not wish to learn about the teaching and theology of Jesus Christ from others. But he wished to know more of Jesus Christ as the Son of God, on the basis of his personal experience. He wanted to have a most intimate and closest knowledge of Jesus Christ. He wished to have a deeper insight in the mind and purpose of the Lord Jesus Christ. He wanted to know Jesus Christ everyday and at present. He was not content with the knowledge of Jesus Christ in the past. But he was seeking daily encounter or personal fellowship with Jesus Christ.

Knowing Jesus Christ as the Son of God or God Himself would have meant many things to St. Paul. He specially wanted to know the power of the resurrection of Jesus Christ. Christians know and believe that God raised Jesus Christ from the dead; it means that Jesus Christ was raised by the divine power. St. Paul wanted to know how that living and dynamic power operated in the event of the resurrection of Jesus Christ and how the same power changes the life of the believers or how the Spirit of the Lord Jesus Christ abides in the mortal bodies of believers. St. Paul somehow was convinced of the power of Jesus Christ that was manifested through the dynamic changes in the life of the believers. However, he wished to know this divine mystery. He wrote to the Christians at Rome, testifying this spiritual fact, in the following words:

> But you are not in the flesh, you are in the Spirit, if in fact the Spirit of God dwells in you. Any one who does not have the Spirit of Christ does not belong to him. But if Christ is in you, although your bodies are dead because of sin, your spirits are alive because of righteousness. If the Spirit of him who raised Jesus from the dead dwells in you, he who raised Christ Jesus from the dead will give life to your mortal bodies also through his Spirit which dwell in you. (Rom. 8:9-11)

When the believers are spiritually resurrected by the power of God, they do not go after the worldly things and the things of the flesh. But they seek the spiritual things (Col. 3:1-2; Eph. 2:5-6). St. Paul wished to know how, in fact, the power of the resurrection operated in the life of the believers.

(B) The second idea of the text is that St. Paul wished to share the sufferings of the Lord Jesus Christ and become like Jesus Christ in his death. What does it mean that St. Paul wished to share the sufferings of the Lord Jesus Christ ? He did not mean that he wanted to share in the vicarious sufferings of Jesus Christ for the redemption of the world, because Jesus Christ was the only one to suffer vicariously for the salvation of mankind; no other man can do so; no man can substitute Jesus Christ. It was not St. Paul's intention to substitute his Lord Jesus Christ. Moreover, there is no salvation in the blood of the martyrs, except in the blood of Jesus Christ.

St. Paul wished to have fellowship with Jesus Christ as Christ suffered to preach the gospel. He wished to have communion and participation in the work of Christ Jesus. He wanted to have a privilege of suffering for the sake of Christ Jesus.

St. Paul suffered for the work of Jesus Christ. He mentioned some of his trials for Jesus Christ, when he wrote to the Corinthians these words:

> Are they servants of Christ? I am a better one - I am talking like a mad man - with far greater labours, far more imprisonments, with countless beatings, and often near death. Five times I have received at the hands of the Jews the forty lashes less one. Three times I have been beaten with rods; once I was stoned. Three times I have been shipwrecked; a night and a day I have been adrift at sea; on frequent journeys, in danger from rivers, dangers from robbers, danger from my own people, danger from Gentiles, danger in the city, danger in the wilderness, danger at sea, danger from false brethren; in toil and hardship, through many a sleepless night, in hunger and thirst, often without food, in cold and exposure. And, apart from other things, there is the daily pressure upon me of my anxiety for all the churches. (II Cor. 11:23-28)

St. Paul wished to become like Jesus in his death. He wished to carry the cross of Jesus Christ as a faithful follower of Jesus Christ; and he was ready to die even on a cross for his Lord Jesus Christ. He wrote to the Corinthians these words:

> [We are] always carrying in the body the death of Jesus, so that the life of Jesus may be manifested in our bodies. For while we live we are always being given up to death for Jesus' sake so that the life of Jesus may be manifested in our mortal flesh. So death is at work in us, but life in you. (II Cor. 4:10-12)

In a similar way, St. Paul wrote to the Galatians about his life in Jesus Christ:

> I have been crucified with Christ; it is no longer I who live, but Christ who lives in me; and the life I now live in the flesh I live by faith in the Son of God, who loved me and gave himself for me. (Gal. 2:20)

(C) The third idea of the text is that if it would be possible that he wished to attain the resurrection from the dead. St. Paul was one of Pharisees, who believed in the resurrection of the dead; therefore, he was waiting for the physical and eschatological resurrection of the believers. As this is going to happen for all the believers, then what resurrection St. Paul wished to attain? He wished to be resurrected in the first resurrection of the saints of Jesus Christ. Concerning this belief, he wrote to the Thessalonians:

> For the Lord himself will descend from heaven with a cry of command, with the archangel's call, and with the sound of the trumpet of God. And the dead in Christ will rise first. (I Thes. 4:16)

All other apostles believed in the first resurrection of the believers. Apostle John wrote:

> Blessed and holy is he who shares in the resurrection! Over such the second death has no power, but they shall be priests of God and of Christ, and they shall reign with him a thousand years. (Rev. 20:6)

The first resurrection of the believers was designed to make the believers the priests of God and to rule with Jesus Christ for a thousand years. This was to share in the power and glory of God.

This divine honour is not without cost; there is no crown without cross. St. Paul wrote about this spiritual honour to the Romans, in these words:

> and if children, then heirs, heirs of God and fellow heirs with Christ, provided we suffer with him in order that we may also be glorified with him. (Rom. 7:17)

St. Paul wrote to St. Timothy the same conviction, in these words:

> Therefore I endure everything for the sake of the elect, that they also may obtain salvation in Christ Jesus with its eternal glory. The saying is sure: If we have died with him, we shall also live with him; if we endure, we shall

also reign with him; if we deny him, he also will deny us; if we are faithless, he remains faithful- for he cannot deny himself. (II Tim. 2:10-13)

Conclusion

St. Paul had belief in the resurrection of the dead; he knew that all will be raised again at the last judgment, done by the LORD God. He wanted to be raised first along with the believers and to reign over a thousand years with the Lord Jesus. He wanted to earn this privilege by sufferings for the sake of Jesus Christ. He believed in that there is no crown or reward without cross.

Christians have to ask some questions such as: Do they aspire to be resurrected in the first order of resurrection and to reign with the Lord Jesus Christ and what they are doing now for the sake of Christ Jesus to be resurrected first? St. Paul bore all losses of his religious prestige and bore all sufferings for the sake of being resurrected first. His aspiration for and conviction about the resurrection are given in the words of the text:

that I may know him and the power of his resurrection, and may share his sufferings, becoming like him in his death, that if possible I may attain to the resurrection from the dead. (Phil. 3:10-11)

Recommended Hymns from the Methodist Hymnal

206   'Christ is risen! Hallelujah!'

211   'Low in the grave He lay'

213   'Thine be the glory, risen, conquering Son'

230   'Rejoice and be glad! the Redeemer'

Recommended Responsive Reading from A Worship Manual for Scriptural or Methodist Order of Service

92 (pp. 217-219).

Endnotes

[1] Paul Lee Tan, Encyclopedia of 7700 Illustrations: Signs of the Times, # 5090.

Chapter - 30

Titles of the Sermon

'The Spiritual Resurrection,'

'The Belief in Resurrection and Leading a Moral Life,'

'Victory over Sin and Death,'

'Baptism linked with the Spiritual Death and Resurrection.'

Scripture

Colossians 2:8-15

Isaiah 55:8-9

Matthew 28:18-20

Romans 5:8; 6:2-11, 23

I Corinthians 15:3-4, 12-14, 17

II Corinthians 5:14-15

Ephesians 4:17-19, 22-24

Colossians 3:5-8, 10; 4:22-24

Hebrews 11

Text: Colossians 2:12

A Few Versions of the Text, Colossians 2:12

buried with Him in baptism, in which also you were raised with Him through faith in the working of God, who raised Him from the dead. *New King James Version*

Buried with him in baptism, by which ye are also risen with him through the faith of the operation of God, who raised him from the dead. *Explanatory Notes Upon the New Testament*

And you were buried with him in baptism, in which you were also raised with him through faith in the working of God, who raised him from the dead. *Revised Standard Version*

Having been buried with him in baptism and raised with him through our faith in the power of God, who raised him from the dead. *New International Version*

For in baptism you were buried with him, in baptism also you were raised to life with him through your faith in the active power of God who raised him from the dead. *New English Bible*

For in baptism you see how your old, evil nature died with him and was buried with him; and then you came up out of death with him into a new life because you trusted the Word of the mighty God who raised Christ from the dead. *The Living Bible Illustrated*

This happened when you were placed in the tomb with Christ through baptism. In baptism you were also brought back to life with Christ through faith in the power of God, who brought him back to life. *God's Word*

Introduction

When the Lord Jesus Christ was resurrected, He appeared to His eleven disciples on a mountain of Galilee and gave them the mandate as follows:

> All authority in heaven and on earth has been given to me. Go therefore and make disciples of all nations, baptizing them in the name of the Father and of the Son and of the Holy Spirit, teaching them to observe all that I have commanded you; and lo, I am with you always, to the close of the age. (Mt. 28:18-20)

This mandate is twofold. (A) The first part of the mandate is to convert the people of all countries, colours or races, and cultures to Christian faith by baptizing them. Christianity is a universal faith, embracing all people on the earth, on equal footing. The intention of converting the people to Christianity is to make them disciples or followers of Jesus Christ.

(B) The second part of the mandate is to teach Christians how to observe what Christ Jesus had commanded. Christians should bear in mind that the Lord Jesus Christ had given a very important place to religious teaching in the life of believers. Christ Jesus was Himself the best Teacher, having divine authority to teach the people (Mt. 7:29). Teaching provides substance or content to preaching; preaching must have substance or biblical teaching.

This twofold mandate was taken seriously by the apostles of Christ Jesus. They taught, preached, and propagated the gospel of Jesus Christ to those, who did not know God and the scripture. Their task was to show light to those who were sitting in spiritual darkness. That darkness was created by the man-centred philosophy. The minds of those people were filled with the philosophy of paganism. The apostles preached and taught Christian principles and practices to the Gentiles; and converted them to Christian faith by baptizing them in the name of the Father, the Son, and the Holy Spirit. However, those converts did not give up their pagan philosophy. This was a challenge to the apostles and teachers of Christian faith.

Introduction of the Text

St. Paul was a distinguished scholar and an outstanding apostle. He taught and preached about Jesus Christ to the people, who had a philosophical background of paganism. He taught churches how to face philosophical problems. He wrote letters to various churches concerning the religious and philosophical issues. The Church at Calossae was facing a problem as to how to face issues of morality against the teaching of the pagan philosophy. As a solution to their problem, he wrote to them the following words:

> **and you were buried with him in baptism, in which you were also raised with him through faith in the working of God, who raised him from the dead.** (Col. 2:12)

This is the text of our meditation now.

The Context of the Text

Christians at Colossae had a philosophical background of paganism. Paganism advocated the people that they should be careless about their spiritual purity and physical chastity; they should not worry about physical or spiritual sins (Col. 3:5-8) because spirit is not defiled by sins committed by body. As sins committed by the body, or by deeds and words, do not affect spirit adversely; therefore, there is no need to lead a moral life. Moreover, as the spirit of a person is not defiled by evil actions of the body, the spirit remains pure for ever. This pure spirit needs no salvation. This pure spirit was free before it took body; it is free while it is in the body; and it will be free when the person dies. The spirit is free at all times and it was never in bondage.

This kind of teaching of paganism was against the gospel of Jesus Christ. Paganism taught against the spiritual need of man to be saved from his sins. Whereas the apostles of Jesus Christ were teaching that man should repent of his sins, and ask God to forgive his sins, and be saved by the grace of the Lord Jesus Christ. The Christian faith was asking its followers to lead a moral life. The paganism was misleading the believers that they should not be concerned with the moral life. To such misguided Christians, St. Paul had to write the letter emphasizing the necessity of moral behaviour, because to him holy and moral life was an evidence of being a new creature in Christ Jesus. Moral life is a spiritually resurrected life; it is the life led by the Holy Spirit. St. Paul had to give a theological reason as to why the Christians should lead a moral life. He gave that reason in the words of the text as follows:

> and you were buried with him in baptism, in which you were also raised with him through faith in the working of God, who raised him from the dead. (Col. 2:12)

This is the context of our text.

An Analysis of the Text

In this text, there are four ideas. (A) The first idea is that when the Christians were baptized, they were buried with Jesus Christ in baptism.

(B) The second idea is that when the Christians were baptized, they were raised with Christ spiritually.

(C) The third idea is that Christians were spiritually raised or resurrected through their faith in the working of God.

(D) The fourth idea is that God raised Christ Jesus from the dead.

Exposition of the Ideas of the Text

(A) The first idea of the text is that when the Christians were baptized, they were buried with Jesus Christ in baptism. This is the first aspect of baptism. This aspect of baptism symbolizes the burial of the believers with Jesus Christ. Jesus Christ carried the sins of the world on the cross; He died for the sins of the world. Reflecting on the death of Jesus Christ, St. Paul wrote:

> But God shows his love for us in that while we were yet sinners Christ died for us. (Rom. 5:8)

Again,

> For the love of Christ controls us, because we are convinced that one has died for all; therefore all have died. And he died for all, that those who live might live no longer for themselves but for him who for their sake died and was raised. (II Cor. 5:14-15)

This is the belief of the Christians that Jesus Christ died for the sinful humanity; He paid the price to redeem humanity from sin and death, by his own death, because wages of sin is death (Rom. 6:23).

In the death of Jesus Christ, the believers have the ground to believe that they too died with him. After the death of Jesus Christ, He was buried in the tomb. The believers have a similar ground to believe that they too were buried with Him in the tomb. The death and burial of Jesus Christ symbolize a death and burial of the former life of believers. The believers die and bury their old nature. These features of the spiritual life are demonstrated in the first aspect of baptism.

In the early or apostolic Church, adults were baptized by immersion in water. The adults, who desired to be baptized, were baptized by completely immersing their bodies in water. The act of complete immersion stands for death and burial of the believers. This means that the old life of the believers passed away and their past life was buried. The believers have to say good bye to their past life, when they are fully immersed in water. The old life is marked by fornication, impurity, passion, evil desire, and covetousness (Col. 3:5). It is described as the life of darkness and ignorance. St. Paul talked about the old life, in these words:

> Now this I affirm and testify in the Lord, that you must no longer live as the Gentiles do, in the futility of their minds; they are darkened in their understanding, alienated from the life of God because of the ignorance that is in them, due to their hardness of heart; they have become callous and have given themselves up to licentiousness, greedy to practise every kind of uncleanness. (Eph. 4:17-19)

This old nature of the believers must die and be buried; this old nature, which belongs to their former manner of life must be put off (Eph. 4:22).

(B) The second idea of the text is that when the Christians were baptized, they were raised with Christ spiritually. This is the second aspect of baptism. In the second aspect of baptism, believers are raised or emerged from water. The rising up of the believers from water symbolizes that Christians are given the resurrected or new life; they become the new creatures in Jesus Christ. St. Paul exhorted Christians to give up their old nature and put on the new nature, in these words:

> Put off your old nature which belongs to your former manner of life and is corrupt through deceitful lusts, and be renewed in the spirit of your minds, and put on the new nature, created after the likeness of God in true righteousness and holiness. (Eph. 4:22-24)

This new nature is being renewed in knowledge after the image of its creator (Col. 3:10).

St. Paul theologically linked the death and resurrection of Jesus Christ with their practical implications for the believers, who were baptized, in these words of exhortation:

How can we who died to sin still live in it? Do you not know that all of us who have been baptized into Christ Jesus were baptized into his death? We were buried therefore with him by baptism into death, so that as Christ was raised from the dead by the glory of the Father, we too might walk in newness of life. For if we have been united with him in a death like his, we shall certainly be united with him in a resurrection like his. We know that our old self was crucified with him so that the sinful body might be destroyed, and we might no longer be enslaved to sin. But if we have died with Christ, we believe that we shall also live with him. For we know that Christ being raised from the dead will never die again; death has no dominion over him. The death he died he died to sin, once for all, but the life he lives he lives to God. So you also must consider yourselves dead to sin and alive to God in Christ Jesus. (Rom. 6:2-11)

The new nature demands moral and spiritual life, because it is the resurrected and spirt-led life. This is the second aspect of baptism.

(C) The third idea of the text is that Christians were spiritually raised or resurrected through their faith in the working of God. God makes the believers "new creatures" in Jesus Christ. God brings a radical change in the life of the believers. This act of God is beyond a comprehension of man. God's acts and His way of reasoning are supernatural; they are miraculous. When God makes radical changes in the life of man, which are beyond human comprehension, man must believe that God does those things by His power. How God's way and reasoning are different from man's way and reasoning is proclaimed by God through prophet Isaiah, saying:

For my thoughts are not your thoughts, neither are your ways my ways, says the LORD. For as the heavens are higher than the earth, so are my ways higher than your ways and my thoughts than your thoughts. (Is. 55:8-9)

Christians must have faith in the miraculous operation of God in their life. They have to believe that as God raised Christ Jesus from the dead, the same God and with the same power, is able to raise them spiritually, while they are in human bodies. Christian faith is the assurance of things hoped for, and the conviction of things not seen (Heb. 11:1). Noah, Abraham, Moses, judges, and the prophets had faith in God (Heb. 11). Without this faith in God, Christians would not feel the reality of the spiritual resurrection in their life.

(D) The fourth idea of the text is that God raised Christ Jesus from the dead. God manifested His miraculous power in resurrecting His Son Jesus Christ from the dead. It is the first event in the history of mankind. All the founders of other religions namely, Zoroaster or Zarathustra (early 700 B. C), Gautama Buddha (568-488 B. C.), Vardhaman Mahavir (540-468 B. C.), Muhammad Paigambar (A. D. 570-632), and Guru Nanak Singh (A. D.1469-1538), died and none of them rose from the dead. The resurrection of Jesus Christ is the most unique event in the human history; there is no parallel to it in our human history. There is an empty tomb, wherein Jesus Christ was buried, as a material evidence of the resurrection of Jesus Christ. There are other evidences in favour of proving the resurrection of Jesus Christ. Those evidences are secondary. The scripture is the final authority on this incredible fact. St. Paul met the risen Lord in a vision. In his testimony to the Corinthians, he wrote the following words:

> Christ died for our sins in accordance with the scripture, that he was buried, that he was raised on the third in accordance with the scripture. (I Cor. 15:3-4)

As God raised Jesus Christ from the dead, He raises the believers spiritually, by using His power.

The apostles, who saw the resurrected Lord Jesus Christ, preached the gospel of Jesus Christ to others; they preached about the spiritual victory of the Lord Jesus Christ over sin and death by His physical resurrection with the power of God. The apostles believed in the resurrection of the Lord Jesus Christ and subsequent resurrection of the believers; and they taught Christians this belief. The belief in the resurrection is not only a theoretical or theological necessity; but it has also a practical implication for the life of believers. St. Paul argued about this point with Christians, saying:

> Now if Christ is preached as raised from the dead, how can some of you say that there is no resurrection of the dead? But if there is no resurrection of the dead, then Christ has not been raised, then our preaching is in vain and your faith is in vain. (I Cor. 15:12-14)

Then he added:

> Your faith is futile and you are still in your sins. (I Cor. 15:17)

The belief in the resurrection of Jesus Christ is linked herein with redemption from the bondage of sin and death. The preaching about the resurrection of Jesus Christ and the faith in the resurrection of the believers are related to one another; and both of them are meaningful in their mutual context.

Conclusion

St. Paul connected the events of the death and resurrection of Jesus Christ with two aspects of baptism namely, immersion in water and emersion out of water. Immersion of believers into water symbolizes the spiritual death of the old life of the believers; and emersion out of water symbolizes the new life or the resurrected life of believers in Jesus Christ. This new life calls for leading a spiritual or moral life. On Easter day, Christians affirm their belief in the resurrection of their Lord Jesus Christ; and they also subsequently affirm their faith in their physical resurrection. Their belief in the resurrection challenges them to lead a spiritual and moral life.

Recommended Hymns from the Methodist Hymnal

114   'Let earth and heaven agree'

204   'Christ the Lord is risen today;'

206   'Christ is risen! Hallelujah!'

209   'On wings of living light'

211   'Low in the grave He lay'

213   'Thine be the glory, risen conquering Son'

215   'The strife is o'er, the battle done; '

230   'Rejoice and be glad! the Redeemer'

Recommended Responsive Reading from the Methodist Hymnal

74 (p. 416),

Recommended Responsive Reading from A Worship Manual for Scriptural or Methodist Order of Service

76 (pp. 189-190).

Chapter - 31

Titles of the Sermon
'Believers Overcoming the World,'
'Victory over the World and Death,'
'Constant Victory of the Believers in Christ Jesus'

Scripture
I John 5:1-5
Psalms 14:1-3; 53:1-3
Matthew 11:19; 26:59-66; 27:38
Luke 7:34; 13:13; 14:3
John 1:14; 14:5-6; 15:18-23
Acts 7:51-53, 56
Romans 3:10-12, 20-24; 8:37-39
I Corinthians 15:53-57
Philippians 2:7-11
Hebrews 2:14-18
I John 4:1-3

Text: I John 5:5

A Few Versions of the Text, I John 5:5
Who is he who overcomes the world, but he who believes that Jesus is the Son of God? *New King James Version*

Who is he that overcometh the world, but he that believes that Jesus is the Son of God? *Explanatory Notes Upon the New Testament*

Who is it that overcomes the world but he who believes that Jesus is the Son of God? *Revised Standard Version*

Who is it that overcomes the world? Only he who believes that Jesus is the Son of God. *New International Version*

for who is victor over the world but he who believes that Jesus is the Son of God? *The New English Bible*

But who could possibly fight and win this battle except by believing that Jesus is truly Son of God? *The Living Bible Illustrated*

Who wins the victory over the world? Isn't it the person who believes that Jesus is the Son of God? *God's Word*

Introduction

Church history tells us that Christian preachers and leaders were persecuted because of their faith in Jesus Christ. Many of them died for their faith. Their martyrdom did not stop spreading the gospel; but, on the hand, many people embraced Christian faith, having seen and learnt about the dedication and sacrifices of those Christian leaders.

(1) Dietrich Bonhoeffer (February 4, 1906 – April 9, 1945) was a Christian leader and a theologian in Germany. He was put in prison by Adolf Hitler (April 20, 1889- April 30, 1945), a dictator of Germany. Benhoeffer was leading his Christian religious life in the prison; he used to pray and meditate on the word of God every day. On Sunday, April 8, 1945, pastor Benhoeffer held a little service with other prisoners. That service touched the hearts of many. When he hardly finished his prayer, the door was opened by two soldiers. They entered the room and shouted, "Prisoner Bonhoeffer, come with us! " This meant that he was to be scaffolded. Bonhoeffer bid his goodby to the fellow prisoners, saying, "For me this is the beginning of new life, eternal life." [1] Bonhoeffer died for his Christian conviction. His death was not vain. He influenced life of others, while he was in the prison.

(2) A brief history of the early church is recorded in the book of the Acts of the Apostles. It states that Christians were persecuted and killed for their faith.

People of the synagogue of the Freedmen falsely charged Stephen to be blasphemous. They seized Stephen and brought him before the council of the Jews. Stephen, in his defence, bore testimony to Jesus Christ. He said to them:

> You stiff-necked people, uncircumcised in heart and ears, you always resist the Holy Spirit. As your fathers did, so do you. Which of the prophets did not your fathers persecute? And they killed those who announced beforehand the coming of the Righteous One, whom you have now betrayed and murdered, you who received the law as delivered by angels and did not keep it. (Acts 7:51-53)

When the Jews heard these words, they were enraged. But Stephen was gazing at heaven and he said to them:

> Behold, I see the heaven opened, and the Son of man standing at the right hand of God. (Acts 7:56)

People then stoned Stephen to death. He publicly witnessed Jesus as the Christ, the Messiah, in a life-threatening situation.

(3) All the apostles faced persecution and many of them were killed. Let us see how they were treated by the unbelieving people and the political authority.

Matthew suffered martyrdom, as he was slain with a sword in a distant city of Ethiopia. Mark was dragged through the streets of Alexandria; and he died of the pain. Luke was hanged upon an olive tree in Greece. John was put in boiling oil; he escaped death in a miraculous manner; and he was banished to Patmos. Peter was crucified at Rome with his head downward. James, the Greater, was beheaded at Jerusalem. James, the Less, was thrown from a lofty pinnacle of the temple; and then was beaten to death with a fuller's club. Bartholomew was flayed alive. Andrew was crucified. Thomas was run through the body with a lance at Coromandel, East Indies. Jude was shot to death with arrows. Matthias was first stoned, and then beheaded. Barnabas of the Gentiles was stoned to death at Salonica. Paul was beheaded at Rome by the

Emperor Nero.[2] These church leaders were firm believers in the Lord Jesus Christ. They died for their belief. Their death was not vain. Churches began to grow because of their sufferings and martyrdom.

Introduction of the Text

The apostles of Jesus Christ and other devout Christian leaders became immortal by their service to the Lord Jesus Christ. The unbelieving and opposing world tried to destroy the cause of the Christian faith; but it failed, because God made Christian believers victorious. John, an apostle of Jesus Christ asserted this truth in the following words:

> **Who is it that overcomes the world but he who believes that Jesus is the Son of God?** (I John 5:5)

This is the text of our meditation now.

The Context of the Text

Apostle John was a leader of the early church, which was facing persecution and theological controversies. It became difficult to preach Jesus Christ as the Messiah crucified by the Jews, because the majority of the Jews did not accept Jesus as their Messiah. Moreover, Jerusalem was under the power of the Roman Empire; in A. D. 70 the holy city was desolate. The Jews were dispersed by the Roman Ruler throughout the world. For Christian preachers, it became difficult to preach the doctrine of incarnation, God becoming man in Jesus Christ, to the Gentiles, who were influenced by Gnosticism. The gnostics believed that the spirit was good, and matter was utterly evil. This implied that any real incarnation of God was impossible. Further, it implied that there was no really vicarious suffering of Jesus Christ on the cross. Because of these trends, some Christian preachers were afraid of ascribing full humanity to Jesus. Those teachers denied the reality of the incarnation of Jesus Christ. Apostle John had to take a firm stand against these trends. Therefore, he wrote to the churches emphasizing:

> Beloved, do not believe every spirit, but test the spirit to see whether they are of God; for many false prophets have gone out into the world. By this you know the Spirit of God; every spirit which confesses that Jesus Christ

has come in the flesh is of God, and every spirit which does not confess Jesus
is not of God. (I Jn 4:1-3)

God gave apostle John deeper spiritual insight into the doctrine of the
incarnation as to how the blood and suffering of the Messiah were
intrinsically required for a victorious spiritual life, when he was
surrounded by sufferings and persecution. He shared his insight with
Christians by asking:

> Who is it that overcomes the world but he who believes that Jesus is the
> Son of God? (I Jn 5:5)

An Analysis of the Text

This text has an idea. This text is an interrogative statement. It can
be changed into an affirmative statement. It will be like this: "He,
who believes that Jesus is the Son of God, overcomes the world."

Exposition of the Idea of the Text

The statement, "He, who believes that Jesus is the Son of God,
overcomes the world," gives an assurance to the Christians that they
would be victorious over the world, if they believe that Jesus Christ
is the Son of God.

Apostle John used the term "world" with a special meaning. He
meant by it the society which is organized apart from God, a society
which functions independently of God, and a society which opposes
the teaching and the principles of God. In short, it is a godless society.
A society, which does not recognize God, teaches that man is self-
sufficient to save himself; he does not need any help from above; he
is a master of his destiny. It teaches that man can save himself by
his good deeds. It preaches against the Bible and its moral principles;
it encourages to be secular. It stands against the Church of God. It
creates laws, prohibiting to preach the gospel and to hinder the
extension of God's kingdom. It advocates the vicarious sufferings of
Jesus Christ as foolishness. This is a worldly philosophy.

How a godless society or the world would treat Christians was
prophesied by Jesus Christ when He said:

> If the world hates you, know that it has hated me before it hated you. If you were of the world, the world would love its own; but because you are not of the world, but I chose you out of the world, therefore the world hates you. Remember the word that I said to you, 'a servant is not greater than his master.' If they persecuted me, they will persecute you; if they kept my word, they will keep yours also. But all this they will do to you on my account, because they do not know him who sent me. If I had not come and spoken to them, they would not have sin; but now they have no excuse for their sin. He who hates me hates my Father also. (Jn 15:18-23)

It seems apostle John followed the teaching of Jesus Christ when he spoke of the spirit of an anti-Christ as follows:

> And every spirit which does not confess Jesus is not of God. This is the spirit of Antichrist, of which you heard that was coming, and now it is in the world already.... They are of the world, therefore what they say is of the world, and the world listens to them. (I Jn 4:3, 5)

The world or a godless society teaches that man can save himself by his righteous deeds. This teaching is centred around man. But this teaching is against the teaching of the Bible. The Bible teaches that man cannot save himself by his righteous deeds because man is spiritually corrupt. St. Paul, who was a Pharisee and had a deeper knowledge of the word of God, argued for the doctrine of righteousness through faith on the basis of the scripture. He quoted the texts when he wrote to argue this point:

> None is righteous, no, not one; no one understands, no one seeks for God. All have turned aside, together they have gone wrong; no one does good, not even one. (Rom. 3:10-12 = Ps. 14:1-3; 53:1-3)

Then he argued, saying:

> For no human being will be justified in his sight by works of the laws, since through the law comes knowledge of sin. But now the righteousness of God has been manifested apart from law, although the law and the prophets bear witness to it, the righteousness of God through faith in Jesus Christ for all who believe. For there is no distinction; since all have sinned and fall short of the glory of God, they are justified by his grace as a gift, through the redemption which is in Christ Jesus. (Rom. 3:20-24)

As these verses tell us that there is no salvation apart from Jesus Christ, the unbelievers cannot be saved. This is an exclusive claim of the Christian faith. When Thomas, a disciple of Jesus Christ, asked Jesus, "how can we know the way?" Jesus Christ replied him in these definite words: "I am the way, the truth, and the life; no one comes to the Father, but by me." (Jn 14:6) This divine claim implies that Jesus Christ is the only way to go to God, the Father; He is the way of the eternal life beyond grave; He is the way of overcoming death and to be with God eternally; He is the way of redemption from death and sin; He is the way of life and truth.

Christian believers must believe that Jesus Christ is the Son of God who overcame the world by His death on the cross. They have to believe that God became man in Jesus Christ as a historical fact. Incarnation of God in Jesus Christ is not a fantasy. It was the reality. Apostles bore the witness to this historical fact. St. John wrote:

> "The Word became flesh and dwelt among us, full of grace and truth, glory as of the only Son from the Father." (Jn 1:14)

When God became a man, called Jesus of Nazareth, He emptied Himself of the divine glory. He took the form of a servant, being born in the likeness of man. As a man, He humbled Himself and became obedient unto death, even death on a cross. (Phil. 2:7-8) He took human limitation upon Himself because He loved and cared enough for the salvation of man.

When God became a man in Jesus Christ, He submitted Himself to the criticism of and persecution at the hands of the godless society or the world. Scribes and Pharisees criticised him to be a friend of sinners and tax-collectors (Mt. 11:19; Lk.7:34). He was judged and blamed for breaking Sabbaths, when He healed the sick people (Lk. 13:13; 14:3). He was falsely charged and judged to be sentenced to die on a cross (Mt. 26:59-66). He was hanged between two criminals on the cross (Mt. 27:38). Thus the world became victorious over Jesus Christ when it killed Him on the cross.

The victory of the world over Jesus Christ lived for a short time from His death to His resurrection. God raised His Son on the third day. God thus made Jesus Christ victorious over the powers of the world, of sin and death. Because God accomplished His purpose of salvation for mankind through His son Jesus Christ, God exalted His Son and bestowed on Him the title "the Lord of all" (Phil. 2:9-11).

What the victory of the Lord Jesus Christ over the world or godless society and sin would have a positive effect on the life of believers in Christ? When God was incarnated in Jesus Christ, He was tempted by the devil. He became triumphant over the temptation. Jesus Christ knows our human weakness and He would make the believers victorious over temptation and trials. They would be victorious over the world and its temptation by the power and mercy of the Lord. This assurance is given to them, in the following words:

> Since therefore the children share in flesh and blood, he himself likewise partook of the same nature, that through death he might destroy him who has the power of death, that is, the devil, and deliver all those who through fear of death were subject to lifelong bondage. For surely it is not with angels that he is concerned but with the descendants of Abraham. Therefore he had to be made like his brethren in every respect, so that he might become a merciful and faithful high priest in the service of God, to make expiation for the sins of the people. For because he himself has suffered and been tempted, he is able to keep those who are tempted. (Heb. 2:14-18)

These verses explain why God took a human form. There are three reasons given herein. (1) The first reason was that the Son of God shares the nature of man. (2) The second reason was that the Son of God destroys the devil through His death. (3) The third reason was that the Son of God becomes a merciful and sympathetic high priests, making expiation for the sins of man. These three reasons were meant for the total victory of the believers over temptations and trial on the earth.

Jesus Christ wants to share His victory over the world and death, with His followers. The believers are promised to have the eternal life beyond the grave. St. Paul wrote to the Christians at Corinth, concerning this hope:

> For this perishable nature must put on the imperishable, and this mortal nature must put on immortality. When the perishable puts on the imperishable, and the mortal puts on immortality, then shall come to pass the saying that is written: 'Death is swallowed up in victory.' O death, where is thy victory? O death, where is thy sting? The sting of death is sin, and

the power of sin is the law. But thanks be to God, who gives us victory through our Lord Jesus Christ. (I Cor. 15:53-57)

This victory of the believers in Jesus Christ over the godless world is going to be a constant victory in their daily life. Jesus Christ will be always with the believers. Nothing would separate them from Jesus Christ. Their mutual love would go on in all kinds of crises. St. Paul wrote to the believers at Rome, concerning this, as follows:

> Who shall separate us from the love of Christ? Shall the tribulation, or distress, or persecution, or famine, or nakedness, or peril, or sword? ... No, in all these things we are more than conquerors through him who loved us. For I am sure that neither death, nor life, nor angels, nor principalities, nor things present, nor things to come, nor powers, nor height, nor depth, nor anything else in all creation, will be able to separate us from the love of God in Christ Jesus our Lord. (Rom. 8:37-39)

Conclusion

The followers of Jesus Christ, who would believe Him as the Son of God, would become victorious over trials and temptations, which they would face in the godless world. They would not be separated from the love of Jesus Christ in any circumstance. The Lord Jesus Christ would be with them; He would empower them to overcome the world; He would be sympathetic with them; and He would mediate for them to the LORD God. The believers would be triumphant in the world and in the world beyond the grave.

Recommended Hymns from the Methodist Hymnal

91   'All hail the power of Jesus' name'

204   'Christ the Lord is risen to-day;'

206   'Christ is risen! Hallelujah!'

211   'Low in the grave He lay'

213   ' Thine be the glory, risen conquering Son'

215   'The strike is o'er, the battle done'

'226   'Look, ye saints! The sight is glorious,'

235   'I know that my Redeemer lives-'

661   'Come, let us with our Lord arise'

Recommended Responsive Reading from the Methodist Hymnal

56 (p. 409),

Recommended Responsive Reading from A Worship Manual for Scriptural or Methodist Services

53 (pp. 153-154) or

100 (pp. 234-235).

Endnotes

[1] Paul Lee Tan, Encyclopedia of 7700 Illustrations: Signs of the Times, # 1046.

[2] Ibid., # 1147.

Chapter - 32

'Appearances of Jesus Christ to His Disciples and Followers, after Resurrection.'

'A Significance of Number 40 in the Bible,'

'An Observance On Fortieth Day after Funeral of a Believer.'

Scripture

Genesis 8:1-19

Exodus 8:18

Deuteronomy 8:3

Numbers 14:5-12,26-32

Mathew 4:1-11 ;14: 26-32; 28:7, 9-10, 16-20

Mark 16:15-16

Luke 2:22-28; 5:10; 24: 2,6,12, 13-35, 44

John20:18,28-29, 21:13, 15-17, 23

Acts 1:1-3,12;9:3-5

Text: I Corinthians 15:3-8,6,8

A Theological Significance of Forty Days

The number 40th has some theological significance for Christians. We shall take note of a few of the 40th .

1. The LORD Yahweh was displeased with man when all people became sinful. He decided to destroy mankind and other living beings by flood. The LORD God found Noah as a good and righteous man. God asked him to make an ark to accommodate his family and other animals to survive after the flood. The rain poured on the earth forty days and forty nights. The whole earth

was flooded so much that no man, beast was able to survive; all died in the flood except Noah and other eight persons, and the creatures, who had given shelter in the ark. (Gen.8:1-19) This event of destruction also had a positive aspect that is the LORD God spared Noah and his family and other creatures so that they reproduce of their kind in holiness.

2. Moses liberated the people of Israel out of the bondage of the Egyptians and led them to the mountain of God, Sinai or Horeb. The LORD God asked Moses to come up on the mountain to receive ten commandments and other statues. Moses went to the mountain and stayed there for forty days and nights. (Ex. 24:18) On the mountain, there was no one to cook and serve him his regular meals. This implies that he fasted during those forty days and nights. There is another version of the same event which says that Moses ate nothing and drank nothing for forty days and nights. (Dt. 9:9) God gave the ten commandments, written by the LORD God; then God asked Moses to go down to see that the people had sinned by worshiping the golden calf. The wrath of God was kindled agaisnt the Hebrews and Aaron; and He was ready to destroy them. Moses prostrated before God to plead Him not to destroy them, for forty days and nights. Moses ate nothing and drank nothing for these days. (Dt. 9:18) Moses fasted twice for forty days and nights. These events remind us that Jesus Christ fasted forty days and nights in the wilderness when He was tempted by the devil. When the Satan wished to tempt Him by turning stone into bread, Jesus quoted the words of Moses, with reference to the hunger of the people and God fed them manna as follow:

> And he humbled you and let you huger and fed you with manna, which you did not know, nor did you fathers know; that he might make you know that man does not live by bread alone, but that man lives by everything that proceed out of the LORD. (Dt. 8:3)

In other words, the real bread for man is the word of the LORD God and man must trust in the provision of God.

3. Moses sent twelve spies, one from each tribe to spy the promised the land. They spied the land and gave both negative and positive

forty days reports to the people of Israel. The spies of ten tribes have a very disappointing report that they would be defeated by the residents of the land. Caleb and Joshua gave an encouraging report that they could possess the land if they believe in the promise of the LORD God. (Num. 14:5-12) The people of Israel were afraid and they questioned the promise of God. God was displeased with them. God made them wander in the wilderness for forty years because of their unbelief. (Num. 14:26-32) Most of the people died without seeing the promised land. Under Joshua, the surviving people were able to defeat the inhabitants of the promised land and possess the land. This event teaches us to believe in the promises of God.

4. There are some more events around the figure forty; but I am not going to mention them. What is important for us is to know the events around the life of Jesus Christ.

5. Jesus of Nazareth was dedicated to God by His parents, when Jesus was forty days old. (Lk. 2:22-28)

6. Before Jesus of Nazareth, who was the anticipated Messiah or Christ, began His teaching and healing ministry, He was taken in the wilderness by Satan to tempt Him in many ways. Jesus Christ overcame all the temptations; He told the Satan that He would not bow down before the Satan because He would bow down and worship the LORD God only.   (Mt.4:1-11) The Satan left Him; and the angels came to strengthen Him. This even tells us that we should overcome all temptations and remain in the fold of God in times of crises.

7. The LORD God raised Jesus Christ from the dead on the third day, after His death on a cross. After the physical resurrection, Jesus Christ appeared to His apostles and the followers forty days. He was ascended to heaven on the fortieth day. (Acts 1: 1-3) His ascension to heaven marked the end of His human bodily existence and the beginning of His supernatural or heavenly existence. This event implies that we should end the period of bereavement and begin to live our normal life by the grace of God in Jesus Christ.

8. We want to know a probable sequence of the appearances of Jesus Christ to His apostles and followers during the forty days in order to convince the that He was resurrected and He won victory over sin and death. Let us know the sequence from the New Testament.

9. We can re-write the sequence of the appearances of Jesus Christ to His followers and the apostles as follows:

10. Mary Magdalene, Mary the mother of James, Salome, and other ladies took spices to put on the body of Jesus on Sunday, very early in the morning. They went to the tomb. They were asking themselves who would roll the stone from the tomb. When they reached the tomb, they found the stone rolled away from the tomb. (Lk. 24:2) They entered the tomb but they did not find the body of their Lord Jesus. Suddenly two angels appeared in the tomb and they asked the ladies a question, "Why do you look for the living among the dead?" They told them that Jesus was not there and he was risen. The angels reminded the words of Jesus that He would be crucified and on the third day He would rise again. (Lk. 24:6) The ladies were on their way to the disciples. Jesus Christ appeared to them; and they worshipped Him. (Mt. 28:9-10) It was the first appearance of the risen Lord Jesus to His followers. The risen Lord Jesus Christ told them that He was risen from the dead and He would meet His disciples on a mountain in Galilee. The ladies went to the disciples to tell what the angels told them and how they met the risen Lord Jesus Christ; but they did not believe the report. It appears that Mary Magdalene did not go with other ladies; she stayed behind, she reported that the body of Jesus was removed from the tomb. Mary Magdalene who was a very devoted follower of Jesus Christ. She was possessed by seven evil spirit. Jesus Christ freed her from the evil spirits; therefore, she became a close follower of Jesus Christ.

11. Having heard from Mary Magdalene, Peter and other disciples went to the tomb. Peter entered the tomb, he found the linen stripes but did not find the body. He was wondering what had happened to the body of Jesus. (Lk. 24:12)

12. When all disciples left the tomb and went home, Mary Magdalene stayed behind. She saw a man; she supposed him to be a gardener. She asked him whether he knew where the body of her lord was kept. The man called her by her name; then she realized that the unknown man was Jesus her lord. This was the second appearance of Jesus Christ to His followers. Mary then went back to the disciples and told them the news that she saw the Lord Jesus. But the disciples did not believe her testimony or report. (Jn 20:18)

13. On the same day, i.e. Sunday, two followers of Jesus Christ, one of them was Cleopas, were going to Emmaus, the village seven miles away from Jerusalem. They were discussing what had happened in Jerusalem during the last two days. Jesus, an unknown man, joined them in discussion. He explained to them about the Messiah with reference to the scripture that Messiah would be raised from the dead on the third day. The hearts of disciples were burning while the stranger was telling them. The followers asked the man to stay with them because it was going to be night. When they sat together for a supper, the stranger took a bread and gave thanks; then their eyes were opened and they recognized Him as the lord Jesus. Then Jesus Christ disappeared from them. Those two disciples went back to Jerusalem to convey the news to the disciples. (Lk. 24:13-35) This was a first appearance of the risen Lord Jesus to His disciples.

14. The disciples of Jesus were afraid of Jews and they were hiding in a house. The followers, who returned from Emmaus to Jerusalem, were reporting how they saw the Lord Jesus to the disciples, Jesus appeared to them. It was a second appearance of Jesus to His disciples. They were frightened believing it was a ghost. Jesus showed them His hands and feet where nails were put through. Yet they could not believe. He asked them for food. They gave Him a broiled fish. He ate the food. Then He told them that whatever was written about him by the prophets and Moses be fulfilled; and He would be raised on the third day from the dead. (Lk. 24:44)

15. Thomas was absent when Jesus appeared to the disciples. He raised questions about the resurrection of Jesus that he wanted to put his fingers in the hands and feet of Jesus and his hand in the side of Jesus to verify the news. A week later, Jesus appeared to his disciples and asked Thomas what he wanted to do. Then Thomas believed in the resurrection of Jesus. He said to Jesus, "My Lord and My God." (Jn 29:28)   This was a third appearance of Jesus to His disciples.

The disciples were doing other works during three weeks. Jesus appeared to other followers; but the gospel writers did not record those appearance of Jesus Christ. (Jn 21:23)

16. Jesus Christ appeared to His disciples by the sea of Tiberias in the following way. Peter. Thomas, Nathaniel, sons of Zebedee James and John (Lk. 5:10), and other two disciples went fishing in the sea of Tiberias. They caught nothing during night. In the morning Jesus appeared to the disciples and asked them whether they caught any fish. They replied to the stranger saying 'nothing'. Then Jesus asked them to throw their net on the right side of the boat. When they did they caught a large number of fish. John said to Peter that the stranger was the Lord Jesus. Peter jumped into water because he was not well covered with clothes. Peter and others took the boat at shore and removed fish from the net. The disciples saw a fire burning coals and fish on it. Jesus asked them to bring some fish to have a breakfast. Jesus gave them bread and fish (Jn 21:13) After the breakfast, Jesus asked Peter, 'Do you love truly love me more than these? Peter replied 'Yes.' Then Jesus said to Peter 'Feed my lambs.' Jesus asked the same question to Peter and then Jesus said to him 'Take care of my sheep.' Then third time Jesus asked the same question; and Peter answered 'You know that I love you.' (Jn. 21:15-17) Then Jesus said to Peter 'Feed my sheep.' This conversation between Jesus and Peter tells us how St. Peter was made a leader of the disciples; and he was given a responsibility to look after the church. This was a fourth appearance the risen Lord Jesus to His disciples.

17. Jesus Christ appeared to more than five hundred followers at one time. (I Cor. 15:6) This event might refer to when Jesus Christ appeared to His followers and disciples on the mountain in Galilee.

18. Finally, Jesus Christ appeared to apostle Paul at Damascus (I Cor. 15:8; Acts 9:3-5)

19. Recall the event when Mary Magdalene; and other ladies went to do the final rite to the body of Jesus. They saw an angel who told them that Jesus was risen and he told them to tell the news to the disciples that Jesus was risen and ask them to go to Galilee. There they would see Jesus. (Mt. 28:7) The disciples went to the mountain of Galilee and they saw the resurrected Lord Jesus. This was a fifth appearance of the risen Lord Jesus Christ. On this mountain, Jesus gave the great commission to His disciples to go all over the world and preach the gospel and baptize the people in the name of the trinity. (Mk. 16:15-16) After giving them the commission, Jesus was ascended to heaven. It was the fortieth day (Acts. 1:2; Lk. 24:51)

Conclusion

The period from the resurrection to ascension of the Lord Jesus Christ is marked with supernatural events indicating the triumph of Jesus Christ over sin and death. The body of Jesus Christ was transformed when He appeared to His disciples. Our bodies will be transformed into heavenly bodies at the time of the second coming Of Jesus Christ. This spiritual transformation gives us hope how we would be in the life beyond grave. Therefore, we should build our faith that we are sharing in the victory of Jesus Christ. This should give us courage to face all kinds of crises and be victorious in life. This conviction should enable us to end our period of mourning and to begin to live a life as long as the Lord God wills for us.

Benediction: Now may our Lord Jesus Christ Himself, and God the Father, who loved us and gave us eternal comfort and good hope through grace, comfort your hearts and establish them in every good work and word.

Bibliography

A) Primary Sources

The Holy Bible, The New King James Version. Nashville: Thomas Nelson Publishers, Inc., 1982

The Holy Bible, Revised Standard Version. London,Edinburgh,Paris,Melbourne, Johannesburg,Toronto,and New York: Thomas Nelson and Sons Ltd.,12th impression, 1962.

The Thompson Chain-Reference Bible, New International Version. Grand Rapids, Michigan: Zondervan Bible Publishers, second printing, 1983.

The New English Bible with the Apocrypha. New York: Oxford University Press, 1971.

The Way, The Living Bible Illustrated. Wheaton, Illinois: Tyndale House Publishers, sixth printing, 1973.

God's Word, Today's Bible translation that says what it means. Grand Rapids, Michigan: World Publishing Ins., 1995.

B) Secondary Sources

Barckay, William. *The Gospel of Luke*. Edinburgh: The Saint Andrew Press, Eighth Impression, 1964.

——————————. *The Letters to the Corinthians*. Edinburgh: The Saint Andrew Press, fifth impression, 1961.

——————————.*The Letters of James and Peter* . Edinburgh: The Saint Andrew Press, 5th Impression, 1963.

——————————. *The Mind of St Paul*. London & Glasgow: Collins Fontana books, 1965.

Campbell, Duncan. *God's Answer: Revival Sermons*. Edinburgh: The Faith Mission, 1960.

Kee, Alistair ed., *A Reader in Plotical Theology*. London: S. C. M. Press, 1986.

The Methodist Hymn Book with Office. London : The Methodist Publishing House, 1933.

Methodist Preacher, *John Wesley the Methodist: A Plain Account of His life and Work*. New York: Eaton & Mains, 1903.

Miller, Basil. *William Carey: The Father o Modern Missions*. Minneapolis, Minnesota: Bethany House Publishers, 1980.

Richardson, Cyril C. ed. *Early Christian Fathers*, Vol. I, Philadelphia: The Westminister Press, and London: S. C. M. Press, n. d.

Scott, John R. W. *The Epistle of John*. Leicester, England: Inter-varsity Press, Reprinted, 1983.

Spitz, Lewis W., *The Renaissnce and Reformation Movements*. Chicago: Rand McNalley & Co., 1971.

Stewart, James S. *A Man in Christ*. Grand Rapids, Michigan: Baker Book house, Third Priting, 1980.

Wesley, John. *The Works of John Wesley*. Grand Rapids, Michigan: Baker Book House, 3rd Ed. 1984. Vol.14.

──────────.*Explanatory Notes Upon the New Testament*. Grand Rapids, Michigan: Baker Book House, 1986. Vol.2

The Wesleyan Bible Commentary. Peabody, Massachusetts: Hendrickson Publishers. reprinted 1986. Vol.6.

C) Other Sources

Concise Dictionary of the Bible. Neill, S., Goodwin, J., and Dowle, A., ed.   London: United Society for Christian Literature, Lutterworth Press, 1966. Vol. 2.

The Complete Who's Who in the Bible. Gardner, Paul D., ed. Grand Rapids, Michigan: Zonsevan Publishing house, 1995.

The Encyclopedia of Religious Quotations.

Mead, Frank S. ed. Old Tappan, New Jersey: Fleming H. Revell Company, 1965.

The Interpretwer's Bible in Twelve Volumes, New York: Abingdon Cokesbury Press Nashville,1952.

The New American Encyclopedia. Philadelphia: The Publisher Agency Inc., 1974. Vol. 20.

The New Dictionary of Thoughts. Edwards, Tryon, orignal compiler; Catrevas, C. N. Edwards, Jonathan,Browns Ralph E. Revised and enlargered by,U. S. A: Standard Book Co.,1960.

Tan, Paul Lee. *Encyclopedia of 7700 Illustrations: Signs* of the *Times*.

Rockville,Maryland: Assurance Publishers, 9th printing, 1985.

"Ebony," January 1986.

"Observer," January 1984.

Appendix

Rt. Rev. Dr. Daniel D. Rupwate has written more than three hundred textual sermons. Some of his textual sermons are published in the books, having different titles, mentioned below. This index booklet includes only fifteen books. Other sermons were privately published; they are excluded from the list. The index will help readers know where his textual sermons be found.

Index Booklet for the Published Sermons

Name of the Book	Book Number
In Remembrance of the Life- Blood of Jesus Christ: Thirty-Six Textual Sermons on the Holy Communion	1
A Meditation on Good Friday: Textual Sermons on Seven Utterances of Jesus Christ from the Cross	2
The Good News of the Bible: Twenty-Five Textual Sermons on the Gospel Of and About Jesus Christ Vol. I	3
The Good News of the Bible: Twenty-Five Textual Sermons on the Gospel Of and About Jesus Christ Vol. II	4
Proven Divinity of Jesus Christ Through His Spiritual Titles and Exclusive claims	
A Biblical Perspective on Mothers' Day, Fathers' Day and Children's Day	6
Biblical Foundations of Scripturally Based Spiritual Revival in the Church: Twenty-Eight Textual Sermons on Revivals and Reforms	7

The Teaching of Jesus Christ Through His Parables	8
A Biblical Administration of the Church and Society: Nineteen Textual Sermons on Administration of the Church And Fifteen Textual Sermons on Administration of Society	9
A Biblical leadership and the Church Discipline: Sixteen textual Sermons on the Biblical Leadership And the Church Discipline	10
The Call of God in Jesus Christ for Holiness and Social Morality: Fifteen Textual Sermons on Lent with Methodist Piety And Social Morality Or Scriptural Holiness of Methodism	11
Sanctified, Sacred, and Saved Life of Christians: Twenty-Nine Textual Sermons on Baptism, Marriage, and Funeral Services	12
Jesus of Nazareth, the Messiah or Christ: Thirty-One Textual Sermons on Proving Jesus as the Messiah or Christ.... (16 Textual Sermons on Christmas, 7 Textual Sermons on the Palm Sunday, 8 Textual Sermons on the Easter Sunday)	13
Covenantal Relationship Between the LORD God and His People: Nine Textual Sermons on Covenant Sunday or New Year Sunday with The Covenant Theology of the Rev. John Wesley and 'An Enlarged Historical Preface the Covenant with God Service	14
Thanking the LORD God on Two Special Occasions: Eleven Textual Sermons of the Thanksgiving Day and Two Textual Sermons on Church Anniversary Day	15

Text	Book No.	Chapter No.
Genesis		
2:18	12	8
4:9	9	20
22:16-18	14	1
24:50-51	12	9
Exodus		
4:13	9	1
14:15-16	9	2
20:12	6	7
Leviticus		
23:23-24	14	2
13:30	7	1
13:30	15	12
Deuteronomy		
5:15	7	2
8:10	15	1
8:14	7	3
16:14	14	3
32:6	15	2
Joshua		
23:14	12	15
I Samuel		
2:20	6	1
12:24-25	10	2
I Kings		
19:12	4	2
19:12	10	3
II Kings		
4:10	6	2

Text	Book No.	Chapter No.
II Kings		
12:15	9	20
17:15	7	4
20:5-6	7	5
23:3	7	6
23:3	14	4
23:3	10	4
I Chronicles		
29:17	15	3
II Chronicles		
32:7-8	7	7
34:31	14	5
Nehemiah		
9:28	11	1
Psalms		
24:3-4	11	2
26:1	10	5
50:23	15	4
51:10	11	3
73:25	12	16
82:3-4	9	21
103:2-5	15	5
Psalms		
111:10	10	6
112:5-6	12	17
116:15	12	18
119:9	6	13
121:1-2	11	4
127:1	12	10

Text	Book No.	Chapter No.
Proverbs		
2:12	6	14
3:27	9	22
9:10	7	8
10:1	6	15
10:7	12	19
11:24	15	6
13:21	9	23
19:18	6	16
20:7	6	8
22:6	6	17
23:13-14	6	9
24:3	7	9
25:4-5	9	24
29:15	6	3
29:15	6	18
29:18	9	25
31:20	6	4
31:30	6	5
Ecclesiastes		
12:13-14	10	7
Isaiah		
4:4	11	5
11:1	7	10
11:1	9	3
25:8	12	20
28:26	9	26
32:17	9	27
66:3	12	21

Text	Book No.	Chapter No.
Jeremiah		
5:30-31	10	8
18:4	11	6
Ezekiel		
11:19-20	14	6
34:4	9	28
Hosea		
6:1-2	12	22
Amos		
3:7	9	4
5:24	9	29
Micah		
5:2	13	1
Habakkuk		
3:17-18	15	7
Haggai		
1:9-10	9	5
2:9	15	8
Zechariah		
4:6	7	1
Matthew		
1:1	5	1
1:21	13	2
1:23	13	3
2:3	13	4
2:10-11	13	5
2:12	13	6
3:11	12	1
5:13	8	2

Text	Book No.	Chapter No.
Matthew		
5:14-15	8	3
5:17	4	3
5:20	9	6
7:14	8	3
7:18-19	8	5
7:25	8	6
7:28-29	3	2
8:8	7	12
8:17	3	3
9:17	8	7
10:32-33	4	4
12:45	8	8
13:8	8	9
13:9	3	4
13:30	8	10
13:32	8	11
13:44	8	12
13:45-46	8	13
13:47	8	14
13:52	8	15
16:16	5	2
16:23	4	5
18:35	8	16
19:14	12	2
20:16	8	17
20:31	8	18
21:8	13	17
21:9	13	18

Text	Book No.	Chapter No.
Matthew		
21:13	10	9
21:16	13	19
21:41	8	19
21:42	3	5
22:12	8	20
25:13	8	21
25:40	9	30
25:45	9	31
25:45-46	8	22
26:27	1	1
26:29	1	2
26:38	11	7
26:64	5	3
26:66	11	8
27:46	2	4
Mark		
1:14-15	4	6
1:22	3	6
4:26-29	8	23
8:35	4	7
10:30	4	8
11:9-10	13	20
16:3	13	24
Luke		
2:7	13	7
2:10	13	8
2:11	13	9
2:21	13	10
2:34-35	13	11

Text	Book No.	Chapter No.
Luke		
2:52	6	19
2:21	12	3
4:18-19	3	7
5:4-5	7	13
7:32	8	24
7:47	8	25
9:62	4	9
10:36-37	8	26
11:9	8	27
12:21	8	28
12:48	8	29
13:5	11	9
13:8-9	8	30
13:21	8	31
13:24	8	32
14:11	8	33
14:28	8	34
15:7	8	35
15:10	8	36
15:32	8	37
16:10	8	38
16:15	10	10
16:25	8	39
17:18	15	9
18:7-8	8	40
18:14	8	41
19:26	8	42
21:3	15	10
22:13	1	3

Text	Book No.	Chapter No.
Luke		
22:15	1	4
22:20	1	5
23:24	2	1
23:42-43	2	2
23:46	2	7
24:5	13	25
24:30-31	1	6
24:46-47	3	8
John		
1:14	5	4
1:14	13	12
2:17	13	21
3:3	7	14
3:16	3	9
3:30	13	13
4:13-14	5	7
4:21	11	10
4:26	5	5
4:42	9	7
6:35	5	8
6:35	1	7
6:53	1	8
8:12	5	9
8:31-32	7	15
8:42	6	10
8:58	5	10
10:7	5	11
10:11	10	11
10:11	5	12

Text	Book No.	Chapter No.
John		
11:25	5	13
12:5	9	32
12:9	13	22
12:14-15	13	23
12:35-36	12	23
13:13	5	6
13:15	9	8
13:18	1	9
14:6	5	14
15:4	7	16
15:10	6	11
15:13-14	1	10
19:26-27	2	3
19:28	2	5
19:30	2	6
21:12	1	11
21:15	13	26
21:18-19	13	27
Acts		
6:3	9	9
19:5-6	12	4
20:24	4	10
20:28	1	12
Romans		
1:16-17	3	10
2:29	14	7
3:25	1	13
5:8	3	11
5:9	1	14

Text	Book No.	Chapter No.
Romans		
5:18	3	12
6:4	12	5
8:18	12	24
10:15	4	11
12:2	7	17
12:9	10	12
13:12-13	4	12
15:18	10	13
16:18	10	14
I Corinthians		
10:16	1	17
10:21	1	18
10:33-11:1	7	19
11:26	1	19
11:29	1	20
13:5	12	11
15:17	13	28
II Corinthians		
2:15-16	3	15
3:9	3	16
4:3-4	3	17
4:6	3	18
4:18	12	25
5:15	1	21
5:17	14	8
5:20-21	3	19
7:10	11	12
9:8	15	11

Text	Book No.	Chapter No.
Galatians		
1:9	4	16
1:11-12	3	20
2:20	4	17
2:20	7	20
3:13	3	21
4:4-5	4	18
5:1	4	19
Ephesians		
1:13-14	4	20
2:13	1	22
2:15-16	3	22
3:6	3	23
3:17-18	13	14
4:3	9	33
4:5	12	6
4:11-12	9	13
5:2	14	9
5:8-9	13	15
Philippians		
1:27-28a	3	24
2:4	9	14
2:9	9	15
3:10-11	13	29
3:13-14	11	13
3:13-14	9	16
Colossians		
1:13-14	1	23
1:23	4	21
1:20	1	24

Text	Book No.	Chapter No.
Colossians		
1:28	4	22
2:12	13	30
3:14	12	12
I Thessalonians		
2:3-4	3	25
5:5:11	9	17
II Thessalonians		
2:15	4	23
I Timothy		
6:11	15	13
II Timothy		
1:5	6	6
1:10	4	24
2:21	11	14
3:5	7	21
3:15	6	20
4:21	9	18
Titus		
2:11-12	7	22
2:11-12	11	15
Hebrews		
2:11	13	16
2:14	1	25
4:9-10	12.	26
8:6	1	26
9:14	1	27
9:22	1	28
10:19-20	1	29
11:9-1	12	27

Text	Book No.	Chapter No.
Hebrews		
12:5-6	6	12
13:4	12	13
13:12	1	30
James		
2:13	7	24
3:17	7	25
I Peter		
1:2	1	31
1:12	4	25
1:17	10	17
1:18-19	1	32
2:24-25	3	26
3:21	12	7
4:17	4	26
II Peter		
1:5-7	4	27
1:8	4	28
I John		
1:7	1	33
2:29	7	26
3:14	7	27
5:5	13	31
III John		
4	12	14
11	7	28
11	10	18
Revelation		
1:5-6	1	34
1:8	5	15

Text	Book No.	Chapter No.
Revelation		
3:16	9	19
5:9	1	35
7:1	1	36
7:16-17	12	28
21:7	12	29

A Word
About the Author and His Book

The Rt. Rev. Dr. Daniel D. Rupwate, B. A. (Hons.), B. D., M. Th., Ph. D., was the General Superintendent of the British Methodist Episcopal Church of Canada from 1987 to 1998. He was born in Maharashtra State in India. He was graduated from the University Pune (Poona) in 1963 with B. A. (Hons.). As far as his training in a theology is concerned, he obtained B. D. in 1967 and M. Th. in 1970, from Senate of Serampore. Whilst in India, he served the Methodist Church in Southern Asia as a Minister in Nagpur, Pune, and Mumbai. He was a lecturer in the United Theological College, Poona, for a year. He served as a Regional Secretary of Maharashtra State of the Christian Institute for the Study of Religion & Society. Some of his essays were published in a newspaper and were later compiled in a booklet in Marathi and published in 1974. The English subtitle for this booklet is *"Christianity in the Context of the Indian Way of Life."*

In 1980 he obtained Ph. D. from McMaster University, Hamilton, Canada. He joined the ministry of the British Methodist Episcopal Church of Canada in 1978 and served as a Minister in Toronto, East York, Brantford, St. Catharines, and Niagara Falls, Ontario. He also served as the General Secretary of the B. M. E. Church Conference from 1982 to 1986. He wrote a few essays for Canadian Methodist Historical Society, which were published by the said organization. He continues to do research and writing on Methodism. His book *"Negro Methodist Churches, Rev. John Wesley's Thoughts Upon Slavery, and His Struggle Against Slavery,"* may help readers know the significant contribution of Rev. John Wesley, a founder of Methodism, toward propagating the gospel and combating racism in the world.

He had an intension to build a better image of the British Methodist Episcopal Church. Therefore, he revised services on baptism, marriage, funeral, ordination etc. and published a book

"The Book of Offices for the Methodist Episcopal Church" in 1998. He wished that the followers of Methodism should know in depth theology of Methodism. Therefore, he wrote a book "A Scriptural Vindication of the Articles of Religion: The Twenty-five Articles of Religion of Methodism…" and published it in 2010. He wanted to maintain the spirit of Methodism in the churches; therefore, he wrote a book "A Worship Manual for a Scriptural or Methodist Order of Service." He published this book in 2005. He began to revise the Discipline of the Methodist Episcopal Church when he was elected as the General Secretary of the B. M. E. Church Conference in 1982. He continued his effort until 1998. He published a book on the discipline of the B. M. E. Church in 2001. These books would keep the spirit of Methodism in the B. M. E. Churches, if they use these books.

His pursuit of writing on biblical theology is evident in his second book, "In Remembrance of the Lifeblood Jesus Christ" This book was published by the Word of Life Publication, Pune, India, in 2002. The I.S. P. C. K. Delhi, India, has published his other books on theology, which are mentioned at the end of this book.

He put together his sermons on baptism, marriage and funeral of Christians. This book, "Sanctified, Sacred, and Saved Life of Christians," was published by ISPCK in 2018. He followed the same trend. He put together his sermons on Christmas, Palm Sunday, and Easter. This book is called "Jesus of Nazareth, the Messiah or Christ." This book was published by the ISPCK in 2018. This book is intended to prove that Jesus of Nazareth was the anticipated Messiah, the Christ (muktidata), and the Son of God. Those religions or sects, who question these scriptural titles of Jesus Christ, should read this book and should have a proper perspective about these titles of Jesus Christ.

Rev. Dr. Balavant Paradkar
Toronto, Ontario, Canada.

Other Works by the Author

Books

Sanctified, Sacred, and Saved Life of Christians: Twenty Nine Textual Sermons on Baptism, Matrimony, and Funeral, Delhi, India: ISPCK. 2018.

A Biblical Leadership and Church Discipline: Sixteen Textual Sermons, Delhi, India: ISPCK, 2017.

A Brief History of the African Methodist Episcopal Church from 1816 to 1856 in the United States of America and in Canada, Hamilton, Ontario, Canada, 2017.

A Biblical Administration of the Church and Society: Nineteen Textual Sermons on Administration of the Church and Fifteen Textual Sermons on Administration of Society, Delhi, India: ISPCK, 2016

The Teaching of Jesus Christ Through His Parables: Forty-one Textual Sermons on the Parables of Jesus Christ, Delhi, India: *ISPCK, 2016*

Biblical Foundations of Scripturally Based Spiritual Revivals in the Church: Twenty Eight Textual Sermons on revivals and Reform and Rev. John Wesley's Theology of 'the New Birth', Delhi, India: ISPCK, 2015

A Biblical Perspective on Mothers' Day, Fathers' Day, and Children's Day, Delhi, India, ISPCK, 2014

The Good News of the Bible: Twenty Five Textual Sermons on the Gospel of and About Jesus Christ, Vol. I, Delhi, India, ISPCK, 2014

The Good News of the Bible: Twenty Seven Textual Sermons on the Gospel of and About Jesus Christ, Vol. I I, Delhi, India, ISPCK, 2014

Proven Divinity of Jesus Christ Through His Scriptural Titles and Exceptional Claims, Delhi, India, ISPCK. 2014

In Remembrance of the Life-Blood of Jesus Christ: Thirty-Six Textual Sermons on the Holy Communion, Pune India, The Word of Life Publication, 2003

Negro Methodist Churches, Rev. John Wesley's Thoughts Upon Slavery, and His Struggle Against Slavery, 1998

The Book of Offices for the British Methodist Episcopal Church, 1998

A Worship Manual for a Scriptural or Methodist Order of Service, 2005

Biblical Solutions to the Problems of a Church: Fifteen Textual Sermons, delivered at Annual and General Conferences of the B. M. E. Church of Canada, 1998

A Scriptural Vindication of the Articles of Religion: Twenty-five Articles of Religion of Methodism with The Reverend John Wesley's Acts of and Thoughts about Baptism, 2010

Booklets

A Meditation on Good Friday: Textual Sermons on Seven Utterances of Jesus Christ from the Cross, Pune, India: Sumitra Prakashan, 2012.

A Historical Significance of the "salem Chapel" with reference to the Underground Railroad Movement and a tribute to Harriet Tubman, Second or Revised edition, 2016

Christianity in the Context of the Indian Way of Life (a book on social, religious, and political issues, in Marathi), Bangalore, India: Christian Institute for the Study of Region & Society, 1979.

Socio-Religious Policies of the British Methodist Episcopal Church of Canada, Toronto: B. M. E. Church Conference, 1990

A Historical Significance of "Salem Chapel" with Reference to Underground Railroad Movement, 2006

Essays

'The Bible and Racism', "Mukti", Bimonthly, Vol. 1, no. 4 and 5, Toronto, 1982, 1983.

Christian Participation in Politics', "Apostle", The B. M. E. Church of Canada Publication, May 1979.

The Covenant Theology of John Wesley, Toronto: Canadian Methodist Historical Society, 1993

Methodist Piety and Social Morality or Scriptural Holiness of Methodism (Toronto: Canadian Methodist Historical Society,1995)

A Versatile Significance of *Rta,* (Poona, India: Bhandarkar Oriental Research Institute, 1982)

'A Theological Significance of Forty Days' in this book, Delhi: ISPCK, 2018, pp. 345-351.